"WILL YOU LEAVE MY ROOM SO THAT I MAY ATTIRE MYSELF PROPERLY?"

Kell couldn't stop himself. He caught her rounded chin between his fingers to hold her still. "Let's begin on your education, sweet thing. When a man's in your room, you don't talk about getting dressed. You've got it all mixed up, blue eyes." He didn't know why the tremor he felt from her pleased him. But he did understand that his body was ready to find out what other reactions he could bring about with his touch.

Annie had had enough. "I decline your offer, Mr. York. There is nothing you could teach me that I would find a worthy contribution to my education. Now leave."

"My pleasure." Kell started for the door, then turned. "Last thing, Muldoon. Put the cost of repairing the lock on my bill."

"Get out! And never fear, Mr. York, I intended to bill you for damages."

But as Kell left the room he wondered if there were some damages that couldn't be paid for. He looked back. **Shall I become a saint or make her a sinner?**

Darling Annie

"A priceless gem, to be savored and cherished."
—*Romantic Times*

"A winner! An absolutely luscious romance."
—*Paperback Trader*

"A special treat from a gifted author."
—*Affaire de Coeur*

ANNOUNCING THE

TOPAZ FREQUENT READERS CLUB

COMMEMORATING TOPAZ'S 1 YEAR ANNIVERSARY!

THE MORE YOU BUY, THE MORE YOU GET

Redeem coupons found here and in the back of all new Topaz titles for FREE Topaz gifts:

Send in:

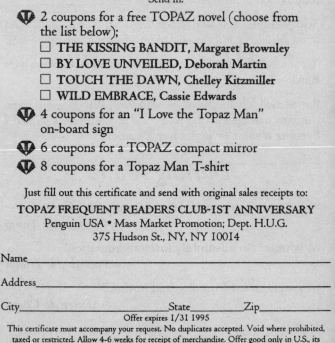

2 coupons for a free TOPAZ novel (choose from the list below);
- ☐ **THE KISSING BANDIT**, Margaret Brownley
- ☐ **BY LOVE UNVEILED**, Deborah Martin
- ☐ **TOUCH THE DAWN**, Chelley Kitzmiller
- ☐ **WILD EMBRACE**, Cassie Edwards

4 coupons for an "I Love the Topaz Man" on-board sign

6 coupons for a TOPAZ compact mirror

8 coupons for a Topaz Man T-shirt

Just fill out this certificate and send with original sales receipts to:

TOPAZ FREQUENT READERS CLUB-1ST ANNIVERSARY
Penguin USA • Mass Market Promotion; Dept. H.U.G.
375 Hudson St., NY, NY 10014

Name_____

Address_____

City_____State_____Zip_____
Offer expires 1/31 1995
This certificate must accompany your request. No duplicates accepted. Void where prohibited, taxed or restricted. Allow 4-6 weeks for receipt of merchandise. Offer good only in U.S., its territories, and Canada.

Darling Annie

Raine Cantrell

A TOPAZ BOOK

TOPAZ
Published by the Penguin Group
Penguin Books USA Inc., 375 Hudson Street,
New York, New York 10014, U.S.A.
Penguin Books Ltd, 27 Wrights Lane,
London W8 5TZ, England
Penguin Books Australia Ltd, Ringwood,
Victoria, Australia
Penguin Books Canada Ltd, 10 Alcorn Avenue,
Toronto, Ontario, Canada M4V 3B2
Penguin Books (N.Z.) Ltd, 182–190 Wairau Road,
Auckland 10, New Zealand

Penguin Books Ltd, Registered Offices:
Harmondsworth, Middlesex, England

First published by Topaz, an imprint of Dutton Signet,
a division of Penguin Books USA Inc.

First Printing, September, 1994
10 9 8 7 6 5 4 3 2 1

 Topaz is a trademark of Dutton Signet, a division of Penguin Books
USA Inc.

Printed in the United States of America

To my editor, Jennifer Enderlin,
for all the right reasons,
this one is for you.

ACKNOWLEDGMENT

While writing *Darling Annie* I asked the help of several people who gave generously of their knowledge and time. My heartfelt thanks to Louise Street Withowiski of the Young County Historical Commission in Texas, who shared her family's history. A thank-you to the ever helpful research librarians of the Broward County Library in Fort Lauderdale, Florida. A very special thank-you belongs to Belinda Jank and her son, Tristan, who exceeded my expectations with their generous and continuous supply of information.

Chapter One

❧

He was only a man, Annie Muldoon reminded herself. One of those mysterious, sinful creatures that were the bane of any woman who considered herself sensible and independent.

There was no logical reason for her knees to be knocking together. She was not a young, simpering ninny, even if Mr. Kellian York had the looks to make her behave like one. But as she repeated this admonishment to herself, Annie wiped her damp palms against the cotton wrapper she had hurriedly flung over her nightgown when shouts of fire erupted hours ago.

She did have the excuse that Loving, Texas, had never seen his like before. Leanly built, he had a dangerous air about him. Peering between the lace curtains of her bedroom windows, she stared down the street and saw Kellian York fling a last bucket of water on the smoldering ruin of the Silken Aces.

And good riddance! But her joy was short-lived. She frowned with fierce concentration. He flung his head

back and was looking directly toward her boardinghouse.

He couldn't be . . . he wouldn't dare . . .

"York, this here's a hangin' offense. Ain't I right, boys?"

Kellian York did not answer Denley Wallace, who owned the biggest ranch to the west of Loving. His gaze raked the smoldering ruin that was all he had left of his unwanted inheritance from his brother, Kyle. He ignored the angry mutterings of the crowd around him and took his gunbelt from his Chinese houseman, Chang Li. Kell knew who was responsible for the fire that had destroyed the Silken Aces. He considered letting the lynch mob talk carry the men around him into action against the witch who had caused this.

But if the fire was reduced to smoldering, his plans for Annie Muldoon were not.

Plans that included a long, slow, exacting revenge for the hell she had put him through in the forty-eight hours he'd spent in Loving. Well, he amended in his thoughts, she had at least been directly involved in all of his hell, if not physically present.

He wiped the grimy sweat off his forehead with the back of his hand. Kell hated being dirty. Almost as much as he hated being broke. He reeked of smoke, but a glance showed that Li had the strongbox tucked under his arm.

Muted colors chased the gray from the sky. Angry mutterings changed to ugly. Kell couldn't stop them. He couldn't blame them. These men and others were going to be denied their pleasures because of the fire.

That was a sin.

Not the pleasures themselves that spinster Muldoon and her gaggle of do-gooders preached against.

"You gonna do something about this, Kell?"

He should have known that Laine would be the first of the doves to demand an answer. Kell settled his gunbelt lower on his hips and faced his brother's lover. Whiskey-warm eyes and a body that had a man thinking of mussed sheets and hot sex made Laine one of the highest-paid daughters of joy in the county. But he didn't forget how vocal Laine had been about the dirty low-down trick his brother Kyle had played by not leaving her the Silken Aces. She was the one who had suggested using the upstairs rooms. She had found the doves for him.

But Kyle was dead and Kell took exception to her thinking. He was the one the trick had been played upon.

His gaze skimmed the other doves. Ruby and Charity, both chestnut-headed twenty-year-olds, stood off to one side being consoled by three cowhands. Their hair color and ages were the only things alike about them. Charity was short, plump, and still managed to keep a wide-eyed innocence despite her five years' work. Ruby, willow slender, returned a hard, brittle stare from eyes that had seen it all and didn't hide it.

Daisy, with long-fingered hands that could make a deck of cards play out five winning hands time and again, huddled with Blossom, the youngest of the doves, and Cammy, whose mournful voice sent a man to the bottle. The three of them stood barefoot in the churned mud of the street.

All the doves were as bedraggled a lot of females as he had ever set his smoke-stung eyes upon. And in his years of drifting he had seen plenty. He owed each one of them a debt for fighting the fire alongside the men to prevent its spreading to the other wooden buildings in town. From the bundles each one clutched, he surmised they had been able to save their scant possessions.

"Well, Kell, what are you gonna do?" Laine repeated. She heard her question echoed by the others.

Kell glanced from face to face. He met the scowl of Pockets, the piano player. Pockets wasn't grinning around the stubby end of the habitual cigar he chewed.

They were waiting for his answer. Kell cursed his dead brother under his breath. They were all his responsibilities now, and his first order was to find them housing. Six daughters of joy (even if right now they looked anything but), Pockets, Bronc the barkeep, Chang Li, and himself.

A loser's hand. Cutting his losses and moving on was ingrained after years of drifting. But he owed Kyle. For Kell it was an unconscionable burden for a man who prided himself on being free of encumbrances. And liking it just fine that way.

The sun rose and formed a halo around the neat two-story frame house at the opposite end of the street. Kell stared. The Muldoon Cozy Rest boardinghouse had rooms, hot water, and food. Lots of empty rooms, since the railroad had passed over the town to build its line east.

"Kell?" Laine ventured to ask once more, touching his rigid, muscled forearm.

Kell didn't answer. He shook off her hand and took his proffered flat-crowned black hat from Li. With a purposeful stride he started down the middle of the street. Li herded the doves in line behind him, his voice softly promising hot baths, food, and rest. Cowhands and townsmen alike trailed along.

"Gonna stop an' get a new rope, York?" someone called out as they marched passed Herman Lockwood's mercantile.

Kell shook his head. "Hangin's too good and way too

fast for that starched string of bones daring to call herself
a woman."

Way too good and way too easy, he repeated to himself.
He wanted to see Muldoon reduced to her knees, learning about humility and true charity all the way down. The
creature had no compassion, no tolerance for anyone who
did not conform to her rigid standard of behavior.

He wasn't a man to advocate using violence against
women. He was tempted to, sorely tempted, but he
wouldn't do it even if he had just cause. Women, to his
way of thinking, were one of the Lord's given pleasures to
man. He couldn't hang a woman, but he wasn't about to
let her get away with this.

Kell strode up the three wide steps leading to the front
porch of the boardinghouse. He set himself to kick in the
door, since he had been forbidden to enter its sacrosanct
walls.

"Always open," Pockets warned from behind.

Kell shoved the door open with a bang, striving to hold
on to his temper. Two overstuffed chairs were in the corner, and the counter, with its neat pigeonhole board behind it, was empty of the dragon he had first encountered.
The small lobby offered no clue that anyone was around,
but he knew better.

"Muldoon!" he bellowed, heading straight across the
polished hardwood floor to the stairs. He knew which
front room belonged to her. He had seen her up there
when he had arrived on the stage, peeking out of her window like a timid mouse. She'd still been up there watching when he left after being refused a room by that old
harridan aunt of hers.

But she wasn't going to have a chance to refuse him
again.

Once before he had walked away. Just once he had

given in to the urge to settle down and buy himself a saloon. He had even considered getting married. But when a traveling preacher whipped up a frenzy against the sins of drinking and gambling, a group of overzealous women wrecked his business and stole his money box. Never again, he swore.

"Muldoon!" he shouted again, taking the steps three at a time easily with his long legs. His boots hit the wood with the force of his anger, which threatened to explode.

Never again was any woman going to dictate to him. He didn't believe drinking, gambling, and bedding a willing woman were sinful. They weren't even vices. Only a dried-up prune of a spinster like Muldoon would think about denying a man an honest card game, some cheap, warm whiskey, and the same kind of woman.

And Annie Muldoon, the ringleader of the prim, starched, corset contingent, not only spoke out about denying a man his pleasures, she had destroyed them.

The upstairs hallway was narrow and dark. But the right front corner held the room he wanted. Kell stood before the door, huffing and puffing. He didn't bother to knock, he yanked and twisted the doorknob. He was not surprised to find it locked, but he gave it one last angry twist. Stepping back, he braced himself against the wall.

"Open the damned door, Muldoon!" he yelled. "Open it or I'll kick it open." Kell positioned himself to do just that.

Three was about as high as he could control himself to count. Not a sound reached him. Despite his exhaustion, every gambler's instinct told him she was cowering inside.

The stout door resisted his first try to the shouted count of one from everyone in the hall. Kell shot a look at Li, for even he had joined in. With his second kick, accompanied by more yelled encouragement, the wood splintered. The door flew open with a crash on Kell's third attempt.

Cheers erupted.

Kell lurched forward, then stopped.

There was a blasted horse pistol aimed at him

His fists braced him in the doorframe, blocking the view of those crowding and pushing him from behind.

With disbelief, he registered the fact that the nightgown-clad woman, trembling so badly that the old pistol she aimed wavered between the juncture of his thighs and his belly, was not Annie Muldoon.

But she was as good to look at as having an ace high flush dealt to him after a losing streak at the poker table.

"Where's Muldoon?" he demanded.

Annie was too frightened to realize that he didn't immediately recognize her. His grimy, overwhelmingly male presence in her virginal room, where no man had ever been, was enough of a shock for her to deal with. She watched his wintry sage-green eyes search every corner before returning to pin her in place. Kellian York looked dangerous. Fury poured from his body and invaded her room. He took a step toward her and Annie forced herself to raise the pistol. She wasn't sure if it was legal to shoot a man who trespassed into her room. But she'd worry about that later. Right now, she could barely press her knees together to keep standing there and not reveal how frightened she was of him.

Kell tipped his hat back. Softly then, so as not to alarm her, he called to Li. "Privacy." He didn't wait to see if his houseman accomplished his order, he knew it would be done in a matter of minutes. Kell stepped further into the room and closed the door behind him. He ignored the rusty little squeak of protest.

"Darlin', there's no need to hold that weapon on me. All

I want from you is to know where that spit-starched prune of a spinster is."

Annie couldn't swallow, much less answer him. Shock doubled and redoubled. He didn't know who she was! She managed to motion him back with the gun. Call her spit-starched and a prune, would he? Is that what he thought, after she had made gallons of coffee and supplied her fried apple dumplings to all the men fighting the fire? The ungrateful lout! Her rounded chin hitched up and she steadied the pistol in her hands.

She had been horrified and bewildered by the fire that destroyed his place. She knew she didn't set it and was certain her small group of women would never resort to violence of any kind.

"Well? Just tell me where she is. Nothing between hell and heaven is gonna protect her from me." Kell scowled at her. He was tired, he wasn't thinking straight, but he didn't think he had seen this woman around in the past two days.

With a rough shake of his head, he became sure of it. He would have noticed and remembered her hair if nothing else. Bright as new copper sprinkled with exotic spices, two braids fell below her hips. Eyes, wide and dark, so heavily fringed with long lashes it was a wonder she could keep them open, were locked on his. And that mouth. It was downright indecent. A sugar-soft mouth with a lush bottom lip that was scored by the edge of her teeth. A deep, unholy suspicion began to form.

"This is Muldoon's room, isn't it?"

His question earned him the cocking of the pistol. Kell ignored it. If she had meant to use the damned old thing, she would have fired it by now. He took a step closer, then another.

"S-stop right t-there. You'd b-better leave."

"Jus' answer me, darlin' an' I will." He wanted the wary look in her eyes gone. Those pretty white teeth digging into her lip were chasing the heat of his temper and quickly replacing it with heat of another kind.

Her wrapper wasn't closed tight enough. He could see the pristine white ruffles of her nightgown, which nearly matched the leaching color of her skin. She wasn't tall; her head would barely reach his chin. He glanced down. Her bare toes curled into the worn carpet. There was something vulnerable about a woman's bare feet. Or maybe, he amended, it was just hers.

His forceful presence alarmed Annie, but the way his snapping green eyes were watching her now sent a deeper, more dangerous warning through her.

At twenty-eight, Annie was resigned to her spinster state after having been abandoned at the altar ten years ago. She had grown up in Loving with her widowed mother and Aunt Hortense, but no one, not ever, had looked her over like a feast set before them. She cleared her throat and tried once more to get him to leave. Nothing came out but another squeaky sort of a sound.

There were scuffling noises in the hallway, but Kell didn't turn around. He knew Li would handle it. No one, but no one, would be allowed in here until he opened the door. Li excelled at protecting his back and ensuring his privacy. And right now Kell had other things on his mind. Things like stalking this snippy little female who wouldn't talk, wouldn't lower the pistol, and wouldn't stop staring at him as if the devil himself had come to call.

"Muldoon's not getting away with what she did. She'll pay and pay for destroying my property." He glared at her, waited for a reaction, then snorted with disgust. "First she denied me a room. Then decent food. Those damn women of hers stopped every customer with their preaching. Lord spare us all from *good* women. And then there's the wagonload of whiskey that went astray. You wouldn't know anything about that, would you? Just tell me where she is and I'm out of here."

"G-go."

"No way."

Annie backed away from him. She knew everyone was aware of her soft spot when someone was in need. She didn't know how to say no. The fault had shanghaied her into being the ringleader of the town's women. They had banded together to close the saloon once Kyle York won it and brought those women in to sell their favors—a condition no decent woman could allow. But this man's need to have revenge for imagined and real slights was not going to touch her. Not when she was his intended victim.

Kellian York, with his thick, sun-streaked brown hair, slightly crooked nose, and mouth that did funny things to her insides was not going to touch her.

Kell was losing it. "She set a fire, damn you! Tell me where she is."

Annie turned and found herself about to be cornered between the bed and the wall. A man like Kellian York would crush her without a thought. He blamed her for the fire that had burned down that cursed brothel of his. She was innocent, but he was in no mood to listen. She prayed nightly for his home-wrecking establishment to be closed. But never would she countenance endangering lives by setting a fire.

She was the one in danger of being consumed by the wolf in her room. He had her cornered like a lamb in a pen.

Annie shot a look at him over her shoulder. Before he could lunge and grab hold of her, she scrambled up onto the bed.

Wrong move. The soft feather tick sank beneath her weight and threw her off balance.

Kell was on her faster than a flea on a hound. He flattened her beneath him before she could right herself.

Then he froze.

Chapter Two

◡

First Kell became aware of the pistol she still held. It was pressed between them, with its thick butt end nestled below her breasts and its barrel aligned with his most vulnerable male part.

His throat worked, and he finally swallowed the lump that rose. He held his breath for a few seconds, then release it, very slowly, careful not to alarm her by any sudden moves. But he was thankful that she didn't know he was afraid to take another deep breath and find his voice level changed to a soprano's high.

"Do tell me, darlin', is it loaded?"

"I am not your darling." Even to her ears, it sounded like a halfhearted protest at best. What was wrong with her? But Annie knew why she was cowering ramrod straight beneath his body and too scared to move. First he had invaded her room. Then her bed. Now, the heat of his lean, hard body was seeping into her as he pressed his full length against her. He was so close, she could see the beard stubble on his narrow cheeks. And that wasn't the worst of it at all.

His most unmentionable body part was indistinguish-
able from the pistol's barrel.

Mustering every bit of courage she had, Annie glared
up at him. "I wouldn't know. Is it?"

Kell's grin beamed a wicked warning as it kicked up one
corner of his mouth. "Since you've got your hand on the
trigger," he drawled in a low, husky voice, "you tell me,
sweet thing."

"Mercy," squeaked past Annie's suddenly dry lips. The
bold brass buttons of his pants closing were indenting
their shape on the back of her hand. The buttons weren't
the only bold, brassy thing making an indentation on her.
She longed to sink out of sight into the feather tick.

"Haven't got an ounce of mercy in me." Kell gazed
down at her flushed cheeks. His grin changed into a wide
smile. There was a dusting of freckles across those flaming cheeks. "Charming little—"

"I'm Muldoon!" Annie confessed, too afraid to hear
what he was about to comment on.

"I," Kell noted very softly, "already figured that out for
myself."

Wicked. Dangerous. His eyes glazed with an intense focused concentration that promised excitement. Annie denied she felt the tiniest bit of it. Disdainfully she wrinkled
her nose against the strong, overpowering reek of smoke.

He moved.

She froze.

Annie briefly closed her eyes. She was fever-flushed
from inside out. A mistaken case of spring fever. But it
wasn't spring. It was summer and long past mating time.
And people were different from animals. Weren't they?

"Mr. York, there is no need for you to maintain your position and prove your greater strength."

"So polite, darlin'?" Kell waited until she looked at him.

Her big blue eyes were dilated and luminous. He smiled. "Make you nervous? Butter won't melt in that dainty little mouth, would it?" He didn't expect an answer and didn't get one. "But I'm not going anywhere, Muldoon. I sure to appreciate a woman who knows her place."

Kell felt proud that he was keeping full rein on his temper. It was Annie Muldoon that he had pinned beneath him, but an Annie that was a good ten years younger than he had believed and been told.

Without the mobcap she wore to conceal every bit of her shining hair and with no spectacles hiding those stunning dark blue eyes, Kell had to revise his opinion of her. She was a freckle-faced redhead, but she sure wasn't as flat as yesterday's flapjacks.

Annie was soft—incredibly so. Lush, actually. He settled more of his weight on her. Her ears were dainty and heated with the same flags of color that reddened her cheeks. And her mouth was not, as Pockets had described it, a pinched-up old dried nut.

She squirmed.

Kell froze this time. "Careful, darlin'. A wrong move could prove my ruination."

Her tiny sound and caught breath enticed him to lower his head and taste the small beauty mark above the left corner of her lip.

Their breaths mingled. Hers was mint sweet and warm. He started to close his eyes. Watching her lips part, seeing for himself the intriguing space between her two lower front teeth, had him licking his lips.

Suddenly he jerked his head back, forgetting all his own caution about moving too fast. What the hell was he doing? He was going to kiss her? This was Muldoon!

A twist of his body brought him to her side. He yanked the pistol out of her hand before she could react. Kell tossed the weapon across the room and placed one splayed hand on her upper chest to pin her in place.

"Don't," he grated from between clenched teeth, "if you know what's good for you, move."

It wasn't the warning in his voice that held Annie in place. It wasn't even the hard strength of his hand spread on her upper body. It was the chilling impact of his eyes that had been so blazingly warm moments ago.

"Next to liking a woman who knows her place, I like a woman who listens and obeys." Her mouth formed a tight, mutinous line, but she didn't move.

"You owe me, Muldoon. And I always collect my debts. I haven't even decided yet how much you owe me. Just rest assured and bet your sweet bottom that you will. What's more," he added, leaning closer, "you'll pay every damned dollar of it."

"No."

"No?" he repeated in a soft voice, so soft that it would take the most discerning ear to catch the quiet fury underlying the word.

Kell brought the tip of his nose to the snooty angle of hers. She had a plucky sort of courage, he admitted. Too bad she didn't have some horse sense to go with it.

"Don't bait me, darlin'. You'll lose every time. Didn't your mama ever teach you not to challenge a man when he's in your bedroom, on your bed, and a hell of a lot bigger than you?"

"My *mama*, Mr. York, supposed the only man in my bedroom and on my bed, would have the right to be there. You sir, are not my husband. You sir, have no right—"

"Maybe not and thank the Lord for that. But, sweet thing, I've got you at my mercy and that gives me a lot of right. What's more, no one is coming to rescue you."

Annie barely managed to inch backward so that his

nose now grazed her chin. Sweet heaven, but he was too close! She squinted up at him. "You don't have any mercy. That's what you claimed. Are you a liar too, Mr. York?"

"Another sin you're lookin' to lay on me? Wasn't enough to call me a gamblin', drunken prince of vices? Don't matter none. I'll lie when I need to."

"Well, I *do not* lie. I had nothing to do with the fire that destroyed your home-wrecking establishment. So I don't *owe* you anything, Mr. York. Now, you had better let me up."

"Or?"

Annie released a shuddering breath. She looked directly into his eyes. "Or I shall expire right before you, Mr. York."

"Expire? You wouldn't dare." Kell didn't move. He searched her features. "You're not the fainting kind."

"Would you believe I could surprise you?"

"Oh, you surprised me all right, darlin'. And if I was a man looking to cause himself some grief and pain I'd find out what other surprises you have in store." The moment the words were out he regretted them. Kell always sensed trouble by the crick in his neck. And the crick said it was time to cut and run. But she was pursing that luscious mouth as if bad taste were contagious. So he told his crick to go to hell.

"I have none for the likes of you. You do not know me, Mr. York. Do not be so arrogant as to lump me with the sort of women you have so obviously been consorting with."

"At least they were women, Muldoon. Damn proud of the fact. Something I doubt you know anything about." Kell pressed his hand harder to hold her still. His thumb and forefinger rested on either side of her neck. A smooth, slender throat, he absently noted, whose pulse was so rapid he couldn't count it. Didn't want to. The heel of his palm was nicely cushioned by the full upper curves of her breasts.

Two thin layers of cotton cloth couldn't hide the warmth or the fragrant scent of her skin rising and flowing inside him with every breath.

He was accustomed to women reacting with fascination, at least intense interest, when they caught his eye. It had been a curse to both him and Kyle until they understood what a blessing their good looks could be. But there wasn't any physical awareness of him in Annie Muldoon's eyes. Her gaze was as steady and about as friendly as a cardsharp's who'd been caught cheating.

Kell had had enough. He rolled off the bed and stood looking down at her. It wasn't even a hardship. Cloth was caught up around her knees, revealing shapely calves and ankles. He grinned, thinking he'd win a bet that no man had ever seen them. Slowly, his body came alive, nerve endings sending an alert surging through him. He was exhausted, but suddenly he was aware of how much woman Annie Muldoon appeared to be.

It was short-lived. He was a man who prided himself on his control. With a snort of disgust for his unruly reaction to her, he turned away.

Annie scrambled off the bed and stood on the other side, clutching her wrapper together. Her senses were clouded, and she had to shake her head to get rid of the feeling that she had just had a close call with more man and danger than she knew how to handle.

"What are you waiting for?" she asked, unable to look away from the tear in his shirt or the way the damp blue cloth clung to his back.

"I'm deciding," he answered after a moment, "whether I believe you had nothing to do with the fire. You can't deny that you lead that gaggle of do-gooders trying to close me down. You tried to do it to my brother before he died. But—"

"We—that is, I—had nothing to do with Kyle's death!"

"Oh, I know that, Muldoon. My brother died a happy man, doing what he loved best. He didn't name his place the Silken Aces for those sweet little winners in a deck of cards. He was thinking about the silken spread of a—"

"Oh, my good Lord! Don't you dare—do you hear me, Mr. York—not one more word about where he got *that name* from."

"It's not an it, but a she. Only you wouldn't understand a man's way of thinking."

"And proudly admit it," she countered. "That is the most positively indecent thing I've ever had to hear."

"Well, get used to it, Muldoon." Kell raked back his collar-length hair, dying for bed and bath, then set his hands on his hips. He refused to turn and look at her.

"Stop interrupting me. There is nothing indecent about a man giving up the ghost while he's in the saddle—one, which you should know 'cause of all your preachin', that the good Lord you're so fond of quoting made expressly for a man." For some reason her gasp of outrage pleased him. "And my brother was with a woman he cared about. But you, Miss Starch and Vinegar, wouldn't know a damn thing about that either."

"That is enough! I want you out of my room this minute. I want you and those people who followed you here to see your unconscionable behavior out of my boarding-house."

Kell spun and came around the bed so fast that Annie slammed against the wall trying to escape him. The difference in their height didn't intimidate her. The blaze of fury on his hard, lean-cheeked face did.

Still, she glared up at him.

He smiled. "Muldoon, let me be the first to inform you that I'm taking up residence here."

"You can't. I do not rent rooms to your sort."

Kell leaned close. "*Sort*? And you dare say it like you just ate a crate of lemons?"

"I like lemons," she whispered, nervously licking her bottom lip.

"I don't." Kell didn't even blink uttering the lie. Fact was, he'd been drawing in the faint scent of lemon from the moment he'd gotten near her. And he didn't like what it was doing to him one damn bit.

"Muldoon," he pressed closer to say, "in case you're blind, look again. I'm not a *sort*. I'm a man."

Annie tried to push out the wall behind her to escape. It was a foolish thought. Almost as foolish as Kellian York's statement that she might be blind and not know he was a man. If her eyes hadn't registered the fact, there were other body parts achingly aware and more than ready to explain it to her.

For the first time in her life, she truly thought she would faint. "Please," she pleaded, raising one hand and fluttering it between them. She didn't have the courage to shove him.

"Aim to, every time, any way I can, darlin'."

"You are crude. I want you to leave."

"Stayin', Muldoon. And you ain't being given a choice." Kell caught her hand, no longer denying his own unexplainable need to touch her. His fingers slid beneath the loose sleeve of the wrapper. The warmth of her skin under his palm tempted him to do more, but he resisted. He'd gotten what he wanted. He rather liked the alarmed look she shot at his hand. Just like a skittish filly coming under her first bridling.

He skimmed the slender length of her forearm. deliberately trailing his fingers down the back of her hand, then stopped.

"Just so we understand each other, Muldoon—"

"Miss Muldoon to you."

"Muldoon. There's a contingent of angry men waiting to hang you for destroying my place. Be nice to me, darlin', or I'll let them have you."

"Do not call me darling. It implies an intimacy that could never exist between us, Mr. York. I would never allow it."

"I ain't asked you to. Like I said before, you'll bring some poor bastard nothing but grief and pain."

Annie was trembling with rage and fear. She dug deep and found there was a small unused store of courage. With a look of disdain she removed his hand from hers.

"I know most of those men. I will explain to them that I had nothing to do with the fire. None of the women who belong to the Legion for Decency and hope for civilized behavior in Loving would condone a fire that could have taken someone's life."

Kell allowed her to slide past him. "They're in an ugly mood. Wanted to stop and get a new rope from the mercantile." He saw her hand creep up and cradle her throat. "You've taken away their pleasures for the next few weeks."

"Pleasures? Ha! Devil's pastimes is more like it. At least their wives will know where they are and have a chance to redeem them."

"Spare me your Sunday morning sermon." *But do let me see more of that frankly arousing hip-swinging walk of yours, Muldoon.* As if she had heard his silent request, Annie stopped pacing. "I've made my decision," he said. "I'm taking rooms here until I can rebuild."

"Rebuild? Rooms here?" Annie repeated. "No! Most definitely not. You can't stay here. And those women who work for you . . . no! I will not have such . . . such—"

"Wash the floor with your sanctimonious attitude, Muldoon. I said you had no choice and I meant it." Kell waited for his threat to sink in. He didn't have to wait long. She spun around and finally faced him.

He lifted his hand and rested it on the canted butt of his gun. "Understand? No choice. The Cozy Rest has enough rooms for my needs. It's the only place in town that does."

"You can't have the rooms. I won't have those women—"

Kell's hold on his temper slipped a few notches. "Say 'those women' in that prissed-up voice once more and I'll wash your mouth out with soap. That's for a start. They've been up all night fighting the fire. Each one hauled water. Don't you dare say they're not good enough to stay here. I oughta haul you over my knee and give you what for so you never do it again."

"Try it and it'll be the last thing you do with those hands."

"Empty threats, Muldoon. And don't I know it. What's got you pursin' that mouth? Worried about the doves? Don't be. They wouldn't think of selling their sexual favors here and soiling your precious virginal white sheets. Likely they'd feel as repressed as I do just being in the same room with you."

Annie stared at him in mortification, eyes wide and color burning her cheeks. No one had ever dared to speak to her in such a crude manner. Not even his brother Kyle (the good Lord rest his soul, if He could find Kyle) had boldly uttered words that had no place in a decent woman's vocabulary.

There Kellian York stood, bold and brassy, gazing at her

without an ounce of apology or remorse. He was unprincipled. Amoral. The man oozed bad with every evil connotation of the word as written in the Good Book.

"So, tell me, darlin'," he murmured in a soft, dangerous voice, spreading his legs in an aggressive stance, hands held out to his sides. "What's it going to be? Me and the doves or the hanging party waiting outside to stretch your pretty little neck?"

Chapter Three

~

Annie stroked her throat, thinking about his threat. She forced herself to swallow the lump choking her. The men had put up resistance to the idea of closing the Silken Aces when the women had begun their campaign. He could be telling her the truth.

How had she ever got herself into this pickle barrel? One look at the stern, almost brooding expression on Kellian York's face and she knew there was no help to be had from him.

"Well?" he prompted. He grinned as apprehension flashed in her dark blue eyes.

Annie didn't understand why she was still infuriated by his remark that she was repressed. His astounding lack of manners, the fact that he was blackmailing her, and his invasion of her room should have been the only reasons she was angry.

"Let me be sure that I heard you correctly, Mr. York. You are threatening me with hanging unless I allow you and those instruments of vice to stay here?"

"*Instruments of vice?* What's wrong with you, lady? The doves are women. Oh," he said, lowering his arms and shoving his hands into his pants pockets to stop from shaking her from her holier-than-thou platform. "How could I forget? You don't know anything about being a woman. But do let me be the first to give you a prize, Muldoon. You got it right on the first try."

"Stop insulting me."

Kell's gaze raked from where sunlight was now glistening on her hair to her bare feet. "Honey, it ain't all that hard to do."

"Enough."

"Muldoon, I'd sell my soul to the devil before I'd take charity or be in debt to you. I'll pay for the rooms at your regular rate."

"I'm sure the devil already owns your soul, if you have one, Mr. York." Annie stared at him with grim relish.

"Darlin', I'll ask the next time I see him. As for the rooms, the doves can share three to a room, so that's two. Pockets and Bronc can double up in one. Li needs—"

"Lee? Who is that?"

"Chang Li, my houseman, right hand and friend. He gets—"

"Why do you call him by his last name?"

"It's the custom of the Chinese to use their family name first." Impatient with himself for bothering to take the time to explain to her, Kell added, "Li gets a room of his own despite his being Chinese." His voice and gaze were laced with the warning that he wouldn't tolerate a protest.

Annie merely nodded, not really accepting that this was happening to her, but understanding his quick defense of his Chinese friend. She felt the same about Fawn, the mute Kiowa girl she had bought from a miner—it was the only way she could get the young girl away from the man's abusive hands. A reluctant admiration formed, but Annie refused to comment. She didn't want to like Mr. Kellian York, and she certainly didn't want to find anything redeeming about him.

"Now we settled everyone but me. I'll want a room of my own." Kell began a slow perusal around the spacious corner room with speculation bright in his eyes. He dismissed her sharp little cry, letting her think that he was considering taking her room for himself. It was small compensation for all the aggravation she had caused. He had yet to decide if he believed her about not setting the fire.

His muddy boots had marked the faded and worn flowered rug which covered most of the floor. Lace curtains, snow white and starched like the woman who had hung them, covered both sets of windows. Sunlight filtered through, streaking across the four-poster bed. Kell stared at the muted shades of the mussed quilt, his body instantly tightening and reminding him of how Annie had felt beneath him. He couldn't dismiss this feeling as easily as he had her cry.

Annoyed with such an unruly response to a prim, prissy spinster, he forced himself to continue evaluating her room.

Elbow grease and oil had resulted in the gleaming finish on the wooden chest, wardrobe, and dressing table. There wasn't a crack to be seen on the plain white china washbowl or its matching pitcher. Natural linen towels, nearly stacked on the washstand's shelf, were embroidered with small flowers.

Kell rubbed the back of his neck and thought about some of the places he had roomed in over fifteen years of drifting. He prized his comfort and cleanliness. While he had stayed at some of the best hotels the western territories had to offer when he was on a winning streak, he'd also bedded down in places where even the bedbugs had fleas.

Ignoring Annie's wary stare, he strolled to her dressing table and picked up first her silver-backed brush, then its matching comb and hand mirror. His back was toward her so she couldn't see him curling one long red hair around his finger, until he caught himself and stopped. Opening the glass bottle of perfume, he lifted the stopper to his nose, and inhaled the faint scent of flowers and lemon.

Still holding the stopper, he turned to her. "Nice, real nice. I like a woman who smells as good as she looks."

There was a hushed, delicate intimacy implied in his voice that Annie couldn't help but react to. She stepped back, chastising herself for showing him a weakness, sensing that he would use it if it served to his advantage. His wicked grin caused her to wonder how many women had fallen all over themselves to please him. *Annie!* she warned herself. *You don't even like this man. You certainly don't like what he does, or what he is.*

Despite the warning, her temperature seemed to be rising. Tension formed a knot inside her, and his gaze appeared lit with unholy glee, as if he knew what was happening to her.

Kell inhaled her scent one more time, smiling all the while he put the stopper back in place. Using one finger, he pushed around the pins in the small dish-shaped china receiver. A froth of white cloth caught his eye and drew him to the upholstered lady's slipper chair in the corner.

"That's not—" Annie's protest died. He was lifting her beribboned, lace-trimmed chemise by its wide shoulder strap.

Kell glanced from the garment he held to Annie, then back again. The ribboned lacing was spread open, and he couldn't stop the image of Annie wearing it from coming to mind.

"So," he remarked, "you can wear the trappings of a woman, but just can't get the behavior part right. We'll need to work on your education, darlin'. Perhaps in the evenings when you're free?"

Annie wouldn't dignify his taunting grin or his repeated "nice" with any comment. She folded her arms across her chest, but nothing could stop the deeper flags of color from flaming across her cheeks when he dropped the chemise and held up her drawers.

"Lord, give me patience and save me," she muttered. Annie rapidly calculated how much money the rent he would pay in addition to the extras for meals and laundry would bring her. The sum was more than she could afford to refuse. Truth was, she needed the money. But she still had a difficult time shushing her conscience and compromising her moral values by allowing him and his sinful entourage residence in her boardinghouse.

Kell noticed her distracted air, and that annoyed him too. He wasn't used to women dismissing him. Even the *good* ones like Muldoon. Not that he had anything to do with that sort. Women like Muldoon only wanted to get a man's ring on their finger to control him and his money. He'd never get caught in that trap even if the bait was so temptingly packaged. He revised his opinion of Annie Muldoon, for everything he observed was soft, feminine, and at odds with the rigid, prim, unappealing appearance she presented outside this room. A most perplexing female . . . and one he had no intention of getting involved with. Kyle had saddled him with enough for any man's lifetime.

Loud voices rose from outside, and Kell reached the window first. There was a confrontation between the men who had followed him to the boardinghouse and a group of women brandishing signs and a few brooms.

The moment Annie tried to push him aside and see for herself what was going on, Kell blocked her way by simply facing her and raising his arms as if he would restrain her physically if need be.

Annie didn't want him to touch her again. Once, she believed, was enough for any woman. Or maybe it was just her unfathomable reaction to him.

"The natives are getting restless, Muldoon. Decision time."

Annie didn't answer him. *Think, Annie, you could finally make a sizeable contribution to the church building fund and maybe have enough left to place an advertisement for a real minister.*

It was her dream to have a real church, not her front parlor, to hold Sunday service.

But Annie, another voice whispered, *he's blackmailing you. Make no mistake, Kellian York will do it again, and again, if it serves his unholy purposes.*

You could fix the leaks in the roof.

He'd be underfoot all the time. You'd have to see that wicked grin and those sage-green eyes that seem to pierce right through cloth.

Even if you didn't have anything to do with the fire, can you call yourself a Christian, charitable woman and still refuse?

The money, Annie. Think of the money.

What would the legion say? They'd all be mortified and maybe not speak to her. They might even ask her to resign as chairwoman. Now that by itself was a tempting thought.

"Muldoon," Kell warned, crossing the room to stand in front of her. She had been backing away all this time, and he had to snap his fingers close to her nose to get her attention. "Your answer," he demanded when she came to with a start.

"Yes. All right. I'll do it." Annie drew a deep breath and squared her shoulders. "Now will you leave my room so that I may attire myself properly?"

Kell couldn't stop himself. He caught her rounded chin between his fingers to hold her still. "Let's begin on your education, sweet thing. When a man's in your room, you don't talk about getting dressed. You've got it all mixed up, blue eyes." He didn't know why the tremor he felt from her pleased him. But he did understand that his body was ready to find out what other reactions he could bring about with his touch.

Annie had had enough. She jerked her head back and shoved his hand aside. "I decline your offer, Mr. York. There is nothing you could teach me that I would find a worthy contribution to my education. Now, leave."

"My pleasure." Kell started for the door, then turned. "Last thing, Muldoon. Put the cost of repairing the doorframe and lock on my bill. I don't want any man wandering in here by mistake."

"Get out. Just get out! And never fear, Mr. York, I intended to bill you for damages."

"Sure, honey, you do that." But as Kell left the room and made sure the door stayed closed behind him, he wondered if there were some damages that couldn't be paid for. Like the flash of passionate anger in Muldoon's eyes that set his blood to warming again. He looked back once on his way down to disperse the crowd. *Shall I become a saint or make her a sinner?*

Minutes after he left her, Annie sagged down on her bed. Tension seeped out of her and she buried her face in her hands. "What have I done? Just what have I done?"

* * *

By late morning the countryside was buzzing with the news that Annie Muldoon had offered rooms at the Cozy Rest to Kellian York and his doves.

Mrs. Herman Lockwood, by virtue of her husband's owning the only mercantile in town, was the recipient and bearer of every juicy detail. She was also a staunch supporter of Annie's decision. And she told her dearest friend, Abigail Duffner, so.

"Let Annie be a lesson for us all. She believes in giving Christian charity. Annie is no fool, Abigail. She's well aware that the example she sets for *those women* may very well be their salvation. We all owe Annie our understanding and our support during this trying time for her. But I have faith in Annie. Girl has strong moral fiber and will allow no devil's pastimes beneath her roof."

"All good and well, Lucinda. But she has invited the devil and his cohorts to dine, and you know what they say about supping with the devil."

Abigail's smug tone irritated Lucinda. She straightened her considerable girth and tilted her spectacles down her long nose. "I know what's said. You forget that Annie is the one who's always telling us that he who sups with the devil will pay the devil his due."

With a quick, birdlike thrust of her head, Abigail leaned close. "Do you ever wonder just what a man like Kellian York would consider his due?"

"Abigail Duffner!"

"Oh, pooh! Admit it, Lucinda. You have so wondered. And it's 'cause the devil has come handsomely wrapped."

"I can't—I just can't believe you said that. I can't even believe you have such thoughts."

Abigail toyed with the cord on her drawstring purse. "I knew his brother was a fine figure of a man. But I swear, when Kellian first smiled at me, I could feel my heart beat faster."

Giving her friend a sharp-eyed glare usually reserved for those daring to request credit on an overextended account, Lucinda backed away until the shelf behind the counter stopped her.

"Are you meanin' to tell me that you're sympathizin' with our common enemy?"

"Don't be a goose, Lucinda. I'm just telling you that the man's good-looking. Not an ounce of fat on him." She heaved a wishful sigh. "Abner, Lord love him, eats too much of my cooking. So even if Kellian York's ways are sinful, he's a handsome devil. You can look at me like I've lost sense, dear, but he isn't cheap about spending his money."

"You took money from him?"

"Indeed, I did. Just like you and Herman did. He marched those women of his into my shop—"

"Abigail, you didn't—"

"I did. He said they could have two new ready-made gowns each when Emmaline refused to sew for them. Paid me up front, too," she snapped, settling her hands on ample hips. "That's more than I can say about some that shop."

"Ladies, ladies," came a softer voice that instantly drew their attention to the wide aisle. Velma Grant rushed as quickly as her high-buttoned, pointy-toed shoes could take her to where Abigail stood near the counter. She accepted their curt nods of greeting with one of her own.

"I came as soon as I heard. My word, what are we going to do about this? Your boy, Abigail, rode out to the house and told me what's gone on." Spreading one gloved hand over her heart, Velma whispered, "Is it true? Did our Annie really take him in?"

Before they could answer, another woman rushed to join them. Ruth McQuary's husband owned the barbershop and sold patent medicines, along with making a few of his own.

"Lower your voice, ladies," she admonished them. "I could hear you shouting while I was walking down the street. This is not a time for us to be fighting among ourselves. We need to make plans."

But her arrival seemed to have drawn other women into the store, and finally Lucinda had to shout for quiet. Each woman wanted to voice her opinion about what Annie had done.

No one noticed the lone figure listening avidly from behind a rough wood table piled high with blankets. Then the figure slipped out without approaching them or making a purchase.

Nor did anyone on the street pay attention to the muttering that was going on in the full glare of morning sunlight.

The fire destroyed that place! They were supposed to leave town. All of them. Damn Annie Muldoon's interfering hide!

Chapter Four

❧

"I'm not hiding from them, Aunt Hortense! And they are guests. Paying guests!" Annie shouted for the third time. She despaired that today, of all days, her elderly aunt was refusing to use her ear trumpet. She generally wouldn't use the hearing aid unless it suited her to do so on the principle of vanity.

"Well, I don't like the looks of them, Annie Charlotte. Not a bit. Not one little bit."

Annie murmured soothing sounds and patted her aunt's shawl-clad shoulder with one hand. The other she used to rub her own pounding temples. In the two hours since she had agreed to—no, been blackmailed into—allowing Kellian York and his people to stay here, she had become more exhausted than a whole week's worth of work could make her.

She and Fawn had heated and lugged buckets of hot water upstairs, more than was used in a month of Sundays. That had been accomplished only after an extensive effort to coax the mute Indian girl out of hiding. Poor

Fawn, she didn't know what to make of the strange men and women prowling the hall upstairs.

One thing Annie knew was that Mr. York had told the truth when he claimed that Chang Li not only could but would help her. The man had been everywhere at once, or so Annie thought, meeting demands for more towels, more food, more coffee, and more of that infernal hot water. Annie had no idea how he had managed to calm Fawn into accepting his presence, but the girl wasn't cringing in the corner any longer.

Annie owed Li, as he asked her to call him, her thanks, and she would see to giving it to him just as soon as she recovered. Much as it annoyed her to admit it to herself, not one of these people had been offensive.

No one, that is, but Kellian York.

He needed an extra pillow; two weren't enough. He had to have his shaving water reheated because it had grown cool while he bathed. He needed his curtains drawn to keep the sunlight out of his room so he could sleep. Get him another quilt in case he got chilled. Mend his shirt after it was washed. Wash his pants and clean his boots.

And when she had so innocently—and so foolishly—commented on the absence of a union suit among the items to be laundered, she should have been warned by his wicked smile. Her ears still felt blistered, not by his honey-sweet, thick-as-syrup-on-a-cold-winter's-morning voice, no, not that, but his words.

"Poor darlin', you do need some educatin'. I don't wear one. Gets in the way. It's just me an' my skin under the pants."

Coward! She was and didn't argue it. Inwardly she cringed to think of how she had fled down the hallway. Despite her denial to her aunt, Annie was hiding in the big front parlor reserved for female guests. If she had to hear that amoral man's husky, seductive, insinuating voice one more time yelling her name for something, she would . . . would . . .

Annie didn't know what she would or could do, but there had to be a way to silence him. Something as wicked as his unholy grin or the gleam in his eyes as soon as he spotted her. She would use it too, just as quick as she found out what it was.

She was grateful that the crowd was gone. It was unsettling to see how fast Kellian York had ended the disturbance. Whatever he said to the men ready to hang her, and to the women who rushed to her defense, they left minutes later.

It was another quiet, late morning on a summer day in Loving.

"Annie Charlotte, if you pat my shoulder any harder, you'll be pulverizing my pore old bones."

"Oh, Aunt, I'm so sorry." Annie whipped her hand behind her and twisted the long ties of her apron.

"Come 'round where I can see you. Swear my eyesight's failing by the day. You'll be needin' to ask Doc Duff for more of his Headache Syrup. I've near finished the last bottle."

"Aunt Hortense," Annie said very slowly, leaning close to the old woman's ear, "Abner Duffner is not a real doctor. You shouldn't be taking any remedies—"

"He's all we've got."

"True. But I don't believe that mixing his syrup of powdered charcoal and molasses in half a glass of whiskey several times a day does your headaches any good. Maybe you need stronger glasses."

"Fiddles! That's what you know. His syrup settles my head just fine. Now come 'round, girl."

Ingrained obedience to her elders made Annie do just

what Hortense ordered. She didn't bother to correct her
aunt that she was no longer considered a girl and hadn't
been for a long time. Aunt Hortense would truly turn a
deaf ear to any protest she made. She had come here to
hide and recover from her emotional battering at Kellian
York's hands. Annie was exhausted from lack of sleep, but
there was no one to pamper her. By the way her aunt's
raisin-dark eyes were studying her, Annie knew she was in
for it.

"Where's your cap?" Hortense demanded. "Don't know
what gets into you young girls. In my day, a girl wouldn't
show off her crowning glory to anyone but her husband.
'Course," she added with a sniff, "you ain't got a husband."

Annie didn't defend herself. This was old territory that
her aunt raked over yet again. It was better to let her have
her say and then make good her escape as soon as she
could.

Peering up through her spectacles, Hortense wrinkled
her beaklike nose. "Have you been fiddling with the devil's
temptation of tobacco? Don't lie to me, Annie Charlotte.
I know the smell of smoke when I sniff it."

"There was a fire, Aunt Hortense. The brothel burned
down last night. That's where the paying guests came
from."

"Fire in a bottle? Whatever for? What fool tried to—"

"No! Listen to me." Annie dropped to her knees, sighing with weariness. There was no help for it. She'd have
to shout so everyone in the boardinghouse would hear her.

"The gambler's place burned down!"

"Oh, my. Girl, what have you done?"

"Me? I didn't have anything to do with it."

"You're a good girl, Annie Charlotte. But why are you
wearing that old faded gray gown of mine today? It's not
Monday. I'd know if it was, 'cause the papers would come

in on the stage. And Monday's the only day you do the laundry."

Cupping her forehead in her hands, Annie prayed for more patience. She had surely used up her store. "It's not Monday. But I had to do extra wash." Annie swallowed, her throat a little raw from yelling. She had to find a place where no one asked anything of her. Covering her aunt's parchment-skinned hands folded over the silver head of her cane with both of hers, Annie forced a bright smile.

"Would you like a nice cup of tea?"

"You're very late with it this morning."

"The guests . . . I'll hurry and get it now." But as Annie rose, the jingle of coins in her apron pocket made her aware that she had never put away the money Kellian York had paid.

Annie glanced at the double door leading out to the lobby. She gazed around the room looking for a place to hide the coins. Eyeing the urn in the center of the mantel, flanked by the two silver branched candlesticks, she shook her head. Her aunt swore that that urn held the remains of her fourth cousin Josh, and Annie to this day had never felt brave enough to test the truth of the statement.

She didn't want to return upstairs to her room, where she kept the strongbox. That thought was reinforced, along with a shiver of awareness, when she heard Mr. York moving around in his room directly overhead.

Heaving a frustrated sigh, Annie dismissed the clutter of vases and china boxes on the tables. Aunt Hortense was the only choice. Bracing one hand on the back of the rocker that her aunt sat in, Annie scooped the coins out of her pocket and placed the small pile in her aunt's lap.

Tucking the end of her shawl to conceal the money,

Annie smiled at her aunt. "Hold on to this until I come back, dear."

With a crafty look Hortense lifted one of the coins and bit it. "Gold?" She glared from the coins up to the flushed cheeks of her niece. "What have you done, Annie Charlotte? Sold my home out from under me? Don't be a-lyin' to me. Your face's redder than Tildy Means's rooster's comb. What've you been up to?"

"Not now, Aunt. Please, not now." Annie scrubbed her hand over her forehead. "Just hold on to the money and I'll go get you a nice, soothing cup of hot tea."

"Key? What key? Come back here, girl! Thought we was all done lockin' up gold from the Yankees." She thumped the end of her cane on the floor, glaring over her shoulder at Annie. "Come back here."

Annie went to her side.

"Your mama, Lord rest her, left you in my care. I'd be remiss in my duty, Annie Charlotte, if I didn't ask. Now you tell me why you're needing my key. You explain what you're up to, girl."

Annie couldn't swallow her moan. Once again she held her aunt's hand and stared at the age spots, willing herself to be patient. Someday she would be old, if she lived through this mess.

"Aunt, all I've done is rent every room in the house," Annie explained with exaggerated care, leaning close. "Do you understand that? I've done nothing wrong."

Hortense lifted her hand and smoothed it over the coiled braids of her niece's hair. "Smart girl. Always liked that about you, Annie. Now, be off. It's long past time for my tea."

Annie straightened slowly, trying to shake off her exhaustion. She made it to the double doors, waiting to be called back, as so often happened. But a glance behind her showed her aunt contentedly sitting and gazing out the window. With a quick twist, Annie set her apron to rights, then touched her hair. Opening the door to the lobby, she thought it strange that she couldn't find her cap. She had left it on the chair in her room.

"Oh, Annie," Hortense called before the door was closed, "find Dewberry, dear. He so likes to curl up on the sill while the sun is hot."

"I'll find him."

Dewberry? When had she last seen her aunt's old cat? She closed the door, frowning as she crossed the lobby and went into the dining room. Annie realized she couldn't remember when she had seen the cat. He had been in the kitchen while she brewed coffee and fried apple dumplings last night. She had been in and out bringing cups and plates to where Lucinda had set up a table. It wasn't unusual for the old tom to disappear for hours at a time, but she couldn't remember seeing him with all the confusion this morning. Aunt Hortense would fuss if she didn't find him, and with a sigh, Annie added "Find the missing cat" to her mental list of chores to be done. Dark as the brush blackberries he was named after, Dewberry could be anywhere.

A quick look at her watch pin showed that she had less than an hour before lunch would be served. Today should have been fried chicken day, but Annie had put a stew to simmer once her boarders were settled. And it was too bad if anyone didn't like it.

A look revealed the Fawn had already set the eight square tables that filled the dining room. Linen tablecloths, white, starched and ironed, lay smooth over each table. The matching napkins were rolled neatly. Teaching Fawn was a pleasure, for she leaned so quickly.

Annie rolled her shoulders to ease her tension. She

would be serving those people in here. She pushed one china plate back a little from a table edge, pleased with the gleam of the silverware. Cups and saucers were set precisely at the tips of the knives, with glasses alongside.

As she walked by on her way to the kitchen, she trailed her fingertips over the backs of the chairs, making sure that no trace of the lemon oil used to polish them lingered. One of the stage customers had complained that her new short cape had been stained by an excess of oil and had made Annie pay for it.

Although she was tempted to stay in the quiet, peaceful dining room, Annie moved on to the kitchen, stopping at the door. Men's voices? In her kitchen? She yanked the door open and rushed in. "Fawn? What's—"

"Like so," Li explained to Fawn, as if he were not aware of Annie. "You push with heel this hand. Turn with other. Now, again." he said, as the girl worked the dough on the table.

Annie glanced from Li's tall, slim body, draped with a loose, square jacket and trousers, to Fawn's slender shape. Li topped Fawn's height by a few inches. Annie motioned for Fawn to continue when she stopped. Li's bright, almond-shaped black eyes met Annie's gaze before he, too, turned his attention back to watching Fawn knead the dough.

"Just so," he praised in his lightly accented voice, one golden-skinned hand pressing over Fawn's to show her again how hard to knead.

Annie noticed the calluses on the outward curve of his palm. But she was struck not only by the similar skin color, that of golden-browned biscuits, but also by the same black, straight hair that they both wore in a single braid. A shuffle called her attention to where Pockets leaned against the pie safe watching them. She returned his nod, thankful that he had not lit the cigar he was chewing. There were rules to be observed in her boarding-house, and no smoking within its walls was just one of them.

Annie hadn't had time to discuss the rules with her new boarders, an omission she intended to rectify as soon as possible.

"Got the makings of a fine little cook there, Miss," Pockets said, removing his cigar to speak, then sliding it back into his mouth.

With a warm smile for Fawn, Annie agreed. "Fawn is quick to learn when someone is patient teaching her." An image of the frightened, cowering girl that she had first known came to mind, but Annie dismissed it. For the moment she forgot that these men had no right to be in her kitchen.

"Was there something you wanted, Mr. Pockets?"

"Me? Nah. Couldn't get to sleep this late. And it's just Pockets. On account of the vest, you know."

Looking at the bright red, yellow, and green plaid vest hurt Annie's eyes. She couldn't imagine why he needed eight pockets, or why anyone would take his name from them. Each pocket bulged with hidden contents, but Annie was not going to pry by questioning him about them.

She walked over to the stove, sniffing appreciatively at the enticing aroma rising from the simmering stew pot. Since Li and Fawn were making the biscuits, she could boil water for her aunt's tea and steal time for herself.

Annie tried to frame a polite but firm statement that she didn't appreciate Pockets' wearing his bowler hat in her kitchen. But when she went to the dry sink to prime the pump, he moved from his slouch to do it for her.

"Allow me. You must be tired after being up all night." Annie forgot about his hat. She held the kettle as he pumped a steady stream of cold water to fill it. "How did you know I'd been up all night?" she asked, heading back to the stove and thinking of the awful accusations his boss had flung at her.

Pockets glanced at her back while she lifted the metal plate to poke the fire and exchanged a quick look with Li. Pockets shrugged when Li shook his head.

"There was leftover apple dumpling sitting on the table, and I remember eating one once we had the fire under control. Then there was a pair of fancy ladies' shoes as muddy as mine and a cloak that reeked of smoke. Stands to reason you were out there, all right."

"Thank you for not accusing me of starting the fire. I didn't, you know. None of the women had anything to do with it."

Annie was unaware of the quick slicing motion Li made with his hand. Pockets shifted his cigar to the other side of his mouth, then took it out. "I've looked around some, and saw a fine upright in the back room off the parlor. Play it yourself?"

"A little. Just enough to pick out a few hymns when we hold service here on Sundays. The doors to the parlor open and—" Annie broke off, flustered. What was the matter with her? She was explaining about Sunday service to a man who worked in a den of vice. She reached for the tin of tea leaves.

"There was nothing to salvage of mine. Since the boss is planning to rebuild, I'll be grateful if I can use yours."

The china cup and saucer rattled in Annie's hands. She hated to say no, but it wouldn't be proper. She turned, ready to utter the word, but Pockets, his heavyset body once more in a slouch, was shaking his head.

"Wouldn't do at all, I guess. We don't want to cause you more trouble. Folks'll be saying plenty 'bout you renting us rooms. If they find out I'm using your piano they'd likely figure it was tainted by the devil's music." He stretched out his long-fingered hands in front of him, wiggling, then shaking them. "Keeps them limber," he explained at Annie's puzzled expression.

But Annie was thinking of what he'd said. After all, it was her piano. It was her boardinghouse. There was such a deep, wishful look in his light brown eyes that she was beside herself. The right thing, the most prudent thing, was to agree with him that it was improper and let it go. But he had been so polite, not at all like his boss. He hadn't accused her of starting the fire, and the piano did sit idle during the week unless she managed to find time to practice.

Before she gave it more thought, or weighed the very consequences he mentioned, Annie made him an offer. "I don't have much time to use the piano on weekdays. There's no real reason why you couldn't use it. Not while meals are being served, of course, or in the early morning, since my aunt's room is next to the parlor, but you are welcome to use it in between those hours."

"Well, thank you. Real pleased to accept your offer," he said, taking off his hat and making her a sweeping bow. "And don't worry none. I'll tickle those ivories like I was—" Pockets stopped himself. He couldn't tell a woman like her what he thought about the keys of a piano. Smoothing down his tightly curled brown hair, he replaced his hat.

Once again he shared a look with Li, and he got the feeling that just as he was revising his opinion of Annie Muldoon, Li was as well. He beamed a toothy smile at Annie and was warmed by the one she returned.

The kettle whistled in warning, and Annie grabbed a folded towel to wrap around the handle, pouring out the boiling water into the small china teapot. She measured out the precious tea leaves into the silver strainer that had been in her family for generations, then placed it into the pot to steep. It took her only a few minutes to gather what she needed to fix the tea tray for her aunt.

But when all was ready, Annie remembered about the cat.

"Since you've been in the kitchen with Fawn, Li, and you've been around downstairs, Pockets, have you seen a large black tomcat?"

Fawn was shaking her head. Li looked up, his hands never still as he shaped the small round biscuits and set them on a tray for baking. "No cat."

"Pockets?" Annie asked. "He's got one ear half torn off—"

"And a pushed-out jaw with a mouth turned off to one side like he's a cocky son of a—"

"Yes! Yes, that's him." Oh, dear! She must speak to him about his language. If Aunt Hortense ever heard him, there would be a fuss to end all others. "Where did you see Dewberry? He's my aunt's cat."

"Ah, well, that's hard to say." He shot a look at Li, and with a sheepish grin around his cigar, Pockets found his boots needed contemplation.

"I don't understand. Where is the cat?"

Li answered her. "A cat's heart is wise, like a mirror it reflects all without being sullied by any."

Mulling over his words, Annie decided she was too tired to try and understand what he was saying. From the incredulous look on Pockets' chubby-cheeked face, he didn't either.

"I'm sure those are wise words. Lovely ones, too. But I just want to know if you have seen Dewberry?"

"The cat is with Kell."

"Oh. Well, I'll just go fetch him." Annie lifted the tea tray, then set it down with a rattle. "He's with . . . the cat is up in . . . the room? The cat's in the room?"

"The boss has the cat or it might be the other way around," Pockets helpfully supplied, but he didn't look up at her, afraid his smirk would cost him the use of the piano.

Annie smoothed down the sides of her apron. "Yes. Well, thank you for telling me. I'll just bring this tea to my aunt, then retrieve our cat."

She made it out of the kitchen and halfway across the dining room before she realized what she had said. Dewberry was in Kellian York's room. She was going to go inside to get him. She was going to do it or there'd be a tussle with Aunt Hortense.

Annie, you are made of sterner stuff than you believe. You played the coward enough today. He is merely a boarder here. You are only going to retrieve the cat. Stop shaking as if you were going into the devil's den.

She stopped by the counter and reached for a key from the bottom row of pigeonholes. Years before, when Aunt Hortense kept losing the keys to rooms, Annie had the locks changed. No one knew that one key fit them all.

Wearing grim determination like a suit of armor while she served her aunt tea and reassured her that she would bring Dewberry to her shortly, Annie marched out of the parlor.

Short and quick. Annie repeated these words to herself as she raced up the stairs and down the hallway to Kellian York's room. She squared her shoulders. She took deep, steadying breaths. She released them shakily.

Just do it, she told herself. *Go in, get the cat, and get out.*

Annie stared down at the key. One last thing. Pray real hard that he's asleep.

Chapter Five

❧

Annie didn't worry that the lock would give her away as she fitted the key into it. She was a good house-keeper who oiled each lock regularly to prevent rust from forming. Yet she hesitated, for she had never violated a boarder's privacy by going into the room while they were inside.

Her earlier encounter with Mr. York made her anxious not only for herself but for Dewberry. What if the man didn't like cats?

There was no help for it; she had to go in there and find out for herself.

Kell was alerted to his unexpected visitor by Dewberry's twitching his ears. His left hand continued stroking the twenty-pound coon-size cat, who purred his contentment with a steady rumble.

His right hand, concealed beneath the sheet, closed over the smooth wood grip of his gun.

Annie heaved a sign of relief as she inched open the door. She had given this room to him not only because it had a large double bed but also because it was at the opposite end of the hall from her room. But as the rooms were opposite, so were the placements of the beds. Mr. York's, unfortunately, was set against the wall behind the door.

"Dewberry?" she whispered, hearing the cat's distinctive rumble.

"Can't be bothered to knock, Muldoon? Some boarding-house you run, barging into rooms without an invite. But come in, I've got nothing to hide."

Staring at the barrier of the door, Annie fought the urge to stick out her tongue. A most childish temptation, one she had not had for more years than she cared to remember. She was furious that he was awake, and worse, that he had caught her.

"I've come for my aunt's cat, Mr. York."

"Like I said, come on inside. If you want this old tom, you'll have to get him yourself. He's real contented where he is."

Taunting, teasing, impossible man! Did he think for one minute that she was afraid of him? Annie pushed the door open completely and stepped inside. She could see the foot of the bed, but nothing of Kellian York.

"Please let the cat go. I shall leave once I have him."

It cost Kell a great deal to keep quiet. Her prissed-up voice grated on his ears. But once more his gambler's instinct came into play, warning him that his silence would draw her in and the wrong word would send her fleeing. Although, for the life of him, he didn't know why he wanted to see her.

Annie strained to listen, hoping for a clue to what he was doing. All she heard was the cat's continuous purring. Well, Mr. York didn't hate cats. Dewberry wouldn't have let the man touch him if that was true.

She couldn't keep standing there with the door open. Being discovered in his room would add fuel to the gossip. He said he had nothing to hide. She wasn't afraid of him.

"Enough of this nonsense," she stated briskly, stepping around the door. "I demand—oh! Oh, my!"

A giddy feeling in her stomach had Annie thinking she was on a swing in the middle of a downward arc. He had warned her. She couldn't blame this on him. She suddenly stopped thinking and stared.

He was sitting up. One bare, muscled arm cradled his head. His chest was bare, too. Well, not quite, she amended. There was a mallet-shaped mat of golden-brown hair crossing the top of his chest. And like the handle of a mallet, the line went straight down to disappear beneath the sheet that barely covered his hips. Even with the shadowed light filtering into the room through the drawn drapes, Annie could see there wasn't an ounce of fat on him. Her gaze tracked the fall of the sheet off the side of the bed, revealing one of his legs, bare to the knee, dangling off the edge. The other leg, covered decently by the sheet, was angled into a vee-shaped cradle where Dewberry lay on his back, paws spread wide, looking like a chicken ready for stuffing.

Annie didn't even realize she had been holding her breath until she released it with a wheezing moan. She snapped her mouth shut. She closed her eyes and fought the blush that was ready to send heated color across her cheeks.

Nothing to hide. He had tricked her. He knew he would be embarrassing her with this blatant display. His image formed in her mind, and Annie opened her eyes in an effort to stop it. Her gaze landed on the framed sampler above his head.

The giddy feeling increased and spread from her stomach down to her legs. Pressing her knees together, she straightened her shoulders and read the sampler to distract herself.

> *'Tis a wisdom you should heed—*
> *Try, try again,*
> *If at first you don't succeed,*
> *Try, try again.*

Samuel Goodrich's words, embroidered by her grandmother, were the best advice Annie could have had at this moment. She would not allow Mr. York to disconcert her. She would not allow him to win this encounter.

"Mr. York," she began, taking a deep breath and releasing it. "Let me start over. I am sorry to have disturbed you, but I want Dewberry."

Kell smiled. He glanced down at the beat-up old tomcat. With his pushed-out jaw, half-torn ear, and mouth in a permanent cocky grin, the cat looked like a perpetual sinner. They were both males, and Kell had an affinity for wayward males.

After all, he was one of them.

"I don't think he wants to leave me, Muldoon. But you're welcome to come and take him."

"Come and take . . ." Annie saw the dark red embroidered words run together before her eyes. "I'm afraid, Mr. York, that would be most improper."

She couldn't help it. She had to look. Meeting his steely-eyed gaze, Annie knew he would not relent.

"Dewberry," she called, "come to me." When the cat didn't obey, continuing his purring instead, Annie took three steps closer and rested her hand on the footboard

"If you would stop petting him, Dewberry would come to me."

"Think so?"

Her only reply to his taunting was to order the cat to come again.

Annie was dismayed. Dewberry's response lacked understanding of her plight. He stretched his head back, offering up his white-patched throat for scratching with a plaintive meow.

She tried to avoid looking at the man while she figured out a way to get the cat without having to touch the odiously offensive Mr. York. She had serious doubts that there was anything under that sheet but the man's flesh and bones. From the parlor below came the thumping of Aunt Hortense's cane. Time had run out. Annie could delay no longer.

She went forward, her eyes spellbound by the stroking motion of his hand. She couldn't control her response. Her heart beat faster, her breath came in huffs and puffs, but there was an undeniable excitement present too. Annoyance with Dewberry's contented rumble for every gentle stroke gave her the courage to reach out her hands.

To her mortification, her hands hovered in the air above the cat.

"Careful, darlin'. You don't want to be grabbin' the wrong thing."

She jerked back. His cocky grin enraged her. "You . . . you . . . I don't know what's bad enough to call you."

"Lady, I'm only trying to protect my ass—" Her gasp made him stop. A satisfied smile curved his mouth. "My assets, darlin', that's all. Just my assets."

"Then I suggest you either wear clothing, Mr. York, or keep your door locked to protect your precious . . ." Annie felt that the airy wave of her hand in the direction of his lap served better than any word.

The thumping of her aunt's cane grew louder. Annie reached for the cat.

"Locking my door didn't keep you out, did it?"

Don't listen to him. Annie's hand brushed against his. A tiny frisson of warmth rippled up her arm. She couldn't help but notice that he had the same calluses as Li on the outward curve of his hand. Not that she cared enough to question him about it. The less she knew about Mr. York, the better.

Dewberry's golden eyes slitted open. Annie knew that look. He was going to hiss at her. Well, it was too bad for Dewberry. She intended to take him, willing or not.

"You know," Kell said, tightening his fingers over the headboard so as not to touch her, "most males don't like being ordered. Not by a female. And not when they're enjoying themselves."

"I'll keep that sage advice in mind, Mr. York, if I should ever find use for it," she snapped in return. There was no way to lift the cat but to slide her hands beneath his fat body. The way Kell's muscled leg cradled the cat, Annie saw that she couldn't avoid having to touch the man. Gritting her teeth, she prayed for guidance. She had to close her eyes, unable to look where she was plunging her hands.

Soft, silky fur met her thumbs and fingers. Solid, hot flesh singed the backs of her hands. It took only seconds, but she snatched up the cat and plastered his hissing, squirming body against her chest. Thankfully, Dewberry was too well behaved to sink his claws into her.

She had done it!

Her triumph was short-lived.

Kell's laughter flooded over her, then suddenly stopped.

Annie had to look at him. The second she opened her eyes and met the unholy wicked gleam in his, she wished she had not given in.

"Call down the hellfire and brimstone. Miss Annie Muldoon went diving in the devil's playground and came away unscathed. Or did she?" he asked, with a knowing look that raked her from head to toe. "Just as virginal as the moment she—"

"What possible concern can it be to you, Mr. York, if I am?"

"Interrupting someone as much as you do is rude, Muldoon."

"I don't need you to teach me manners." With her arms wrapped around the cat to stop his escape, she glared at Kell. "The state of my morals, the state of my being, Mr. York, has no bearing whatsoever."

She turned and with military precision rounded the door. "Good day to you."

Kell kicked the door closed, but didn't bother to get up to lock it again. He had watched her run from him for the second time today, and his smile grew wider with satisfaction. He had really been guessing about her virginal state. Poor little darling. Now he knew why she bristled around him.

Temptation lured him. He could tame that prissy little hedgehog.

Kell tossed off the sheet he had snatched up for her benefit, afraid she would expire if she walked in and found him buck-naked, and stretched out full length on the bed. He cradled his head with both hands and stared up at the ceiling.

He could rescue Annie Muldoon. Somewhere in the Good Book that she was fond of quoting when it suited her, there had to be a sin against wasting all that lush femininity. He would be performing a sweet mission of mercy. It might even be exciting.

Why he should want to rescue her, he didn't know. The woman hadn't shown him an ounce of mercy. She had invaded his room. She had left behind the delicate scent she wore. The inside skin of his thigh still throbbed from the momentary brush of her hand when she grabbed hold of the cat. Thank whatever sanity prevailed that she hadn't been aware of his slight movement that had prevented her from grabbing hold of his pride and joy. He could imagine the prim little darling's screeching if she found herself holding something more unruly than that squirming cat.

"Ah, Muldoon, if only you were a different sort of woman," he muttered with regret. "We could've spent a pleasant few hours pursuing your education."

Far from being discouraged, however, Kell knew there would be other times, and other places.

"For sure," he promised himself, closing his eyes.

Closing her eyes was not a luxury Annie could afford as the lunch crowd arrived, even though the avid way everyone's eyes seemed to follow her every move made her want to hide.

On a usual weekday she served one sitting for lunch. On Tuesdays and Thursdays, Lucinda, Abigail, and Emmaline, her very best friend, would get together once the other diners had been served their meals. But today, which was not at all a typical weekday, Annie had not seen Emmaline, and she couldn't spare the time to talk to Lucinda or Abigail. She even had to smile when Velma Grant fibbed about coming here to taste her fried chicken and stayed when informed there wasn't going to be any. Annie had given Velma her special family recipe. And Velma never came to town during the week. She came

Saturdays to shop, and she always attended Sunday service. Now she held court at the table in front of the windows with three members of their group.

If this wasn't enough to give Annie's stomach a sour dose of nerves, cowhands that she never served during the week were standing in line in the lobby waiting for a place to sit. Not one of them left when she informed them that there was only stew to eat, not fried chicken.

It didn't take the brain of a peahen to figure out what they were all up to. She knew they had come to whisper and gawk at those women. If the good Lord had not heard one of the prayers she had offered throughout this trying morning, at least he had spared her having to deal with the presence of those women, too.

It was all Kellian York's fault that she was being made the sacrificial goat. Sometime, somewhere, that man had done a good deed marked by the Lord. It was the only reason Annie could find to account for the Lord's placing her within one inch of the man. Either that or Kellian York had brought the devil's strong wiles into her boardinghouse thereby rendering her prayers useless. She had to think of this as a test of her beliefs and fortitude. Nothing else made sense.

For try as she might, Annie could not escape the image of him forming in her mind. Even the golden-brown biscuits that Li and Fawn were turning out reminded her of Kellian's bare skin. Shameless, that's what he was. Tempting her like some wanton.

Entering the steaming-hot kitchen just as Li removed another tray of baked biscuits from the oven set Annie to muttering under her breath.

Fawn rushed to take the empty plates and silverware from her, and Annie forced herself to smile. "Seems we're having a booming day, Fawn. I'll need four more plates."

She turned to find that Li was watching her with opaque black eyes. "How is the stew holding out?"

"You should tell them there will be no women. They will leave quickly."

"You're right. I should. But I'm not going to." She didn't know why she didn't put him in his place. He had no right to give her advice when he was just as much at fault as his boss. Perhaps it had something to do with the way he worked, an economy of motion, readying serving plates, each with two biscuits on top of the stew.

Annie went to the pie safe and took down two tins. From one pocket she removed the bills and coins that paid for meals and went into the household tin. The other pocket held her tip money, which she shared at the end of the week with Fawn. Frowning as she slid the smaller amount of coins into her tin, she wondered if she should offer to share it with Li.

"I will not require the money," Li said.

Annie almost dropped the tin. How did he know what she was thinking? Replacing the lids, she set the tins back in place, realizing as she did so, that she wasn't concerned that Li should know where she had put the money.

Wiping the sweat from her forehead with quick little pats of her hand, she faced him. "Why don't you want me to pay you? You're working every bit as hard as Fawn and myself. You should have something—"

"I do," he interrupted to say. "The stew grows cold from the pot."

She would have liked to stand there and argue the matter, but he was right—the food would get cold. Annie did intend to take this up with him later.

The time flew. Once the cleaning up was finished after the last diner left, she and Fawn tackled the laundry. Annie did the mending while Fawn ironed. Aunt Hortense and Dewberry were taking their afternoon nap, and Annie had to think about supper. Li disappeared once the kitchen was clean. She had not seen Pockets again, so she assumed that he, like Mr. York and the women, was in his room asleep.

It gave Annie a perverse sense of satisfaction to put up a kettle of bacon and beans. She could have still made the fried chicken, but she was tired and she didn't think those who only came to gawk would notice what they were eating.

Annie tripled the amount of corn bread and hot peppers she usually made as Fawn made trip after trip to bring the clean piles of laundry upstairs. When there were only Kellian's clothes to be returned to him, Annie asked Fawn if anyone was awake.

With graceful motions Fawn showed herself knocking and tilting her head to listen. She bent down as if placing an offering, then straightened and slowly shook her head.

"Say a prayer they all stay that way," Annie said, jabbing the thread through the needle's eye. "If we have another crowd for supper, you'll have enough money for that new calico material you've been wanting." She bit off her measured thread, knotted it with a roll and practiced twist of her fingers, then stared at the rip in Kellian's shirt.

It was unfortunate that Fawn, always eager to learn, moved closer to watch her. Annie longed to stroke the fine, high-quality weave, but she refrained from doing so with Fawn at her elbow. The linen was buttery soft, almost silky, and she could not stop the image coming to mind of him wearing it.

Her once-to-be-husband had been broader in his shoulders and chest, but he had never sent the type of unfurling warmth through her that the sight of Kellian York brought like a fever-flush. Before Annie could take the neat darning stitches needed to mend the tear, she had to still the faint trembling of her fingers.

The house was quiet, the room cooler now that the oven was off and Fawn had left the back door open. Annie could see a bit of her garden from where she sat at the work table. She didn't have much time to tend a real flower garden, but her seeds were sprouting among the vegetables. The drone of bees lulled her as she began her chore, but once she looked down at the material again, Kellian York's image returned.

Fawn pulled up a chair and sat close by, Annie smiled at her, searching for something to distract her thoughts. The only thing she came up with was the new book her ladies group had presented her on her last birthday. *Woman: Her Power* was a series of sermons on the duties of the maiden, wife, and mother, and their influence in the home and society, written by Reverend T. DeWitt Talmage, D.D., pastor of the Brooklyn Tabernacle in New York. The publisher, Mr. Ogilvie, was a distant cousin to Velma Grant, who had obtained the book once she had learned about it.

Annie treasured the book almost as much as she treasured her Bible. The sermons were a proven source of inspiration to her, one that she eagerly shared with the ladies sewing circle at their first-Wednesday-of-the-month meetings. As was often her habit, Annie also shared her thoughts with Fawn. It was anyone's guess how much the girl understood. But her black eyes would sparkle whenever Annie talked about the women's role.

"Do you remember, Fawn, I told you that the women's group was still discussing the first section of the sermons of Reverend Talmage?" Fawn fluttered her fingers near her mouth, as she always did to describe someone talking rapidly. Annie laughed. "Just so, like the twittering of the birds. But I explained to them the meaning of women who fight the battle alone. Truly, my dear, it is uplifting to know that there are men in this world, like the good reverend, who believe it heresy that a woman is thought to be a mere adjunct to man, a sort of afterthought.

"We know that is not true. It is a foolish notion entertained and implied by most men. The reverend agrees with my own view, that a woman is an independent creation. She is intended, if she chooses, to live alone, walk alone, act and think alone, and fight her battles alone."

Becoming excited, Annie forgot to watch the needle and jabbed its point into her finger. A tiny stain of blood appeared to mar the fabric of the shirt.

"Fawn, quickly, please, a cup of cold water."

That man was now interfering with her most precious thoughts of woman's independence. As Annie had pointed out to Abigail when she took exception to the very idea of independence, the Good Book said it was not good for a man to be alone, but never had it said that it was not good for a woman to be alone.

Knowing every secret of the married women in the circle made Annie realize that too many of them should have remained single even if society didn't approve of the state for women.

She liked being in charge of her life, and she resented being called a spinster, for it sounded ugly. She hated the term "old maid" equally, for she was not that old.

Fawn tapped Annie's shoulder lightly to get her attention and pointed at the open doorway.

Startled, Annie upset the cup of water the girl held. "No, Fawn, don't fuss. It won't hurt the shirt," she reassured the girl while taking the measure of the man who stood and watched.

He was tall, thin as a bean pole, filthy as could be, but Annie never turned a hungry drifter away.

"May I help you?" she asked, setting the shirt aside and rising from her chair.

" 'Preciate a bucket of water to wash, ma'am. I'm Bronc the barkeep—"

"Oh! I thought you were upstairs asleep."

"No, ma'am. Don't want to muddy up your floors, so—"

"Certainly not," Annie interrupted. "Where have you been? The whole county turned out for lunch here."

"Boss sent me back to watch over things." Bronc sniffed and licked his lips. "Something sure smells good."

"You missed lunch. Supper won't be ready for at least an hour." Annie pumped a bucket of water for him, relenting about her own rule that no meals or food of any kind was served except at set mealtimes. "I believe there might be a slice of pie left, though, and I could get you a glass of buttermilk from the springhouse."

"That's fine, ma'am. Real fine," Bronc said, taking the bucket from her.

"Towel's hanging on the peg," Annie reminded him, lingering in the doorway.

"Boss awake?"

"I have no idea. I do not make it a habit to keep track of the comings and goings of my boarders."

Bronc splashed water all over his face, bending low to toss a few handfuls over his sparse, rust-shaded hair. He shook himself like a wet hound, then reached for the towel.

"Need to find him real quick. He'll be mighty interested in what I found near the fire."

"And what was that?" Annie asked, with a little curiosity.

Bronc unfastened the two middle buttons on his shirt

and pulled out a mud-stained bit of cloth. For a moment her held it crumpled in his large, bony hand, then he shook the cloth, holding it up for her inspection.

"Can't rightly tell who it belongs to, but for sure, it's a woman's."

Annie couldn't stop her involuntary reaction. Her hand jerked up to touch her head. It was a woman's mobcap and could be her missing one.

"Please, may I see it?" she asked Bronc, holding out her hand.

"Hang on to that piece of evidence, Bronc," Kell ordered as he came into the room. "Did you find that near the fire?"

"Evidence?" Annie whirled around to face Kell. "I told you I didn't have anything to do with starting that fire."

"Close enough, Boss." Bronc withdrew the cap and once more held it crumpled in his hand.

Annie looked from Kell's impassive expression to the cap. "Evidence?" she whispered again. "But why?"

"Tell it to the sheriff in Graham," came Kell's reply, reaching out in front of Annie to take the cap from his barkeep. "The sheriff should be interested in seeing this. Whoever lost it might have set the fire. Then again, Muldoon," he added, facing her, "maybe whoever was wearing this cap saw who did set the fire."

"No! And I refuse to deny it again." But Annie couldn't look at him.

"You can deny it all you want, Muldoon, but you'll have to talk to the sheriff."

"That's how much you know, Mr. York. The sheriff is once again chasing after the cattle-rustling Marlow brothers. If they rode for Indian Territory like the last time they escaped jail, he could be gone for weeks."

"Guess that leaves me to find justice on my own." Kell

doubted that Annie had started the fire. What bothered him was that someone was trying to make him believe she was responsible. If Bronc found this cap anywhere near the fire, then someone had planted it there. The cap stank of smoke, but it wasn't singed.

"So, tell me, is it your cap, Muldoon?" he asked, waving the cloth beneath her snooty little nose.

Chapter Six

❧

"D"on't you dare wave that cap under my nose, you bounder!" Annie made a grab for the filthy cloth, only to have Kellian whip it high over his head.

"Bounder, Muldoon? Me? Who saved your neck?" Kell danced backward to dodge another attempt by Annie to snatch the cap.

"Who blackmailed me, Mr. York?" Annie advanced on him. "You . . . you . . ."

"Stop wasting time trying to think of names to call me, Muldoon. You don't have the talent for it."

"I'll call you whatever I like!" Annie yelled, too angry to care that his eyes sparkled with amusement. She lost her temper and shook her finger at him. "You're nothing but a strutting rooster who—"

"Rooster?" Kell stopped and shook his head. "Why, you little—" He started toward her.

"Yes, a rooster," she repeated, stepping back, then skirting the table. She kept looking at the cap he held out of her reach. "And I'll say it again, Mr. York, you strut while herding your hens."

"Roosters don't herd!" Kell shouted. With his free hand he raked back his hair, eyeing her across the table. "And they're not hens. I call them doves, lady."

"Soiled ones, too," Annie countered. She shot a look at Bronc, but the man stood with his arms folded over his chest, impassively watching from the doorway. Well, she didn't need a man to speak for her! "Mr. York, you're as bad as those quacks who sell fake patent medicines from their wagons."

An insult to any decent man, she knew, and she edged back from the table. She saw that Fawn wisely took herself off to the corner, out of the way. From the scowl on Kellian's face, Annie wondered if he would do her harm.

"Do you know what you are, Muldoon?" Kell began, his teeth gritted as he circled the table after her. "You are a vigilante leader. And you like dictating. You and that stifling group of corset-cinched, dried-up old hens are jealous."

"Don't you dare call my friends 'hens.' "

"They're hens, Muldoon. And what's more, you're jealous of the doves."

"Jealous?" Annie stopped and whirled around to face him only to find he, too, had stopped on the opposite side of the table. Adjusting her position to glare at him, she slammed her hands onto her hips. "I am not jealous." Even as she made her declaration, Annie was aware of Kellian's stillness. She was not blind to the life-and-death struggles played out by nature in the land where she lived. Kellian had the look of a predator, and she was the only prey in sight.

Despite his narrow-eyed gaze and the way he had flattened both hands on the table, pulling his shirt taut to reveal the finely honed muscles of his arms, shoulders, and chest, Annie dismissed him as a threat.

"Since you are so intent on furthering my education, Mr. York, let me add to yours. There is nothing for me to be jealous about. I would not sell myself."

"You," he leaned closer to whisper, "wouldn't be given a chance to. No man," he taunted, "could be so desperate as to want the likes of a shrew like you." *Liar! You want her. Want Miss Annie Muldoon just as she is now—with those dark blue eyes flashing a challenge, those golden freckles on blazing pink cheeks, and those other generous endowments created to torment a man heaving with every breath she drew and huffily released.*

His insults stung, but Annie refused to acknowledge either his words or her hurt. She would attack. "You will not malign my friends under this roof, Mr. York. They are all good women—"

"Yeah?"

"Yes! But someone of your ilk wouldn't know anything about good women. And there is nothing wrong with the fact that they wear corsets. Real ladies do!"

Annie didn't need Bronc's sudden spate of coughing or Kellian's smug look to make her cover her flaming cheeks with her hands. What was this man reducing her to? Here she was, yelling about ladies' unmentionables in her kitchen to a man she didn't even know!

Kell jumped up on the table, tossed the cap to Bronc, who caught it easily, then turned his attention on Annie.

Bewildered, she stared at him. "What are you doing? Get down from there."

"With pleasure, Muldoon."

He was down and hauling her up against him before she could utter a sound.

"Unhand me! Of all the gall! Your behavior is a disgrace. You're nothing but a bold, brassy parish-stallion!"

"Ah, Muldoon, *now* you've got the name right."

Annie gasped like a caught fish, and felt about as helpless as one flopping on a stream bank, struggling to get free of Kell's hold. She reared back as far as she could when he leaned his face closer, then bared her teeth at him. She refused to dignify her bid for freedom with the verbal abuse she longed to heap on him.

Kell moved fast. He slid his hands down her sides to grab hold of the corners of her apron, avoiding a kick to his shin. With an upward yank, he had the generous material of the apron twisted around Annie, imprisoning her arms against her sides. Quickly bringing the ends together behind her back, Kell held her captive with one hand.

"Now I've got you at my nonexistent mercy, Muldoon." He drew her closer to his body, his free hand caressing the rigid line of her shoulders. Gazing at her upturned face, Kell smiled. She looked mad enough to shoot him. Her luscious mouth was pressed into a tight line. Her brows were drawn together in a furious scowl, and her eyes promised retaliation. He couldn't wait.

"Did Dewberry steal your wasp's tongue, darlin'?"

Annie didn't answer him. She was smart enough to know that she was no match for his practiced wiles. She ignored the spark that kindled the moment he touched her. *Remember how mean he is,* she warned herself. *And stop looking up at his sun-streaked hair, thinking how it would feel to touch it!*

"Cad," she snapped, her gaze lifting to meet his.

"Do you know," Kell whispered, tunneling his fingers into her coiled braids to keep her head still, "how I'm going to shut you up, Muldoon?"

"No." Annie didn't bother to elaborate. She didn't call

him another name. She couldn't. Something was happening to her breathing, her heart and her legs. She wished she knew what made her feel so warm, shivery, and tense at the same time. Rushing back was the image of the intimate press of Kellian York's body against her own this morning. Was it only this morning? But this time it was worse. This time Annie knew what lay beneath his shirt. Swallowing against a mouth that was as dry as summer grass, Annie tried to block out the recollection of what the rest of his sheet-draped body had looked like.

"Muldoon," Kell murmured. He lowered his head until his lips hovered just a hairsbreadth from her mouth. He heard her swift in-drawn breath. Her reaction forced him to bury his laughter. Annie's squinting gaze dropped from his to target his mouth. Being so close, he saw her eyes nearly cross with impotent fury as she realized that he wasn't going to stop what he intended to do.

Her mouth was sinfully indecent. Red, luscious, and pure temptation. She parted her lips, exhaling huffy, heated little breaths. Kell didn't doubt it was excitement and not fear that caused each hitch in her breathing.

"Ever been kissed, Muldoon?" He didn't know why he asked her when he already knew the answer—not by anyone like him. If ever a woman looked ready for kissing, Annie was that woman. He wanted to kiss her—needed to do it.

A slight move to the side gave him a glimpse of Bronc's frown. Kell closed his eyes and touched his lips to Annie's.

"Oh, my! Goodness! Gracious goodness! What are you doing to my niece? My glasses—where are my confounded glasses?" Hortense demanded, banging her cane on the floor.

Kell lifted his head, but didn't release Annie.

"Ma'am," Bronc answered before anyone else, "them glasses is tied to the ribbon around your neck."

"Yes. Of course they are." Hortense snapped them in place, gaping at Kell and Annie. "I can hardly believe what I'm seeing. And in my kitchen, too. Unhand that young woman at once, my good man."

"There is nothing good about him, Aunt." Annie responded on one level to her aunt's upset, but on another level she wished her aunt had waited just one more minute. As for the lie she had just uttered, Annie didn't believe anyone had to know that there was a great deal good about Kellian York. He looked good. He felt— She stopped herself, suddenly realizing what she was doing.

"If she had waited a few minutes more, Muldoon, you wouldn't be able to say that."

"Oh, yes, I would, Mr. York." Annie twisted to escape and he let her go. "On top of every other sin you have committed, you have humiliated me before my aunt."

"And I wasn't half trying, Muldoon. Imagine what I could do with a little time and privacy." *Where the hell was Li when he needed him?* Kell raked back his hair and turned at the sound of a slight shuffle from the doorway leading to the dining room.

"About time you showed up," he said to Li, not in the least surprised that he was there.

"I have been here. You would not have listened if I told you a caged nightingale does not sing sweetly."

"Not only wouldn't he have listened to you, Li," Annie said, annoyance lacing her voice when Fawn quickly moved to stand beside Li, "but the arrogant Mr. York wouldn't have the intelligence necessary to understand you."

"Annie Charlotte!"

"Yes, Aunt Hortense?" But even though she answered

her aunt she refused to look away from Kell. Her fingers curled with the itch she had to wipe the smirk from his lips.

"Niece, I demand to know what is going on here."

"Ma'am, afore you do," Bronc said from where he still stood in the back doorway, "would it be all right if I had that piece of pie first? I'm powerful hungry. You can forget 'bout the buttermilk. Water's jus' fine."

"Annie, do you mean to tell me you've let this poor man go hungry?" Without waiting for an answer, Hortense said to Bronc, "Come in and sit down at the table, young man. Have you washed your hands?" She was not satisfied with his curt nod. Hortense moved closer to the table and lifted first one of Bronc's hands, then the other. Her spectacles slipped as she inspected, then released him.

"They will do. Fawn, give this young man a piece of pie. Not too big, it's close to supper. You will stay to supper," she informed Bronc. Sliding her glasses off, Hortense faced her niece. "Annie Charlotte, I will see you and Mr. York in the parlor." Hortense pivoted with the aid of her cane, straightened her slender shoulders, and walked to the doorway, where Li stood with Fawn beside him.

"Young man," Hortense said, glancing up at Li, "you were very kind to help my niece and Fawn with preparing lunch this afternoon. But I caution you against trying to cage birds. They were meant to be free so that all may enjoy their songs."

Annie found the bewildered look on Li's face priceless as he watched her aunt's dignified exit. Though she was short and petite, with silvered hair, Aunt Hortense was still a presence to be reckoned with. Her gray-blue gown with its crocheted collar and cuffs was as old-fashioned as her beliefs. Beliefs that Annie shared.

But Annie refused to give in to the urge to smile when

Li glanced at her with puzzlement. She still had to deal with her aunt and Mr. York. Chin up, shoulders back, and spine straight, Annie walked past Kell.

"Now you have done it, Mr. York," she muttered, hurrying after her aunt. "If you don't want to find yourself spending the night sleeping outside, you had better come along."

Kell sauntered out after the two women, not because Hortense demanded it or Annie threatened him. He simply wanted to gaze at Annie's enticing, hip-swaying walk. It was a torment, but he felt he deserved such punishment for what he had done. No, what he had almost done. This morning—was it only this morning?—he couldn't stand Annie Muldoon. Now, for the second time in one day, he was surprised at how close he had come to kissing her.

What was wrong with him? He had been without sleep before, but he had never thrown all caution to the wind. He had enough problems to solve before he left this back side of nowhere town without the added complication of Annie.

He certainly shouldn't have been tantalized by kisses that had never happened.

And make no mistake, he warned himself, Annie's a woman who'll expect involvement and demand commitment from a man. She'd be after the forever kind of promises. You don't ever make promises. She's a good woman, the kind that would want a man's name, his ring, and a free hand in his pocket. You don't like that kind of a woman. You avoid them.

He had seen enough in his own family of what happened when men gave up their dreams and indulgences because of marriage. They couldn't smoke in the house, couldn't play cards—either because of lack of money or because their wives, all good women, didn't like it. Sneaking drinks out behind the barn like kids. Not him. He wasn't going to be tied down by some woman's apron strings. He'd never get so bogged down in worry that he forgot how to smile. That's what marriage did to a man. Why, he would have to give up his wanderings ways—and for what? To be paraded like a prize at a church social? Never happen. He'd take a pleasure-loving woman any day of the week.

Kyle had taught him that. His brother had lit out the night he turned sixteen and came back a year later sporting fancy duds and jingling gold coins. Kell didn't need much persuading to take off with him. And once he had, he found a life he loved.

Annie Muldoon was a woman to avoid at all costs. He would even bet the contents of his strongbox that she was as green as meadow grass about men and sex. She'd need a great deal of seducing and he had no time for it.

But the moment he had himself convinced as he crossed the lobby, Annie stopped in the open doorway of the parlor and faced him. With a saucy toss of her head, her eyes issuing a challenge no man in his right mind would acknowledge, she crushed every warning he had just given himself.

The dare aroused him. Annie disappeared inside the room. Kell followed, but slowly, as if he suddenly had all the time he needed or wanted.

Annie left the parlor seething with resentment. Not only had her aunt called her to account for her behavior, she had reprimanded Annie in front of Kellian York. The humiliation was not to be borne in silence. But silence was all she had, since she refused to create another scene. It was enough that she had verbally protested her aunt's invitation for Mr. York *to* stay and visit with her.

How could Aunt Hortense have been taken in by that snake charmer's ingratiating manner? Annie had no answer, and as the long afternoon wore on, and the dinner hour approached, she found that the day could grow worse. Could and did. By the time she retired to her room with a blinding headache, hunger pangs, and a walloping dose of self-pity, she knew what a state of abject misery truly was.

Since she had forgotten to bring up hot water, she had to be satisfied with a cold cat's wash from the water in the pitcher. It added another black mark against Kellian York, and at this rate, Annie knew she couldn't find a card big enough to hold all the marks against the man.

Sinking into her bed with a weary sigh did not bring relief that the day was finally over and she could rest. Annie tossed. She turned. She closed her eyes, attempting to block out the sight of her dining room crowded again with those who had come to gawk and whisper.

The only blessing was that, once more, Mr. York and his birds failed to come down and provide the show everyone seemed to expect. But it was no thanks to any consideration on Kellian's part. Annie knew it was Li who had taken supper trays upstairs to keep those women away. Li, she decided, was a decent man, one of great sensibility, the complete opposite of Mr. York. Why they were together was a question she would like answered, but asking anything of Kellian York was not possible. Not after what he had done to her.

Annie sat up, bunching her pillows behind her. With an angry kick she rid herself of the twisted sheet and wrapped her arms around her raised knees.

The matter of her cap being found near the fire preyed

on her mind. Bronc had allowed her to examine it, and Annie found the small red X she marked all her clothing with on the bottom edge of the cap. Someone had stolen it. But why?

Resting her chin on one knee, she worried her lower lip with the edge of her teeth. Why would someone want her to look guilty of starting that fire? It made no sense. But the fact remained that her cap had been stolen from this room.

A chilling shiver ran up her spine. Now that she was alone, Annie had no need to pretend she was brave, resourceful, and didn't need anyone. It violated her to think that her room had been entered. And there was no one she could turn to and confide her fear.

One of her fears, she reminded herself. The other was a fear on a different, but no less frightening level. She couldn't dismiss Kellian York from her mind. Like a thief, he slipped into her thoughts, boldly and brazenly making his presence felt.

And she had no one to confide in about him. She had wanted him to kiss her. There! She admitted it. But far from making her feel better, her admission let Annie know she was in trouble.

Rarely did she allow herself to think about her almost marriage, but she was restless, though exhausted, and the long-ago day's disaster came rushing forward from where she kept it buried.

Adam March was everything she dreamed of wanting in a man. He had been tender, gently courting her, winning her trust and her love. She had been so sure that marrying him was the right thing to do. He had a steady job as a cattle buyer for several ranch owners in California. The lush land of the Loving ranch and its fatted cows had drawn him to this far north corner of Texas. Annie rented him a room, found herself spending time with him whenever he was in town, and lost her heart to the black-haired scoundrel he turned out to be.

She adored the bounder, fool that she was. He wanted a quiet wedding, claimed he had no family and intended to stay right there in Loving with her when he wasn't traveling. Annie agreed to every one of his plans. She hadn't the sense of a goose being fattened when Adam looked at her with those dark eyes of his and sighed her name so that it sounded like music, need, and desire all rolled together.

But the night before their wedding, screams erupted from the back porch. Annie shivered now, recalling how she had run downstairs through the kitchen to investigate what was going on. The shock of seeing a woman on her knees, pleading with Adam to come home, had nearly caused her to swoon.

Even now, so many years later, her stomach churned with nausea. No matter how she tried to block the sight of that woman looking up at her, claiming to be Adam's wife, Annie knew it was a memory burned in time that would never be wiped away. Annie didn't believe her, she couldn't. The woman was scrawny, wild-eyed, and dressed like the meanest farmer's wife.

Rubbing her arms, she increased her pacing as the hours that had followed slammed back full force as if it had happened yesterday.

Adam's denials. Annie's own acquiescence to his request that she leave him to handle everything. She had been so in love with Adam, and she had never dealt with a hysterical woman. It was the excuse she offered herself then, and now, for meekly allowing Adam to usher her out of the way that night.

Then came morning. What was to have been the happiest day of her life. Her wedding day.

When she went downstairs, the woman was gone. But so was Adam. Annie's anxiety turned to fear. It wasn't until Aunt Hortense had gone looking for the strongbox to gift Annie with her mother's pearl earbobs, that Adam's other perfidy came to light. He had disappeared with the strongbox, which held money, jewelry and some worthless stocks. The sheriff still had a wanted poster for Adam, and Annie wished he would rot someplace hotter than Texas in the summer.

No one saw the scars he had left on her. Annie knew her pride was a sin, but it was all she had to wrap around herself when she had to face everyone and announce there would be no wedding. Pride was the shield she had hid behind whenever a word of pity came her way.

In the years that had passed, few dared to mention that Annie had been abandoned at the altar, and her pride was all that allowed her to scoff at any mention of marriage for her.

She was an independent woman. She did not need a man to clutter up her life. She had no wish to find herself forced to ask some man's permission before she wanted to do something.

Her pacing gradually slowed, then Annie stopped near the window. Her life was full. She was content. But even as she thought this, there was a restlessness rising to plague her.

She knew she was plain. She certainly did not follow the dictates of Godey's that claimed a woman's waist should measure one inch for each of her life. She was twenty-eight years old but her waist still measured the same eighteen inches that it had on the day planned for her wedding.

Perhaps she had been foolish over the years to turn aside the least hint that a man was interested in courting her. But Adam March had betrayed her trust. He had made her believe that she was not a woman a man could love. No one had ever understood how he had shaken her belief in herself, until she had retreated from any man who attempted to court her.

Annie knew she was set in her ways, having been called a prude more than once. That, too, had become her shield to hide behind. She had come to think of her desires and passions as a weapon to be used against her. Curbing them with the firm standard of behavior she adhered to made her less vulnerable. Her only regret was that there would be no family. She would never have the children she longed for, the ones to carry on with her dream. Yet, she was determined to leave a mark on Loving by seeing to the building of a church, and then, having a real minister preach on Sunday.

Nothing was going to get in the way of that dream. Too restless to sleep, Annie picked up her wrapper and draped it over her shoulders. Dragging up the past about Adam only reminded her that Kellian York was likely cut from the same cloth. Mr. York had no scruples.

But Annie, a little voice corrected, *at least Kellian York is honest about it.*

"True," she muttered. "But his constant insults sting. I didn't need to hear from him that no man would want me. I know what I am and what I look like. Facts that won't change. Who cares a nickel what his opinion is? And I certainly don't like the way he looks at me."

Ah, but Annie, you can admit the truth. No one will know. It's a little frightening, but deep down you get excited about the way he looks at you. Remember today? This morn-

ing, and later. Remember how he almost kissed you twice? You felt shivery and tense, and warm at the same time.

"Well, that's a crockful!" she whispered. "I do not like the way he looks at me. I do not like Kellian York. He's a necessary evil means to a good end. That's all."

But she stared at the door, where she could barely make out the shadow of the straight chair she used to prop against the door. "I'll be on my guard," she warned herself. "He won't force his way into my life the way he came bursting into my room."

He won't, she repeated, before finding sleep.

She was still trying to convince herself when all hell broke loose in the morning.

Chapter Seven

❧

Annie didn't have her corset strings tied when the first crash alerted her to trouble. The sun was still a small eye on the far horizon when a wild yell echoed from somewhere downstairs. Barefoot, Annie left her laces undone and tugged on her shirtwaist, trying to do up the buttons and make sense of the loud noises. Footsteps pounded in the hallway, warning her that the boarders were aroused too.

She didn't bother with shoes or stockings, leaving her room at a run. Annie never knew what made her look up just as she reached the stairway, but she was sorry she did. A woman was standing in the doorway of Kellian's room. There was not enough light to see who she was, but the sheet barely draped around her told its own story of why she was there.

Blushing like a rose in full bloom, Annie stared a hole through the sheet and rushed down the stairs.

"What happened?" Annie demanded as she reached the bottom step. She had not fully understood what it would mean to have the women from the Silken Aces in her boardinghouse. Now she did. In various states of undress, four of them clustered around the counter. Two had on wrappers, but Annie could have sworn they didn't have a stitch beneath them. The third wore a chemise and petticoat, and the last, like the women upstairs, was draped in a sheet.

Good Lord! Annie silently muttered. *York had had two of them in his bed!*

Clearing her throat, she again asked what had happened. This time her demand was loud enough for the women to separate.

Annie clung to the newel post. Pockets leaned against the counter, pressing a cloth to his jaw. Kellian York stood beside him, barefoot, bare-chested, and turned toward her with those sage-green eyes promising hell to the next one who crossed his path. Unfortunately, that was Annie.

"I'm trying to find out what the hell happened here, Muldoon."

With her breath lodged in her throat, Annie didn't answer him, didn't say a word or make a sound to protest his use of profanity in her boardinghouse. Annie was positive that the position of his hands on his hips was all that kept the threadbare denim pants covering what they were meant to. She amended her thought. The glove-soft fabric clung to his body in a way that struck sparks in her fertile imagination.

Annie!

For just a few moments she ignored her own silent warning.

His body did fascinate her. His subtle move caused all sorts of stirrings inside her. She knew it was wrong, but all she saw, all she could think about, was Kellian's body. A body so lovingly created that it confirmed, by all she held dear, that he was formed to be a woman's temptation.

It was not her imagination but Kell himself who shifted his stance so that he stood with his legs spread, radiating an aggressive, arrogant, and taunting attitude.

Annie tried to swallow, but the lump in her throat remained.

He raked a hand through his sleep-tousled hair. The movement drew Annie's gaze upward to his stubbled cheeks, and from there it seemed a natural progression to look at his eyes. Annie was drawn to their deep green color, but at the same time she wished she had never looked. There was an immediate sense that Kell was aware of her reaction to the worn pants that hid nothing of his muscular legs and left nothing for her to speculate about—not when only two buttons were closed.

She rubbed her damp palms against her skirt.

When Kell's heavy-lidded gaze raked her from head to toe, then lingered on her bare feet until she curled her toes, Annie longed for another two inches on her skirt hem to hide them.

Heart pounding, mouth dry, flushed from the heat spreading inside her, Annie was fascinated and a little frightened of the total awareness they had of only each other. He looked up and her gaze locked with his. The breathlessness she experienced was due to his look—which promised excitement—and to his cocky stance that seemed to whisper, *Come an' get me, darlin', an' I'll make sure you have one helluva ride.*

Helluva? Well, that was right. He was hell, and . . . Annie came to with a start, suddenly conscious of the others, murmuring all around them. Quickly offering up a prayer for strength and salvation, she asked again what had happened.

"Went out to the shithouse—" Pockets began.

"The what!" Annie slammed one hand over her pounding heart.

"Help me out here, Kell. What do ladies call—"

"Ain't that the berries," Cammy said, coming forward to stare at the red flags of color on Annie's cheeks. "Pockets was sayin' that he went out to the honey-house—"

"She's a lady, Cammy," Ruby cut in, eyes twinkling with laughter as she tugged her sheet tighter. "Try the chapel."

"No, no," Daisy said, resting her hand on Pockets' shoulder. "Ladies call them privies."

"Enough." Kell didn't raise his voice, but his look at each of the doves silenced them. Blossom never said a word, but she moved closer to Cammy and whispered something. The two then stared at Annie. With his uncanny sense, he knew that Li was there without turning around. "What did you find outside?"

"What I expected. No one," Li answered. His gaze took in the sight of Kell's aggressive stance and the obviously aroused state of Annie Muldoon. To watch Kell with Annie was to see a master with a novice. An innocent novice who cried out for protection without being aware of it.

Kell glanced again at Pockets' swollen jaw. "You're sure you didn't see who hit you?"

"Didn't see a damned thing," Pocket mumbled, working his swollen jaw with one hand. "Ain't broke. Just hurts like hell. Reckon you can get a few more chips of ice?" he asked Daisy, then glanced at Annie. "That all right with you?"

"Yes. Of course it is." Distracted, Annie backed up the steps. How could those women remain so uncaring of their undressed state in front of three men? No sooner had the question formed than Annie realized what she

was thinking. These women made their living being undressed in front of men!

"Running again, Muldoon?" Kell taunted.

"My shoes . . . there's chores and . . ." Annie stopped
herself. The slow, curling grin on his lips was enough to
send her up the stairs at the same run she had come
down them. It promised to be another day of unrelenting
headaches.

Kell left Pockets to the care of the doves and followed
Li into the kitchen. He accepted the mug of coffee that
Li handed to him. Leaning against the edge of the table
while Li picked up the chair he had knocked over in his
rush to get outside, Kell continued the conversation that
had been interrupted by Pockets' shout.

"Since Muldoon is careless enough to leave the front
and back doors unlocked, we know anyone could have
stolen that cap from her bedroom. And it made perfect
sense that I would suspect her and her group of starting
that fire."

"Why do you keep calling her Muldoon?" Li asked, filling his own cup with coffee. "Is that the way you distance
yourself from her? You know she does not realize what you
are doing to her, Kell."

"I'm not doing a damned thing. She's a burr and I want
to focus on the fire, not on that prissed-up excuse for a
woman."

Li's speculative gaze rested on Kell. He grinned, then
sipped his coffee.

"Don't be getting any ideas about Muldoon," Kell
warned him. "If you can't say anything more about the
fire, don't say another word."

"Right, Kell, the fire. You were saying that if you were
to blame Annie, you would look no further for the real
culprit." Li met his friend's gaze. "What about Laine?"

"She's got the most reason to hate me. She expected Kyle to leave the Silken Aces to her. If Kyle hadn't been thinking with what was between his legs instead of the good sense he had, she wouldn't be badgering me to cut her in for half a share when I rebuild."

"You're set on doing that? We could leave, Kell. I have wanted to travel east again." Li moved to the dry sink and tossed out the last of his coffee. Working the pump handle to rinse his cup, he thought of the many years he had been with Kell. Nearly eight, he recalled, remembering how Kell had won him in a poker game. In all that time, Kell had never lied to him. Li wondered if Kell realized that he was lying now not only to him but to himself about Annie Muldoon.

"It's hard to explain," Kell began, joining Li at the sink and rinsing out his own cup. "You know I never wanted the place. I gave up trying to settle down a long time ago. But I feel like I owe Kyle. And there's the doves, Li. I can't just go off and leave them without work, without a place."

"Good reasons, I am sure," Li agreed in his slightly accented voice. He dried the cups and hung them back on the hooks in the cupboard. "You once told me that you had been run out by a women group—"

"Yeah, I know. Maybe that's part of the reason why I'll rebuild. Make up your mind that we're staying. What's more, we're going to find out who tried to burn us out. I can't see Laine as being behind this. She risked her own life that night."

"We all did. Shame it was too dark for me to see much when I went outside. Perhaps Bronc had more luck than I." Li stared blankly at the wall for a moment, then added, "I saw Cammy, Ruby, Daisy, and Blossom. Where were Laine and Charity?"

"Laine was in my room. I didn't see Charity at all."

"Your room?"

"Not what you're thinking," Kell was quick to say. "She came in to talk."

"In the middle of the night?"

"She heard me moving around. Like you, I couldn't sleep for long. And that's all it was, Li." But Kell's gaze followed his Chinese friend's upward toward the ceiling. "If you thought that—I guess Muldoon—"

"Had similar thoughts?" Li finished for him.

"Who the hell cares what she thinks?"

Li watched him, silently laughing. *You care, Kell. You may not know it as yet, but you care.*

"I do not care that he had two women in his bed. You understand that, Fawn," Annie said, while she and the young woman made up Aunt Hortense's bed. Pounding the sides of the goosedown pillows to fluff them, Annie continued. "I must tell him that I cannot have such behavior here. I will not tolerate it. He can go someplace else to conduct his affairs. If that's even what they're called. I run a decent, respectable house and he must abide by my rules. Fawn," she declared, smoothing down the pillowcase, "it's high time Mr. York was informed of what he may and may not do here."

Leaving her aunt's room, Annie paused to listen to the tune Pockets was picking out on the piano. She didn't recognize the music, but it was pretty and she hummed along as she went upstairs. Patting the coiled braids at the back of her neck, Annie forced herself down the hall and stood in front of Kell's room.

She tried to rehearse exactly what and how she would set her rules before him. It was a pity that the sight of him in those denims would not leave her. But she had delayed long enough. Annie knocked on the door.

"It's open."

"Mr. York, I have come to discuss—oh, I didn't realize you had someone here." Annie remained where she stood, in view of the bed where Kell lay prone on his stomach while the woman Annie had seen in his doorway draped in a sheet earlier, proceeded to rub his back. His bare back. And she wasn't just rubbing him, she was working long fingers into his muscles and causing him to groan. If that wasn't enough to mortify Annie, the woman straddled his hips.

"Yeah, Muldoon? You can talk. Laine knows when to pretend she's not here."

"Would that I could do it as well," Annie snapped, losing whatever hold she had had on her temper.

"Bother you, does it? I'm sore and she's a wonder."

Recalling the fact that another of the women had also been draped in a sheet, Annie didn't dispute or ask what he was sore from—obviously his bedsport had been strenuous.

"I did not come here to discuss the merits of Miss . . . Miss—"

"Laine, Muldoon," Kell drawled, deliberately keeping his eyes closed. "And Laine is very, very good at what she does."

Annie couldn't understand why the deep, rumbly sound of his voice made her think of mussed sheets and beds. She found it more and more difficult to keep her mind on what she had come to see him about. Sprawled as he was, and with Laine never once pausing in her stroking, Annie felt she was an intruder on their intimacy. But the fact remained, that was the very thing she had come to discuss.

"I realize you may feel comfortable with Miss Laine

hearing what I have to say to you, Mr. York, but I do not. Since I have no intention of leaving, she will have to."

"Bossy little critter, ain't you?" Laine said.

Annie met Laine's amused look with a direct stare learned at her mother's knee. It should have been enough to quell Miss Laine's smile. It didn't. Plain talk was all she had left.

"You may think so. I do own this boardinghouse, and it has always been a respectable place. I wish it to continue being regarded as such. There are rules and—"

"Leave us, Laine," Kell interrupted her to say. He waited until she raised herself up, then he rolled out from under her. Kell came off the bed and with a stalking grace headed straight toward Annie.

Lord help! Annie closed her eyes, chiding herself for being a coward. He was still wearing those pants, and they still weren't securely fastened. *Didn't the man have any morals? Why, his appearance could have an adverse affect on a woman. Namely one. Herself.*

Annie heard the door close behind her; she emitted a rusty squeak but didn't move. "The door—"

"Leave it closed, Muldoon."

She knew he was near her. Not that he made an attempt to touch her, but Annie knew how close he was because there was a rise in the temperature around and inside her. When she had requested to speak to him alone, she hadn't given thought to her own unruly reaction to Kellian York.

"It's improper to keep the door closed."

"And it's damn improper for you to come into my room, Muldoon." Kell mimicked her starched voice, then added, "Say whatever it is you need to get off your chest." The instant the words were out Kell regretted them. His gaze slid down to her breasts, and he was disappointed to see that she was tightly laced and layered, unlike the charming picture she had presented him with this morning.

"There is no need for you to ridicule my speech." Annie had to look at him. She tried to focus on his jaw, but its stubborn set annoyed her. He still had not shaved. Annie decided that his earlobe, visible beneath his mussed sun-streaked hair, was the only safe place for her to look.

"I'm still waiting," he reminded her.

"I intend to finish. I always finish what I start."

"Well, well, who would believe we have something in common, Muldoon." Kell paused, most deliberately, snagging her panicked look for a second before she stared off at a point past his shoulder. "So do I. You might want to remember that."

"Don't threaten me. I never had the opportunity to discuss the rules of living here. You must consider the other residents in my boardinghouse, Mr. York, namely, my elderly aunt who would not have withstood the shock of the scene I had to witness earlier. There is Fawn, who has already been subjected to terrors in her young life and is a most impressionable young woman. And, Mr. York, there is myself. I demand—"

"Demand, Muldoon?"

"Yes, demand, Mr. York. You must dress properly when you are out of your room."

"No restrictions about what I wear when I'm in it?"

Annie steeled herself against the taunting note in his voice. "Now you mock me. I'll not have that. I expect you to tell those women the same. I do not restrict kitchen privileges, but I won't have people traipsing about the house at all hours in various states of undress. It is improper. Do I make myself clear so far?"

"In the clear, ringing tones of a medicine wagon preacher. But tell me," Kell asked, hooking his thumbs into the loose waistband of his pants, "did you expect Pockets to knock at your door in the middle of the night and ask politely for your permission to use the outhouse?"

"There is"— Annie squeezed her eyes closed, trying to hold on to her temper—"no reason for you to be sarcastic. I most certainly am not implying that anyone should have to ask my permission. I do not wish to be informed of their need to use the outdoor facilities."

"It's an outhouse, Muldoon," Kell whispered, leaning closer but still not touching her. "Open your eyes and look at me, then say the word. It's damn polite enough. Even for you. And do try," he added, when she finally looked directly at him, "not to talk like you've eaten lemons. For everyone's sake."

There stirred within Annie a strange feeling. Her fingers curled and itched with the need to do violence to him. But he was not going to make her flee. She had responsibilities. His behavior had to be curbed. "Since I have not come here to win your approval, my speech is not important. I am trying to make the best of this temporary arrangement you have foisted on me. I demand that you control the behavior of the people you have boarded here."

"Or?"

She stared at him blankly for a moment. "If you don't, you'll have to leave."

"Will I?"

Annie stole a hurried glance at his hands and gulped. She thought the pants had slipped a little. "Plain talk. I am attempting to gain your cooperation." Her fingers showed white knuckles with the effort she had to use to control herself. "Your attitude shows I have wasted my time. You refuse to help make this unfortunate association the least bit pleasant."

Kell lightly tapped the tip of her nose. "Darlin', you've got that all wrong. I'm all for makin' this *association* just as pleasant as can be. Problem is, Muldoon, we have very different ideas of what's pleasant."

Annie batted his hand away. "Don't take what I said and twist it around to suit your evil purposes. I don't want any intimacy between us."

Only a small step separated them. Kell didn't think. He took it. She backed up two steps. "Pleasant, Muldoon, remember?" Kell smiled and followed. Annie ended with her back against the door.

Her head whipped from side to side. His left hand came up, palm flat against the door. Her nose brushed his right hand as he moved it to imprison her. Annie sucked in her stomach to avoid touching him. It was the wrong move. His bare chest met the rise of her breasts. Through the light cotton shirtwaist and corset cover Annie felt his warmth. The wicked, knowing gleam in his eyes defeated her. She sagged in place, sending silent pleas to the Lord to free her from the trap of the solid door behind her and the substantial devil in front.

"We were," Kell said, absently noting the change in his breathing, "discussing how to make things pleasant between us. And I did say I'd take care of your education, darlin'. This is as good a time as any. Let's begin with your concern about intimacy, Annie. There's degrees—"

"But I don't want—"

"I think you do. You just aren't aware of it yet." Kell trailed the back of his left hand down her flushed cheek. "You have the most charming freckles."

Annie had turned to follow his left hand, but jerked her head to the other side when his right cupped her shoulder. "You," she said in a small, anxious voice, "have more moves to watch than a fencing master."

"What do you know about fencing, Annie?"

"Oh, I saw a traveling troupe—there's thrust and parry—Why did you poke fun at my freckles?" Her lashes fluttered to feel his lips nuzzle the stray curl at her temple. "They're the bane of my—"

"Thrust" and "poke" were the only two words that Kell managed to retain. His mind sent a message. His body, to his annoyance, quickly responded. Too quickly. And to Annie Muldoon! He was supposed to be teaching her a lesson.

"Let's get back to intimacy, Annie. You're in my room. Alone with me. Understand so far?" Her widened eyes, their deepening color, and the swift darting of her tongue touching her upper lip made his pulse race.

"Let's not get back to it. Let's not discuss it at all. I'll just leave."

"Oh, no. You came here without an invitation, Muldoon. You made your point. Said your piece. Now, darlin', it's my turn."

Kell touched his forehead to hers. His voice dropped to a smoky, rumbled drawl. "Think about pleasant, Annie. Think about intimate."

It was most unfortunate that Annie did just that. She looked up to find that his eyes were closed. His lashes were darker at the base and lighter at the tips. They even curled. She knew his words were calculated to have the effect he wanted on her. She didn't know how to defend herself. This wasn't a physical attack. Kell undermined and dissolved all her good sense.

With a brushing motion the back of his fingers lightly caressed her chin. She had never known her skin could be so sensitive to touch. He overwhelmed her—his size, the warm male scent of him that filled her with every ragged breath she drew, his smile and the slow way he lifted his lids to look at her. His eyes were bright and—and hot. *Foolish, Annie. Eyes can't be hot.* But his were just that.

Lord! Oh, help! The buttons on her shirtwaist restricted her breathing. Her corset with its baleen stays no longer acted as armor. Blood began to pound in her temples.

Annie longed to push him away. Needed to. To that end she raised her hands and touched the bare skin of his waist. Her quick gasp brought one of his grins. But she didn't move her hands. He was as smooth and hard as the walnut parlor table. And he felt as heated as the tabletop did when the afternoon sun had been absorbed for hours into the wood.

Kell caught the back of her head, her hair an amber fire that he wanted to see free. His fingers discovered the warmth of her skin, as fine and soft as a blossom's petals.

"Annie,"—he tilted her head to the side— "like your lesson so far?"

"Lesson?" she repeated in a dazed voice.

His thumb brushed the lush curve of her bottom lip. "Hmmm, lesson, darlin'. That's what I'm trying to teach you." Kell whispered a kiss across her cheek, barely touched the heavy fringe of her lashes, her brow, and once more nuzzled the fine, curling hair at her temple.

"Such a fast learner," he murmured, working his way back with light, scattered kisses. "Educating you may turn out to be my pleasure."

Heat spread inside her. There was unexpected hardness to his body when she measured it against the soft, unhurried murmur of his voice. *Oh, Annie, my girl, don't forget each gentle touch of his lips.* But she tried. She didn't want to admit the strange feelings blooming to life inside her. She certainly did not know how to deal with them. Or with him.

"Touch me, Annie. Let's see what degrees of intimacy I can teach you."

"I've . . . learned quite enough."

"Not nearly, darlin'. Not at all. We haven't got to the good parts yet."

With her insides melting like a sugar topping in the sun, Annie didn't think there could be more. But he nuzzled, he murmured, his voice coaxing her to touch him. Shades of a snake oil drummer! Of their own volition, her hands stroked up his sides, then slowly fluttered down. His skin was smooth, taut and warm. She had never touched a man like this, had never seen a man half-dressed and didn't even know if it was right to touch him.

Just by the way he was encouraging her, Annie knew it couldn't be right. But instinct guided her. Instinct and the strange tension that coiled into a hard knot, and his damning voice that rumbled with wickedness urging her to keep on.

When she heard the catch in his breathing, Annie stopped thinking about right and wrong. He lifted his head, his amused expression bewildering to her.

"Such a small, secret smile. One I like, Annie." He brought his lips to hers. Briefly. Tasting and breaking, only to find he had to come back for more. "That's right," he murmured, "keep smiling for me, Annie."

She turned her face away, not wanting him to see her slide her tongue over her lips to ease the throbbing.

Kell cupped her chin and brought her mouth back to his. "Nothing hurts. Nothing will. I promise."

Annie couldn't deny it. The shiver that came from feeling the light brush of his hair against her sensitive skin didn't hurt. Not painfully. But a slow spreading ache brought forth a sound she had never made. Her hands opened and closed on his body. She thought she could feel his own smile before he strung kisses along the edge of her restricting collar. She longed to ask him what he was smiling about, but all she managed was another funny little sound.

"Sweet, darlin' Annie." Kell felt the warmth of the sun at his back coming through the window to raise the temperature of the room. Under the gentle ply of his mouth Annie's skin became heated and moist, bringing him the faint scent of lemon and flowers, and the more enticing taste of kindling desire.

He drew back, gazing at the luscious red of her lips, damp with the repeated touch of the tip of her tongue. Temptation. Pure and simple. He admitted that. Admitted it and pushed aside the warning that he didn't want anything to do with her. He forgot his own caution to regain good sense when her hands stopped their kittenlike kneading and slid around his waist. Her fingertips barely pressed his skin, yet he was full, hard and aching. She aroused him faster with her tentative touches than another woman's practiced wiles would have.

But Annie had no feminine wiles. Annie was as innocent as a wobbly-legged spring lamb.

Kell forgot about that too.

He was close to being obsessed with how she kissed. How she would taste.

He never denied himself anything he wanted.

The delicate little shiver that passed over her, the quickened pace of her breathing, made him gently cup her shoulders and bring her fully against him.

"I promised nothing would hurt, darlin'. But you're so tense." Her wide, dark blue eyes, glazed with the first stirring of passion, stared up at him. Kell smiled. "Close your eyes, Annie. That's the next lesson." He was still smiling as he angled his head. "When a man's about to kiss you—no, sweet, don't pucker up. Open your mouth, Annie. Just a little. I'll show you. You'll understand better that way."

His mouth touched hers softer than a whisper. "And here wants kissing, too." Kell breathed the words over her slightly parted mouth, brushing his lips against the charming little beauty mark above her lip.

"We shouldn't be doing this." Annie sighed with despair when she heard herself. Her voice wasn't firm. Wasn't strong. More like a thready whimper. "The rules—"

"There's none where pleasure's concerned. And this—ah, yes, sweet, give me your mouth just like that."

She felt the rasp of his beard stubble against her cheek and the smooth, heated texture of his mobile mouth skimming butterfly kisses that lured her into forgetting who she was and who he was.

With mesmerizing slowness Kell lifted his lips from hers, smiling to see a quick frown. He cupped her chin, lifting her face. "Annie, don't think about rules and should nots. You'll miss out on all the good things. Don't you want to know what you're missing?"

Rich promises were in his voice and his eyes. Annie was tempted. She felt herself wavering. His kisses only made her want more. She didn't know where she found the will to resist him.

"I can't do what you ask. It's not right."

"The hell with right. I made you feel good, didn't I?"

"Don't swear." She had thought his features sharp, but now there was softness that enticed her. Bright was his hair, and his eyes gazed at her with a look that made no secret of his desire. *You're strong, Annie. You can overcome this, but oh dear, do watch his mouth.*

"Conscience at war, darlin'?"

She nodded, angry that body and mind were indeed

warring, annoyed that he knew it. Her hands snapped down to her sides and clung to her skirt as if it were an anchor that would ground her firmly in reality. She refused to look away from him, refused to give in to the clamoring little voice that begged her to let him kiss her once more.

"Guess the lesson's over for today." Kell stepped back and away from her. He squelched his laughter at her chagrined expression. Rubbing the back of his neck, he glanced at the stitched sampler hanging over his bed. Well, he had tried.

"Since I'm obviously out of practice at seducing virginal curiosity seekers, the schoolroom's closed." Raking back his hair with both hands, he turned around and snatched up his discarded shirt. It was just as well she had stopped him, she wasn't anywhere near ready to make use of the bed, and he had had enough of this insanity.

He wished he could quell his arousal as quickly as she had caused it. A first for him. The desire was vivid, accounted for, he thought, by the fact that she stood there and watched him. Every intention to have nothing to do with her came rushing back.

"What are you waiting for, Muldoon? An encore? I said the lesson's over. Since I'm paying for the privacy of this room, leave."

His abrupt turn from seductive to dismissive set Annie's teeth on edge. She couldn't recover as quickly. She wanted to leave as much as he wanted her to go. Despite the feeling that her knees were about to crumble, she felt along behind her until her hand closed over the doorknob. Her gaze held the flex and play of his muscles beneath the shirt that covered him. She retained the imprint of his heated mouth on hers. But, most damning, Annie was now left with the coil of strange tension that lured her into staying right where she was.

Foolishness! She twisted the knob just as a sharp rap sounded on the door.

Chapter Eight

~

"Kell? You inside?"

"The door's open, Li." Kell turned around, still buttoning his shirt. Annie moved toward him with a start. "Hold it. Out you go, Muldoon."

"I intended—"

"Just tell me one thing. You have a rule that covers your presence in a male boarder's room?"

"I've never needed one." Annie spun as the door opened and scooted past a surprised Li.

"You wait for an invite next time, Muldoon."

Fencepost rigid, Annie froze, then faced Kell through the doorway. "There will not be a next time, Mr. York."

"Don't go bettin' on it, Muldoon. Innocents like you are easy pickin's."

Disdain laced her voice. "And you must not judge everyone else by your lack of morals."

He started toward her. "I'll show you what you can do with your morals."

"Kell." Softly said, Li's voice held warning.

"You're right."

With a look of apology to Annie, Li closed the door.

Annie was torn between allowing Kell the last word and demanding the chance to say her piece. Still shaken, she muttered, "The man has no morals. I would only waste my time."

"You're right there, honey."

Annie turned around and found Laine leaning in the open doorway to her room. Smoothing her apron front, Annie bought herself a moment. She didn't know how to answer the woman who had overheard their conversation.

"Best you remember what you said. Kell is more man than you'd know how to handle. Kinda like baying at the moon."

"You're mistaken," Annie snapped. "I have no intent of *handling* Mr. York. And baying is something wild animals do."

"Yeah," Laine answered. A smug smile came with a direct look. "That's Kell, all right. Wild."

"You are welcome to him." Annie didn't wait to hear more. She walked rapidly toward the stairs.

Since neither woman had made any effort to lower her voice, both Li and Kell heard them clearly.

"Kell, I will speak to Laine."

"No, leave it. Anything and anyone that serves to keep that prissed spinster away from me has my full approval."

"A man lies to his enemies with good reason, there is none for lying to a friend. And a man who lies to himself is a fool."

Shoving his shirt inside his pants, Kell shot Li a damning look. "Don't read more into this. The woman irritates the hell out of me."

Li glanced from the mussed bed to the obvious proof of

Kell's lie. "Does she take the hell out of you or put you there?"

Kell paused and with a rueful smile glanced down, then at Li's amused expression. "A little of both, since you won't stop until you have the truth. But you didn't come here to discuss Muldoon."

"Muldoon? After what I have seen—"

"Muldoon she began and Muldoon she'll end. Now, I'm a man in dire need of a drink, so if there's nothing more—"

"There is. I discovered our missing dove, Charity, and with her, Pockets' attacker. I may even," Li said, settling himself on the single straight chair in the room, "have some information about the missing wagonload of whiskey."

"At least you've made some accomplishments."

"Do not discount what you accomplished, Kell. Miss Muldoon will certainly not darken your doorway again."

"Your point is taken, Li, but save your breath. Muldoon is a green meadow I've no intent of plowing." Too restless to sit, Kell refused to give Li the satisfaction of seeing him pace. He settled himself in a slouch before the window, leaning back against one side of its frame with his long legs extended and crossed at the ankles.

He was about ready to kill for a glass of good whiskey. Something strong enough to remove the lingering taste of Annie from his mouth.

Meeting Li's knowing look, Kell scowled. "Am I to be treated to one of your silent studies or are you going to tell me what you found out?"

"Tell you, of course. You are a complex man, Kell. The more I believe I understand you, the less I do."

"Well, be at ease, friend. There's times when I don't understand myself."

Li let the remark go unanswered. "Our missing Charity was the cause of Pockets' injury."

"Charity socked him?"

"No. Her young man did. He thought they would be discovered together, something I gather your brother frowned upon. Jessup Beamer is young, believes he is in love with Charity, and is a sometime stage and freight driver."

"My missing whiskey?"

"That, too. An interesting tale," Li added, stretching out his legs, then folding his arms over his stomach. "Beamer claims he was delivering the whiskey, but he was met on the road outside of town and told to take the load down to Fort Worth to sell it. I believe he said the Bank saloon was mentioned as a possible customer."

"He was *told* to sell my whiskey? Don't tell me he got religion and voices whispered to him?"

"Nothing so imaginative. Beamer said he was stopped by a man driving a buckboard. He did not have a detailed description to give me, for it was dusk. Beamer remembers he thought it strange that the man was bundled in a coat with a hat pulled so low he wondered how the man could see. But that is who gave him the orders, from you, I might add, to sell the whiskey."

"Hell!"

"Not quite. The whiskey's outside around the back of the house."

"He never sold it? This doesn't make sense, Li."

Contemplating the tips of his boots, Li murmured agreement.

"Did this Beamer say why he changed his mind?"

"He was almost to the fort when he realized he had never been told what to do with the money from the sale. Once that thought entered his mind, he claimed he smelled a rat. An odd saying, that. I do not believe one can smell the rodent."

"News for you, Li. I smell one, too. Who could have given such an order? And why?"

Turning to brace his hands on the sill, Kell looked out on the dusty street below. Heat waves shimmered, and the only sign of life was a skulking, emaciated brown mongrel near the mercantile. Thin wisps of clouds floated in the distance of the bright blue sky. His gaze swept over the buildings once again. It appeared as if time had stopped and frozen this moment to remind him that he wasn't going to be run out of any place again.

"Have you then decided that Miss Muldoon and her group are not responsible?"

"I haven't ruled them out entirely."

"I believe Beamer. He had no way of knowing that that order did not come from you. He had not seen you. Kyle's dead and you are the new owner. The story is too simple—"

"The best lies sometimes are."

"True, Kell. But once more I say I believe him. He is waiting with the wagon. Talk to him."

"How far would Muldoon go?" Kell mused, half to himself. "I can't see her dressing up like a man to divert a wagonload of whiskey."

Li glanced quickly at Kell, a dusky silhouette standing against the window's glare. Interest brightened his eyes. The speculative note in Kell's voice told him that his friend was imagining the very thing he denied. Or something more. It was unusual for Kell to dwell on one woman for any length of time.

"If you ask for my opinion, Miss Muldoon in a man's pants is as likely as my discovering the man who abandoned my mother to a life of slavery. Were you to mention it to her, the mere thought might send her into a swoon."

The words were matter-of-fact, but Kell closed his eyes briefly. Li's search would never end, though he had long ago lost the bitter hate that had fueled him. But Kell bit back a groan at Li's deliberate need for his pound of flesh. He didn't want to picture Annie in any man's pants. Except maybe his. Damn that woman! He gripped the sill, forcing her out of his mind, angry that he had to make an effort to do it.

"Point by point, Kell, we agree that she had nothing to do with the fire. Since the front door is always open, anyone could have come in that night, gone to her room, and taken the cap Bronc found. Like you, I thought of a woman because of the bulky coat Beamer mentioned as being worn by the one who stopped him. If that is true, someone does want you out of Loving."

"Of course it's true." Kell turned around. "Only a coward would use a fire. Fine, I know men who would do it."

"There is still Laine. She knew about the whiskey. She has reason to want you gone."

"Sure. That makes the best sense of all. No building, no whiskey, no business. I leave, Laine starts it up again, and this time she doesn't have to share the profits with anyone."

"Sound reason. Yet I hear doubt in your voice."

"I won't rule out someone in that corset contingent that blindly follows Muldoon." Kell shot a studying look at his friend. The rough beginning of a plan formed. One that Li wasn't going to like. "Even if you're against my rebuilding here, you do intend to help me, right?"

"You ask that of me? I owe you my life, Kell. No. Do

not make that dismissive motion. There is nothing I would not do for you."

"There's damn little you haven't already done. I've told you and told you that you've repaid me more times than I want to count, Li. No one has a better friend to protect his back and share a fire with. But be at ease. I don't want you to kill anyone. I've got a plan."

"Why can I not find comfort in your words?"

"Beats me." Kell shrugged and glanced down at the floor.

Li patiently waited. When Kell looked up at him, Li sat up straight in his chair. He knew that smile. It was one the angels would envy. His dark eyes narrowed. Kell's smile boded no good for him. But he listened. Kell's first words, his cajoling manner, only reinforced Li's warning to himself.

Minutes later, when he left Kell, Li knew himself to be a fool. "A wise man," he muttered, heading down the stairs, "learns to listen to his inner voice of wisdom. An intelligent man understands there are times when ignorance can bring peace. Lastly, only an unworthy man embraces friendship with conditions."

"Pardon?" Annie asked, finding it difficult to look up at Li. Busy with her account book behind the lobby's counter, she saw his frown. "Is there something wrong?" She removed her spectacles, chiding herself for being afraid to face the man. She would have to do it sometime.

"I spoke aloud to clear my thoughts. Have I alarmed you?"

"No. Not at all." Annie tried to smile and failed. Just as she failed to hold his gaze. "When I'm vexed, I do that, too."

"Just so." Li paused, and thought about what he had

witnessed between her and Kell, but loyalty to Kell kept him silent. With a curt nod, he continued on his way toward the dining room.

Annie sighed and reached for her spectacles just as the soft strains of a waltz tune came from beyond the closed back parlor doors. Pockets was talented, and he had been entertaining Aunt Hortense for most of the morning with his playing. Fawn had taken the shopping list and would be gone for at least an hour, since Annie had urged her to buy a length of calico for her new dress.

For the first time since the fire, a peaceful solitude descended. Annie wished she could enjoy it. Images of Kellian York formed in her mind, some as thin as mist and others as solid as the floor she stood on. His features tantalized her, especially his mobile mouth that went easily from wicked grin to sensual snare. The sweet taste of desire appeared to have seeped below the fragile layers of skin that formed her lips, for no matter how she licked them, the taste remained.

Her body was under the siege of some malady akin to the dreaded influenza. She could account for the sudden onset of feverish tremors, chills, and aches no other way. *Don't forget the breathing, Annie,* a small voice reminded her.

How could she? She hadn't drawn a normal breath from the moment he'd set foot in her room.

Admonishing herself to stop being no better than a flower stalk buffeted hither and thither at the mercy of the wind, Annie set her mind to dismiss him.

The neat columns of numbers made no sense, despite her fierce concentration.

Own up to the fact, my girl, that removing him from thought requires aid. If you sat in a patch of cactus, you couldn't pull out the spines without help. A painful but necessary process.

The creak of the stair startled Annie. She glanced up and saw the tips of boots. Kell's boots. *Not now. It's too soon.* She ducked down, crouching low behind the counter.

Nothing short of physical force could make her face him now. She was humiliated to remember she had put up as much defense as a cotton crop attacked by dark brown stainers.

She counted his footsteps, heard him pause, and thought he was standing near the front door. It was hard to determine the direction of sound when her heartbeat pounded like the wings of a frightened bird trying to escape a stalking Dewberry.

What was he waiting for? Why didn't he leave the lobby? Now that she had hidden herself, Annie felt foolish, but she was not about to let him discover her.

Her calf began to cramp. Annie gritted her teeth. She was afraid to move, sure that along with everything else, Mr. York would have an acute sense of hearing. Holding on to the small shelf beneath the counter for balance, she tried to count slowly. Her damp palms slipped, another sign that her nerves were growing more agitated with each passing second.

The cramp spread down to her toes. Annie bit back a moan. Too much time had passed. She couldn't suddenly stand up. If the cramps squeezing her muscles continued, she would never stand at all. The thought of falling out from behind the counter in a sprawl at Kellian York's feet lent her new strength.

"It's reassuring to know what a meticulous housekeeper you are, Muldoon," Kell called out softly.

The fiery sheen of Annie's hair popped into view. But

her stunned look as she raised her head above the counter filled Kell with an immense satisfaction and enough amusement that he had to stop himself from laughing.

"I offer you the sincerest of compliments, Muldoon. From the moment I met you, you haven't managed to bore me. A rare woman, indeed."

Still beset by the agonizing cramp, Annie couldn't stand up and face him. But she refused to allow his remark to go unanswered.

"I am boring. And the only thing rare about me is the way I cook my steak for Saturday night's supper."

"We have more in common than you think, Muldoon. I wish I had time to discuss appetites and disprove your claim, but I don't. Later, perhaps."

Annie croaked a protest, struggling to rise. She heard him open the front door, but the pain in her leg demanded her attention.

At the door, Kell found himself face to face with a petite dark-haired woman. He stood aside to let her pass once she recovered from seeing him. Her reaction made him take a closer look, and then he placed the shadowed eyes and scrawny form as belonging to the dressmaker who had refused his money when he ordered new gowns for the doves.

Annie glanced up in time to see her best friend, Emmaline, inch through the open doorway, carrying a large basket in front of her. Emmaline had a delicate constitution, and Annie wanted to protest the intimidating stare that Kellian leveled at her as she sidled past him.

It was on the tip of Annie's tongue to call out reassurance to Emmaline that Mr. York wouldn't touch her. He reserved that torment for Annie alone. But, having an idea

that his reaction would be anything but pleasant, Annie
kept silent.

Her gaze met his, but she read nothing in his expression. With a flip at his hat brim he closed the door behind
him. Annie released a breath she hadn't realized she was
holding.

"Thank goodness he's gone. Emmaline, I have never
been happier to see you. But where," Annie asked, now
free to rub the spasm in her calf, "have you been? I
haven't seen you since the night of the fire."

"My throat." Emmaline freed one hand from the basket
and pointed to the swathe of cloth around her neck.
"What's wrong?"

Annie glanced up. "Cramps. But now that he's gone,
the pain's easing." She stamped her foot a few times, trying to wiggle her toes in the confining leather of her
shoes. Concern for her friend's pale skin made her set
aside her pain.

"I hope you haven't been taking Biglow's Kickapoo Indian Cough Cure. I know Ruth McQuary and her husband swear by his remedies, but Emmaline—" Annie
stopped. Emmaline was shaking her head. Annie watched
with interest as the woman peeled back the linen towel
covering the basket.

Inside were two pies, but it was a tin in the basket that
claimed Annie's attention. She withdrew the tin with one
hand and reached for her forgotten spectacles with the
other. Once the glasses were in place, Annie read the la-
bel.

"ALLEN'S COCAINE TABLETS. For Colds, Sore
Throats, Nervousness, Neuralgia, Headache, Sleepless-
ness, Dyspepsia, Indigestion, Heartburn, and Flatulency.
Used by Elocutionists, Vocalists, and Actors." Frowning,

Annie slowly removed her glasses, then set them aside on the counter.

"I suppose this is another of the wonder medicines that Mr. McQuary ordered from a newspaper advertisement? I have no doubt that this will cure sleeplessness, Emmaline. If you are drugged, you will sleep. As for indigestion, if you're sleeping, you certainly couldn't eat, so these tablets would eliminate that problem as well. As for the rest of these claims, I believe taking these will do you more harm than good."

With a slight shake of her head, Annie returned the tin to the basket. "You and Aunt Hortense will try anything that Mr. McQuary recommends. Has it helped?"

"Sleep a lot."

"And your throat? Its claim is to cure a sore throat."

"Still sore."

Sympathy for her raspy voice made Annie pat the woman's slender gloved hand. Despite the heat, Emmaline wore gloves, a golden-brown poplin pleated walking skirt, and a cream-and-brown striped basque. Alternating rows of ribbon and lace formed the yoke. Emmaline always sewed wide bands of ruffled lace to the yokes of her shirtwaists and basques. She felt that nature had cheated her of a proper feminine silhouette. Annie envied her. She had to bind herself due to nature's generous endowment.

Lifting the basket, Annie limped out from behind the counter. "Come into the kitchen with me. I'll make you a strong tea of horseradish and yellow dock root sweetened with honey. It's my grandmother's recipe and will relieve your throat. We'll have a nice visit, and I'll tell you everything that has happened."

Walking slightly ahead of Emmaline, Annie silently amended the last with a vow not to tell anyone what had passed between herself and Kellian York. It was a good thing today was Friday. She wouldn't be serving any meals for the next three days. Except to her boarders.

"Emmaline, you must be as curious as the others about why I let those people stay here. I do hope that you won't be judging me."

Annie set the basket down on the kitchen table. She folded the linen towel, then took out the pies. "Pecan! Oh, you are a dear to have made my favorite."

"Friends," Emmaline whispered, reaching out to squeeze Annie's hand.

"Of course we are. The best. I'm sorry. I know you won't judge me. I've been on edge since they arrived here." Annie pulled out a chair. "Set yourself down while I put up the kettle."

Tempted to have a slice of the pie now, Annie resisted. This was her punishment for allowing Kellian liberties that no lady who called herself one should. She wouldn't be much of a friend to indulge herself with pecan pie when Emmaline couldn't swallow a bite. Taking the pies to the pie safe, she set them on the empty shelf.

It took her a moment to realize that the pie safe was empty. Not a crumb remained of her baked goods. Annie closed the door with a bit more force than necessary.

"It's a good thing I don't have meals to serve today. There would be no desserts offered. Gone, Emmaline. Pies, breads, muffins, and all."

Moving from dry sink to stove, then to the pantry, Annie kept up a running commentary of all that had happened. She did not reveal that Kellian had blackmailed her into letting him stay. Even to her best friend, Annie couldn't reveal her own weakness.

Grating the horseradish into the mixture of honey and powdered yellow dock root, Annie said, "Now that was all bad enough, being accused of starting that fire, but when Bronc—" A rap on the table made her look at Emmaline. "He's the barkeep. The tall, skinny one. He found my cap near the burned remains. Mr. York threatened to haul me to the sheriff. He—Mr. York, that is—didn't know that the Marlow brothers had escaped jail again. But he did inform me he would see justice done."

Emmaline's startled move made Annie hasten to reassure her. "No, he didn't do anything more. I really can't blame him for being angry, dear. Much as I wanted to see that place closed down for good, I didn't want anyone's life put at risk."

Glancing down at the bowl just as the kettle whistled, Annie decided she had the mixture about right. She poured the boiling water into the teapot and added two spoonsful of the thick, clouded honey mix.

"Just a few minutes more and you can have your cup of tea. Truth to tell, Emmaline, aside from having money to fix the leaks in the roof, I will have enough to make a sizeable contribution to our church fund."

Annie drew a chair around the table so she could sit next to her friend. Keeping her voice to a whisper, she continued, "I hope to have an opportunity to speak to those women about finding a new direction. This life of sin they lead may be all they know. I am counting on you to help me with them, Emmaline. You've been widowed. You know what it is like to make your own way and remain respectable."

Pouring out the tea, Annie was not comforted by the look Emmaline gave her. If she couldn't convince her best friend to help her, there was little hope of gaining the other women's support. And if she thought any more about Emmaline's strange look—near to horror, Annie thought—she would stop right now.

"I've given a great deal of thought to this, and I believe that Mr. York has no real direction in his life, either. The man appears to live for pleasure and little else. Perhaps I should invite him to attend our service on Sunday. I could find a most fitting passage to read. Something that would enlighten him. What do you think, Emmaline?"

Choking, Emmaline rattled the cup in her attempt to set it down without spilling the tea. "Not wise. The ladies—"

"I suppose his presence would upset them. But we have never limited attendance." Noticing how dark the room was becoming, Annie rose and lit the coal oil fixture above the table.

A sudden gust of wind swept through the open doorway, bringing with it a gritty dust. Annie rushed to close the door, sending a searching glance at the clouds piling up dark and roiling for a summer storm.

She had no sooner returned to Emmaline's side than the door burst open to admit two of the doves and Bronc crowding behind them.

Emmaline knocked over her chair in her rush to stand. "Leaving."

"Emmaline! You can't leave. If you get soaked, you'll end up in bed again." Puzzled by her friend's strange behavior, Annie stared at her.

"Gonna rain like a sonofa—" Bronc caught Annie's warning look—"hard. Gonna rain real hard, ma'am."

"Won't stay here with them."

Annie felt her mouth open, but no sound came out. She faced Emmaline. Raspy as her voice was, Emmaline had made herself heard. How could her friend, her very best friend, do this to her after she had told Emmaline her plans? Annie was counting on having Emmaline's support with the other ladies. How could she act as if being in the same room with the doves would taint her?

To Annie's mortification, she found four pairs of eyes avidly watching her to see what she would do.

Chapter Nine

❧

Emmaline snatched up her basket and spun around to march from the room. Annie jumped up from her chair and ran to stop her.

"Please don't go. You're my best friend. If I can't count on you—Emmaline, you're not listening to me."

"Those women—"

"Aren't doing anything wrong." But even as Annie defended them, she looked to where the two women stood, both watching her. They were decently gowned, if she discounted the expanse of bare skin from the rounded scoop necklines up to their chins. The gowns were ready-mades from the mercantile, plain as could be, and neither woman wore paint on her face. The wind had left their hair mussed, but Annie didn't find their appearance offensive.

And they were her paying boarders. Emmaline was her friend. She caught Bronc's gaze on her from across the room.

"If you'd like, I'll escort her home," he volunteered. "That's if she don't mind."

Annie ignored Emmaline's whispered refusal. "Come with me to get the umbrella." Not giving her friend an opportunity to protest, Annie latched onto Emmaline's wrist and pulled her along after her.

"Honestly, Emmaline, you didn't have to be rude. I know you don't like them, but they are boarders in my house. I have enough to contend with. Jumping up like you'd sat on a hot griddle!"

"Annie!"

"Don't try talking now. Your throat hurts, remember? You won't stay and I won't ask you to, but you will accept his escort home."

Annie found the umbrella, tucked behind the corner chair in the lobby. She still wouldn't let go of Emmaline. The parlor doors were still closed, but Pockets was no longer playing a sweet tune. The music was lively, and as Annie marched back into the dining room with Emmaline in tow, she thought she heard singing. Surely, that can't be Aunt Hortense? She glanced back, but thunder pealed and rattled the windows.

"Still want to leave?"

"I won't stay here with those women."

"Suit yourself, Emmaline. But frankly, I'm disappointed."

"Don't understand."

"I do, Emmaline. But I thought our friendship—never mind. Take my shawl." Annie made sure the light wool was wrapped to cover her friend's neck and throat. She avoided Emmaline's pleading gaze and turned to Bronc.

"Mrs. Rutland has been ill, so do try to keep her dry since she insists on returning home now. And if you would, Bronc, please stop by the mercantile and see if Fawn is ready to come home. Storms frighten her."

"I'll take care of her, ma'am." Bronc gazed down at

Emmaline's heart-shaped face. He never had any truck with the town women, spending his days off in Graham. But this woman's brown eyes made him think of a wounded creature. She was tiny. The top of her head just reached his shoulder.

Clearing his throat, he said, "You'll be safe with me, ma'am. Won't give your husband no call—"

"Oh, Emmaline's a widow, Bronc." The shy looks Bronc cast her friend's way had not gone unnoticed by Annie. Even if Emmaline had angered her with her unbending attitude, Annie did wish she could find some happiness. When she had arrived in Loving almost four years ago, Annie thought her the saddest woman she had known. But loving and losing someone dear accounted for her grief. And her bitterness, Annie added to herself, recalling that too.

"Best be off," Annie said.

Bronc found the catch and started to open the umbrella.

"No!" Emmaline cried out, striking his hand.

Annie rushed to grab the umbrella as a started Bronc let it go. "It's bad luck to open one in the house," she told him, pushing Emmaline aside to get it first. She remembered Aunt Hortense's warning that a woman who picked up a fallen umbrella would remain a spinster all her life. Since Annie was already considered one, it didn't matter for her.

She handed the umbrella back to Bronc. "Wait till you're outside to open it."

"Li said that silly superstition started in his country."

"Cammy," Bronc warned.

"Well, it's true. He did so say that."

Annie shooed Emmaline and Bronc out the door, closed it behind them, then turned. Neither young woman showed any intention to leave the kitchen. She saw that one was eyeing the teapot.

"Would you like some tea?" Annie's impulsive offer was met with an exchange of looks between the doves. "Emmaline brought over pecan pie too. I was going to save it for supper tonight, but we can have some now."

Annie, what are you doing? I don't know, she answered herself, but whatever it is, those two smiles say it was the right thing.

"I'd like to hear more about the umbrella—Cammy, is it?"

"Yeah. I'm Cammy and this here's Blossom."

"And I'm Annie." Bustling about the kitchen to make fresh tea for them as well as Aunt Hortense, Annie knew the Lord had given her the perfect opportunity to begin her role. She had been forced to take the position of leadership among the town's women, now she would prove to them that she was worthy of it.

"Cammy, I really would like to know what Li told you."

Licking her lips at the generous slice of pecan pie that Annie set before her, Cammy looked up. "Really?"

"Really."

"Well, he didn't say it was an umbrella. He called it a—"

"Sunshade," Blossom supplied, wondering how long they had to wait until they could have the pie.

"Yeah, that's it. He said that only rich folks used them in China. That's where he's from, you know. Anyhow, he says if you had to use a sunshade out in the sun and the sun don't come inside, it was bad luck to open one 'less you were out."

Annie, having finished fixing the tea tray for Aunt Hortense, added another cup and saucer, along with a plate and fork. "Pockets," she explained, although no one asked, "has been playing the piano for my aunt all morning. He might enjoy some refreshment, too."

"I could take that to them. That's if you don't mind."

Blossom's shy offer caught Annie by surprise. "Ah—I—"

Ducking her head, Blossom added, "Guess you think it wouldn't be fittin'."

"No, that's not why I . . . I hesitated." The kettle's whistle gave Annie the excuse to turn her back. *Dear me, what would Aunt Hortense say?* She's dressed decent enough, and maybe Aunt won't notice. But for the moment, Annie did not understand why it mattered that she not offend Blossom.

Pouring out the boiling water into the pot, Annie knew they watched her every move as she added the tea leaves to steep. She repeated the process for their tea, set the kettle and tea tin back in their places, and cut a slice of pie for Pockets.

"I didn't accept your offer because you are a paying guest here. But I would be grateful if you would carry the tray in to them. Just don't let my aunt start questioning you. She doesn't hear well—won't use her ear trumpet—and you'll have to yell things over and over. Even then," Annie finished with a sigh, "she's likely not to understand what you were saying in the first place."

Annie watched Blossom take the tray and leave.

"She won't drop it," Cammy said.

"I guess I was a bit anxious." Goodness! Now she was apologizing! "I'm sure she'll be fine." Casting about for something safe to talk about, Annie pulled out a chair and sat across from Cammy. "Can you tell me why Li was talking about umbrellas? It seems a strange choice—"

"For women like us, you mean?"

The young woman's directness was disconcerting.

Meeting the gaze that was leveled with the same directness on her, Annie's innate honesty made her nod.

Cammy smiled. "You're not like the rest of the old
biddies in town."

"Thank you, I think. But you mustn't have a hard opinion of them. They want a good place to raise their families
and feel that drinking, gambling and . . . and—" Annie
stopped and stared at Cammy. What did one call what
she did to her face?

"Kell said we wasn't allowed to get your back up about
what we do. Guess talking about umbrellas is better for
both of us." A smirk tilted the corner of her mouth when
Annie merely nodded.

"It started 'cause of Laine's new parasol. She sings—we
all do some—an' wanted to use it. It was the prettiest
thing you ever did see, all black lace ruffles with bright
red bows. Even had her name spelled out in silver beads
underneath. But Kell said no. He didn't want any bad
luck—"

"Mr. York believes in superstitions?"

"Kell's a gambler. They all do. He ain't no knave, either.
Kell's an ace." Cammy eyed the pale tobacco-colored liquid that Annie poured into her cup. It was hot, but that
was the only good thing she could say about it.

"Don't suppose you have something stronger to flavor
it?"

"Stronger?"

"Like whiskey?"

"In tea?" Annie caught herself doing it again. She couldn't
keep sounding critical about everything or she would never
be in a position to convince Cammy or the other women to
turn away from the life they led. And what did she know?
Perhaps putting whiskey in tea was the way they drank it.

"I don't have whiskey, but Aunt Hortense likes a little blackberry brandy on special occasions."

"Fine. That'll be just fine." Cammy sighed with relief when Annie went to the pantry to get the brandy and Blossom rejoined them. "Blossom," she whispered as the girl sat down beside her, "what's blackberry brandy taste like?"

"Fruit. My ma used to put some up after she made jam. Pa'd drink it if he couldn't get no 'shine." And to Annie, she said, "They didn't hardly notice me. Pockets's got Ruby an' Daisy in there, singing with your aunt. That big ol' cat has himself draped on top of the piano—"

"Dewberry?"

"Guess so, 'less you got more'n one. Ruby brought him down with her. He was hollerin' in front of Kell's door."

Catching the sly looks, Annie was too generous with the brandy. They knew! She sat down and, without thinking, poured a measure of brandy into her own cup. Well, she would just brazen it out if they said anything about her going into Kell's room to retrieve her aunt's cat.

"Blossom, you ever see Bronc color up like he just did?"

"Bronc? Can't say for sure. He's so quiet most times, a body wouldn't know he's 'round. Even when he's tossin' some drunk out, he does it quietlike."

"You don't need to worry about your friend with him," Cammy said to Annie.

"I realize that. Seems I'm learning all the time that I shouldn't make judg—" The wind rattled the window so hard that Annie stopped. Even the door shook under the repeated gusts of wind hammering against it along with the heavy slash of rain. She sipped her tea, absently licking her lips to capture the added taste of the brandy. Pushing away from the table, she rose.

"Wher'ya goin'?" Blossom asked. "I say something wrong?"

"No. It's nothing either one of you said. This storm appears to be a lasting one. The roof leaks, and if I don't get buckets under the worse of them now, I'll be mopping up puddles all night."

Once again, Cammy and Blossom exchanged looks, then turned to Annie. "We can help," they both offered.

"Help?"

"Don't take the brain of a peahen to set a bucket 'neath a leak," Blossom answered. "Could be our beds gettin' wet, too."

The offer was kindly meant, and Annie found herself accepting it with a smile. "The quicker it's done, the sooner I can get supper started for everyone."

"Shucks, let Cammy help you set your buckets. I'm a fair hand at cookin'. That's if you don't want nothin' fancy."

"Fancy?" *Really Annie, stop parroting them.* Did someone like Blossom think fried chicken was fancy? And why should she be surprised that Blossom could cook? *Follow your own statement and stop making snap judgments about these people.*

"I planned on having fried chicken—"

"With taters an' gravy?"

"Mashed, of course."

Blossom licked her wide, mobile mouth, moaning with delight while rubbing her belly.

Cammy started laughing. Annie joined her, laughing even harder when Blossom jumped up, dancing around the kitchen making claims, each more outrageous than the one before, about how good her fried chicken was.

It was minutes before they all stopped and Annie showed Blossom where everything she would need was kept. From the pantry Annie hauled out two stacks of buckets, dividing them evenly with Cammy.

"I just hope these will be enough buckets."

"Sure looks like you've got a heap of leaks in that roof."

Leading the way out of the kitchen, Annie tossed back, "You don't know the half of it."

"Buckets?" Li repeated. He glanced at Kell, hammering yet another stake. "How could buckets hold this much rain?" With a sweeping motion of one arm, Li indicated the downpour beyond the open sides of the stretched canvas they had labored to erect.

"It's just an expression. Another saying that folks have regardless of whether or not it makes any sense." Kell stared in disgust as rivulets of water snaked their way over the level ground clearing. When he had gone out scouting for a place to reopen while the rebuilding went on, he had wanted to pick the first clear spot he found, for the ground was higher, but it was nearly two miles out of town. For his purpose, he needed to be as close to Loving as possible.

"At least the whiskey'll stay dry," Kell muttered, taking another swing at the last stake. He checked the ropes on his side of the open-sided tent and saw that Li was doing the same across from him.

He had muscles aching that he had forgotten he had. And he was still annoyed that Li had paid so much for the canvas. "Still can't understand how you let Lockwood swindle you into paying so much for these moldy old wagon covers. He should have paid you to take them off his hands. If any more rain collects up there, the whole thing will come down."

"Barrels would be better. We could have put them at

the corners. I should have asked Lockwood if he had any empty ones."

"Barrels? Who the hell said anything about barrels?"

"I did. To collect the rain." Li used his booted foot to tamp down the dirt around a stake, then moved on to the next one. "If you feel cheated by my bargaining, Kell, you should have done it. Lockwood is a man who believes it is his duty to cheat anyone who's not his race."

"There's too many of his kind, Li. Don't think about it. Christ, you know, you're real touchy today."

Li didn't answer him, and as the silence between them grew, it bothered Kell. He started toward Li, just as the other man spoke.

"There is a bitter taste on my tongue."

"Ah, so that's it. I wish you'd said something before, Li. Can't see why it should bother you. You've lied for me before this," Kell reminded him.

"Lied to protect you, yes. And I would lie again. These words you asked me to say against you were hard to speak. I truly do not believe you are fit only for the worms to feast upon. To say that you beat me—"

"Is the damn truth! You haven't won one poker game yet. And you know why you had to begin with Lockwood. He sees everyone in town and outside it. If someone is looking to drive us out, who better to approach than you, Li? You're discontented. You haven't got the good sense God gave a mule 'cause you're a pigtail-swinging Chinaman. You're the only one who'd be believed."

Kell set his hammer down and walked to his friend. He met Li's black, almond-shaped eyes with a level look. "You know it isn't true. I know it isn't true. Who the hell else matters, Li?"

"No one."

"Good. We agree. Let's break open a bottle and have a

drink to that. Besides, I want to taste what my brother paid for." Kell moved to the wagon's side and lifted the canvas. Li used his hammer to pry open the wooden slats on a case of Old Crow and lifted out the first bottle.

Kell took it, pulling the cork. "Might be the real thing, after all." He sniffed the top, took a small taste, then upended the bottle for a healthy swallow. Wiping the back of his hand across his mouth, he handed it to Li.

"Not bad. Not bad at all. At least it's not that Shelby Lemonade." Kell grinned. "Can't figure how a man bellies up to the bar and drinks that booze-blinding stuff."

"Good for the heart, I have been told," Li answered, passing the bottle back.

"Strychnine's good for the heart?"

"You do not agree? Perhaps it is the tobacco juice?"

"Alkali water, for sure." Kell guzzled another drink. "Don't forget the alcohol. Can't make any coffin varnish without it." He waited until Li lifted the bottle to his mouth. "Did you really tell Lockwood I wasn't fit for a worm feast?"

His timing earned him a whiskey shower. Li started choking. Kell pounded him on his back, laughing when Li began a rapid-fire accounting of exactly what he had told the mercantile owner about him.

"Getting into my ancestry was a bit much, Li. But you could be right. There may not be a noble, honorable person among them."

"We are still friends?"

Kell eyed the hand Li held out to him. He caught the gleam in Li's black, almond-shaped eyes and shook his head. Backing away, he began to circle Li, even knowing the man could beat him any day of the week, drunk or sober. When Li set the bottle on top of the crates in the wagon, Kell darted to the side.

Too quickly. His boots hit a mud patch and he went down.

This time it was Li who laughed.

"Well, don't just stand there. Help me up."

"Leaving you there will save me from exerting myself to place you back on the ground."

"Sure of yourself, aren't you? One of these days, Li, I might surprise you."

Clasping his hands in a prayerlike pose, Li then bowed low. "Upon the day you beat me, this most humble master will give forth his most honorable title. This will bring me great joy to see my most worthy student honor my teachings."

"Honor, hell. And you don't sound very humble to me." Struggling, Kell managed to get to his feet, leaving behind mud prints on his pants and shirt.

"Li, we've done all we can today. You go back and I'll stand first watch."

"You go."

Kell wondered why Li was refusing. The man had no liking for mud and rain, having slept in the open too many nights without even a blanket to ward off a chill. It was a long time ago, long before Kell had won him in a card game, but Li had a long memory.

He wasn't about to go back to the boardinghouse. The less he saw of Annie Muldoon, the better for him. Li had no such problem, and Kell said as much.

"I do not wish to leave you here alone. I am not ready to part company with you, Kell. You believe these people are not killers. I do not share that belief."

"Fine. Send Bronc to stay." Kell lifted out his rifle and a box of shells from the wagon's planked seat. "Or tell me the reason why you don't want to go back to the boardinghouse. There's a false note in your voice, Li. I learned to read that from you."

"So the student becomes the master."

"Stop handing out your vague statements that tell me nothing. No," Kell amended, "that's not true. By not telling me why, you confirm there's more to it."

Kell set his loaded rifle back on the wagon seat and began pulling off the canvas that covered the cases of whiskey.

"If you're staying, help me unload so we can have a dry bed of sorts."

They worked in silence, stacking the crates against the side of the wagon until the flatbed was empty. Kell jumped up and spread out the canvas, eyeing it with distaste.

"You, at least, could have a dry, comfortable bed to sleep in."

"I will not—" Li stopped and looked up at Kell. "My reasons are much like yours. I do not wish to spend time with the little one."

"Annie? What the hell is that supposed to mean?"

"Annie, is it? No longer Muldoon?"

"Never mind what I call her. What has she got to do with you not going back to the boardinghouse?"

"The thought makes you angry?"

"Damn right it does, Li. Now answer me."

"She has nothing to do with my reason for not going back. When I spoke of the little one, I thought of Fawn."

"Fawn?" Kell repeated the name, but he caught Li's grin and realized what he had admitted. Nothing he could say would be believed. Not by Li. Still, he made an attempt.

"It was the whiskey talking. I couldn't care less what you or anyone said about Muldoon."

"Yes, I am sure you believe that." Li gazed out at the unabated rain. "Fawn is a wounded bird."

"So heal her, if it matters so much."

"Your Annie does not know what made her silent."

"She's not my Annie. Muldoon's a joker in a poorly dealt hand. That's all she is, Li," Kell added in a voice laced with warning.

"She is so young. Her eyes bring to mind an ancient one who has lived too long and has seen too little of joy."

"She's not that young. If she's given you a bad case of horn colic, mooning around here won't cure it."

"Fawn trusts me."

"What the hell has that got to do with anything? If you want her—"

"I am a prudent man, Kell."

"News for you, my friend. You sound more like a smitten swain to me." Kell bunched up one corner of the canvas to pillow his head. He knew he wasn't going to sleep, but he settled himself down on the planked bed and closed his eyes nevertheless.

Minutes later Kell sat up. Li was still staring out at the rain. He swore to himself that Li had mentioned Annie. He wasn't going to get any rest with another Irish toothache. It was bad enough when it happened near the woman, but he had come to a poor pass when just the mention of her name disturbed the fit of his pants.

"If you're not going to sleep," Kell called out, "grab that bottle and we'll finish it."

The whiskey was warming, enough so that Kell dozed off, but when he awoke, damp and aching, he found that Li still stood watch. Groaning and cursing that old age was finally catching up with him, Kell left the wagon and joined Li near the edge of the canvas.

"Damn rain's enough to send me heading down to Mexico."

"You have become a creature spoiled by comfort, Kell. Go back to the boardinghouse. It is long after midnight. I will stay and keep watch."

When Kell didn't answer him, Li turned to look at him. He could not make out his features, but only the tired set of his shoulders. "You have not slept in too many nights. If you push yourself now, who will watch tomorrow night?"

"All right. I give. You don't want my company, I'm out of here."

It wasn't that far to walk back to the boardinghouse, and the thought of a dry, soft bed, even without a body to warm it, enticed Kell like four pilgrims at a poker table.

CHAPTER TEN

～

hilled to the bone by the time he entered the darkened lobby, Kell reminded himself to tell Annie to start locking the doors. Tonight, though, he was glad she hadn't. The last thing he needed was another no-win confrontation with her. Li had been right; he had pushed himself too hard the last few days.

His boots made sloshing noises as he wearily climbed the stairs. He felt like a man who'd been hit by a wall-eyed bronc gone loco. The whiskey, the cold, and his dogged tiredness had him staggering into his room. He didn't bother with the lamp, and only the thought of sleeping dry made him bother to kick off his boots.

He felt his way around the room until he reached the washstand. Stripping off his wet clothes, he managed a few swipes with the towel before the thought of sleep beckoned him to find the bed.

He hit his shin on the corner post of the bedstead. "Damn it! It's as black as a full house of spades," he swore, pulling back the quilt and sheet. He ignored the pain racing up and down his leg, his eyes already closed when he flopped stomach down on the bed. Kell barely had the strength left to yank the quilt over him.

Something cold and wet tickled his ear. Kell drew the cover up to his neck. Sleep was all he wanted, all his body craved. His head nestled deeper into the soft, goosedown pillow that smelled of something sweet and warm as sunshine. And feathers. Wet feathers.

And the pillow wasn't warm. It was damp. Kell inched over and grabbed hold of the other pillow, shoving it beneath his head.

"Better," he grumbled.

Moments later he struggled to open his eyes. His lids felt as if the grit of every two-bit town he had hit in the past year had settled on them. A drop of water trickled down his forehead. Kell rolled over, gave the pillows a halfhearted punch, and settled himself again.

Water rolled down his cheek. "Shoulda dried hair," he muttered. Something was wrong. His body was dragging him into the sleep he craved, but his mind kept sending him some message.

Water. There was something wrong about water . . .

Another drop trickled from his forehead, rolling back into his hair. A one-eyed squint was all he could manage.

Plop! Water hit his eye. Kell snarled, knuckled his eye, and forced his lids up. Wide-eyed, he stared, trying to make sense of what was happening to him.

He could still hear the rain. No longer storming, it fell in softer, but steady patter. The pillow had already been damp when he hit the bed. This much thinking taxed his weary mind.

Water fell on his nose. He raised his hand to wipe it away and caught another drop. Kell looked up. He couldn't see the blasted ceiling in the dark, but he knew—as sure as any gambler knew when lady luck up and left him to flirt at some other man's table—that he was not going to get any sleep in this bed.

Not tonight.

Aware that his temper was never being far from exploding, Kell fought to remain calm. As the drops dribbled down his chin though, he could feel the temper surge inside him.

"Muldoon." Just whispering her name from between his clenched teeth sent exhaustion fleeing. He kicked off the covers and wore a sheet of goose bumps.

"This time I will strangle her." Water hit his shoulder. Another drop wove a cold path down his beard-stubbled cheek.

"That does it!" He bounded off the bed. "First it's stealing. Then someone tries to use me and mine for a down-home barbecue. This isn't a town. It's a pit full of rattlers. And now that damn witch is trying to drown me!"

Kell flung open the door to the hallway, and a cold draft swept over his naked body. It wasn't the chill that sent him back into his room. Only the thought that one Annie Muldoon would likely expire of apoplexy if she saw him in Adam's glory and thereby cheat him of the pleasure of killing her sent him searching for a pair of pants. Dry ones.

She wasn't in her room. Kell discovered that when he didn't bother to light a lamp and tripped over a chamber pot in the middle of the rug and landed on the bed which was empty of the body he had designs upon—murderous ones. His prey wanted serious tracking.

Subjected to a steady dripping shower while he stood in the middle of her room, figuring out where she could be hiding, he began to think about other designs for her body. The kind they hanged a man for doing.

No one, but no one, would blame him for killing her. And at this moment, he knew he didn't give a damn what happened to him. He wanted his hands around her neck.

He didn't bother to check the doves' rooms. She'd no more seek them out than she did him. Finding the bathtub empty was no surprise, but he thought to check the small room. Li's room was empty. Everyone was asleep because their beds were dry. He wouldn't put it past that devious, prissed-up witch to have deliberately knocked a hole in the ceiling above his bed. The woman was born to torment man.

It was about time she found out she had picked the wrong man.

Every step added a number to her sins. Muldoon wouldn't admit she'd committed any, but a man had to protect himself with the weapons at hand. The top of the list: she caused him a steady Irish toothache. The annoying state caused him to lose sleep. She was the added reason he dug in his boot heels about staying in Loving to rebuild the Aces.

And that mouth. *You're slipping,* he warned himself. *Can't forget that sugar-soft mouth that teased and tempted you.*

Prowling into the front parlor, he checked beneath the sofa, then moved into the back parlor, all the while thinking he was racking up an impressive list.

If he was ever brought to trial, he'd have a defense ready. It was a good thing women didn't have the vote. An all-male jury would acquit him faster than he could spot a marked deck of cards. From the top of her bright-as-new-copper hair to the tips of her high buttoned shoes, Kell managed to add nine more attributes of Annie Muldoon that offended him.

"Freckles," he muttered, opening the door to her aunt's room. He could barely make out the low trundle bed where Fawn slept, but he wouldn't discount the cowardly Muldoon seeking refuge here. The woman wasn't aware that she couldn't hide. He was determined to find her. Tonight—or what was left of it. And he wasn't going to forget about her freckles. The serious question of finding out if she had them all over had caused him all sorts of agony.

Over the years Kell had done his share of sneaking into and out of too many rooms. He stepped inside, controlled his breathing and listened. Fawn's breathing was soft. But he received an earful of Hortense's snoring. If another body was hiding in there, it wasn't alive and breathing.

A light thud amended that. Dewberry meowed and tried to twine himself around Kell's bare feet. He scooped up the cat before he woke either of the women and closed the door softly behind him.

With Dewberry settled in the crook of his arm, Kell walked out into the lobby and spotted the weak sliver of light that showed at the far end of the dining room.

"Euerka, cat. We hit the right pocket." His voice was as soft as his hand absently stroking the big tom. Now that his prey was close, Kell took his time walking to the closed kitchen door.

"Accommodating lady. She's far enough away from the others so I won't have a witness when I strangle her. That's what I call lady luck, cat."

Dewberry purred. Loudly.

"Nice to know you approve. She probably beats you when no one's around." Kell set the cat down on one of the dining room chairs. "Stay there. I need both my hands free."

A plaintive cry made him shoot a glaring look at the big cat.

Kell leaned down and whispered in the cat's ear, "You want to see justice done, don't you?" Dewberry flicked his ear, then settled his haunches with his front paws tucked neatly out of the way, face turned toward the door. "Good boy."

Kell jerked up straight. Christ! Now Muldoon had him talking to a cat!

Closing his hand over the doorknob, he took a deep, calming breath and released it before he shoved the door open. He was ready for anything.

Or so he believed.

Muldoon waiting with her horse pistol would not have surprised him. He was ready to duck if she attacked him with a broom. He was even prepared to dodge flying china—a very brief affair that had gone sour had taught him how and was best forgotten—the affair that is, not how to dodge, and nothing would stop him from having his satisfaction.

Except Annie Muldoon herself.

Each scene he imagined disappeared when he opened the kitchen door. He had found his quarry. She was accommodating him by being alone. She sat at the table, facing the door, her head bent, a fretful hand wiping at her face. Muldoon crying?

"If you've come for a bucket, there's none left. Not a pot. Not one pan. There's not even a bowl to be found. Unless you want the cracked one. But that's of no use. It leaks."

"Pity I'm not interested in the contents of your kitchen." Kell closed the door and leaned against it.

Annie looked up. "Oh, it's you."

The dismissive tone and her obvious fascination with

the table stung. "Should I apologize? Help me out here, Muldoon. Were you expecting someone else perhaps? An angel of mercy? A knight to rescue you? Who, Muldoon?"

"If I was expecting one of them, I'm doomed to disappointment. All I got was you."

"An unrepented sinner."

"How true. I tried to empty the flour crock, but there's nothing left to put the flour in. These," she said, a stabbing motion of one finger indicating the crooked row of teacups on the table, "are all that remain."

"Teacups for showers? Who would've thought? Much as I hate to dampen your brilliance, Muldoon, don't make that offer to anyone else. Despite what your lowly opinion is of us, I wouldn't drink from a cup that's filtered water through your ceilings."

Annie sniffed. Her shoulders sagged and she had to rouse herself. "You've likely had ample opportunity to drink from the most disgusting vessels. Take them and leave. They are all I have."

Kell almost argued the fact. Her weary sigh stopped him. "Poor Muldoon." And if she had looked up at him in that moment, she would have found genuine compassion in his eyes. "While I could debate the issue of your assets . . . I'll admit, you look like something even Dewberry would reject bringing home."

Her head fell forward into her cupped hand. "Dewberry, I'll have you know, is a male. He has no taste. Even you would be surprised by what he brings home." Annie jerked herself awake. "Then again, maybe not. He's very much like you."

Into Kell's sleep-starved brain, the slurring tones of her voice slowly penetrated. He sniffed the air. Spirits? Was he truly smelling liquor in Muldoon's kitchen? His eyes brightened with interest. It was something fruity. But then, he was staring at a woman who claimed she liked eating lemons.

The pooling spread of the lamplight on the table helped his eyes pick out details—the tangled fall of her red-gold hair that nearly hid her back and shoulders, the plump curves of her breasts hiding the edge of the table while her damp, pristine white and too-thin-for-his-peace-of-mind nightgown revealed the darker shade of her nipples. He noted the faint trembling of the slender hand that held up her head. As if she became aware of his intense scrutiny, Annie lowered her hand to the table and looked up at him.

Kell added the overly bright blue eyes, lashes—dark and thick as molasses—fluttering with the effort to hold his gaze. The flush on her cheeks hid her freckles and he had to avoid looking at her mouth. Fragile as a battered wildflower, she appealed to a softer, gentler side of him that had not been awakened in some time. He tilted his head to one side. There beneath the table her bare feet were hooked around the chair rungs. The hem of her nightgown was caught high enough to reveal dainty ankles and curled toes—damn Annie Muldoon and her bare feet!

He had come looking for her to strangle her, not to feel this vulnerable tug of compassion for her beaten state.

She shivered and briefly squeezed her eyes closed until the chill passed. From her lap, her right hand appeared holding a small cut-glass bottle. Too tired to make herself tea, Annie had tried liquor to get warm.

Kell's avid gaze couldn't hide his surprise. Muldoon drinking? The Bible-thumping leader of the Loving corset-contingent? He settled himself in a slouch against the door, his arms crossed over his chest. His need for sleep disappeared. He never expected to be entertained. Murder was no longer the option he considered. But, oh, he still had designs on that body.

She lifted the bottle, grunted, then glared at it for a few seconds before she raised it to her lips. Kell's gaze followed her move. And so much for his need to avoid looking at her mouth.

"Tell me, Muldoon, did you intend to finish the bottle and use it for your flour?"

Annie shot him a disdainful glance, took a swig, and coughed. In a most unladylike fashion, she wiped the back of her hand across her mouth, then licked her lips. Focusing her gaze—and she retained enough sense to realize that it was an effort—she hiccuped.

" 'Scuse me."

The giggle that followed made Kell grin. "It's all right. What's a little hiccup between friends?"

"Friends?" That was too much for Annie. She took another tiny sip.

"You didn't answer me, darlin'." A blank look made him add, "about the flour."

"Mr. Stork—no, that's not right. Ah, York. That's it. Well, what you know about a crock of flour would fit in a . . . a . . . a thimble!"

"Maybe not, Muldoon. But flour, darlin', ain't the only thing crocked around here."

"It's not?" Eyes wide with this startling announcement, Annie sent a searching gaze around the kitchen. She reared back in her chair, but trying to sit up straight was too much to ask of her aching body. She slumped forward again. *What had he said? Pay attention to him,* she warned herself. *He'll tangle you up in words and looks, then hang you out to dry.* Dry? Maybe it wouldn't be so bad. She could use something dry. But he said crocked . . .

"Did you accuse me of being crocked?"

"No offense, honey, but you're—"

"I'll have you know . . ."

"Yes?" he prompted when she appeared lost.

"Ah, that ladies don't get crocked."

"Much as I hate to correct a lady, crocked is what you are."

"Nooo," she groaned. "Tip-sy." Annie blinked. Shoving aside her tangled hair, she leaned forward, staring up at him. "Your hair's all west."

"West?"

"Wet. It's wet." She gently shook her head. Had she accused him of some misdeed?

"Annie, it's raining outside." Her moan had him add in a gentle tone, "Raining inside, too."

"Oh, I know. I know." His gaze waited for hers like a trap set for a mouse. Annie could no more avoid looking at him, than she could stop another hiccup. "I tried. Really I did. But the rain wouldn't stop."

"Annie," he said in that same gentle tone, but now undercurrents of laughter shimmered in it. "If you had all the buckets, pots, and pans from every kitchen in Texas, you couldn't stop the rain."

"Stop the rain? Have you indulged in the evils of drinking?"

"I've done my share. But, darlin', you can bet I hold my liquor better than you. Need some advice on coping?"

Listen! He'll talk rings around you. "You're most deliberately trying to confuse me. I wasn't trying to stop the rain outside. I know you don't have a very high opinion of me." A buzzing began in her head. Annie had to speak with extreme care. "I'm a woman."

"I can see."

"Don't interrupt. I may be only a woman, but I'm perfectly intelligent. I was attempting to stop the leaks in the house."

"Ah, that accounts for it then. I wondered what you'd been doing. I wouldn't have guessed unless you told me. Were there a great many of them?"

Having exhausted herself trying to speak coherently, Annie laced her fingers together over the top of the bottle and rested her chin on them. "Ever so many. I couldn't keep up emptying the buckets. Everyone tried to help, but I sent them to bed."

"I can see that you're very tired. Why don't I take you up to bed?"

Annie bolted up from the chair and sat down as quickly. She caught the bottle before it spilled, wondering why her knees felt as if the stuffing had been taken out.

"Bed?" she repeated.

"As in to sleep. To rest your weary little . . . ah, head. To—"

"Oh. You were being kind." Tears welled up in her eyes. Annie never cried if she could help it. Crying made her nose stuffy. She couldn't manage dainty tears, not like Emmaline, whose eyes sparkled prettily if she cried. Annie's eyes became red. The rims of them already burned as if she had used her scrub brush on them. Sniffling, she heard the buzz in her head increase. Her head ached from all this thinking that *he* was forcing upon her.

Had she really told Kellian York that he was being kind?

Annie pulled back and eyed the bottle. *This is what happens when a body makes free with spirits. You feel fever-flushed and cold at the same time. Your mind resembles Aunt Hortense's succotash. Pay attention, Annie Charlotte. The man is talking about bed. And you thought he was be-*

ing kind? He wouldn't know kindness if it sat up, tapped his stubborn set chin, and kissed him!

Kissed . . . him? Why would she think about kissing? Through the sheen of tears, Annie focused on his mouth. It was a nice mouth, as mouths went. Maybe his was a little full on the bottom. And there were those charming indentations when the corners lifted. Annie stared at his forming smile—all honey innocence and comfort, his smile could have sweetened every cake in the county.

The upper half of his face was shadowed, but the light from the table lamp spilled a flowered glow on his bare chest. Really! The man had to do something about his lack of shirts.

As with his mouth, Annie tried telling herself that he was made of skin and bone. Nothing at all special. But a small voice—one she swore was inebriated—countered that that wasn't true. The patterning of hair on his chest appeared soft as goosedown, golden and so inviting to her weary head that her fingers curled with the need to touch him.

She attempted to give herself a mental kick to beat back the enveloping haze from the little blackberry brandy she'd had. It didn't work. She knew that exhaustion accounted more for her state than the brandy.

Staring at the canted jut of Kellian's hip sent warmth unfurling inside her. The room seemed suddenly warmer, but a shiver raced over her. Annie squeezed her knees together. Cold drafts touching her through the damp nightgown had not caused shivers; they came from excitement stirring. Her blood sizzled awake body parts, all the ones unmentionable even to herself.

But she couldn't stop looking . . .

"You must be cold standing there with nothing on."

Kell's smile became a wicked grin. He glanced down at himself, then slowly straightened away from the door. A few short steps would bring him to the opposite side of the table from her. His hesitation lasted all of a moment. Then he stood in front of Annie and placed both his hands palms down on the table.

"Open your eyes, petunia. I'm wearing pants."

"Most men do," she snapped, aware, as she had never wanted to be, of the loving fit of cloth to his body. She couldn't remember ever being concerned about the fit of any man's pants, but then she had never met a man like Kellian before. And not one man that she knew had a body . . .

Annie!

Hush. It's true.

And she silenced that little voice, losing the battle at the same time. Her gaze slid down to his waistband. She didn't know if she should feel thankful that the top button was fastened or disappointed that the cloth hid an intriguing swirl of hair encircling his belly button. Every button was snugly closed. Her eyes opened wide, then closed. The fit of his pants had changed to a decidedly pronounced state guaranteed to bring about heart palpitations. Her hand rose and curved over the upper slope of her breast as if to contain the quickening beat of her heart.

Merely by his close presence he had effectively routed her again. She was frightened of her own reaction to him. Any intelligent female could deal with the likes of Kellian York. All her life she had thought herself rational, logical, and most practical.

So why was running the only solution that came to mind?

Like the thick, unstructured puddle of succotash she

had likened herself to, Annie found she couldn't order all
body parts to move. Some parts put up resistance at being
taken out of his sight.

He was still watching her with a calm, remote expression, but his eyes were narrowed and strangely intense.

"Did you come to complain about your bed?"

"The thought crossed my mind. It's wet and while there
are times I don't mind the sheets getting soaked, it's usually because—"

"I don't want to hear this."

"Wouldn't make any sense to explain it to you. You
wouldn't know what I was talking about anyway. Would
you mind if I sit? No! Don't look at me like I suggested
taking a broom to your backside."

"Mr. York!"

"And you can call me Kell."

"It's easy finding names to call you, but using your first
is not proper."

"Darlin', you're sitting there in a nightgown that hides
as much as strawberries swimming in cream—oh, Lord,
now I've made you realize how ridiculous your talking
about propriety is."

He raised a distinctly skeptical brow. She sat with her
arms crossed over her chest like some about-to-be-set-
upon heroine from a bad play or one of those penny
dreadfuls that the doves had Pockets read to them.

Annie looked down at herself. Dismay filled her. She
rearranged her forearms. The new placement offered no
better concealment. When she glanced up to find his eyes
had darkened to the green of sweet spring grass, she was
spurred by a new surge of modesty to hide her breasts
with her cupped hands. Kell's groan told her she had not

achieved success; if anything, judging by the flush tinting the skin stretched tight over his cheekbones, she'd done the opposite.

Hunching forward, she drew as much of her hair around her as she could. "Have you no shame?"

"Not a penny's worth."

"I wish you would just go."

"Not for all your teacups, darlin'." His lips twitched as the color rose in her cheeks. The lamplight burnished her skin and hair to a golden hue, and he had a sudden impulse to reach across the table to touch her cheek, to feel the warmth beneath his fingertips.

She had the damnedest way of lifting her chin, almost as if she read his thought and dared him to touch her. Her move revealed the slender line of her throat, her pulse beating erratically in the smooth hollow. Knowing that he made her nervous gave him a feeling of primitive power. It was when she defended herself against any admission that she was a sensual woman that she aroused his hunting instincts.

And there was the annoyance that she could also arouse him so easily and remain unaware of it.

The mindless surge of lust—for that was all it could be—angered him. Kell immediately tried to suppress it. Why her? What was it about Annie Muldoon defending her virtue that made him want to kiss her senseless and wring an admission from her that she was a passionate woman with needs? What had she done to him? His reaction to her was too strong, and nearly uncontrolled. When he had first met her, he'd wondered whether he would make her a sinner or she would make him a saint.

Annie steeped in pleasure—pleasure that he could

bring to her—despite her calling it a sin, was too great a
temptation for him to resist.

Desire came, so powerful that he knew he wasn't going
to try to temper it.

Chapter Eleven

〜

"You are not going to leave, are you?" Annie's gaze sent
a plea that briefly touched his eyes. Strands of his
hair were drying, she could see the lighter hues as he
shook his head.

"Not on a bet, darlin'. Shall we see who outlasts the
other? I should warn you, I've gone without sleep for days.
Have you?"

"Yes!" Pathetically eager, Annie embarked on tales of
childhood illness. Near breathless when done, she saw
that he was not impressed. "Last year, Aunt Hortense had
a bout of grippe. I didn't sleep for almost a week until she
was better. Then there was the time I forgot to tell Fawn
that I washed the stairs. She had a fall and suffered a bad
sprain."

"Is that it?"

Annie searched her memory, even as she wondered
why. "I had a terrible toothache once. The pain kept me
awake plenty of nights, but then it could have been some
of the cures."

Shifting the moment she mentioned toothache, Kell once more shook his head. "Annie, have you ever stayed awake all night for pleasurable pursuits?"

"Unlike you, I do not have an avocation for pleasure." Annie exhaled a short, exasperated breath. "Is that all you think about?" She knew better than to let him see her anger. Any reaction from her would only add to his obvious enjoyment. Why he would find baiting her a pleasurable pursuit, Annie didn't know. But the man seemed to thrive on doing it. In silence she watched him move around the table to her side and lean against the table's edge, his long legs inches from her hand.

"Annie, you make educatin' you a difficult task. A lesser man could get discouraged."

"And you, of course, are not one?"

"No, darlin'. I'm a man who loves a challenge."

Her eyes watched his hands rake back his hair, until the flax to burnished brown strands appeared as if a hot Texas wind had combed it. Every move was filled with sensual grace, an affront to a decent woman. He was a man born to raise hell and a few eyebrows—hers being the first—not to mention the feelings of dangerous excitement from his wicked smile and the restless heat of his eyes. Annie pursed her lips, trying to find the strength not to respond. Far easier to give up her goal to see a church built here. He always looked as if he had tumbled out of bed.

And the devil's imps were at work tonight, for she thought with longing that it would always be someone else's bed.

"Annie, have I told you how inspiring I find your samplers?"

"My samplers?" she parroted. Annoyance crashed with vivid disappointment. *Her samplers?*

"Have you stitched all of them hanging around the house?"

She searched for a trap in answering him and found none. "Some are mine, a few my mother and grandmother sewed. Aunt Hortense never cared for needlework." Confused, she stopped.

"I like them, Annie. Truly I do. Is that one yours on the wall behind you?"

Annie wasn't sure what she was hearing and seeing in front of her. The effort to remember what was behind her was simply beyond her capability at this moment. She swallowed, then rising like a fish to unresisting bait, she nodded to his lure.

"Busy Hands Are Happy Hands," Kell drawled, flicking his gaze back to hers. Her embarrassment brought his reluctant admiration—Annie might be exhausted and crocked, but the lady was still sharp-witted. "Do you believe that's true?" He glanced from Annie's clasped hands to his own. "Of course you do, otherwise you wouldn't have it there. Darlin', if we don't find something to occupy my hands, it's gonna be a long, long night."

"Well, then Mr. York, you can help me empty the buckets." Annie made her announcement with the smugness of a thrifty housewife getting the best of a bargain.

"Then up you go." Kell was not immune to her need to escape. He reached down and drew her tense body out of the chair.

"What are you doing?"

"Don't do a modesty bit with me." Kell uncrossed her hands and forced her arms down to her sides. "I'm trying to behave like a gentleman, Annie."

"Well," she demanded with flaming blue eyes, "who asked you to?"

"Ah, Annie. Darlin', unpredictable wilted flower." His voice a soft, seductive caress, he hooked his finger beneath her chin and lifted her face. "Look at me. Don't hide with fluttering lashes." This close, he could see the shadows that curved under her eyes. "Let me take you upstairs to bed. No, don't panic. You rest, I'll tend to emptying the buckets. If you stop moaning, you'll hear that the rain's almost stopped."

She didn't seem to have the strength left to stand and Kell drew her closer. Sainthood did not sit well on his shoulders. He needed a shot or two of whiskey; holding her so near was too much to ask of himself. A tremor shook her body and Annie leaned against him, her red-gold hair caught between them.

A glass or two wasn't going to be enough. He needed a bottle—what's more, he needed it right now.

She didn't utter a sound. The crick in his neck warned him he held an armful of trouble. He was too aware of her, had been from the moment he found her in her room, the feel of her shoulders and back beneath his hands, the soft fullness of her breasts against his bare skin, that worthless bit of thin cloth leaving none of the precious modesty she needed to protect her. The curve of her belly fit below his as she settled herself against him, her head at rest below his shoulder, her long hair draped over his arm.

Fragrant and silky soft, her hair enticed him to bend his head and rub his chin over the tumbled curls. "Scented with flowers and sprinkled with spices," he murmured despite his repeated silent warnings to himself.

"Are we cooking?" she asked in a distracted voice.

"Bubbling like a pot about to boil."

Annie lifted her head and looked at his face. Lamplight loved his features. She struggled to see the telltale marks of his sleepless state. Her hand moved of its own volition to cup his beard-stubbled cheek.

"Kellian?"

The meld of fear and plea in her eyes ripped his control. He knew he wasn't a saint. He wanted to prove to Annie she wasn't one. His mouth closed over hers, a tempered kiss, a few strands of her silky hair caught between their lips.

Under her palm, Annie could feel the curving muscle of his chest and the steady heart rhythm mating with his breathing. Her own had the erratic pace of an overworked horse. Under the subtle, clever pressure of his thumb, her lips parted, and she was rewarded with his mouth stroking the open softness. Long, slender fingers played in the wisps of hair at the side of her head and traced the outline of her ear, toying with the sensitive earlobe, then he gathered her hair at the back of her head, as if to hold her steady against the spinning sensations she was feeling. Gently then, he turned her head from side to side, dragging her mouth across his.

Her small, involuntary whimper brought a reassuring stroke to her shoulder, the cupping of her waist that urged her closer to him. Her shivering body warmed against the heat of his skin. His arms tightened around her, and Annie gave him her mouth, swaying under the powerful feelings he unleashed.

Insistent and urgent, his mouth tutored hers, his hands sliding down to cup her buttocks and lift her to him, the thin cloth that separated his wanting body from hers of no use to still the flow of desire that caused her to move instinctively nearer. He fed on the

sugar-sweet, generous offering of her lips. Desire
heightened, his hand shaped the curve of her waist,
narrow and tight beneath his questing fingers. The
swell of her hip invited exploration, the tips of his fingers delicately sculpting flesh and bone so rich with
warmth, he could almost taste it.

Annie cried out when his palm gently cupped her
breast. It was shocking to have him touch her, but she
was steeped in a deliriously pleasant cloud where his
knowledgeable touch both soothed and brought to life a
tension that ached. The sensation was too much, and
she cried out again, her breath sharp and hurting.

"Gently, sweet, gently," he murmured. "Nothing
hurts. I promised it wouldn't." The backs of his fingers
brushed back and forth over the tip of one breast, his
lips pressed coaxing kisses on her temple, her flushed
cheek, the corner of her mouth. And just as gently, he
nested the full softness of her breast in hand, his thumb
forming slow, hot circles that brought her mouth seeking his.

Behind her lids, Annie held the image of his hard, lean-
cheeked face, hair streaked by the sun, thick and unruly,
begging for a woman's hand to tame it. Her hand. She
parted her lips at his urging, but even as the blood rushed
with sizzling force through her, she felt like a cloth torn in
two. His touch promised pleasure, his mouth offered
heaven, but a sane voice of reason warned her back from
this seductive trickster.

"Annie. Annie, open your mouth, sweet. Let me taste
you."

The hot glide of his tongue on her bottom lip sent
shocks racing. The slow, heated throb of her mouth was
soothed and yet burned for more. The nudge of his powerful thigh between hers filled her with embarrassment.

Below the pit of her stomach the tightening ball of tension frightened her.

"Please. I . . ."

"I'll do the pleasin', darlin'. Just open your mouth for me. That sugar-soft mouth drives me—" Kell silenced himself by taking her lips in a hard, exploring kiss, feeling the bite of short, neat nails digging into his shoulder. Her trembling thighs rode his, soft, hidden heat scalding him. *Nothing hurts.* Foolish words for him to tell her. He was hurting. Passion unfurled with the changing cry he wrung from her, his ending kiss forced her to draw air as though she were starving for it, the rapid rise and fall of her breasts fitting snugly against him. He thirsted for the honeyed moisture of her kiss, unable to think about anything but the need to bury his aching flesh in Annie. He was hot and hard, and the charming effort she made to capture his tongue told him the night wasn't long enough for the ride he wanted.

He drew her head to the side, his mouth gliding against the petal soft skin of her neck. His thumb and forefinger caught one end of the night gown's ribboned tie. A light tug and the cloth obligingly fell open, bringing the warm fragrance—floral, feminine, and heady—to intoxicate his already aroused senses.

With tender kisses and murmurs he brought her up to another peak, every tremor of her body a caress to his. He enjoyed women, and willingly lavished every moment spent to bring them pleasure, having learned after a misspent youth, just how much he had denied himself.

There was acquiescence, not resistance, in his darlin' Annie. He could feel the passion smolder to life in her as his mouth trailed lower to kiss the curve of one pale,

rounded breast. Greedy, sharp-set passion led to his savoring her; his reward was a pleading litany of his name.
Her fingers were curled within his hair, then slid down
to his chest, open and kneading his skin like a purring
kitten. Kell smiled and whispered every encouragement.

"Please," Annie pleaded through lips too dry and
heated. "I implore you."

"Don't beg, love. I'll give you—"

"No. No, you won't listen." Annie struggled to untangle
herself from the web of sensuality that held her ensnared.
She pushed at his chest, shaking her head.

Kell wasn't so far gone in his desire to bury himself
within her that he didn't stop. His head lifted slowly
while he noted the effort it required to breathe nor-
mally.

"This," he said the moment she looked up at him, "is
what I get for kissing a woman who likes lemons and
blackberries."

"There is nothing wrong with my liking fruit." Annie
closed her eyes, licking her lips and feeling ravaged by the
need to bring his mouth to hers.

Kell clasped her hips in a gentle fashion, ignoring her
renewed struggle and freed his thigh. Before she knew
what he was about, he swung her up into his arms. "This
time you are going off to bed." He took a moment to settle her weight and order his unruly body to resign itself to
abstinence.

Annie didn't have the strength left to argue or question
him. Her arms tightened around his neck and she snug-
gled her head against the warm curve of his shoulder.
Why she trusted him, she didn't know. Closing her eyes
against the sway of his body finally moving out of the
kitchen, she knew she could not get upstairs without his
help. Thinking of what happened between them was be-

yond her. Sleepily she murmured to his skin, "Why don't you like fruits?"

"I didn't say that, petunia. There's nothing wrong with fruit unless you try to pick 'em green."

"Green?" Annie shuddered. The mention of the word made her stomach roil. She would expire if she was sick on him.

"That's what I said." Kell found he had to struggle up the stairs with his charming burden.

"Pickin' green fruit," he explained in a whisper as he entered her room and quickly lowered her to the bed, "can give a man an Irish toothache."

"Wasted effort . . . ripe is sweeter . . ."

"I know, darlin', but there you have it. Green equals ache. And don't tell me you have a cure for it."

"But I told you . . . I did tell," she mumbled sleepily, curling up on her side.

Kell drew up the quilt to cover her. "Trust me on this one, Muldoon. You aren't ready for the cure. And somehow I'll survive the ache."

He stood watching for minutes until he was sure her breathing was deep and even. Reaching down, he brushed a few stray curls from her cheek. "And you were wrong, Annie. The only one I don't have a high opinion of is myself."

What was left of the night brought dreams to Annie where Kellian York whispered love words that led her needy spirit into believing something good and true might bloom from his seeking her out. There was the disturbing presence of green apple images that brought an ache she couldn't quite disperse.

But morning—late, to judge by the turn of the sun in

her room—brought Annie to a saner time when she chastized herself for having had absurd wishes.

Never, she swore, struggling out of bed, would she touch another drop of liquor. Every pamphlet, every sermon that proclaimed the evil effects of indulging in spirits had bespoken the truth.

She had to cast aside any thought that Kellian York was about to give up his sinful ways to become her helpmate. He wasn't going to denounce his pleasure-seeking life to join her in good deeds. It was hopeless to dream. Utterly hopeless.

Just like her effort to recall exactly what had happened after he entered the kitchen last night. No, she amended. It was long after midnight, after she had given up her fight with rain and buckets.

Her feet slid on the sopping carpet, and Annie caught the post of the bed to keep herself upright. She bent down slowly to push the chamber pot back under the bed, her gaze just as slow to find the leak in the ceiling. The plaster was stained a dark, unbecoming yellow, crazed by minute cracks and a most definite sag. One more expense to be taken from her church fund.

The first deep breath she drew brought a slight moldy odor rising from the carpet. Her shoulders sagged at the thought of rolling the carpet, then hanging it to dry. Not only her own, but the carpets from every other room where the ceiling leaked.

Daunted, Annie eyed the bed. Just once it would be heaven to have someone else take up her burdens.

But standing there brooding would not get the laborious chores done. Annie turned and found the tall mirror reflecting a wanton-looking creature that bore little resemblance to herself.

Sunlight streaming in from the windows penetrated the

frail cotton nightgown to reveal the darker shadow of her body. The image held her, for seconds or minutes, she didn't know. There was a strange compulsion overriding her natural embarrassment, and she was compelled to move forward.

This was the woman Kellian saw last night. The knowledge came with a clarity she could not deny. Her hair was a riotous mass of tangled curls framing her face, then draping over her shoulders to hang past her waist. Staring back at her were wide, dark eyes marred by shadows and lips that appeared to be bee-stung. But it was the reddened spots on her cheek and chin that drew Annie closer to the mirror.

She touched her face, and fate was kind; only fragments of the time in the kitchen came back to her. Dark murmurs, kisses that . . . No!

Annie turned her back. She was not that woman. She was a lady. Committed to fighting Kellian York and his damning ways.

"Air. I need fresh air in here," she muttered, rushing to open the windows. But no matter how deeply she breathed, a tear had been made in the shrouded lost hours, and her mind was set on recalling them.

Needing the distraction, Annie swept the street below with a gaze that searched for Kellian York even as she denied it.

Far from the quiet scene of a weekday, Saturday found the town crowded with ranchers and farmers come in for their weekly shopping. Wagons were drawn up along one side of the street, narrowing her view. Ruts were filled with water, faint rainbows shimmered on the muddy puddles, and walking across the street required a great deal of care. Near the harness shop, Otis Fenway and Noel

Bower played their weekly checker game to the advice of the crowd around them.

Two boys swept the wooden walk in front of the mercantile, keeping it clean of the mud that clung to every pair of shoes. Lucinda Lockwood couldn't abide dirt in her store, no matter how it got there.

Loud voices drew her attention to the far end of the street, where men labored to clear the area of the fire. A high-sided wagon was loaded with burned timbers, and two men raked the blackish area where the Silken Aces had stood.

Annie shaded her eyes with her hand, making out several men in a line, passing along the debris to fill the wagon. She could see that another waited behind it, the seat empty and Li coming into view. He motioned to one group; she was too far to hear what he was saying, but despite his black braid gleaming in the sun, the men scrambled to move. The resemblance to an industrious ant colony came to mind, not only the men but also the women walking along with their market baskets.

Nowhere did she see Kellian. Annie was about to turn away when a wagon departed and revealed a small group of women at the edge of the wooden sidewalk sheltered from the sun by the overhang in front of Emmaline's dress store. Likely, the women were speculating about Kell's plans to rebuild.

"You," she warned herself, "are not going to think about that man."

Annie dressed with undue haste, ignoring the way the crisp white linen collar and apron over her gray washday gown made her look like a Quaker. She attacked her hair until it lay smoothly coiled and pinned to the back of her head.

She had dawdled enough. Knowing she had to leave her room for the last to be cleaned, Annie headed for the door.

A piercing scream halted her. More screams and shouts sent her flying back to the windows.

Chapter Twelve

❦

Annie stared with horror at the scene of confusion that reigned below. At the far end of the street, near Emmaline's shop, a horse reared in its wagon traces, screaming as though in pain. The women had backed to the front of the store away from the animal while two men fought to hold the horse still.

The maddened horse's screams had other men scrambling to the line of wagons along the street as those teams of horses tried to bolt. There were shouts and yells until no sense could be made of them.

A woman crossing the muddy street tugged on her child's hand. The little one she carried held her neck in a death grip. Annie saw the woman slip, then free her hold on the little girl. The horse cried out again, its hoofs rising to slash, and one man went down as the horse bolted free.

The child struggled to get back to the middle of the street. Bearing down on her was the runaway wagon team, the seat empty of a driver to control the frenzied horses.

The child's face was a frozen mask of terror as she stood holding a muddy rag doll.

"Do something!" Annie screamed. The mother had shoved her other child into someone's arms, but two women held her back when she tried to run into the street. With disbelief Annie saw the townspeople freeze.

The child was going to be crushed beneath the horses. Annie heard a shout below her window just as she caught sight of Li racing parallel to the runaway team. Black braid flying behind him, he moved with incredible speed, his feet appearing not to touch the ground.

Annie yelled for him to hurry just as Kell came into view. Li made a leap for the horses' headstall. Kell dived into the muddy street, rolling the small body beneath his own. Without a second to spare he had them out of harm's way, but Li's lunge brought another scream from Annie and more shouts from the crowd. Li slipped in the mud, only one of his hands solidly gripping the headstall. He was being dragged and was too close to the hooves of the crazed horses.

Stricken with terror, Annie couldn't make a sound. Then Kell appeared in the wagon bed. She didn't look at anyone else. He was struggling to climb over the seat. In moments the wagon was out of sight. Annie ran.

There had been no time for Kell to think, only act. In the tense minutes before he managed to seat himself on one horse, he saw that Li had pulled himself up on the other. They held their voices to soothing murmurs and with reassuring touches they calmed the animals until they came to a shuddering standstill a little way outside of town.

For long minutes after they dismounted, Kell struggled to regain his breath. Li had the same trouble. There was no backslapping, no shared laughter to relieve the tension, no joking about their mud-strewn appearance.

Kell wiped his face, realizing too late that by doing so he smeared mud across his cheek. "Why did the horse suddenly bolt?" He stroked the quivering animal's hide, working his way down the foreleg to make sure there was no injury to the horse.

When no immediate answer was forthcoming, Kell saw that Li, with a thoughtful expression, was duplicating his motions on the other animal.

"What the hell happened, Li?"

"I do not know." He straightened and went around the wagon to stand at Kell's side. "I gave the order to move this empty wagon to the other side of the site. The driver was leading the horse and stopped near the group of women by the dressmaker's shop." Sweat mixed with the mud blotches on his face, making him itch. Li tried to find a clean spot on his shirt to wipe it away. There wasn't any.

Shaking his head, he recalled the moment someone had yelled his name. "I turned for a moment, then the horse bolted."

"Can't understand it. From what I saw walking toward you, the animal wasn't spooked." Kell suggested they check the hoofs in case the horse had picked up a nail.

When Annie arrived, breathless from running, she skidded to a stop at the way they both turned accusing looks on her. Her insides felt like churned buttermilk left in the sun and she had to swallow several times before she approached them, thankful that neither man was injured. Behind her came a murmuring crowd of townspeople.

"What happened?" she asked, unable to stop herself from visually inspecting Kell. The only recognizable feature were his eyes; everything else was coated in thick mud.

"We were trying to figure that out, Muldoon."

"I saw from my window. The horse took off as if a bee had stung him."

"Bee?" Kell repeated, glancing at Li.

"I cannot remember if there were any."

Impulsively, Annie untied her apron and handed it to Li. "You can share it." She accepted his murmured thanks with an absent nod, growing uncomfortable with the way Kell was staring at her.

"Li," Kell began, holding his gaze steady on Annie, "you said those women were near the wagon just before the horse bolted?"

"That's right." Li flipped the apron over to the clean side and handed it to Kell. "Here, use it. You need this more."

Keeping her voice low, Annie stepped closer to Kell. "You can't mean to accuse my friends of this? Those women are mothers. They would never do anything to endanger a child's life. Whatever can you be thinking of, Mr. York?"

"I'm thinking," he answered, wincing at the pain spreading from his shoulder, "that I have someone who doesn't want me here and will go to any lengths to prevent my staying."

There was dissent from the men in the front of the crowd that half circled them. Annie turned, looking for support, but the mother and child were being ushered forward and all attention was focused on them.

Annie recognized Clovis Littlewood. Her halting manner as she tried to thank Kell was touching. Her little girl, Mary, usually shy, stepped out from behind her mother's skirt and held out her muddy rag doll to Kell.

"She's not hurt?" he asked, going down on one knee to bring himself level with the child. Dark brown eyes stared back at Kell. Someone had attempted to clean her face, but a few dirt streaks remained. He lifted his hand and touched one bruise on her forehead.

"Mama says I . . . I . . ." Helplessly she turned to her mother.

"Thank him, Mary."

"Oh, yes, and for Cora Mae, too."

More thanks were given him and Li, and Annie listened and watched as Kell merely nodded to acknowledge them, his concentration focused on the child. His smile for the little girl wasn't one she had witnessed before. Gone was the wickedness. Even his tone was gentle as he listened seriously to how much the rag doll meant to Mary.

She sensed rather than saw that the crowd was drifting back to town, and she turned to leave. Later, she promised herself, she would talk to him about his unfounded suspicions. Her friends would not deliberately have injured a horse. The man was reaching for straw in a mud puddle even to think such a thing.

"Your apron," Li said, coming alongside Annie. "It is in a sorry state."

"I can wash it. He's wrong, Li. I just know that he's wrong."

"Perhaps. He has reason to feel angry."

"Yes, I know. The fire."

"There is that, but more." He glanced at her and smiled. "Would hot baths be too much trouble to ask for?"

"No. I'll tend to it." She paused and knew the question would have to be asked. "Why else is Kell angry? You've been with him so long—"

"It is not for me to tell you."

His voice was soft, but there was dismissal. Annie

glanced back to where Kell now stood alone. "I don't think he ever will. I shouldn't have pried."

"*Li.*" Kell barely kept the impatience from his tone.

"Kell calls me."

"I'll see you back at the house," Annie said, walking away, thoughtful and not looking back.

"What did Muldoon want with you? More denials of her friends being involved?"

"She is loyal. Loyalty is to be prized."

"She's blind, and that is to be pitied. Anyway, I want to show you what I found." Kell opened his palm. "Interesting?" Kell looked from Li to Annie's retreating figure. "Even honeybees have stings."

"Stings! I said stings, Aunt Hortense. That's the way the horse bolted. Like a bee stung him." Annie huffed her way into Kellian's room, despairing that in addition to being exhausted from cleaning up the mess that the leaks made, she had her aunt feeling spry and following her around.

"Why would a bee sting a horse, Annie Charlotte?"

"Ask me why the moon is round, why don't you? I don't know. It just looked that way to me." Annie stripped the bed and tossed the damp sheets on the floor. She rolled the top thin feather tick and carefully felt along its underside to see if the water had penetrated. The one below felt dry, but she would have to take this one outside and hope the sun lasted.

"If it doesn't," she muttered, struggling to roll the tick tight, "he'll have to sleep on one." Blowing the hair that escaped her coil out of her eyes, she spun around to find her aunt poking with her cane at Kell's things on his dresser top.

"Aunt Hortense! Stop that. You can't poke in a boarder's things."

"I haven't broke anything. Did you know that your grandfather always said you could tell a lot about a man by the way he keeps his razor?"

Bundling up the sheets and quilt, Annie shot her aunt a bewildered look. "No, I didn't know. What's more, I don't care. The less I know about Mr. York, the better for me."

"A man who keeps his razor sharp keeps his mind the same way." She met Annie's gaze with a blank look. "There was more, but I seem to have forgotten what it was."

"Fine, dearest. Mr. York has a dull mind. Are you sure you wouldn't be—"

"No, no, Annie. His razor's nice and sharp. And see," she added, lifting the strop with her cane, "the leather is of good quality."

"Then I hope he cuts his throat," she muttered, spreading a fresh sheet over the bed.

"Now why would Mr. York want to cut a rope?"

"Aunt, he can hang himself with one for all I care."

"That so, Muldoon?"

"No. Oh, no," Annie whispered to herself, tucking in the corner of the sheet. Why did he have to bathe so quickly? With a heartfelt sigh, she straightened and turned to see Kell come into the room carrying his muddy clothes.

"Is this the laundry pile?"

"You know it is." Nothing could stop her from glaring at him. She knew he relished tossing his clothes on top of the pile that would have her washing for another two hours.

"Aunt Hortense, it is a pleasure to see you up and about."

Hortense nodded, glanced from Kell to her scowling

niece, then came forward. "You're just in time to escort me downstairs. Your arm, young man."

"Aunt!"

"Now, now, Annie Charlotte, you know I'm in your way."

"No, aunt. I . . ." Annie shook her head and bent to finish making the bed. It was a blessing that her aunt removed Kell from her sight. The less she had . . .

"Muldoon."

The soft, caressing way he called her made Annie stand at rigid attention. "What now, Mr. York?"

"About last night—"

"Last night? Don't you dare mention last night. If you attempt to touch me again—"

"I did more than that, Muldoon. You were sailing four sheets to the wind."

"I was exhausted, Mr. York. And wipe that smirk off your lips. I do not want you to kiss me again. Do I make myself clear?"

"Blazingly so. So tell me what you'll do, if I steal another kiss."

"I'll . . . I will evict you!"

"Fightin' words, darlin'. The whole town thinks I'm a hero. They wouldn't be pleased to know you tossed me out."

"I am in charge of my own life, Mr. York. I know that thought must shock you right down to your, er, well, the thought is shocking. But I'll do it." Annie wouldn't look directly at him. She pinned her gaze on his shoulder, trying not to notice how his damp hair curled over the white shirt. "Why did you come back here? To torment me?"

"I forgot my string tie." He proceeded to the dresser and opened the top drawer. Watching her in the mirror, Kell drew out the black tie and slid it beneath his flipped-up collar. Then his nimble fingers stilled. He suddenly knew how hard Annie was fighting herself. Her gaze locked with his—a moment, no more, but it was enough to reveal the budding desire he had awakened last night.

"Why do you call it torment, Annie? It's a basic fact that when a man is attracted to a woman and that feeling is mutual—"

"It's not!" With a rough shake of her head, Annie bent to the pile of laundry. She almost groaned when she saw Dewberry, his tail high, come prancing into the room and go directly to Kell.

Remember, she told herself, *that the man is kind to animals and children. He can't be all bad. The wickedness is yours. And the sooner you remove yourself from his sight, the better off you will be.*

Dewberry's loud purring as Kell crouched down to rub behind the cat's ears had her peering over the bundle of sheets. A heated quiver ran up her spine and seemed to make her chest swell as if the air were suddenly gone. She didn't want to think about those slender fingers stroking her last night. Or how they made her feel like imitating the cat. She was made of stern resolutions. The Lord had sent Kellian York as a test of her beliefs.

Head high, shoulders back, Annie left the room. She had been tested quite enough for one day.

"There, cat, goes the bewitching backside of a prickly little hedgehog. What would it take to tame her?" Kell's skin felt tight. Hot. That fast. He rose with the groan of a man in pain, ignoring Dewberry's battering paw when he was no longer being petted.

Why the challenge in her eyes aroused him, he didn't know. But he could see the image of her eyes, dark blue with flecks of gold lighting the depths. The thought of Annie Muldoon looking up at him as he moved over her in bed sent heat flooding his body. His heart pounded hard and fast. Just the way he thought about taking her.

Damn the woman!

Trying to make that corset-wrapped spinster purr could be his undoing.

Only a fool would try.

But then, he'd be the only one to know.

And Annie hadn't been wearing a corset last night . . .

"Keep her warm, cat. I've got work to do."

Annie nodded to Emmaline, who had substituted for her as accompanist this glorious Sunday morning, as the last of the hymn died away. She rose to take her place in front of the small group gathered in the parlors. The knowledge that Kell had opened for business last night outside of town weighed heavily on her mind. From the stern regard of those women and few men that made the congregation this morning, she knew she would be censured for giving those people shelter and thereby allowing the evils of drink, gambling, and whoring to continue.

The motivation to build a proper church lent strength to her voice as she began:

"We are like-minded Christians of the same convictions, using prayer and good living to further our vision of bringing civilized order to our town. We are being tested and found wanting by our lack of charity, lack of vigorous belief, and lack of courage. We have a strong vision of what we can accomplish together. We cannot falter in that vision by allowing doubts of our strength to sever us from our purpose.

"I know the gentlemen here share the belief that women can now assume positions once thought to be inappropriate for females. When the Civil War came and hosts of men went forth to defend our homeland, women conducted the business in our cities and towns during this patriotic absence. From that time a mighty change took place favorable to female employment.

"It is by the example of these courageous women who refused to give up their places that I speak today. We have been given the mission to redeem those who know no other life than the ways of sin. Women are, by Divine arrangement, the first teachers of every child that is born. It is our duty to continue the role of teacher each blessed day that we arise."

Annie paused and judged the silent response. A few nods of encouragement came her way, but Abigail Duffner, along with her husband, Abner, and Velma Grant, still regarded her with stern faces. Aunt Hortense, to Annie's mortification, was gently snoring on the settee in the front parlor. Fawn, her dark eyes bright with interest, stood at the doorway. Her smile bolstered Annie's decision to continue.

"I implore those of you who resist the call to go forth and lead by example to remember that this is work no one but women can do so appropriately. Examine your hearts and minds to be of a clear purpose. Remember that the Lord will arrange all, and all we have to do is our best and trust the Lord for the rest. I read from Luke: 'Lord dost Thou not care that my sister hath left me to serve alone? Bid her, therefore, that she help me.'"

Annie turned to Emmaline to begin the closing song, hurt when she realized that her friend had not been moved by her sermon. She closed her eyes, the words coming softly from her lips, silently praying that she would have the strength of her convictions.

The blending voices, Lucinda Lockwood's soprano, clearly the highest, couldn't drown out the sudden thundering beat that penetrated the room. For a moment Annie glanced heavenward, thinking she had been given some sign, as a hushed, bewildered silence fell on the group.

The all-too-human swearing sent her running out to the lobby. The shouting was louder here. So was the hammering.

"Annie Charlotte! Whatever is that racket?"

And it was the all-too-human sound of Kellian's voice that sent Annie marching to the front door.

"Believe me, Aunt, it is not the Lord coming to call. More like the devil," she muttered to herself, opening the door.

She had to go halfway around the porch to find him. The sight of him was as appealing as the warm sunlight after the storm. It struck Annie that he hadn't lied to her about staying up all night repeatedly. The man didn't look any the worse for not having returned until now. He had not seen her—or was ignoring her. It was no more than she expected; she almost welcomed it for the moment.

Kell balanced easily on the top rail of the porch, one arm hooked around the post. His white shirtsleeves were rolled up to his elbows, revealing forearms lightly burnished with blond hair. The string tie was gone, and the top buttons of his shirt lay open, a veed frame for the strong column of his throat. He leaned his graceful body at a dangerous angle to yell orders up to the men on the roof who hauled boards by ropes.

Sunlight caressed him much as her gaze did and sent an infusion of warmth to flood her. And, that quickly, her body felt tight as a drum's skin. The words of her sermon took flight like the sparrows from the cottonwood that shaded the back porch.

"What are you doing?" she finally demanded, wondering

why the simple act of breathing became such a difficult task when she was near him.

"Bring it up slow or you'll hit the window," Kell shouted. With a half turn, he pivoted around the post to face her. "Good morning to you, too, Muldoon."

His move drew her gaze to the long length of his legs. Grace and power, she thought, trying to dismiss his smile, as inviting as a goosefeather comforter on a cold night.

"I asked what you are doing to my home, Mr. York."

"It should be obvious. I'm repairing your roof."

"Repairing *my* roof? Why? I never asked you to." Being forced to look up at him did not settle Annie's temper. The heat of battle raced over her. "I intended to take care of the repairs this week."

"After I paid my rent?" Kell almost chuckled at the bright flare in her eyes. Temper sent faint color, like the shadow of a rose in a mirror, to hide her freckles. She was as alluring as a peach this morning. A very ripe one. Her hair framed her face in a softer, upswept style, but his gaze drifted lower, slowly savoring her long, slender neck circled by cream lace, draping her shoulders as delicately as a cobweb.

"You look lovely this morning."

His compliment seemed to take them both by surprise, and Annie was slower to recover.

"You're supposed to say, 'Thank you, Mr. York.' "

"I do thank you for the compliment. If only I weren't worried what advantage you'd try to make of it."

"Smile for me, darlin'. When I want to take advantage of you, you'll know."

The explicit promise in his voice had Annie wipe suddenly damp palms down the sides of her blue serge skirt. She had no choice but to ignore his comment.

"Annie, stop looking for a polecat in the woodwork. I

like sleeping in a dry bed. Be gracious. I've saved you bother about it. And if payment is worrying you, don't let the matter cause you to lose sleep."

As rich and buttery as the golden crust of a cobbler, the words spilled forth. Annie lowered her lashes, hiding his face from her sight the only way she could.

"We can work something out about the payment."

His engaging grin caused a hitch in her breathing. The brightness of his eyes as she lifted her gaze to his brought unwanted images of the unholy ways Kell would exact payment.

"Such a difficult decision, darlin'?"

"Stop calling me that. What you're doing isn't proper," she whispered, stepping close and feeling as if every pair of eyes in town were targeting her back.

"Proper ain't fun."

"Rules governing behavior bring order to one's life."

"Rules are boring," he countered.

Kell sent his gaze skimmering over the enticing length of her body and smiled to see the tip of one black shoe beating out toe-tapping impatience.

Think, Annie ordered herself, unable to tear her gaze away from his sun-streaked hair. It was too long, curling over the back of the collar. Long and soft and silky. Her fingers curled at her sides in memory of how it felt to hold his hair, drawing his head closer, feeling the silky length slide through her fingers when his lips . . .

Stop this! The warning came too late. She wet her bottom lip with the tip of her tongue, soothing the heat that memory caused.

"Annie, answer me this. If Lockwood came with a crew of men to repair your roof, would you tell him it wasn't proper?"

"No. Neighbors help each other in times of trouble."

"Must I remind you that I'm a neighbor, too? Just as soon as I get the Silken Aces rebuilt."

He offered an acceptable out and Annie knew it. "This is a neighborly kindness to your credit, Mr. York. But I will pay you. Now, send your men home, for this is the Lord's day. One that is set aside for prayer and reflection as well as the enjoyment of one's family and friends."

"I've had all night to reflect, and we're not family. I can't think of you as a friend, darlin', much as you'd wish. But enjoyment, Annie, now there's a thought to my liking."

Annie, sure that wicked, whispering voice of his had reached no one else, was tempted. *"Rules are boring," he had said.* Watching him above her, recklessness a halo he could no more shed than an angel, she was lured into agreement. She did all she could to hide the delicious shiver of temptation that threatened her moral fiber.

She looked out over the neat rows of her vegetable garden. "You ask too much of me." Regret laced her voice, but she had to be her own best example. "I do appreciate your help with the roof repair, no matter what your reason."

Li pulled up around the side of the house with a wagon full of cut boards and two ranch hands that Annie knew. She murmured a greeting and used the distraction to leave.

Why did her convictions falter in Kell's presence?

She needed to take her own advice and spend the day in prayer and reflection. But not here. Not when Kell would be close by all day.

And Li, knowing that Kell would go after her, refused to help unload the wagon, forcing Kell to do it. For now, this was the only protection he could offer Annie from her moral dilemma.

The only question was, For how long could she hold out against Kell?

Chapter Thirteen

❧

In the end Annie found it surprisingly easy to escape. Aunt Hortense corraled the ladies in the parlor for the refreshments Fawn served. Despite her aunt's most selective hearing problem, Annie knew there was nothing wrong with her eyesight. When Annie hid nothing of the turmoil that this latest confrontation with Kell had caused, Hortense ordered her out of the room and closed the door. No one dared object, given Hortense's age and her imposing presence.

The chicken had been fried early that morning to avoid the heat, and Annie helped herself to a few pieces. Carrying her napkin-wrapped lunch, a quilt, and her favorite book, she slipped out the back door.

Fawn sat on the back porch, studying the E. BUTTERICK & CO. summer catalogue borrowed from Emmaline, and eagerly pointed to her selections.

"Hmmm, the pattern costs twenty cents, but maybe Emmaline will have this one. I like the shirred waist blouse, too. The calico you picked out will be pretty. We could even trim the cape collar with a bit of lace. Would you like that?"

Dark eyes shining, Fawn nodded rapidly, then pointed to the opposite page, holding up two fingers.

"Why do you want two corset covers? You don't like to wear a corset." Fawn's scowl as she shook her head made Annie pause. "You can't have these made in the calico, Fawn. It's not proper to bare that much skin. See here," Annie said, tracing the small pattern with her finger, "there's no sleeves, nothing to cover most of your shoulders but these thin bands. This one is better. The combination chemise and drawers will button right up to your neck. And we won't need to spend thirty cents for a pattern."

The Indian girl's bent head brought Annie to crouch beside her. "Don't be sad. Show me what it is you want. Something very pretty, I warrant." Meeting Fawn's gaze, seeing her shy smile, told Annie she was right. She stroked the glossy length of Fawn's thick braid. "It's Li, isn't it? But you're so young, dearest. I do not want you hurt."

There were times, Annie thought, when no words were needed. The softened light in Fawn's eyes, the gentle way she covered her hand, sent the message that Annie was wrong this time. It was uncanny the way she had trusted Li from the first meeting. Examining her own feelings about the man made Annie's warning die aborning.

"We'll go see Emmaline tomorrow afternoon once the meal is done. I'm sure we can find the prettiest pattern for you. Something that will make a man take notice of how lovely you are."

Annie left then, wishing that was all it would take, just a bit of lace or ribbon trimming to make a man notice. But that was not her problem. Kell noticed too much.

Hugging her quilt and book against her too-tight chest, Annie strolled down the lane, thinking of how he looked when he called her lovely.

And Li, setting the pole brake on the wagon as he drew it around to the back, watched her go. This was the last of the wood that was to have begun Kell's rebuilding, but when he had pointed this out, Kell merely shrugged and said he had more coming.

Troubled by his observation of Kell last night, Li did not see Fawn slip inside the kitchen and watch him as he began unloading the wagon.

During the years Li had been with Kell, he knew the man never drank whiskey when he gambled. Drawing a crowd, once word spread that he was reopened for business outside of town, should have pleased Kell. But a little past midnight, Li had watched him prowl restlessly from table to table where the doves dispensed cards, whiskey, and promises all with the same avarice. Kell left his glass at Laine's table when her attempt to flirt with him failed and began drinking from the bottle.

Li could have warned her not to taunt him when ice wintered in his eyes and edged his voice. But he had kept silent. Some lessons were best learned by those who repeated them. And she did repeat it. Going to Kell once again and leaving him with hate glittering in her eyes.

Kell's lack of interest in Laine's generous body gave cause for grave concern. Irish toothache, horn colic—no matter what name Kell called it, Li held to the belief of his own people that a jade stem too long denied the pearled essence of its chosen garden brought disharmony to the body, the mind, and the soul of a man.

He could never claim to truly know Kellian York, for no man could say this without walking in another man's boots. What he did know about him were unshakable truths. Kell always weighed the risk of any action. Doubly so, his words. He never threatened, promised, or swore unless he could back it up. The man's sharp mind was to be admired. Li learned from him to figure all probabilities.

But the moment Kell had come into contact with Annie Muldoon he had changed. The strong attraction she held for Kell blocked the man's logic. Li knew that if he mentioned this, Kell would dismiss it as the worry of a man who spent his life in shadow. That was true enough, but Li also recalled that it was Kell who often reminded him that it was the little things that trip up a smart man.

The afternoon wore on, hot and humid, the breeze as warm as heated syrup soaking a stale biscuit and leaving a man with that much less energy. He tucked away the many times Kell sent a searching gaze over the yard, or glanced in a window looking for Annie. When Kell approached Fawn after a cold lunch of fried chicken and sweet lemonade, Li made himself scarce as he questioned the young woman about Annie. The measure bought him a little more time.

He knew Kell would eventually find him. Just as he had drawn the conclusion that no matter what he did or said, Kell would pursue Annie as thunder followed lightning; just as close, just as heatedly. And, Li thought with a wicked grin, the resulting tempest might lay waste to a woman's virtue as if it had no more substance than a cobweb or it might bring a strong man to his knees.

Annie Muldoon would appreciate the latter.

So he placed himself to wait, and finally Kell came to him.

"You've been avoiding me, Li."

"It seemed the wise course." Leaning back against the trunk of the cottonwood, Li set the wide-planked swing that hung from its limb by thick ropes to swinging. Without looking at Kell, he mused, "If I tried to warn you, would you listen to me?"

"I always listen."

And Kell did. Patient for now, quiet as Li finished. He caught hold of the swing's rope and stopped it. "My friend sees shadows where there aren't any. There's nothing complicated about my feelings for her, Li. And you know the likelihood of risk always makes a game interesting to me. Otherwise, I'd be upstairs right now enjoying Laine's bed."

"Then why do you not do just that? The safer course is at times the best chosen."

"You also know I don't like playing with a deck that someone else has marked. Takes all the excitement away."

"Is that all Annie is to you, Kell? An exciting game?" For the moment Li wished to recall his questions. Kell's eyes narrowed, their gleam chilling enough to lower the heat of the day.

"Does she appeal to some latent need I've been unaware of? Take my word for it, Li, Annie doesn't need your protection. She doesn't need any man's."

"You never answered me." Li sent a searching gaze over Kell's features. He marked the impatience he knew too well. "Kell, leave her be. Her world is narrow and she is safe within it. If you cannot answer me, that could be an answer itself."

In a voice he couldn't manage to keep under control, Kell said, "All right! You'll wear away at me like water dripping on rock in that so polite soft voice until I say it. And the answer is that I don't know what the hell she is. But I intend to find out. Now, where is she?"

Studying the dusty toes of his boots, Li thought hard what to say. Every minute that he kept Kell away from Annie allowed her to knit the holes in her faltering convictions. To flip the coin, every moment that he delayed allowed Kell's impatience to build and shred whatever caution still governed him.

"Will you tell her what we have found out?"

"No. And quit stalling, Li."

Stepping away from the tree and staring down the path that Annie had taken, Li tried again. "She would have to believe you if you showed her what—"

"Li."

The warning made Li turn to Kell. His survival instincts were as finely honed as a coyote's, while Kell's patience was thinner than a whisker.

"I won't tell her anything, Li, because I don't think I can trust her."

"Then you build an empty house without trust."

"Who the devil said anything about building a damned thing! Just tell me where she is."

"Visiting the sick?"

"You're reaching for a line you don't want to cross. And," Kell added to soften the reminder, "the only one sick around here is me."

"Ah, Kell, if that is true the illness is of your own making." But in the end he knew he would tell him. Li's debt to Kell was an abiding one that could never be fully repaid. Within his inner vision there was no repayment for Kell, who had, with a lucky turn of the cards, freed him from the role as a flute player to walk again as a man. Yet he couldn't stop himself from giving one last caution.

"Annie does not fully understand what she does to you."

"That is the most profound wisdom, and what's more it makes two of us. But it's long past time she learned."

Kell discovered Annie's refuge at the edge of the shallow, bowl-shaped meadow an hour's walk from town. The center was waterlogged from the rain, tips of summer-browned grasses rising to reach the sunlight.

Annie lay on a quilt dappled by shadows from the leaves of a cluster of young saplings. From where he stood and watched her, she was in profile, holding a whispered discourse with butterflies that hovered near a cluster of wildflowers. It was a charming scene. Part of him wished she didn't look so innocent.

Her high-buttoned shoes were neatly placed side by side on the far edge of the quilt, but it was the slight breeze fluttering her dark stockings hung from a limb above her that sent Kell's gaze skimming over the water again. *Annie at play.* Too easy to imagine. And need arose that he had not been here to capture the image.

He had told Li the truth. He didn't fully understand what Annie did to him.

The blue ruffled folds of her skirt were bunched above her knees, a spilling froth of white petticoats nestled her hips, and her bare legs, slender ankles, and dainty curved calves languidly moved back and forth like a lazy pair of scissors. Propped on her elbows, she held her chin in her hands. Her head was tilted to one side as she watched the butterflies, unaware of his presence.

Innocence. Nothing sexual at all. But he found his senses seduced as though by the first sweet, heavy lungful of opium. There was the same raking pain inside his chest as the initial taste had brought, but Li wasn't here to steady him as he had been then.

With the same kind of sharpened clarity that opiated senses sometimes gave, Kell saw her innocent pose so firmly etched that he realized he was an intruder on more than this scene. This was a time and place for a lover to come courting.

Annie denied him the status of lover and he had no intent to perform the rituals of courting.

It had been too many years since he had allowed a woman to make this kind of an impact on him. Annie, with those wide bluebell eyes full of a woman's sensual secrets, would not stay out of his mind.

Kell backed away, resolved to leave this unspoiled place, when fate—laughing cruelly at his attempted noble gesture or smiling kindly with pity on his starved senses, as Providence was wont to do—intervened.

A brownish blur shot out of the woods between them, and hot on the rabbit's powerful hindquarters came the town mongrel. With a beastly growl, the dog lunged at his prey, and Annie cried out, turning and shouting for the rabbit to run faster. The chase sat too close to her own predicament.

The rabbit veered off around the deeper water in the middle of the meadow, but the dog's momentum carried him forward to be bogged down by the mud and grasses. The rabbit was gone by the time the dog slunk out of the water, and Annie, feeling pity for his hunger, tossed him the uneaten chicken from her napkin.

Following the mongrel's progress into the woods with his prize, Annie saw Kell standing in shadow.

Some hunters lost their prey and others caught it. The thought lodged itself in her mind, but she couldn't decide which applied to her. To see the object of her long afternoon's contemplation in the flesh—*Annie, Annie, how the lofty are fallen to think only of flesh*—raised the welter of emotions she had almost ruthlessly dealt with. And since the flesh was gloriously packaged in the lithe, shadow-graced form of Kellian York, she could not deny herself the sight of it.

The cost of her gazing at him was nearly the shredding

of her carefully rebuilt moral fiber. He didn't move and
Annie blessed whatever held him still, allowing her time
to adjust to the stirrings of her poor overworked body.
Blood flowed like a newly primed pump until its warmth
and speed made her dizzy. The sultry air, charged as if a
storm brewed, offered no surcease to her laboring lungs.
Longings, apparently suppressed forever, awakened and
whispered through her. Their coaxing entreaty blended
with yearnings she could not fully name yet denied until
she trembled.

But it was Kell's continued, absolute silence that gave
her pause. She was reaching conclusions about his sudden appearance with all the base substance of a cloud.
He could have been out walking and found her by accident. He could have come looking . . .

"Has something happened? Is that why you're here?"
she called out.

"Nothing's wrong," Kell answered. *But something had
happened.* Fate decreed confrontation, his purpose at the
start, but as he walked toward her, he knew nothing
would ever be simple again. His instincts were strangely
silent, but it was the absence of the warning crick in his
neck that worried him. Annie had not moved, but her every breath started a war with his emotions too complex to
sort out now. Perhaps, as any good gambler did, he should
stand pat and let her decide the ante.

"Spending the day in prayer and reflection?" he asked.
He'd stopped short of the quilt, his gaze drawn to the
bare length of her legs. "You've chosen a quiet spot where
the view is . . . breathtaking."

Annie, following the direction of his gaze, knew the ex-
posure was accidental. She had twisted around quickly to
watch the dog and never realized that Kell was close by.

But that did not explain why she was so slow now to shift and free her petticoats and skirt to cover her legs.

Embarrassed that he had watched, she sat up and clasped her knees, the move protective. "I needed a great deal of time today to do that and more. Did you know," she asked, wanting a safe topic, "that when I was little Aunt Hortense told me butterflies received their name because they're milk thieves. How could anyone think these delicate creatures are elves or witches in disguise, come to steal milk or butter?"

"Now that is a subject worthy of hours of discussion. May I join you?" He lowered himself to the quilt, facing her with his long legs stretched out, his head propped on one hand. "Perhaps someone began the tale because of their color? But then all things with butter would mean that elves or witches were concealed within."

"Like butter-and-eggs which is just toad-flax?"

"Or butter-ale? I've never had it. Somehow flavoring ale with butter, spices, and sugar doesn't appeal."

The whimsy in his voice invited her smile. Annie shot him a smug look. "And the butter-bean, butter-boat, and butter-box."

"Ah, you require a man to be sharp. Let's see . . . there is a butter-bird."

"Butter-bird? You are making that up."

"Swear it's true. There is a bunting in Jamaica called a butter-bird."

"Have you been there?" she asked, eyes bright as she turned to look at him.

"A long time ago. A lifetime, it seems. The island is lush and lovely, with water so clear you can see beneath it." *And the shades of blue would match every emotional change your eyes reflect, Annie.*

"I've never left Texas. But I'd bet I could still name more buttery things than you."

Safe. Her protection. His choice. Kell smiled at her. "Bets need a prize for the winner."

"Well, I shall choose mine if I win and you decide what you would like."

"Fair enough." Annie, he thought, what am I going to do with a woman who has the survival instinct of a week-old kitten? And it was the other side, the needy one, that refused to let him ask her.

"Shall I begin? It's only fair to warn you that I have four already and you only two."

"Since I'm putting my reputation in your hands, Miss Muldoon, you must promise not to take advantage."

"As you do?" Annie glanced away, sorry she had spoken.

"Not today, Annie. You have all the advantage on your side."

Wishing it were true, unwilling to pursue it, Annie hugged her knees and faced him. "Buttercup, buttermilk, and a butterbox."

"Butterfly and butter-fingers."

Her gaze went immediately to his long fingers. She would bet they were never clumsy no matter what use he put them to. Annie reached out one hand and picked up a twig. She pushed the edge of the quilt on her side closer so she could keep score.

"Don't you trust me to keep count?"

"No, and I'm still ahead. Make up your mind to lose, for I have buttermold and butter-pot." She thought a moment. "And butter tongs."

Kell racked his mind for something else. "Butter, butter everywhere," he muttered, turning to lie on his back with his hands cradling his head. "In the city a butterman sells butter."

"That gives you one more."

"Well, I'm trying, Annie. Butter's not my—"

"Cup of tea?" she finished, laughing at his mock scowl.

"You'll pay for that one, Muldoon. There's butterscotch candy and a butter tub and we need someone to make all this butter, so let's try a butterwoman."

Annie pounced on him before she thought. "No. You can't be so desperate to think I'd allow that."

"If we have a butterman, we need to give him a butterwoman, Annie."

"We have—" Annie lost her thought with her breath. She lay across Kell's chest, her mouth inches from his lips. All she could think about was the buttery shades of his hair that her fingers wanted to touch.

Kell, feeling the spreading need from where she rested against him to every nerve ending in his body, held his breath lest she leave him. "A man for a woman," he whispered, his gaze holding hers. "If you've won, tell me now what you'd have as a prize, or I'll claim the win is mine."

To herself, Annie wouldn't lie. She had known what she wanted. Two words would give it to her. The expression in his eyes dared her.

"Ask me, Annie. Just ask me."

With all the languid substance of smoke, his husky voice whispered through her. *Just ask.* "A kiss."

The breath he had been holding eased out, and with it went the tension that gripped him. "Remember you've got to close your eyes, Annie." He reached out with one hand to slide his fingers into her thick, loosely coiled hair, angling her head to one side and dragging her closer. His gaze played over the feathered velvet of her brows and lashes and the deep satin rose lips. Shadows drifted across her brow, her cheek, and hid the faint freckles from him.

Her half-closed lids flew open when he brought his

other hand to her cheek, one finger smoothing over her skin. She thought he would kiss her quickly, but his eyes were narrowed, filled with a drowsy look that, far too late, set off an alarm.

"One kiss, Kell. Just one."

"Enough to challenge a saint, darlin', but I'll try. Just see if I don't. We need to arrange you a bit closer." One finger trailed suggestively over the most sensitive fold of her ear. Kell didn't count the tiny shiver as a reward for his effort. Her skin flushed under his gentle touches, her lips slightly parted and waiting for his kiss. But waiting, Kell had learned, heightened pleasure immensely. With his thumb he coaxed the trembling swell of her bottom lip, and she leaned forward, eyes enormous before her lashes drifted down to hide them.

"One kiss, Annie. Only one to pleasure you." He slowly dragged her mouth across his. "And me. There's pleasure here for me, too."

Kell traced her mouth with his fingertip, and Annie's move to follow brushed her lips against his. Hesitantly, her hands came up to frame his face, and with a sigh her breath mingled with his. She had never initiated a kiss in her life, but the idea tantalized her. Kell was so much more skilled than she. The teasing touches of his mouth circling hers provoked a rising need to feel his lips on hers. One kiss. That was all she wanted. The problem was not impossible to resolve. After all, she was on top. She could hold his head still. She could . . . *just do it, Annie*.

Wiggling to settle her weight on him, Annie slid her hands into his hair, making him still. Her eyes closed, and releasing a shaken breath for what she was about to do, she aligned her lips with his and kissed him.

There was nothing to fear, she was in control. But her soft, tentative kiss to his enticing mouth that languidly altered pressure only made her want more. Dreamily parting her lips for his voluptuous pleasuring, Annie relinquished herself to him. His slow, compelling rotation of her head deepened the kiss, filling her with wild, sweet imaginings and the promise of unveiling answers to all the forbidden riddles.

Warmth rose within, but Annie was suspended in tenderness, as desire softened and shaped their mouths and she opened to the heavy stroke of his tongue.

And she learned that the ancient force of passion, once unleashed, would wrest control from her foolish belief that she could bend it to her will. For surely it was this force that brought her hands twisting into the thick, silky length of his hair, fighting to heighten their kiss.

Each moment both sated and increased her need until she felt helpless. Her body was ruling her mind, hushing the voice of caution that warned she was stepping over a line of safety. But her blood was spinning through her with aching pleasure, Kell's hands a whisper against her body, drawing it more fully into alignment with his. Shocked and burning with budding desire, his hot, open scattered kisses coursed over the flushed skin of her cheek, the sensitive curve of her chin, murmuring pleasure sounds into her ear before he reclaimed her mouth.

She was drifting and turning, lifting heavy-lidded eyes to see him above her, freeing her hair from its pins. His thumb stroked her bottom lip and his head dipped down to taste. She knew she should stop him. Annie willed herself to say the words. But his eyes, dark green and brilliant with desire, brought only his name.

"Kell?"

"Who's counting? One kiss? Two? You've won, Annie. Give a beggar a prize." He cradled her head, nibbling at the paleness of her exposed throat, feeling her swallow beneath his mouth. His tongue stroked the light pulse of blood so close to her skin and felt the soft moan that escaped through her parted lips.

He kissed her with a caressing intensity that stole her will, and Annie knew Kell was wrong. She was the beggar who wanted more of his mobile mouth tutoring hers with kisses that left her trembling.

Through the fine linen weave of his shirt, Annie felt the heat of his skin beneath her fingers. Tempted to explore the powerful hardness of his body, yet unsure, her hands slid over his shoulders, stilling to feel a tremor.

"Annie. Annie, don't stop. Pleasure," he murmured, glistening her lips with the tip of his tongue, "that's you touching me." Kell allowed her the needed escape to turn her face, but cradled her cheek with one hand.

"Do men . . . like . . . I can't say this," she whispered, keeping her eyes closed.

"This man does. A lot." Her shyness was touching. She was so anxious to give pleasure and so uncertain how. Kell leaned back and gently lifted her hand to his mouth. "Look at me, Annie. Let me," he coaxed softly, turning her slender hand palm side up, "show you how pleasurable touching can be." And he waited until she turned back to watch him with sensual curiosity that tightened every nerve ending in his body. With his gaze holding hers, he pressed an openmouthed kiss to her palm, calling forth an involuntary shiver from her. Using the tip of his tongue, he circled the sensitive skin before he gently bit the fleshy pad below her thumb. Her blue eyes dilated, and Kell smiled to know how intensely aware she was. "That's pleasure, Annie."

"Yes." The word was a mere whisper of sound, and Annie couldn't look away.

"Someday darlin', you'll do that for me. But not now." He drew her hand around his neck and lowered his mouth to hers.

Soft heat curled inside her. The taste of him swept over her as she learned to savor again the hot glide of his tongue over hers. The delicate twinings and retreats brought to mind a graceful duel, but Annie knew she was an uneven match for his skill.

Deliberately Kell shifted his hands, arching Annie against him. For a moment she twisted, then her hands were searching over his back, fingers digging into his hard flesh under the explosion of passion. He encouraged her with hoarse words, the deepening bite of her fingers a hot promise he wanted, needed to have.

The feel of his strength covering her body raced through Annie, making her moan deep in her throat. It was the only sound she was capable of making, because her mouth was wholly involved with the taste of him in an utterly new way. With the violent clarity of lightning against a night sky, her shocked senses absorbed the hard smoothness of his lips and the primitive serrations of his teeth as he caught her lower lip. The sensual roughness of his tongue brought a hunger to capture the heat and taste of his mouth biting into her. She tried to get closer to him, wanting to burn him as he was burning her.

Kell felt the instant change in her body as she released conflicting emotions and surrendered herself to the desire that had her body a taut, supple curve branding him from his knees to his mated mouth. Hunger prowled in a wave of heavy, wild heat bringing a groan of need. There was the rational caution that whispered he couldn't take her here, in an open field where anyone could discover them. But he couldn't order his hands to stop caressing her resilient body, couldn't stop rocking his violently aroused flesh against her hips.

This is what he wanted.

Not here. Not now.

Chapter Fourteen

~

K ell?" Annie whispered his name against his cheek, her
rioting senses making every word a strug-
gle. "You said nothing would hurt. But I ache, Kell. I—"

At war with himself, Kell rested his forehead on hers.
"Annie, I never meant things to go so far. I didn't want . . .
Christ!" he groaned, his hands stilling the provocative
arch of her body to his. Her eyes revealed confusion and
he released an explosive breath, counting, and needing
more to still the fever raging through him. "It's all right.
I'll make it all right," he promised recklessly. "Show me
where you ache, Annie," he murmured, easing his body to
her side, unable to let her go. He curved his hand over
her slender waist, scattering kisses on her flushed face,
while he closed his eyes for a few moments denying himself the sight of her breasts stirring with her ragged
breaths.

Unknown need dictated her move to draw his hand up
to rest below her breast, where blood seemed to rush and
swell that most delicate feminine flesh. Twenty-eight

years of moral lessons struck a warning for her brazen manner, but Annie, nestled in desire's cloud, sought her pleasure from his lips again.

He came to her with a groan, seduced as he had never been by the cost to Annie to show him where she wanted him to touch. Kell consigned warnings to hell and wished her corset there as well. Using skilled touches to heighten her arousal, he knew she was still far too shy to let him undress her. She made those little sounds that drove him to a new edge, and he coaxed and praised her by turn.

It was his murmuring voice that pierced the sensual veil that softened Annie's world and narrowed it to senses filled with Kell. But rather than the lover's incantations that dragged her deeper, to the edge of passion's realm, she kept hearing his denial. *"I never meant things to go so far."*

And with each repetition, sharpened clarity made the meaning very clear.

Annie shoved aside his hand and tore her mouth from his. "You never meant . . . you followed me here? This was deliberate!"

Kell was slow to react, ensnared by his own heightened senses and a body that was needy. When she landed a punch on his shoulder, he opened his eyes to see her eyes shift from passion's glaze to a slow, blazing fury. Regret was brief. Hunger still prowled, demanding surcease.

"Christ, Annie! Stop hitting me. I stopped, didn't I?" He caught hold of her hand and moved quickly to reach for the other. "Yes, I came here looking for you. No, this wasn't deliberate. I was leaving without you ever knowing I'd been here when that damn dog came racing out of the woods."

"You came here to seduce me!"

"I'm not a green boy who needs to flip a female's skirts

in a field. And if I wanted to seduce you, Annie Muldoon, I'd have had you on the kitchen table, and then again upstairs in your bed."

The memory of that rainy night brought flags of color to her cheeks. "You would have taken advantage of my exhausted state?"

"Exhausted? Hell!" Her accusing voice stung. "You were drunk, darlin'."

"Tipsy. And let go of my hands."

Kell flung himself away from her. He didn't trust himself to remain very civilized. "Come to think of it, you weren't. You stopped the action, petunia, and that's where it ended. If I had been bent on seduction, bet a week's rent and double it that I'd have succeeded."

Annie glanced to where he lay on his back, one arm shielding his eyes. His chest moved with the same erratic breaths that had hers heaving. Heightened senses, so newly awakened, goaded her gaze to drift lower. She stared at the damp patches that made his linen shirt almost sheer, becoming aware that her body was dampening her clothing with the heat still flowing through her. On the side facing her, his shirt had pulled free of his pants revealing an intriguing amount of golden-brown skin. The sight made her hand curl around the quilt. Gloving his body from his powerful thighs and flat belly, the provocative fit of his pants held her gaze for long moments.

"Have pity, darlin'," Kell said without looking at her. "I can't help being aroused, but save your expiring until I'm gone. Right now, I don't trust myself to touch you."

Annie flung her arms over her head, hiding like the coward she called herself. She had accused him to save her own pride. She had never ordered him to leave when she saw him. Not once did she ask him to leave, to stop.

The kiss was her invitation, her need to appease the longings he stirred. This was her fault, not Kell's.

"The things you make me feel and do frighten me, Kell."

"Yeah? Well, for your ears only, darlin', I'm scaring the devil out of myself."

Before she lifted her arms to look at him, Kell rose in a controlled rush, dragging sultry air into his lungs.

"Thanks for your charming company, but you'll pardon me for not escorting you home. In my condition, I'm most likely to draw out one of your sermons on the evils of sin, damnation, and hell . . . and no thanks, Muldoon. Once a day on the rack is enough for any sane man."

"Muldoon? How can you call me . . . after what you . . . what I—" Annie struggled to sit up and saw the last of his back disappear in the woods. With her feelings in chaos, she fell back against the quilt. "What possessed me to ask for a kiss? One little kiss?"

Asking for that one little kiss had led to some great big answers. And more questions.

What was she going to do? An afternoon spent in prayer and reflection to strengthen her moral fiber had proved to be a waste of her time. By his mere presence, Kell sliced through the carefully knit fabric that constituted her life.

"Since I've been tested and failed," she whispered, lingering as dusk came, "I shall have to savor the fact that I bedeviled Kellian for a change."

But within minutes, Annie left for home. There were too many questions she needed answered. Emmaline was the obvious choice. She had been married and would know—what? Emmaline wouldn't have an inkling of how to deal with a man like Kell. And her best friend had been suspiciously lacking in support during this trying time.

No, Annie knew she could never tell Emmaline about what she had done, what she had allowed Kell to do. Aunt Hortense would be no help. The whole town would hear Annie shouting to make her aunt understand one question.

Who could she go to?

As Annie rounded the corner of the boardinghouse, she stopped. If she wanted a gown made, she went to Emmaline, who was extremely talented in hiding a woman's faults and accenting whatever made her attractive.

And if she wanted to know about men, Kellian especially, who better to ask than the doves? After all, men were their . . . well, their business. She had to get over this utter reluctance to admit that or she'd never get far enough to ask them anything. Someone had to help her understand what was happening between her and Kell. And she wouldn't mind knowing how to repay him for every sleepless night he caused her.

If she hurried, she could catch them before they left for Kell's temporary establishment. Tossing the quilt on the laundry pile in the pantry, Annie rushed through the rooms and upstairs.

Intent on finding the phrasing for her request, Annie almost barreled into Kell coming from his bath.

"No! Deuces to aces my luck's deserted me. Before you dare utter one word, Miss Starch and Vinegar, I followed every damn rule you have posted in there." With a glare, he pointed over his shoulder. "I emptied the tub. I put the soap back. I'm wearing my towel, but rest assured you'll find it with the laundry and no, I didn't leave hair in there. I didn't leave a damn thing but the skin I tried scrubbing off!"

Annie did the sensible thing. She backed away from him. Unfortunately for her, Kell had had time to raise his frustration to a new high. He went after her, pinning her against the wall. He caught hold of her chin, and took her mouth with his.

He didn't kiss nicely. He didn't coax her. Didn't try to seduce her mouth with his. He took. Hungry and lusty. He wasn't kissing her like a man who had more women than he could handle. Annie felt as if he kissed her like she was the last woman in sight and he was dying. He had to be dying, from the sound of his groaning, before he jerked free but kept her pinned in place.

"What the hell does it take to keep you scared and away from me?"

"Just one moment. I wasn't . . . I'm not . . . afraid of you." *Confused, Kell. That's what you make me feel.*

"You should be afraid. You will be. You keep this up and I'll take it as an invitation to bed you down."

"No. I—"

"Bed, darlin'. Not once. Not even twice. Hell, the way you make me feel, a damn week wouldn't do. Understand? I won't say no again. I'll take every advantage I can."

Staring at the wild sugar-sweet mouth that was shaped like a small, enticing 'o' drove Kell closer to the body that triggered a landslide. Flash floods. Mine cave-ins. Kell ran out of natural disasters. Explosions and fireworks came next. What he had told her should be scaring the drawers off her. *He* should scare the drawers off her.

Kell moaned. In pain. All he could think of was the other pleasurable ways to get her drawers off.

He closed his eyes, his head sinking down to rest on his forearm. She made him swim into immoral daydreams that left him no peace.

Immoral?

What the hell was the matter with him? He was immoral!

If he had one ounce of good sense left, just one moral in his conscience, he would leave and never come back. Annie had no self-preservation instincts with regard to him. A peek out of one eye revealed her watching him with luminous fascination.

That did it! She had no sense of the danger she was in. No fear about him. He should . . .

"I warned you, Muldoon. That's all you get. I don't owe you a damn thing more. I never owe anybody anything!"

The door to his room slammed closed before Annie dared to move. Kell had warned her about himself. Hope was renewed. He *did* have redeeming qualities. Her time spent in prayer and reflection had been answered in the strangest way. And if Kellian had seen her slow, understanding smile of satisfaction as she passed his closed door, he would have caught the next stage out of town.

Far from the warning lesson he attempted to impart, his outburst gave Annie the needed courage to follow through on her idea. She nearly tripped with haste to get to the room that Cammy shared with Blossom.

Hairbrush in hand, Cammy answered her knock, giggling when Annie stammered out an apology for interrupting her toilet.

"Toilet?" Cammy repeated, motioning Annie inside.

"That's what ladies call getting gussied up."

"Oh, Ruby, I'd expect you to know. But come in, we're all dressed."

Annie took Cammy's word, and avoided looking at the basque of her gown that was fastened at the waist and veed open over a sheer scoop-necked chemise. The "all" included Blossom, sitting on the straight chair, white as Annie's linen sheets while Daisy—at least Annie thought it was—worked rouge over her cheeks with a hare's foot. Cammy stood before the mirror brushing out her dark brown hair, as thick and straight as a horse's tail.

"What's she want?" Ruby asked, snapping the red lace garter that held up a stocking the like of which Annie had never seen. She shot Annie a hard, brittle stare from eyes that had seen too much and didn't care who knew it. "Somethin' wrong?"

"No." Annie added a quick little shake of her head. "Your stocking—"

"Pretty, ain't they?" Ruby hiked up her gown to show off the other one. "Fella bought these all the way from St. Louis for me."

"An' red's her favorite color." Cammy lifted the sides of her long hair and with a few expert twists formed a loose topknot. Once she had it pinned in place, she shook back the rest of her hair. Meeting Annie's gaze in the mirror, she smiled. "Most men like a woman's hair loose."

"Makes 'em think of havin' hot puddin' for supper."

"Or stabling his naggie, Ruby," Cammy added. She shared a quick look with the other doves at the way Annie touched her own neatly pinned hair.

"That's not for the likes of you," Ruby told Annie, shaking out the folds of her petticoats and the bright red skirt that barely reached her calves. She slipped her feet into black-heeled shoes and sighed. "Sure wish I had a pair of fancy buckles like Laine's."

"Don't bother asking her to borrow them," Daisy warned, stepping back to admire her work on Blossom's pale cheeks. "Laine don't like lending her things. 'Fraid some other gal might look prettier."

Pinching her cheeks and turning from side to side in front of the mirror, Cammy nodded and faced Annie. "You never did say what you wanted."

Annie was distracted, trying to figure out why a woman's loose hair would make a man think of having hot pudding for supper. She offered an absent sort of smile, thinking her own description of Cammy's hair made sense of a man stabling his horse. But she caught the look they were exchanging and knew they were sharing a laugh at her expense. Well, she had come here to learn, and if she didn't ask she would never know.

But the words just wouldn't come. She glanced helplessly at Blossom, who sat still, softly groaning. "What's wrong?"

"She's got the collywobbles," Cammy answered.

"Collywobbles?"

"The misery," Ruby explained, then asked Annie, "What do you call it? Ladies have different names for everything."

"Woman's doom. Monthly misery," Daisy supplied.

Red-faced, Annie whispered, "A lady is indisposed."

"I'll say."

"Seconded by me, Daisy." Blossom whispered, wrapping her arms around her waist.

"Would you like me to heat a brick for you?" Annie asked, trying to overcome her ingrained lessons that forbade such frank talk. "Or I could make you a nice hot cup of tea? With some blackberry brandy," she added, remembering that rainy afternoon.

"They said you weren't like the others." Daisy, with her clever slender hands on ample hips came to stand in front of Annie. "Tea and a hot brick would help Blossom."

Fascinated by Daisy's unconcerned manner over her dress or undress, Annie nodded. The woman's cleavage was exposed by the lace scalloped edge of a bright blue gown that about equaled the length of Annie's drawers and was pinned up on one side to reveal nearly all of the woman's thigh.

"You didn't understand what we said, did you?" Daisy's golden-brown eyes searched over Annie's flushed face, and after a few moments she nodded, as if satisfied. "I was once just as sheltered as you, but my uncle figured I cost him too much and wasn't earning my keep. He put me to work, only I didn't see any of the money, so I took off on my own."

There was silence in the room, and Annie felt the tension as the four women waited for her reaction. Compassion was her only thought, and it spurred her to put her hand on Daisy's arm.

"Surely there was someone who could have helped you? Other family, a friend, a neighbor? Couldn't you have him arrested?"

"Honey, you are innocent," Ruby said, sitting down on the edge of the bed. "Would you have taken her in? After all, the bastard made sure everybody knew what she was doing. She's lucky she didn't get a belly full of some bastard's seed."

"Or work a crib," Cammy added, joining Ruby on the bed. "That's what happened to Laine. She never said how she got away, but she swore she'll never go back to it." Rubbing her arms, Cammy looked at Annie.

"It's a dirty little shack with a blanket on the floor. Two bits a toss and the rest goes to whoever owns the crib. You work six-, maybe eight-hour shifts every day."

"My Lord! How can anyone—this is why we banded together to close down—"

"Don't be comparing Kell to the likes of crib owners. First off," Ruby said, holding up her fingers and folding over her thumb to the palm, "Kell doesn't touch a penny we make. Only takes a cut from the whiskey we sell and whatever we earn at cards. He don't beat us. Won't let any man use his fists on any of us. If we say no to dancing the mattress jib with some plowboy, the jerk takes no for an answer or Bronc'll get rid of him quick."

It was too much for Annie, and she backed up until she could lean against the door. "I don't understand. I thought that Kyle made money from you."

"That's right. He did once Laine brought us together. But Kell said right off that what we did upstairs at the Aces was our business. Right?" Daisy asked, looking at the others.

Murmurs and nods confirmed it.

"Shucks, Annie," Blossom whispered, rocking back and forth as her cramps worsened, "even you know that Kell is different. He's got manners. Treats us like we were good folks, talkin' and laughin' with us. Why last night this cowpoke wouldn't take to understand that I don't do French tricks and when I tole him where he could put his bald-headed hermit I figured his fist was meetin' my jaw. 'Tween Li and Kell, that man was gone in a minute an' Kell tole him not to bother comin' back till he got his ears flushed out to hear good."

"Yes, I admit Kellian York has some redeeming qualities. But I'd better get you that brick and the tea."

"Oh, don't go. It's easin' up some an' we ain't had no chance to find out what you wanted."

Courage, Annie. There were genuine smiles on four pairs of lips. Their honesty invited hers. But Annie couldn't look at them.

"I'm in need of learning a bit more about men, and I thought that . . . er, in your profession, well . . . you could answer my questions."

"Move over, Daisy." Ruby patted the bed next to her. "Come sit yourself down. We got a little time before we go to work. And when you leave here, you'll know all about giving juice for jelly."

"Or playin' pickle me, tickle you."

"Plowin' clover."

"Sliding carrots up the board."

"Stop it," Ruby warned, barely able to contain her laughter. "You'll have her dazed and crazed without knowing why. Set your fanny down, Annie Muldoon. You'll have the best educatin' a woman can have. And the first thing you learn is how to tell a goose neck from a gully-raker."

"Yeah. Let Ruby tell you that," Daisy said, curling up by the headboard. "She can size—"

"And that's the secret," Ruby cut in. "See, you look at the size of a man's thumb to make sure you're getting the best leg of three."

Annie jumped up off the bed, the meaning quite plain. She rapidly rethought her plan, but Ruby coaxed her to sit again.

"We'll take this real slow."

"Maybe if you told us exactly what the problem is," Daisy suggested.

Annie was silent so long, her total concentration on her fingers plucking at her skirt. She didn't see the looks the doves exchanged or the conclusion they came to, but she lifted her head when Ruby slipped an arm around her waist.

"Females stick together. Men think they're in control, but honey, even a man like Kell ain't seen the tricks we know.'"

"Dazed and crazed about sums up the feelings Kell stirs and keeps at a boiling point. But you see, doing anything about it is very difficult for me." With a sigh, Annie looked at each one of them. "I truly believe that a woman should keep herself chaste until she weds. Not that I was looking for a husband. Or mean that as a judgment against you. But when Kell—"

"Wantin' a man ain't nothin' to be shamed 'bout. 'Less he don't want you. The good Lord made a woman like he did so's she could have her pleasurin', too."

"Pleasuring, Cammy?" Annie couldn't help the disbelief that filled her voice. "But the women I know, I mean there's very little talk about what exactly a woman is supposed to do. But I never heard anyone mention pleasure." Biting her lip, hesitating, Annie knew she had to make a full confession. "Kell keeps talking about pleasure."

"Landsakes, Annie!" Ruby starting laughing, then stopped. "If a man like Kell crooked his little finger in my direction, I'd be on my back faster than a match gets lit."

"Put wishes like that in a thimble, Ruby," Daisy said with a sigh. "He's turned Laine down more times than I can count."

"Laine? Wants Kell?"

"Don't worry, Annie. He doesn't want anything to do with her. Wouldn't be right anyhow," Ruby explained, patting Annie's hand. "She and Kyle had a thing going for a long while. Now, we're going to tell you what we know. Maybe our way won't be as pretty as you'd be used to hearing, but there's plenty of satisfied customers between us coming back for more."

The exchange that followed was at times confusing to Annie, since each women had her own opinion to voice, often edging Annie toward shock as the detailed descriptions and variations left nothing to her imagination. Nothing, that is, but the true state of ignorance that women of her acquaintance were kept in. Within thirty minutes she stopped blushing and flinching at the frank terms for body parts, all the unmentionable ones that had never been a part of her vocabulary. She was treated to giggles and laughter, and a great many sighs as incidents were recalled that had left behind fond memories.

When a breathless and pink-cheeked Charity arrived, she barely hesitated at seeing Annie there. Dreamy-eyed, she explained she had spent the afternoon and most of the early evening with Jessup Beamer, who wanted to take her away from all this.

As the excited cries and hugs stopped, Charity sadly told them that it wasn't likely to happen any time soon. She wanted a little ranch of her own, and Jessup didn't have much put aside from his monthly wages.

Li's knock hushed them as he called out that the wagon was in back and ready to go.

One by one, the doves fussed a bit and turned to leave.

"Blossom," Annie said, "if you don't feel well, why not stay? I'll make you tea."

"You're real sweet, Annie. But Li'll bring me back if I can't deal. Ain't up to more'n that."

Ruby had a last bit of whispered of advice. "Honey, you think hard about what you learned. Try it out, and I swear you'll leave Kell with an Irish toothache that'll have him on his knees."

But it was Charity who lingered behind the others and sent Annie into a spin. "Jessup and me saw that widow friend of yours with Bronc. They was walking along the lane holding hands. Bet Bronc's sweet on her. They all meant well with what they was telling you, Annie, but when you're in love with a man it's just different."

"Oh, but I'm not—"

Charity's dimpled smile cut her off, and she closed the door behind her, leaving Annie shaking her head, denying the only thing that made sense.

She was falling in love with Kellian York.

She couldn't be in love with him!

The thought was so shocking that Annie began to straighten the room without realizing what she was doing. Picking up a pillow to fluff, she hugged it tight.

Redeemable Kell would never again make vague remarks, then tell her she didn't understand. If she put just a little of what she had learned tonight into practice the next time they were alone, he would know she had the perfect cure for his *Irish toothache,* even if she wasn't ready to act on it. She'd wanted information, and now she had an abundance of it. She'd show him who was an innocent.

The next time. And with that possibility in mind, still hugging the pillow, Annie went to her room.

She never saw the shadowed form on the stairs, flattened against the wall. Annie, in her blissful dreaming, remained unaware of the bitterness and hate that was aimed at her back.

Chapter Fifteen

❧

Monday was washday. Annie's least-favorite chore, and as she scrubbed towels against the washboard, Annie wondered who had begun the ritual of beginning the week with laundry. Swiping a hand dripping with suds over her sweat-sheened brow, Annie refused to look at the piles still waiting for her. All over the town, sheets and union suits were flapping in a sultry breeze that promised a scorching day.

So it was an hour later, after the sheets were hung to dry, that Annie found herself bewildered when Aunt Hortense came to the back door and called her from her labor.

"My dear child, what have you done this time?" Hortense began, shaking her head. "The ladies have come to call and are in the parlor."

"Ladies? What ladies?"

"Abigail, Lucinda, Velma, and Emmaline. They want to talk to you. And I might warn you, Annie Charlotte, they look madder than wet hens. Puffed up like a few old sitting ones, too."

"But it's Monday!"

Looking out at the yard, Hortense blinked, then nodded. "Why, so it is. Come along, dear. I admit I'm curious what brought them away from their own wash lines. But do put on a fresh apron, Annie. You're all wet."

"That's too bad. If they can come to call at the wrong time while I'm working, they'll make do with my appearance."

Annie didn't wait for her aunt. Something must have happened to bring them here. Something that she was going to be lectured about. The feeling that her thought was true was confirmed the moment she opened the parlor door. Pockets was in the back parlor playing the piano, a tune that brought a smile to Annie but obviously found no favor with the four women facing her.

From Abigail's frown to Lucinda's tut-tut sounds of disapproval, Annie gazed at Velma's pursed lips and sought an answer and support from Emmaline. But she couldn't look at Annie.

"Ladies. It must be something very important for you to call on washday. And so early," she reminded them, annoyed by their lack of greeting. Perversely, Annie folded her arms over her chest and stood there, waiting until her temper cooled.

"Annie, dear, do close the door," Lucinda suggested. "What we have to say should be kept private."

"Oh? And why is that? The whole town knows you have come to call. Far too early, I remind you. Why mustn't anyone hear what you have to say?"

"Oh, dear, I was afraid that you would be put out with us," Velma said. "But please, Annie, do come and sit. I'm getting a crick in my neck twisting around to see you."

"All right." Annie turned and saw her aunt hovering

near the dining room. "Coming, Aunt Hortense?" she
yelled, and was dismayed when her aunt shook her head.
It was just as well, she thought, closing the door and moving to take the chair near the window. If they had to shout
and repeat everything for her aunt to understand, these
women would never get to the point.

"We've interrupted your wash," Emmaline said, squirming in her place on the settee. "I had finished mine when
Velma summoned me to join her and—"

"I'm sure you did, Emmaline, but please remember, my
dear friend, that you live alone and I wash for a full
boardinghouse."

"You should make that little Indian girl do the heavy
work, Annie. Let her earn her keep here."

"Abigail, I appreciate your concern," Annie replied
with an overabundance of sweetness. "I assure you that
Fawn does indeed earn her keep." She knew that Abigail was miffed about the miner having turned down her
offer to buy Fawn. If Annie had not been in the store
that day and heard the pitiful amount that Abigail had
offered and impulsively doubled it, Fawn would have
gone from one slaveholder to another. She could never
make any of them understand that she didn't think of
owning Fawn. She had offered her a home and taught
her whatever skills she could, as well as educated her.

But Annie was not going to let them distract her from
why they had come here. "Will one of you explain the reason for this visit? Emmaline?"

"Lucinda will speak for all of us."

"My dear Annie, this is a matter of grave concern for
us. When the men were caught up in their foolishness the
morning of the fire and threatened to hang you because
you rose to the need and assumed leadership of our legion, we stood behind your decision to take those people

in. But the time has come when you must make them leave."

"We supported you then," Velma and Abigail chorused.

"And what, may I ask, has changed? I explained to Emmaline my reasons. I am able to contribute to our church building fund which, much as it grieves me to say, very few have been doing." Annie stood up and studied each face by turns. They had come in full battle finery, hats and gloves, and borrowing from Kell's favorite description of them, they were a rigid corset contingent of do-gooders. Annie didn't even realize that she was aligning herself opposite them. They had come into her home to tell her what to do. That raised one battle flag. The second was out before she stopped herself.

"And where were the four of you when I spoke yesterday?"

"Why, here. You know we were here, Annie."

"Yes. You were here, Lucinda. You all were, but did one of you listen to what I said? We have an opportunity to take these women and show them a better way. Why won't you help me?"

"This charitable notion is to your credit," Velma said when the silence became uncomfortable. "But we have spoken with other members of our group, and they feel as we do. You must ask them to leave."

"If they have no place to stay, Annie, that man would reconsider his plans to rebuild that awful place."

"Emmaline! You expect me to throw them out, too? Why are you doing this now? Why didn't you all say something from the start? And as far as my *charitable notion* is concerned, Velma, you are wrong. I believe in what I'm doing—hear that, ladies—what I am going to accomplish." Annie couldn't get to the door fast enough, but then she turned. "And I will do it with or without your help. Good day."

Annie swept into the lobby, only to stop. Pockets stood near the back parlor door. From his frown, she knew he had heard. His cigar, unlit of course, since Annie had made her no smoking within the walls of her boarding-house rule clear, was clenched between his yellowed front teeth. At a sound she glanced up and found the doves arranged on the stairs, even an angry-looking Laine. Thankfully, no one wore a sheet this morning, even if their wrappers were scanty and could hardly be considered decent.

Undecided about saying anything, Annie nearly laughed when Pockets swept her a bow.

But she lost her smile when he softly said, "You are a truly gracious lady Miss Muldoon. Misguided, but a lady."

"Why, thank you, Pockets. And I do apologize to all my boarders for the early-morning disturbance. Now, you'll have to excuse me. I have laundry to finish and lunch to serve."

She ignored the shocked gasps behind her.

Lucinda's "Well, I never!" followed by Abigail's "What else did you expect?" to Velma's "We need to have another meeting, ladies."

What hurt Annie the most was Emmaline's silence.

Silence was not Kell's reaction when Li told him what had happened. After he had exhausted every curse, every swear and even borrowed a few of Li's, only to find that his temper still wanted satisfaction, Kell decided he would call on those *ladies*.

Li's cooler head prevailed. "They will not listen to you. I told you Pockets said she tickled their ivories with a rousing tune that earned his approval. And that of the doves as well, to judge by their talk."

"Plaguing old biddies! As if I don't have a plateful to deal with. It's enough to send a man to the bottle."

"You already drink enough."

"Thanks for the reminder, old wise one. Then I'll start smoking again."

"Forgive your most humble servant asking, but why are you angry? The woman is nothing to you. Or was that the bottle who spoke to me last night?"

"Woman? Who?"

"Annie."

It was the soft, knowing intonation in Li's voice saying her name that snapped a leash on Kell's temper. "You're right," he agreed in a calm voice. "And it wasn't the bottle but me talking last night. It's nothing to me what Muldoon does with her bunch of do-gooders."

Kell turned back to marking off the new, larger floor plan of the building. Li stood and watched him lay out the floor beams with a sharp eye that allowed no room for error. He gave a passing through to telling his friend about the intriguing conversation that Annie had had with the doves.

He thought about it. He thought about Kell's denial. And he recalled Kell's favorite words: "If a man is so blind not to see high stakes, he deserves to be taken. It's his misfortune and none of my own."

Li went back to work. Annie might be a greenhorn, but she could have beginner's luck.

Luck is not what Annie called it when Cammy arrived just as she was getting ready to serve and asked for hot water for Kell to wash. Annie was not ready to see him, and after the disturbing incident with her friends this morning she felt the edges of her temper fraying. But Cammy reminded her of their talk, and

how a woman had to take advantage of any chances that
came her way.

Armed with his laundry and a pitcher of hot water, she
headed up to his room. Laine was sauntering down and
stopped her.

"I heard you had a talk with the girls last night."

"That's right."

"I warned you once, and you didn't listen. You might
as well whistle for the wind as set your cap for Kell.
He's six feet of trouble, but all of it's a man. Just remember this. Like the wind, Kell won't come to heel
worth a damn."

"I will once again take your sage advice to heart, Laine."
Annie continued on her way, but she felt the power of
Laine's gaze follow her.

Laine's warning made Annie remember that she had
been told before of Laine's interest in Kell. Did he return
it, despite the doves' saying he didn't?

Annie's hands were full, so she used the heel of her
shoe to tap against Kell's door. In the few moments she
waited, Annie bolstered her courage by repeating the less
outrageous instructions she had been given.

Kell opened the door. "I hoped it would be you."

Far from an encouraging smile, Annie saw his scowl.
Oh, well, simpering was an art she had never mastered.
"And why is that?"

"I'm hot and tired and hungry. There's a rule around
here that says I can't come into the dining room unless
I'm clean and dressed. Tell me, Muldoon, do you stand by
the door and inspect every pair of hands before you let
them eat?"

Annie sailed past him and set his laundry on the
chair. His hair still looked like a hot wind had combed
it, and she could see he was tired by the way he rubbed

the back of his neck. Annie forgot about flirting with him.

"I can tell you're hungry," she said, pouring the water into the washbowl and turning around. "You couldn't wait to take a bite out of me."

She was rewarded by his perplexed frown, and then his equally perplexing laughter. "There's an intriguing thought." Kell flung himself on the bed and locked his hands together beneath his head. It was one way to stop the temptation of putting his hands on her. There was something about her . . . Her hair. No braids tightly coiled, but a softer upsweep that had her looking like a woman who fixed her hair so a man could mess it up.

"I heard what went on here with your *good ladies.*"

"Think nothing of it. I did what I thought was right. Besides," she added, smiling at him, "how could I bear to be without your charming company?"

"And the money I pay you."

Annie slowly gazed at the tips of his dusty boots and leaned back against the edge of the washstand. She took courage to try a simple lesson since the door was still open and she could run fast. So her look reflected the judgment any good housewife gave merchandise she intended to buy, and she inspected Kell from ankle to hip.

"Annie."

She didn't respond to the note of underlying warning but lingered over the fit of his dirt-smudged shirt, noting a small tear in the sleeve and the way a drop of sweat pooled in the hollow of his golden-brown throat. It was a reflex to lick her bottom lip, but it also reminded her that she had only fragile walls to shield her from the temptation he presented.

"What the hell do you think you're doing?"

"A little tit for tat?" she answered, distracted by the tightening ripple of his arm muscles.

"You'd better leave while you can, darlin'."

Wide-eyed with innocence, Annie met his gaze. "But I'm only doing what you pay for, Mr. York. Service includes clean laundry," she said, airily waving toward the pile on the chair. *Do it, Annie. Just try.*

"And water. I supplied the *hot* . . . water."

The breathy little catch in her voice sent an alarm that once again had a perplexed frown marring Kell's face. *Hot.* What the devil had gotten into Annie Muldoon? And the devil answered—*it wasn't you.*

Kell smiled. It wasn't wicked. It was downright nasty.

"Full of sugar traps this morning? Guess I'd better nibble carefully on you. Skitter on out of my room, Annie, before I offer to plant your sweet little tail in my bed and do some servicing of my own."

Annie barely managed to still the heat that flooded her. She ordered herself to the door, placed one trembling hand on the knob and started to draw it closed behind her. If you run, she warned herself, you'll never have the courage to tease him again. Annie glanced over her shoulder and mustered confidence from his blatantly aroused body.

"Whatever would you do, Mr. York, if I ever said yes?"

Kell bolted upright from the bed. "Did I hear . . . wait, damn you! Annie. Muldoon!" The door slammed in his face. He was tempted to wrench it open and go after her. He threw back his head and laughed. So she wanted to know what he'd do, did she? "Oh, darlin', my darlin' Annie, you're going to find out."

He timed his entrance into the dining room when Annie would be almost done with serving. She had her back toward him when he took a chair at the far corner table, sitting with his back to the wall. It was an old habit—to place himself with a full view of the room, as well as the doors—and one he'd never broken. The lone drummer engaged her in conversation, obviously reluctant to let her go.

Annie's laughter alerted Kell again to the change in her. She started to move back to the kitchen, and he had a clear look at the man. Slick pomaded dark hair and a gaze filled with male calculation watching Annie's hip-swaying walk made Kell stifle a possessive urge to yank his darlin' out of sight.

The drummer glanced at Kell and, hearing the door close behind him, said, "Better try your luck at the tent outside of town." He raised a wine glass filled with pale yellow liquid in a toast and drank it down.

Kell smiled with satisfaction. "Yeah, you do that. The doves are accommodatin' an' the whiskey the best to be found." *And leave Annie to me.*

From his thought to presence, she pushed through the kitchen door, gaze intent on the change she carried to the drummer. But Kell had a feeling she had seen him and deliberately ignored him. The man left, and Kell asked for his meal.

"Pork roast, green beans, and biscuits," Annie answered, clearing off the table.

"Fine. And bring me a glass of that wine the drummer had."

"Wine?" Annie looked over at him.

"Yeah, Annie. Wine." He wondered at her doubtful look before she nodded.

"It will take a few minutes."

"I'm not going anywhere. But remember, I'm hungry."

"Not likely to forget that," she tossed back and disappeared into the kitchen.

Kell had the room to himself. He wasn't in any hurry to get back to the site, since the lumber he'd ordered wouldn't arrive until late afternoon. Most of his meals had been eaten on the run or up in his room, so this was the first time he had allowed himself to study the various samplers hanging on the walls.

Most were rules that he read with a half-smile creasing his lips. All began with *do not*: spit on the table or on the floor, drink from the saucer, lift meat to your nose to sniff, use the fork or knife to clean your teeth at the table, use the linen to blow your nose. But it was two older ones that reminded him he had to do something about Annie's prissy ways. The cloth yellowed with age, letters faded so he had to squint to read brought his chuckle. *"Put not thy hand in the presence of others to any body part not ordinarily discovered."*

Annie came out carrying a full plate and a wine glass.

Kell waited until she served him, making a trip back to the kitchen for a small pitcher. "Don't run off, Annie. You can't have a rule about joining me."

She offered an absent sort of a smile and poured liquid into his glass, then stood back.

"I do want to talk to you about—"

"Try the house wine," she encouraged.

Doubtful of the expectant look in her eyes, Kell lifted the glass to his lips, frowning at the cloudy color. He wouldn't put it past Annie's prissed-up spinster ways to serve him piss-warm leavings to get even with him.

He sipped. "Wine, hell!" he bellowed, spitting it out. "This is lemonade."

"Yes, Mr. York, that's right." Annie backed away and smiled, nearly choking on her laughter. "That's the house wine of the South. And please, if you want to dine here again, follow the rules." Pointing to the sam-

pler over his head, Annie made good her escape when
he tilted his chair back and twisted his head to look up.

"Drink is a sin against the Lord and leagues one with
the devil. We serve none." Kell turned back to look at
the closed kitchen door. He could still hear her laughing. "You won this hand, Annie, but I'll have a sweeter
dessert," he murmured and then relished every slow
bite of his food.

He was nearly done when Annie came back, hurrying
with a pile of towels filling her arms. "Li's in the kitchen.
I think he wants you."

Kell gave her message a moment's thought. Li could
wait. He hadn't finished his meal.

Annie raced up the stairs, wishing the flirting business did not include removing herself from Kell's presence. She would have loved to sit with him while he
ate, but Ruby had been firm about the first rule. Tease
and retreat. Setting the stack of clean towels on the
marbletop stand, Annie took the few that were left on
the shelf and placed them on top. She had just straightened and was about to rub the ache in her back when
her stomach lurched. Kell was near. Her body tensed as
anxiety pressed in and the cause of it moved closer. His
breath skimmed the top of her head, and her scalp
prickled with awareness.

"You're a poor hostess, Muldoon," he murmured in a
soft, oh, so soft, caressing tone. "You didn't offer me anything sweet for dessert."

The edge of the stand offered help to steady her and
Annie eagerly grabbed hold of it. "There's pie."

"What kind?" he whispered, kissing her nape.

"You can't . . . go around kissing me wherever and
whenever—"

"I'm in a mood for lemon pie, Annie. Sugar sweet

lemon pie. And the only way I can get to taste that," he informed her, gently making her face him, "is to kiss you."

His mouth fully covered hers, and Annie forgot all the lessons she had repeated and vowed to put into practice. When he had her toes curling and her heavy lids barely able to lift to see his blistering smile, he broke the kiss and with one gentle finger, tilted her head to the side and nibbled her neck.

Remember your vow, Annie. You are going to burn his boots off. "More," she whispered.

"I really did want to thank you," Kell whispered between kisses rimming the dainty shape of her ear, "for your staunch support in letting the doves stay."

Since Annie was draped against him like a sheet on a bed, her murmuring agreement was true. "As I am for yours."

Kell slid his hands around her waist and lifted her to sit on the marble stand's top. His lips sought hers just as his hips nestled between her parted thighs.

"You wanted to talk," she managed as soon as he lifted his head.

"Yes. I had the thought." Kell angled his head back, and Annie placed a kiss on his chin. He drew her closer, stroking the slender length of her back, loving the small sounds she made. It crossed his mind that Annie was not behaving like a prickly hedgehog but was being quite accommodating to his every move.

"You make me feel sinful, Kell." And she smiled before boldly dragging her fingers through his hair to bring his mouth to hers.

Alarm from the crick in his neck made the kiss brief. "Is that what this is all about, Annie? You're curious about all this sin you keep preaching against? Must be," he answered himself, watching her drowsy bluebell eyes open to his. "You talk about it, you harp on it, you even dare the devil and make him sin."

His words drifted through the sensual cloud with the thickness of honey. Annie merely smiled. Just like the doves said, this was easy. Her fingers played against his nape and the damp length of his hair. "Are you warm? Why do you talk about sin," she asked, nuzzling his throat, "when you sell sin?"

"Sell sin?" Kell narrowed his eyes. His grin was slow, but it kicked up the corner of his mouth. "Honey," he drawled, gripping her upper arms and holding her away from him. "I don't sell sin. I don't promote sin. I'm sinful, I'll admit. Have a heap of sinful thoughts about you and won't deny it. I've even done my share of sinful deeds and right now, darlin', I'm all for putting all this sinning to good use." He drew her close, tilting his head, her startled eyes blurring as he kicked closed the door to the bath room. "Have I told you that I changed my mind?"

"Your . . . mind?" Panic set in. She was supposed to control the how and when and where of kissing him. Her grip on his hair tightened, but that didn't stop him from brushing his lips against hers.

"I don't want lemon, sugared or not. Annie. Annie, you've got the most luscious, cherry-red lips, made for kissin'."

Do the unexpected! The advice saved her. Annie caught his bottom lip between her teeth. Kell shifted closer, his hands rubbing up and down her thighs. For a moment she was swimming in the heated sensations of his touch and the swift rise of tension so that she all but forgot what she was supposed to do next. Tease him. Flirt. Seduce . . . Annie jerked her head back.

"I can't do this. It's all wrong."

"Practice, darlin'. I promise you'll have it perfect before long."

He muffled her protest with a kiss that send need rocking through his body. Kneading her hips, he dragged her closer to the edge of the stand, the move spreading her thighs to the fit of his. She made those passionate moaning sounds that told more of her want than she could ever put into words. Kell stroked up her sides and nearly groaned at the perfect way her breasts filled his palms. He could hear the pounding of his heart when Annie slid the tip of her tongue over his lip, then shyly retreated.

Breaking the kiss to coax her, Kell heard another pounding and let loose a growl of frustration.

"Annie. Annie, you in there?"

Hearing Li, Kell lifted her to stand on her feet and fought his need to do murder. Flinging open the door, he shot a look back at Annie, who stood gripping the stand. "This had better be good," he all but growled to Li.

"Oh, it is for a very good reason that I seek her. Your cat has taken his prey into the parlor and frightened your aunt. He refuses to give up his mouse, and she has demanded that you be found, Annie."

Rioting senses quickly cooled. Annie sent one long look of regret in Kell's direction, unable to meet his furious gaze. Despite the aching need of her body, she knew this had happened for the best. It was becoming harder and harder to say no.

Kell stepped out into the hallway and, like Li, watched her go.

"You know, Li, I understand exactly how that old tomcat feels."

"You do?" All innocence, Li stepped away from him. He knew that soft, ingratiating voice. It boded ill for him.

"Oh, yes," Kell said, leaning against the doorframe. "He feels possessive. And he's angry that he's being cheated of his catch."

"Ah, so. I would not have thought of this. Perhaps it would be best if I go help Annie."

"You do that, Li. Although, in my opinion, you've helped her enough today. And Li," he warned as the man walked quickly toward the stairs and far from him, "I'll go hunting the pigtail the next time."

Li spun around and held his braid out to the side. More than once in the towns that they had drifted in and out of over the years they had been together, Li had been chased by men bent on doing that very thing. He saw that Kell had not moved, but for all the underlying warning in Kell's voice, the fury was absent.

"You no likee," Li singsonged. "You bad white devil takee hatchet to chinee man's pride and joy."

"Remember that, my friend, for the next time you put mine between a rock and a hard place."

"A wise man would tell you to marry her, Kell, and so end the—"

"Marry? Me?" Kell started after Li. "Marry her?"

Li took the steps in agile leaps, never once looking back to see if Kell followed him.

He didn't. He stood at the top of the stairs and tried to laugh it off. "Marry Annie Muldoon." Ridiculous. This was the first sign that Li's mind was fermenting into mush from all the opium he had been forced to use.

As if he wanted to marry anyone! Shaking his head, Kell returned to his room. It was just a thought too funny for words. He was a free man and all for keeping himself that way. So what if Annie was turning out to be curious about pleasure between a man and woman? It wasn't enough to get him trapped. So why wasn't he laughing?

Chapter Sixteen

Frustration strengthens resolve—Annie's new motto after three days of not seeing Kell and of being unable to get her ladies group to support her efforts of redemption for the doves.

She could not tease, flirt, or attempt to seduce a man she could not find. Much as Annie hated to admit it, Laine had been right. Kell was harder to bring to heel than the wind. Li had taken to bringing Kell his meals during the day while they worked unceasingly with hired hands to rebuild the gambling house. She couldn't even thank him for sending the supply drivers to the boarding-house to eat. She had a nagging suspicion that Kell deliberately came back to bathe and change for the evening while she was busy serving supper.

Why was Kell avoiding her when he had her on the verge of capitulation and her emotional state swinging from high to low? And in the evenings, while she paced and plotted or fell into an exhausted sleep only to dream about Kell, he was gambling the night away in the tent outside of town. Annie's mornings began early, just when Kell came home for a few hours of sleep. Then he would be gone again.

A lesser woman would simply have given up. Punching down the bread dough this blessedly cooler Thursday morning, Annie determined that she was made of stern principles, stubborn backbone and an awakened desire that interfered with everything she had to do.

Today had to be better. Forgetting to mix the yeast in the warmed water was not a sign that the day would go badly. She stopped her kneading. Was she now absorbing some of Kell's gambler's superstitions? No. She knew better.

But from the moment that she had bodily hauled a protesting Dewberry from the parlor with his mouse—prey that she was certain the cat had brought in from the field to torment her for lack of attention, calmed her aunt with a double dose of her tonic, and taken Fawn for her promised dress fitting, Monday was a day to forget.

She and Fawn had surprised Bronc coming out from Emmaline's private quarters behind the dress shop. His hurried greeting served as a confirmation that what Charity had said was true. Bronc courted her. And if Annie needed any more proof, her friend's bee-stung lips and bright eyes gave her that. After all, Annie had seen the same look in her own mirror enough times since Kell had taken up residence in the boardinghouse.

Once she had explained what Fawn wanted made with her new material, Annie attempted to gain her friend's support.

Just the thought of Emmaline's rigid stance was enough for Annie to attack the bread dough with renewed anger. The woman wanted Kell and his entourage gone from Loving, and no amount of reasoning, no pleading on Annie's part had been able to shake Emmaline from her high-and-mighty perch. Annie had thought to point out that if Kell left, he would likely take Bronc with him, but such meanness was beyond her.

Tuesday she had called on Ruth McQuary to renew her aunt's tonic and state her cause to enlist Ruth's aid. That woman's parting comment still smarted.

"Tell me, would she, that I'd have as much success turning those women respectable as Abner fooling with his compounds would in finding the secret of making gold? I'll show her. I'll show them all."

Having worked herself into a sweat, Annie let the dough rest and herself along with it. She wiped her hands on a damp towel and went out the back door. With a sigh she leaned against the porch post. It seemed hopeless.

Visiting Lucinda yesterday afternoon had been another wasted effort. Lucinda's lecture that she was too young, even if they had voted her president of the legion, to understand the consequences of her action. She at least had been kind in pointing out that Annie's opposing view caused them all grave concern.

There had been a time, just a few short weeks ago, when Annie would have gladly relinquished her position. Trying to walk a middle line and do what she believed was right, yet keep the friends she had known all her life, left her in a quandary.

If only there were someone she could turn to for help.

"Annie. Annie Charlotte."

She turned to smile at Hortense and went back inside the kitchen.

"Bread's near ready for baking," Hortense announced after poking her finger in the dough. She pulled out a chair and sat down, peering up at her niece. "You're troubled, girl."

"The ladies group—"

"Ah, yes, those dear ladies. You didn't like what they had to say, did you?"

"They're wrong. I just know that with time and patience I could help these women."

"You've a stubborn streak near as wide as your dear departed mama's. She set her cap for your papa and wouldn't settle for anyone else. Reformed him, made our papa accept him and married the man she wanted. Pity she couldn't see how you turned out."

Annie having heard this before, continued with shaping the dough to fit her greased bread pans, nodding as her aunt reminisced, worrying over her problems.

"Well, answer me, girl."

"About what?"

"Whose the deaf one around here?" Hortense demanded.

"I'm sorry, Aunt."

"Get your pans in the oven and then sit down." Hortense waited until she did so, then adjusted her spectacles and studied her niece. "You're working yourself to a frazzle. You need to find yourself a husband. And what I asked you, Annie Charlotte, is Mr. York your chosen one?"

"Aunt!"

"Don't 'Aunt' me. Just answer me, girl. After all, I'm the only family you've got. The man will need to be spoken to. Someone has to ask what his intentions are."

"You don't want to know," Annie muttered under her breath.

"What's that?" Hortense asked, leaning over the table. "You don't fool me none, girl. I'm a bit hard of hearing and my eyesight's a mite frayed, but I'm not ready for a pine box. I see and hear more than you know of what's been going on."

Annie couldn't look at her. Bits of dried flour stuck to the table and occupied her eyes and her hands to remove it. It was daunting to think of what her aunt may have seen and heard.

"I was a good cook in my day, Annie. Taught you how, didn't I?"

"Why, yes, but what—"

"Recall the first time you tried making cream gravy?" Annie's frown annoyed Hortense. "Pay attention, girl. You curdled the cream. Added it too fast, wouldn't listen worth a darn about needing to keep stirring, and threw it out."

"Yes, but what has making gravy got to do—"

"Listen up, girl. You've been doing the same thing. Stirred up the pot, threw everything in, and forgot to add it all slowly. Now, is Kellian York husband material?"

"I want him to be." Annie looked up at her. "I think I'm in love with him. I know he has good qualities."

"Well, if he hasn't bedded you yet, I'd be inclined to agree."

"Aunt!"

"Hush, girl. Plain talk's needed. You've got the ladies riled at you, the man running scared so's he won't show his face, an' you mooning about."

"That about sums it up. But what do you propose that I do?"

"You've got it all backward, girl. I'm not the one that needs to do the proposin'. Now, first off, you want the ladies' help. And this is how you'll have it. Pay close attention, girl, 'cause I'm not repeatin' this. At my age it's hard enough to figure a way to save curdled gravy."

Annie had to wait until late Saturday afternoon to put her plan into action. She had enlisted the aid of the legion and the doves, but neither group knew of the other one's contribution until it was too late.

From the crowd of ranch hands and drifters in town, Kell would do a booming business. Since what Annie intended was for the best of causes, she was sure he wouldn't mind sharing his profits with her.

Across the road leading to his tent a barricade of borrowed tables forced anyone intent on reaching Kell to stop. Within an hour, word spread that there were baked goods for sale, and just as Aunt Hortense had predicted, there wasn't a man who could resist the luscious array of cakes and cookies the legion had contributed. What Annie never mentioned was that Blossom, Charity, and Ruby had baked right along with her. Their motives were less than pure, for they simply wanted to put a few noses out of joint after the way those women had spoken to Annie.

But Annie wasn't going to look for worms in the garden that had her cash tin filling with the constant ring of coins. Every dollar spent would be used for good works and would leave a little less for gambling and drinking.

As dusky shadows and nearly empty tables warned Annie it was time to clean up, she noticed the unwelcome return of several ranch hands who were less than sober. Velma and Abigail were the only women left to help her, and once they had moved the tables to the side of the road, folded their cloths, and gathered up empty plates to be returned to their owners, they left Annie alone, fending off the suggestions that she join the men for a drink.

Greed would always get one in trouble, Annie told herself, trying hard to ignore the most persistent of the four men hovering near her. She didn't know them, but she was sorry now that she had coaxed them with smiles into buying the baked goods.

Pockets had his harmonica out and a lively tune came

from the woods behind her, where the road curved. Loud whoops and laughter made Annie cast anxious glances around her. She had three plates filled with the remains of the muffins, cookies, and slices of cakes to juggle along with her cash tin and Aunt Hortense's second-best table-cloth.

Two of the men drifted off, and she breathed a sigh of relief, only to find that two remained behind. Taking courage in hand, Annie stacked the plates on top of the cloth, tucked her cash tin in the crook of her arm, lifted her tottering burden, and prepared to leave.

But her way was blocked.

Annie eyed the wiry cowhand, arms extended to the sides as if he would crush her in a bear hug the moment she took a step forward.

"Stand aside," she ordered in her best scolding voice. "You've had too much to drink and will be sorry for this in the morning."

"Sweet thing, you come a little closer an' ain't either one of us gonna be sorry 'bout nothin'."

"You've made a terrible mistake about me. I am not one of the doves." Annie sidestepped, only to find that he moved with her. She wasn't truly frightened—not yet, but she was getting there. "You must let me pass. My aunt will be worried if I'm late."

"Gal, I'm so horny I couldn't last longer than a cricket in a chicken yard. Have you home in two shakes of a lobo's tail. So come 'ere to ole Lige an' give us a kiss."

"Oh my good Lord!"

"Honey," said the other man from behind Annie, causing her to spin around and lose the top plate, "that's what all the gals say when they see Lige."

Annie backed away. The ruined plate crunched under her shoes, but she had no time to think about it. Thanks to the broadening talk of the doves, she had no trouble understanding what they wanted with her. Not that any woman being stalked by the two of them could have any doubt. There wasn't a soul around, the noise from the tent would drown any call for help that she made. *Think of something*, she told herself, angry that fear made her shiver.

"The doves," she began.

"All got taken. Obie an' me don't mind sharin'."

Annie glanced at the man to her left, big and burly with a neck thick as her thigh. "Obie, you don't want a woman that is not willing. I'm not willing. I'm not a dove. It's the evil of drink that clouds your thinking. Take your friend Lige and go sleep it off."

"Lordy, Obie! You hear that? We got us an all-night gal. Sleepin's the last thing I'm gonna do." He lunged for Annie.

She threw the cake and its plate at him. The plate unfortunately missed, but he wore the icing from the cake.

"Why'd ya do that for? We aim to pay you right."

"Pay me! You won't get close enough to do anything to me." Annie hefted the last plate, a solid stoneware, and let its contents fall. "I'm going home. If either one of you dares to touch me, I'll clobber you." Lamplight spilled from the back quarters of Emmaline's store and beckoned her. Annie looked from one man to the other and started to back away.

She tried to orient herself now that it was nearly impossible to see. Kell's building site was strewn with obstacles, but she had to stay close to the shell of the building to reach Emmaline's.

They closed in on either side of her. Annie threw the plate and ran.

She might have made it—she would look back and

wonder if the Lord or the devil had intervened—but two shots rang out. The sudden thunder of hoofs was the only warning she had as a group of riders swept out from town, bearing down on her.

Still as a fawn in a thicket, Annie realized too late the new danger she faced. Her pristine white shirtwaist acted as a beacon for the lead rider, who swerved and scooped her up in front of him. She had no seat to speak of, just a hard muscled arm banded around her waist, leaving her legs dangling like a broken rag doll's. Clutching her cash tin and Aunt Hortense's tablecloth close to her chest, Annie almost uttered a prayer of relief for her unknown savior, when he landed a sloppily wet kiss on her ear. The fumes of his liquor-foul breath made her catch her own.

She felt herself sliding against the hot, sweaty side of the horse, but the thought of struggling free was impossible with the press of the other horses around her. She squeezed her eyes closed, knowing where they were going and dreading it. A spark of independent spirit resented the need to depend upon Kell for rescue, but she had to counter this with the fear that he might do nothing at all.

Whoops and yells announced their arrival, and Annie's eyes flew open and her gaze flitted from one startled dove's face to another before she became aware of the growing silence. There were at least fifty or more men clustered around the makeshift tables and bar, all slowly turning around to look.

Into the tension-fraught stillness, Daisy's whispered "Get Kell" was passed from one dove to the other, and Annie found herself sagging with relief that she would not be abandoned.

The men near her dismounted. Annie had her first look at them in the spill of the brightly lit lanterns. From unshaven faces to the worn, dusty clothing and the guns that each wore, there was not anything reassuring about them. No longer denying the need for Kell, she searched the crowd, unaware of the plea in her gaze when she found first Bronc, still as could be with a bottle in hand, then Pockets, who shook his head and disappeared around a high-sided wagon.

Annie tried to swallow and found that she couldn't. In front of her, a sweet-faced cowboy was dispossessed of his chair near Daisy by one of the men, who grabbed him by the scruff of his neck and hauled him out with a shove. Hands on gun butts, the other three moved through the crowd toward the bar. Annie felt herself suddenly released and sliding toward the ground on knees that threatened to buckle. But the man dismounted and grabbed hold of her arm in a brutal grip that jerked her upright.

Her cry was so soft, but it carried to Kell as he rounded the back of the wagon and stared in disbelief.

If Annie hadn't been so frightened, she might have found humor in the way men looked from Kell to her captor and backed away. Her arm was numb from the man's tightened grip holding her by his side. She shot a quick look toward Bronc. One of the men held a gun on him, and the other two stood on either side of him, guns drawn and facing the crowd. Her gaze snapped back to where Kell stood unarmed, but when her eyes met his, a chill made her tremble. He looked ready to kill.

Daisy tried to stand, but she too, was forced to remain in place by the man at her side. He did nothing to stop the other ranch hands at the table from getting up and backing off to the waiting crowd.

It was then that Annie noticed none of the men who had been drinking and gambling was armed.

"Take a bottle and leave," Kell softly intoned. "If you five plan to stay, the guns go."

"No one takes Noe Hillerman's gun."

"Then you leave," Kell answered, his voice husky. Despite his determination to avoid trouble if he could, his body was responding to the sight of Annie—the subtle fire shades of her hair tumbling free over one shoulder, the too bright blue eyes, the tear at her lace-edged neckline revealing a patch of creamy skin.

"I'm not a patient man," Kell added, his voice roughened by the heated racing of his blood. She was his, and the thought of any other man's hands on her blinded him with a rage he was fast losing control over. He wanted her, and only the whisper of Li's voice urging caution from behind the wagon stopped him from rushing forward to the certainty of a bullet.

Li was right. He had dealt with his share of men like Hillerman—too old to be called a boy and excused but far too undisciplined to be called a man. Hillerman's friends at the bar egged him on with a string of coarse comments that made the doves wince—and they had heard it all. Annie was struggling, trying to unlock the thick fingers Hillerman had around her arm.

Kell waited, knowing what he had to do. Every second brought a change to the world around him. Li's lessons to allow time to stretch while he freed himself were accomplished in seconds. He moved forward, leaning over to grab a half-empty bottle from a table, and without warning he tossed it to Hillerman.

In a reflex as old as time, Hillerman made a grab for the bottle and freed Annie. She didn't need Kell's quiet order to run, she managed a few steps before Pockets was there to hold her.

The man sitting next to Daisy rose, his gun aimed at Kell, just as he launched himself at the two men. Annie

screamed a warning, fear for Kell blocking out Pocket's reassurance that Li and Bronc were helping.

Kell's hand flashed out and the man's gun went spinning. Another blow from Kell had the man grabbing his
arm with a cry of pain. Hillerman rushed forward, ready
to crush Kell with his thick hands, but Kell's foot lashed
up and out, catching Hillerman's chest to stop him. The
blow left the man swaying where he stood, shock visible
before a roar of rage exploded and he lunged at Kell.

With a speed and coordination that left Annie stunned,
Kell sent Hillerman crashing into the nearest table, glasses and bottle tumbling to the ground. Kell's moves were
too fast for her to separate them. Only the results were
visible: both Hillerman and his friend were disarmed and
down. It was only then that Annie dragged her gaze away
to see that Bronc held one of the men up by his shirtfront, delivering short jabs to his dough-soft belly, while Li
was already holding another by the seat of his pants and
shirt to toss him outside the tent.

Hillerman managed to get up on his knees, only to fall
forward gagging. Kell grabbed hold of the other man near
him and lifted him to his feet in a single motion. It was
only Kell's grip on his shirtfront that kept the man standing.

"Take your friends and get out. Don't bother coming
back. *Gentlemen* don't assault the ladies in Loving. Do I
make myself clear?" Soft, ever so soft was his voice, but
every man there heard the threat implied. "Bronc," he
called, "clean this scum out."

"Gladly, Boss."

"Then serve a round of drinks on the house." Kell
waited a few moments while the men returned to the tables, voices subdued, speculation bright in eyes watching

Kell, then Li as both men converged on where Annie stood with Pockets.

"Get Cammy to sing, Pockets."

"Sure thing." He slid his harmonica out of his vest pocket and waved it at Cammy.

Bronc already had three of the men on their horses when other men moved to remove Hillerman and the last man. Slaps to the horses' rumps and a few yells sent the five on their way, and it was then that Li spoke.

"I'll take Annie home."

"No," Kell snapped.

Annie looked at him. Shock upon shock had shaken her this night, but what she saw in Kell's eyes sent yet another, more feminine awareness of the danger he presented rippling through her.

"Damn fine piece of fighting, Kell. Let me buy you a round."

Without taking his gaze from Annie, Kell refused. "Buy the drink for Li, Denley." With no more than that, he snared Annie's arm with one hand and ushered her outside the tent to where horses were tied.

"Take mine, Kell," Denley called out.

"Kell," Annie ventured, sensing that he wouldn't listen, but needing to try. "Please let Li take me home."

"No way."

The horses had been standing quietly until Kell approached. Their snorts and restless stampings were the result of the tension she felt pouring from him.

"I've never seen a man fight like that. The callus on your hand and Li's—"

"What about it?" he snapped, facing her.

"I couldn't help but notice them. I wanted to ask. I . . . please, Kell, this wasn't my fault. I was going to go home.

Two men came back from here and they were drunk. They tried to—"

"Not another damned word, Muldoon." Kell tore the reins free of someone's horse and backed the animal out of the line.

"Muldoon? You only call me that when you're angry with me. You have no right. Do you hear me, Mr. York? No right to blame me for what happened. It's you and the damn liquor you sell that makes men behave like animals!"

He dropped the reins and dragged her close so quickly that Annie barely had time to catch her breath. Heat and tension from his hands melded and spread inside her. She couldn't see him clearly, his upper body and face were shadowed, but there was an escalating sense of danger that had her trembling.

"Kell?"

He shook her none too gently. "Quiet, Annie. Just once. You think liquor's needed to make a man forget all the fancy rules of behavior you'd like governing your safe little world? Wrong. Do you know," he grated from between clenched teeth, "what it did to me to see you mauled?" His fingers tightened and he shook her again. "Do you?"

"N-no. I . . . c-couldn't. I was frightened."

"You haven't got the good sense to be frightened." One more shake and he saw the last pins securing her hair fall. Kell couldn't stop himself. He caught up the fiery mess of her hair and drew her head back, lowering his until his mouth was nearly touching hers. "I've tried to stay away from you. I—"

"Why, Kell? Why?"

"If you need to ask, you prove you haven't any sense. You should be running, darlin'. Running like hell away from me."

He felt as well as heard the startled intake of her breath. Beneath his thumbs her pulse was a rapid beat that made his body tighten in a wild, sweeping rush, one that happened only when he was near Annie.

Kell took her mouth in a fierce, devouring kiss meant to punish and warn. But Annie only knew that barely contained passion was added to the tension and the danger consuming her with a raw sensuality she couldn't fight, didn't even attempt to stop.

She felt a vague tremor coursing through his body find an answering response in her own. The tin she still clutched pressed painfully against her breast as he deepened the kiss, but nothing mattered except Kell and the wild hunger that shimmered inside her.

As quickly as he had begun it, Kell abruptly ended the kiss, his hand still tangled in her hair. "You haven't got the self-preservation instincts of a week-old kitten." The whiskey-tinged warmth of his breath stirred over her hair, fanned her flushed face, but Annie couldn't look away from him.

"Maybe I don't want them."

His hand slid slowly down the curve of her neck, caressing her shoulder before he cupped her breast, where the wild rhythm of her heart beat in tandem with his. "You don't know what the hell you want, Annie." His voice was thick with the roil of passion coursing through him. "But I do."

The promise in his voice coupled with the intimate touch of his hand on her breast, finally broke the spell she had been under and Annie stumbled back, to find the horse behind her.

"Please, Kell, take me home."

He closed the distance between them, his hands fitted to her slender waist, and he started to lift her, only to place his lips and tongue on the tender flesh revealed by the tear at her neckline. She trembled, whether from fear or desire he didn't know, didn't care. "Run, Annie," he whispered once more, as the sudden snorting and stampings of the restless horses brought his head up.

Annie touched his cheek. "I can't run anymore, Kell. I don't think I want to."

"Then I'm taking you"—his breathing was suddenly labored as he fought a battle he was already losing—"home."

Chapter Seventeen

～

On the silent ride home, cradled in Kell's arms, surrounded by his warmth, Annie tried to untangle the emotions the last hour had raised. She didn't want the time to think, she didn't want the desire to cool, but Kell made no move to kiss her into a swirl of heated passion that allowed no room for thought, only feelings.

It was only as they rounded the corner of the boarding-house that he spoke. "Did any of them hurt you?"

He drew rein and slid from the horse before she managed to answer him. "No. Not the way you mean."

Kell lifted her down, deliberately letting her slide tight to his body, letting her feel how aroused he was.

"I can't promise I won't. I want you. Too much to have much control left."

Annie tried, truly tried to think of all the good advice the doves had given her about seducing a man. Kell trailed kisses down her cheek, nuzzling the underside of her jaw. Blood seemed to rush, heated and thick, to where his lips lightly pressed. Honesty was all Annie could muster.

"Kell, I've never been with a man."

She watched his head rise, slowly, as if he were unsure of what she had said. Annie wished the dark away, needing to see his face, wanting to know what his eyes would reveal.

His hand cupped her cheek, tilting her face up. "I've always liked anticipating my pleasures, Annie." His forehead dropped forward to touch hers. "Didn't anyone," he said, his voice lowered to a sensual softness, "ever explain to you that the primitive male enjoys being the first?"

"First?"

"First, Annie."

Scattered thoughts rushed together. "Are you a primitive male?"

"I'm getting there, darlin'." Kell moved quickly and scooped her up in his arms. "Maybe I've always been one. Then again," he noted, heading for the back door, "maybe it's you who has me feeling this way."

Inside the kitchen, Kell set her down and started for the lamp that Fawn had left lit. He glanced at Annie, the nervous way she smoothed out the wrinkles in the cloth, the jerky moves setting the tin she had carried first one way, then another.

"We should talk, Kell."

"Not now, darlin'."

Her hands stilled and his gaze rose to the rapid rise and fall of her breasts to the flush that colored her cheeks. It would be easy to seduce her, he could almost feel her need to have that from him, but not this time. Annie had to come to him on her own. He wanted no recriminations later. And from the hints that Pockets let fall, he gathered Ruby and the other doves had given Annie one hell of an education. He had promised her lessons. Maybe she'd be teaching him a few.

The thought brought a wicked grin to his lips and Annie saw it. "Stop laughing at me."

"I'm not laughing at you, Annie. When a man wants a woman as much as I do you, it's real hard—" Kell felt as if her gaze would burn through the tight fit of his pants. She looked up and he smiled. "Yeah, you see how it is. Damn hard to think about talking bringing any enjoyment."

"I'm not naive," Annie managed, feeling that was exactly what he thought her.

"Oh, I know that, Annie. You're a regular hellraiser, full of unbridled lust just waiting for the right man to set it free." Kell rounded the table to where she stood.

"No." She shook her head and repeated the denial. Two steps back, then two more closer to the doorway. *Annie, Annie, what has he done to you? Now you're lying to yourself.* Just once taste what it's like to be wild and free. Just once know the promise of passion. Annie stopped at the doorway. "All right, Kell. I am everything you said."

"What, Annie? Say the words for me. Say 'I'm a lustful hellraiser.' Say 'I'm a woman who knows what she wants.' Say it for me," he demanded softly, walking toward her. "But mean it, Annie. Mean every word."

She searched his sage-green eyes, bright with flecks of hidden sunlight, and knew he would give no quarter. The teasing was over. Kell was a man, not a boy. He wanted a woman who knew what she wanted too. Wanted and was willing to take as well as give.

But the ingrained moral lessons of a lifetime were not so easy to dismiss. The words stuck in her throat, leaving her mouth parched, and with a cry, Annie spun around and rushed through the door, running for all she was worth.

He had pushed. Too hard. One clenched fish rested

against the doorframe and he fought himself not to go after her.

Annie needed no light to guide her escape to her room, and once there, she wanted the darkness to shield her. In seconds she had stripped off the damaged shirtwaist, her hand shaking as she poured water into the bowl. The tepid water cooled her heated skin, but nothing would cool the thoughts and senses filled with Kell.

Behind her, the door opened. "Light the lamp, Annie. I want to see you." Kell stepped inside the room and closed the door behind him.

"I didn't hear you come up the stairs," she whispered breathlessly.

"I didn't want you to." He could almost taste the tension that surrounded them. "Light the lamp, Annie."

And she made him wait before the strike and flare of the match touching the lamp's wick pooled a golden light to reveal her. Kell's breath locked somewhere deep inside him. Her tangled hip-length hair tantalized his gaze with the wanton tumble that spilled like a fall of fire over the pristine white chemise. Annie's hand shook replacing the glass, then she looked up at him, her eyes dark blue, wide and beckoning him to discover virginal secrets. Damp patches made the thin cloth cling to the pale skin, tiny droplets of water sliding down her throat and he ached to lick every bit of moisture from her skin.

"I thought you left."

"I was going."

"And?" she prompted, unable to tear her gaze from his.

A rueful grin teased his mouth. "Much as I wanted to go, there's something here I wanted more."

With unaccustomed directness, Annie asked, "Me?"

"You. That's as honest as it gets."

She didn't doubt him. Not this time. Not with a blaze

of hunger lighting his eyes. She straightened, and with a brazen move so unlike her, slowly raised her hands to lift the mass of her hair back and away from her face. Her gaze never left his, despite the chill of cool air touching the bare flesh revealed by the scooped neckline of her chemise. She had to fight to draw breath, her body suddenly some unknown thing, blood spinning with a quickening force that left her burning.

"Christ, Annie. I was wrong. So damned wrong. It's not words I need from you. Show me, Annie. Come here and show me what you want."

Impossible! was her instant thought. Then, her own words came back to her. *"I can't run anymore. I don't want to."* Another moment's hesitation was all she allowed herself. Kell had been honest. She couldn't give him less.

Even as she took the first steps around her bed, she knew he wasn't going to make this easy for her. He wouldn't coax. Kell wouldn't seduce. He wouldn't even meet her halfway. He waited, tense and powerful, not moving at all.

Did she want him so badly she was willing to forget every moral tenet she had lived by and believed in?

Countering that was the fever that burned inside her and she knew Kell could ease the ache that left her tossing night after night. A few steps more. So simple to do. But it meant crossing from the safe world she knew into one that would leave her defenseless.

"Did I ever tell you that you walk like a woman?" At her frown he added, "All woman, Annie. Watching you arouses me like hell's on fire." His smile was pure male satisfaction when her lips curved. Kell held out his hand, making no attempt to hide the slight tremor from her. "That's a small bit of what you do to me. If I told you the rest, you'd run."

Annie stood before him, lifting her her head, her gaze direct on his. "No more running, Kell." His words had given her confidence, exposing his vulnerability to her washed a measure of her fear away. But it was his eyes, filled with a hot, bright desire for her, that made Annie revel in being the woman who aroused him.

She reached for his hand, drawing it up to her lips and slowly turned his hand until her mouth caressed his palm. She closed her eyes when he cupped her cheek, his long fingers sliding beneath her hair, curving gently around her neck to pull her closer to him.

Kell's gaze narrowed with a vicious fury when he spied the vivid bruise on her arm. "I should have killed him for touching you," he whispered, his mouth searing a kiss on the marred flesh. Her hand glided into the thickness of his hair, pressing him nearer, heated scents rising from where their bodies touched. Kell battled his need to bury himself deep, hard and fast. He discovered new pleasure in watching Annie awaken to her own sensuality.

She swayed against him, the brush of body to body sending a tremble deep inside her. "See," she murmured, scattering kisses against his hair, "I'm shaking too."

Kell caught her hair, drawing her head to the side, leaving her slender neck exposed to his lips. With exquisite care he bit her, feeling how deep the tremble went against his mouth. "No promises of forever, Annie. But the shaking goes deeper, that I can promise you. That, and," he whispered, kissing the sweet satin skin bared by the thin strap of her chemise, "I promise you won't be shaking when I'm finished with you."

Held against his powerful body, Annie felt another of the primitive caresses shiver through her. *No promises of forever.* The words replayed over and over while she tried to stop them.

As if Kell sensed what happened, he spun her around, pinning her against the door, crowding her there with his body. He took her mouth, leaving her no choice, no way to fight his skill. Suddenly she was clinging to him. Her fingers moved convulsively, digging into his biceps as she braced herself against his power.

Annie felt as if the door, the floor, the world had simply dissolved around her and all she had was Kell. She couldn't let go, on some instinctive level she knew if she did, she wouldn't get him back.

Kell knew he could release her from his fierce grip now and let her slide down his body like hot, sleek satin. He knew, but he didn't let her go. Only the kiss changed, his lips rocking softly, slowly, filling the heat of her mouth with his taste, even as he consumed hers. Her hands eased their harsh, biting grip and caressed him with the same rhythms as the kiss they shared, stroking up to cling to his shoulders, finally sliding up to hold his head. The tremors increased, and he returned caress for caress, the tips of his fingers delicately tracing the dainty shape of her ear. With near exquisite restraint his teeth sank into her bottom lip.

Annie drew back and opened her eyes to find Kell's filled with a heat that nearly took her breath away.

"No promises, no lies," she whispered, her voice husky visibly shaken.

Kell slowly let her slide back down his body, making no effort to hide the thrusting evidence of his arousal. He hid nothing from her, shuddering openly with pleasure when her hips moved over his as her feet touched the floor.

With a muffled cry Annie lifted her mouth to his, hungry to lose herself, to hold him and stop caring about tomorrows. She understood want, or thought she had. Now every claiming sweep of his tongue taught her another depth to wanting. And needing. She had never been so needy. His body against hers, hard and tight with restraint. The sleek thickness of his sun-streaked hair sliding through her fingers. The strength and power of his arms wrapping around her. And her need was to give.

To Kell. Who took everything he wanted from the sweet, sugared mouth that had been slowly driving him crazy. But it wasn't enough. Somewhere deep in his mind, he knew it would never be enough.

But he took her mouth again, then again, until all she could whisper was his name between kisses, his name a ragged litany as she clung tight to him, forgetting everything but him and a desire that burned hot and bright, only to flame higher.

She had more to give him than any other woman, any other kiss shared. Generous and loving, Annie's pleasure was his, new, increased with every heartbeat until it expanded into a timelessness he couldn't begin to question. He could only delve deeply and take more.

Annie was learning to take, too. Kell's male scent was inside her with every breath she drew. She knew he was filling her world in some elemental way, and she was reassured and frightened by its power at the same time. No logic. No sense. Kell was there, drawing her into a place where nothing lived but heat and hunger until she wanted to curl inside him and fill her senses with him. Only him.

And passion's lure that drew her deeper and deeper with every savoring caress of his mouth against hers, every slow, sweeping thrust of his tongue.

Finally Kell lifted his head, his hands framing Annie's face. He looked from her dark, wide, midnight-blue eyes to her mouth, reddened and swollen from his kisses. Generous. And so giving. Kell found himself wondering how he had ever thought he knew all there was to know about men and women and passion. Annie had needed lessons to learn how to kiss. Annie just proved an apt pupil, and surprised him with a few new lessons. He thought what other discoveries awaited them.

The narrowed blaze of Kell's eyes as he stared at her mouth made shimmers of sensation ripple down Annie's back until she pressed her legs together to keep from falling.

"Kell?" she whispered. "What's wrong? Don't you want to kiss me again?"

"Want to?" Kell couldn't control the husky groan that escaped him. He was fighting for control, for every bit of the discipline over mind and body that he had taken for granted. "Do you want me to kiss you again?"

"Do I . . ." she began, shivering and then laughing softly, almost wildly. How could she make Kell understand the feelings that were coursing through her, too new, too fierce, so that she had no names for them. This wasn't the soft, sweet sensual pull of the other times he had kissed her. There was a raw power, a force she could feel coming from him, tightening her own body.

She raised herself on tiptoe, brushing her mouth against his, over and over. "I want what you want. Everything there is for a man and a woman to share."

With a rough sound, Kell bent and took Annie's mouth, giving her his in turn. The first tentative touch of her tongue against his made his arms tighten, lifting her up against him in a searing caress. His hips moved slowly, once, twice, and he had to set her down to fight his own wild response. Kell tried to break their kiss, but the intense pleasure of sliding his tongue into Annie's sweet mouth was too much to give up.

A soft, hungry moan escaped Annie. She didn't want the kiss to end. She needed more of his taste, more of his male passion. She sought to capture him and from the deep recess of her mind Ruby's voice, sultry and laughing, came to her rescue. Very gently, her teeth closed over his tongue, a demand that he stay within her. Annie would have smiled when she felt the shudder that ripped through Kell at her caress, but his hands shifted on her body, stroking the sides of her beasts, sending a burst of pleasure through her. She had to release him, another cry leaving her filled with shock and passion that left her trembling.

The strength of her response was almost violent and she clung to his arms, crying raggedly, "I can't stand, Kell."

"Don't try. I'll hold you." Dark, rough and deep with the barely leashed passion he fought to rein, Kell caught her against him. Hard and hungry, his lips claimed hers again, his body moving to the same rhythms of penetration and retreat as he stroked the sultry heat of her mouth. His hands cupped the full lushness of her breasts, long fingers caressing and teasing her nipples until the thin cloth of the chemise couldn't hide the velvet hardness peaking for his touch. With one arm around her waist, Kell held her and used the thumb of his other hand to stroke down the length of her slender spine. Need clawed him and he tried to slow down his own wild response to her.

There was a warning whisper reminding him of her innocence, but Annie melted into him like a hot river of honey, and his own body tightened with sheer pleasure. Kell tore through the tapes holding her skirt and petticoats, pushing the cloth down.

"Hold me, Annie," he ordered, his voice rough. His hand stroked her from hips to shoulders and back again, pressing her against him as if he could absorb her into himself. Her shy but instinctive move, supple, feminine, and so damn hot, dragged another groan from him. He held her close, moving against her before he found the control he needed to sweep her up into his arms and carry her over to the bed.

"The light?"

"Leave it. I want to see you, Annie. I want to watch you change into my woman."

Her head nestled his shoulder and she held him tight, her mouth his in a meld of hunger that tore through him as he lowered her to the soft waiting feather tick.

Annie knew the sweetly coaxing lover was gone, but she had no desire to call him back. She loved Kell. Loved the wildness and hunger she called from him and unleashed within herself. This was passion, this fire that burned hotter and hotter with every touch, every kiss until she thought she would die from it. She was filled with a fevered ache that made her vulnerable, yet flushed with the first taste of a woman's power. It was her touch that made Kell groan, her kisses that sent his hungry tongue plunging deeper and deeper so she longed for another, more intimate joining to come.

And she wanted to taste him, wanted to know if the tiny, exquisite love bites that made her melt and shiver would do the same to Kell.

Her head tossed wildly back and forth with the need she had to know, but he wouldn't release her mouth. The unexpected heaviness and hardness of his body that her own instinctively cradled sent streamers of fire streaking through her. When he finally lifted his head, his breath hissed out from between his teeth. Annie raised eyelids suddenly heavy to look up at him, defenseless against the blazing passion in his eyes.

"I've never wanted another woman until I shook with need," Kell whispered, his voice rough with his own arousal. He gazed from her mouth to the fierce pulse beating in her throat down to the taut nipples pressing up against the thin white cloth of the chemise.

She turned her face and pressed a kiss to his shoulder. Her hand moved without thought to the buttons that allowed cloth to hide the skin she wanted to taste. Kell instantly leaned to the side, his smile hot, wholly male and enticing when Annie touched the first button.

In the end he had to help her, for her fingers shook. His soft, knowing laughter at her sudden impatience sent her shyness fleeing.

Kell tossed his shirt aside, turning back to take her mouth in a hard, quick kiss. Annie's murmur of protest made him reluctantly pull back, but her lips sliding against his shoulder made his breath ragged.

"Christ, Annie! You'll burn me alive."

"You don't want me to . . ." Glazed with passion, her eyes met his.

As much as Kell wanted to hear the words from her, he knew he was asking too much. "Go ahead. Kiss me, Annie. Touch me. I'd kill to have that hot, sweet mouth all over me. Anywhere, Annie," he added, seeing the shock and the sensual curiosity in her deep blue eyes. "That's how I'm going to taste you. All over. Until I taste like you and you taste like me."

And he forced himself to lie down, locking his hands behind his head to stop himself from pulling her hard against him.

This time he expected the first tentative touch of her lips. He wasn't surprised by the tiny lick of her tongue nuzzling his neck. The shock should have been there, but if Annie was even half as aroused as he was, she couldn't stop. And if he had learned anything at all about her, Annie never did anything halfway. She murmured her pleasure, kneading his chest, her fingers sliding through the wedge of soft blond hair. His breath stuck in his throat. With the same exquisite care, Annie bit him, soothing the tiny mark with a hot foray of her tongue. His fingers ached with the demand he made not to move, not to grab hold of her and shift her beneath his hard, hungry body.

The need to touch her was violent, seething through him with every damn-near-purring sound she made. The silky drag of her hair against his body made him tighten like a bow. The hard peaks of her breasts burned his chest when she found and caressed his own nipple to a tiny, aching point. Pleasure had never been such agony. He wanted the sweet, lush weight of her breasts in his hands. His teeth were almost grinding together with the need he had to taste and suckle and tease her until she cried out.

Needs. They shimmered, heated and coiled, multiplying until he couldn't bear more. But all he did was slide his right hand beneath the weight of her hair, holding her mouth against him while his left stroked her back from nape to waist, drawing her closer to the growing heat of his body.

Annie was lost in discovering the different textures and tastes of Kell's body. She wasn't aware of shifting her legs to accommodate his powerful thigh. Annie was driven by the unabated fever that consumed her. Her body rocked to the slow, thrusting rhythm of his, a new tightening taking hold of her so that she moaned with the ache of it.

Kell smiled against her hair, the primal ripple of her response to every caress telling him her whole body had now become sensitized to passion.

Rough and husky, his voice praised her, feeling the slow, seeping, sweet heat of her dampening the rigid muscle of his thigh. His hands shaped the flare of her hips, his fingers flexing deep, rewarded with a shudder that swept her until he caught fire from it.

He never knew that pleasure this intense could kill, but he wouldn't deny he was dying by inches. He bit her gently on the curve of her shoulder when she focused her attention to turning his other nipple into another hard point. Like a brushfire, he burned from every place they touched, but it wasn't enough. Nothing would be until he buried every aching bit of flesh so deep inside her he wouldn't know where he began and she ended.

With slow pressure, he eased her hips over until she cradled him and the heat of her was a new flame that made his hands shake. He waited for her retreat, had been unconsciously waiting all this while, but when Annie rubbed her cheek in approval against his chest, he slowly gathered her close, sliding her up his body, ignoring the pleasure-pain of his own need.

Slipping his tongue between her lips, he mated his mouth with hers, turning her until she lay beneath him. He trailed kisses to the dainty curve of her ear, biting the lobe, her ragged breath and the tightening of her fingers on his shoulders all he wanted from her.

"My turn, Annie," he whispered, closing his teeth delicately around one of her nipples. He could almost feel the streak of pleasure that ripped through her, arching her up against him in sexual reflex. And Kell arched his body into her, raising his head to watch her while he opened the small ribbon tie, dipping down to kiss the flesh revealed with each lace that he tugged free until she lay exposed to him.

A spattering of golden freckles lay across the pale skin of her breasts, nipples tight with hunger, a deep rose that begged attention. But Kell saw the heated flush that stained her cheeks, the instinctive move she made to cover herself before she looked up and stopped.

"More lovely than I dreamed about, Annie." He heard

the husky approval in his voice, his lips warm as he pressed a kiss to one peak then the other.

Annie gasped. Something deep inside burst into fire and she forgot that she had never let any man see her, had never thought to give herself to any man this way. There had been passion, and male approval, in Kell's eyes. She cried out again when he skimmed the curves of her bare breasts. Once more he bent to take her into his mouth, and heat pulsed through her with each sweet move of his tongue. She heard the cries and knew they were hers, just as she understood that hunger was reaching a new peak, demanding a release. She wanted to tell him, wanted to call out, but her breath was lodged in her throat.

Kell felt the change in her heartbeat, heard the ragged breaks in her breathing, and he took her more deeply into his mouth, tugging on her rhythmically, shaping her to his intimate demands until the shyness was burned away.

Passion lived in her voice calling his name, begging for an end to the coil of tension that held her.

And he knew if he didn't slow down, he would take her too fast, hot and deep, and lose the gift of seeing her come apart for him.

She twisted slowly beneath him, tiny wild sounds forcing him to stifle a groan. Like hammer blows, desire fought him for control. Blood, thick and hot, surged as he soothed and teased her breasts with the same skilled motion. He suckled harder, knowing she was too aroused to feel a lighter touch.

He had promised her pleasure. Promised that she wouldn't be shaking when this was over. Stupid promises. He was being torn apart to keep them.

"Kell, please . . ."

"I'm here, right here, Annie." He rose, tugging the strap

of the chemise off her shoulder, scattering kisses over her bare flesh.

"No one . . . told me," she cried out. "They didn't say it was like this."

"Tell me, Annie," he coaxed, stroking the restless shift of her body with one hand, clutching the quilt with the other. "Tell me what it's like for you."

Chapter Eighteen

❧

Annie's eyes opened slowly and she looked at Kell. Passion had flushed the high curves of his cheeks. His eyes were a dark, near black-green, glittering and hot watching her.

"Tell me," he whispered, still and waiting.

"Like a storm." She licked her lip, his gaze so intense it demanded nothing but honesty from her. "Wild thunder and heat lightning. All hot promise without relief."

"Then we'll make it rain, Annie. A hot, silky rain that will end the storm."

"Yes. Now." The words and demand were hers. And she knew, even before he dipped to kiss her that it wouldn't be now. So she poured her longing, her need into a kiss that he broke with a muttered curse.

"I don't want to hurt you. And I want to sweep over you like that storm taking—"

"Kell," she whispered, her fingertips silencing him. "I'm twenty-eight years old. 'Spinster' is such an ugly name and so is 'old maid.' How much longer must I wait to know what it feels like to make love to a man?" Her fingers trailed down his chin, one barely touching the pulse in the hollow of his throat before both hands caressed the damp pelt of hair wedging his chest.

She rimmed the pebble-hard nipple, a slight smile of feminine satisfaction curving her lips when his breath broke and he muttered a few choice swears. Annie lifted one of his hands and drew it down to the curve of her belly. "I hurt, Kell. Here. Deep inside. And I trust you," she added softly, holding his gaze with her own. "You could never hurt me. I know that. You're a man, not a boy. You would never use your strength against me. You never have."

Her trust was a gift more brilliant than the passion that flared between them. Every word carried her truth, it was in her eyes, and it snapped the leash on the savage need that clawed at him.

Kell came off the bed in a rush, kicking off his boots. Annie rolled to her side watching him, her long hair shielding her breasts. White cotton drawers covered the sleek curves of her legs, but he saw the restless, telltale signs and found his hands shaking with the need to stroke her thighs, to tangle his fingers in the fire-gold hair at the apex of her legs, learning the heat and hunger of her.

He tried to slow down, remembering all too well Annie's threat to expire in this room the first time he held her beneath him. But Annie wasn't expiring. She watched him with half-closed eyes, her fingers curled tight around the quilt. Kell slid the first button free. Her gaze burned a path over his body until he couldn't hide the shudder of pleasure that rippled over him.

"You're so beautiful, Kell."

"Not me. You."

"Would it shock you to know that I dreamed about you?"

The second button bounced to the floor. Annie's eyes drifted closed and she curled her legs tighter. "Every time you touched me, each time I saw you, I dreamed. And you're wrong, Kell. You're all male power like a lightning storm."

Kell ripped the remaining buttons free and kicked off his pants. He fought to use every calming ritual that Li had taught him as every word and sigh shredded whatever rational thoughts he had left.

"I promised I wouldn't hurt you, Annie," he whispered, one knee on the bed.

"I'm not afraid. I want you too much." And she prayed he wouldn't know what it cost her to fight the first stirring of fear as he gathered her close to his hot, hard body.

"Kell, I don't want to wait anymore to know."

"That's all I've been waiting to hear." He bent and brushed his lips over hers, the curve of her chin, the hollow of her throat, drawn to nuzzle aside the tangled curls of her hair and find the taut dusky-rose tips of her breasts. Soft, wild cries came from her, cries that fed him as he smoothed the thin cotton drawers from her, his hands as gentle as he could order them. His hand bunched the damp cloth between his fingers, pulling it away from the hot secrets he longed to claim for his own.

When Annie felt the last protection she had slide down her legs and the heat and hardness of Kell's thigh rubbing against her, fear reared once more. There would be no turning back. She loved him, but not once had those words escaped his lips. No promises. Her legs clamped together, trembling as need and fear waged war for dominance.

"Teasing me, Annie?"

"No. I—"

"It's all right. I like the way you tease."

"But I'm not, Kell." His hand stroking down her leg, only to return to shape the dip of her waist and flare of her hip both calmed and aroused her.

"Annie, love," he noted softly, passion and laughter in his voice, "one of us is sure as hell being teased. Give me your mouth. I need to be inside you. *Now, Annie.*"

She gave him her mouth, just as the unconscious, graceful shift of her hips gave her body to his caressing hands. With every shudder that racked Kell's body, Annie felt an answering one deep inside her. She clung to him, moving with him, her breath shortened when he stroked the warmth of her inner thigh. His voice was rough, husky with arousal, coaxing her.

His hand curled around her, holding her intimately, and drew a startled gasp of pleasure from her. His murmuring sounds of approval, the heated love bites he soothed with the heat of his tongue before he claimed her mouth again and eased his long fingers between her legs, brought a broken cry from her.

Annie tried to catch her breath, it broke, caught and broke yet again as Kell gently traced her layered softness, praising the damp heat that had her burrow against him. He teased her until her hands moved restlessly over him, fingers combing the silky wedge of male hair that covered his chest. Her short fingernails scraped over hard male nipples. His groan sent her hands searching lower, needing to know that he was as caught as she by the passion's web that was both pleasure and pain.

Her hands shaped power; hard, damp, male skin.

Kell moved gently, rocking against flesh that melted against him. The heat of her response, her broken cries, had him kissing her again. He drank her throaty sounds of passion that called to him in a siren song older than time.

Annie felt the hot, gliding penetration of Kell's tongue and his finger at the same time. Shimmering heat seemed to gather itself inside her. She tossed her head from side to side, breaking their kiss, defenseless to stop the sudden shudder that claimed her body.

"Kell," she cried, feeling the strange, tiny convulsions building again. "I—"

The word was lost as another tremor, then another shook her body as he deepened the twin caresses, pleasuring and exploring her with slow movements until all thought of shyness fled in the grip of enthralling passion. He skimmed the edges of her softness, probing sweetly, discovering the aching nub hidden between sleek, silken folds, rubbing slowly, hotly, stealing her breath, her thoughts.

Annie twisted against him, straining to know more of the desire she felt, but it wasn't enough, it was driving her mad. Kell was driving her into a world she had never known, never dreamed of, gently stealing into her, retreating, only to return and send shimmering lightning through her.

Ignoring the violence of his own unsatisfied need was nearly impossible. Watching Annie come apart was the only pleasure he allowed himself. Every breath he took was scented with her fragrance, warmed by the heat of her body, a body that made him burn. He'd never been driven to claim and possess every cry he could call from her, to increase the intensity of her body's response to the hot, intimate caress of his hand.

The tight rosebud begged for his mouth and Kell bent his head to her. Patience stretched thin, he tasted her, making her shudder repeatedly with each soft stab of his tongue, each gently restrained caress of his teeth. This was for Annie, he understood that now, for he could never give this gift again to her. Her fervent pleas incited him to tease her, urging her deeper and deeper, drawing the tension tighter and tighter as his thumb slid over the sleek, hard nub of desire he called from her heated softness.

She rewarded him with the litany of his name that broke repeatedly, the frantic moves of her hands drawing him closer until the tiny convulsions began, and she melted for him like a hot, sweet rain that scored every nerve in his body.

Nearly stripped of his control, Kell gathered her tight, fighting himself, wanting the pleasure never to end, needing it to, just so he could begin again.

Defenseless against the storm shaking her, Annie held on to his sweat-sheened body, the only solid presence in a world that shimmered with too many sensations to understand. She heard the sounds that rippled from her, husky with passion, and curled against Kell as he stroked her trembling body with hands that shook, kissing her until she drew even breaths.

She wanted to see him, and her lashes stirred and finally with effort lifted, revealing eyes near black with desire. She almost lost her breath watching him. His cheeks were stained with heat, the wicked curve of his lips drew her own to press a kiss there, and his eyes, when he slowly opened them to look down at her, held sin and heaven within them.

The caress of his hand shaping her back soothed her and yet started the tension to coil again. "Kell," she whispered, licking her lips from a too dry mouth, "words aren't any good, are they?"

"Pleasure, Annie. That's all I can say. Watching you fills me with pleasure. Touching you is pleasure."

"And me?" she asked, cupping his cheek. "Does my touching you bring you pleasure too?"

"Annie, if it gets any better, I'll do the expirin'."

Her lips curved with feminine satisfaction, and Kell stole the smile with his lips, taking the generous giving of her mouth and giving back a sexual excitement that made her cry out when he lifted his head.

"I taste like you," she murmured, closing her eyes as a shimmering wave crested inside her and the tremors began again. "But no one really dies from this."

"I'm coming close, my love." Kell settled her beneath him, smiling when she instinctively cradled his violently aroused flesh. "Annie. Annie look at me," he demanded softly, huskily, taking both her hands in his and nestling them on either side of her head. "There's a little death, Annie. One that's born in fire." He rocked his body against hers, dipping his head to take her mouth, leaving her whimpering when his lips trailed down the arched slender line of her throat and took one taut peak in his mouth. He shaped her with the changing pressure of teeth and tongue, loving her responsive flesh, groaning with the clenching of her thighs, the sudden arching of her back, and tremors racked her body once more.

It cost him to let her accommodate the heavy weight of his body on her smaller, infinitely softer one. And Kell lavished praise and attention to her other breast, wondering if he had lied to her.

She was so hot, wet and silky against him, that he thought he would die if he didn't sheathe himself inside the incredible heat he called from her.

Knowing there would be pain, he shifted to his side, sweeping his hand over the restless move of her legs, caressing the swollen, sultry flesh that had known only his touch. He groaned when she did, burning only to find himself needing to know how hot the fire could get, how high the flames would be.

Caught in a wildfire that consumed her body, Annie heard his savage voice coaxing her from far away. A little death, he had said, born in fire. No one really died from pleasure this intense. Instinctively she moved her hips, slowly rocking as Kell settled himself over her. She wanted to get closer to the male flesh that tantalized her. Annie opened her eyes.

His were closed and his features revealed both intense pleasure and pain. Without thought, she brought his hand to her mouth, curling her fingers so that his palm was exposed. She circled the tip of her tongue in the center, then gently closed her teeth over the fleshy pad below his thumb.

Kell surged against her with a long, torn groan, his eyes meeting hers. "Annie. Don't move. Don't do anything. I don't want to hurt you."

"You did that to me and made me feel it deep, deep inside me. That's how I want you, Kell. Deep. Inside me."

He was nearly undone by her trust, total and as honest as it could be, that took him to the edge. He shook with emotions that he couldn't ever remember feeling, emotions he couldn't even name. All he knew was that they were more devastating than the desire between them.

He watched her for signs of fear, settling himself deeper, sensitive to the pain that he couldn't help. But Annie, closing her eyes, came apart with a long, shivering acceptance at the first gentle probing he made.

"Pleasure, Annie. Me loving you."

"Loving . . ." Her voice broke. *You, Kell. I love you.* But the words went no further than her mind as he claimed her mouth, as his body made its first claim on hers. Fever spread and she wanted the scent and heat of him filling her until all she knew was Kell.

"Sweet. Hot. Perfect," he whispered, trailing his lips to her ear, gently biting the lobe. He shuddered as his flesh nudged against Annie's moist, vulnerable core. He ached to taste her, to know every bit of her with a shivering intimacy that he never thought about sharing with another woman. But now, it was too much to ask of her, too damn much to ask of himself.

As it was, he teased them both, the hungry, hot length of him rubbing over her, stopping at the edge of fully taking her. He barely penetrated her, making her wild, and himself as well for more. Her ragged cry, both demand and plea, shot through him. Her hands gripped the hard muscles of his arms, sliding down to capture his hips, and Kell jerked reflexively, sliding a bit more deeply into her, stopping just short of the instant he would claim her as his woman.

Annie twisted wildly beneath him, her body too hot, a mist of passion covering them both that intensified the sensitivity of skin rubbing against skin. With a near growl he took her mouth again, pinning her still, letting the shaking wildness wash over them.

With a cry he wrenched his head up. "Annie, don't fight me. I want to go slow. *I don't want to hurt you.* Later," he promised, his voice thick and gritty, "later I'll take you hot and fast, and so deep you won't be able to tell where you begin and I end. But not now. Now I want to—"

The words sliced through Annie. She struggled to look at him. "No. Slow is hurting, Kell. I want what you want. Everything. Nothing held back." She arched helplessly into him, felt him going deeper and shivered as his heat became a part of her. She knew he trembled with the effort to control himself. She couldn't whisper a sound as fire raced through her.

The flames went deeper, tearing aside the veil of innocence, tearing free a wild, sweet cry. Kell took her gift, and gave her himself, all restraint gone, filling her and finding that his pleasure wasn't sated. Hunger couldn't be leashed. He caught her hips with one arm and arched heavily into her again and again, trying to bury himself in her so deeply that the pleasure exploding through him would never stop.

If there was pain, Annie didn't feel it. Piercing emotion filled her as Kell became a part of her. She loved him, loved him as she had never loved another man. The dying came with a savage burning that was another pleasure in itself. Hearing her name torn from him time and again brought her to ecstasy that stripped everything away but Kell and the deep, endless wildness that destroyed and created. Hot. Untamed. Sweetly violent as the cries that echoed the pulses of his release.

In the shivering aftermath, there were no sounds but that of broken, gradually slowing breathing. Annie held Kell tight, shaking still, but when he finally stirred and scattered kisses over her face, then moved as if to roll aside, she refused to let him go.

"I'm too heavy for you," he murmured.

"Please, just stay, Kell."

He wanted nothing more than to drown in the silken heat surrounding him, but there was a deeper, underlying plea in her voice that brought his head up.

"Annie, love, look at me."

She fought the demand of his words, just as she fought off her mind's attempt to make her realize the enormity of what she had done. Kell was her lover. But he didn't love her. He had given and taken pleasure and now he would leave her.

"Annie, don't hide from me." This time he wouldn't let her hold him; he rolled to his side and slid one arm beneath her, drawing her close to his body. Pressing a kiss to the reddened curve of her mouth, he smoothed back the damp tendrils of hair from her cheek and used one finger to tilt her chin up. "Are you ashamed? Full of guilt and sin? Ready to have the fire and brimstone pour down from heaven?"

The words weren't meant to hurt her. She knew that, knew it as surely as she knew she was empty without him. "No hell. And the only fire," she whispered, turning her face to his hand with a sigh, "is what you bring to me making me come alive, Kell."

Annie knew the cost of her admission, and she paid for it with a return to the reality she wished would never return. And she suddenly knew how to stop it. Her eyes opened to find him watching her with a blazing intensity that started a coil of tension escalating with every halting breath she drew.

"Kell, you promised you'd take me hot and deep and fast. Later, you said. Don't you want me like that now?"

"Christ! What the hell did those doves teach you?"

"Not them. You, Kell. You just taught me about dying and being reborn in fire. Does it happen again? Will you show me?"

Her eyes, luminous with newly awakened sensuality, beckoned him with a dark passion. The subtle shift of her silken body sent shafts of fresh desire lancing through him. And for the first time, Kell admitted he felt helpless. He couldn't leash the sudden rise of hunger prowling his body. An elemental hunger that burned through his control. He thought he knew every woman's game there was, but Annie wrote new rules. Sweet, heated murmurs of approval were whispered over his skin with every stroke, each lovingly tendered caress she offered him. His name was a plea and feminine demand that he couldn't fight, couldn't resist.

But he tried, sensing that if he didn't, he was going to make her so deep a part of himself he wouldn't let her go.

"Where's all that starch and vinegar, Annie?"

"Scorched." Her teeth scraped his pebbled hard nipple and wrung a groan from him.

Kell caught her hair with one hand, gentle, but still forcing her head back. "What the hell are you trying to do to me?"

"Seduce you. Make you keep your promise, Kell." Annie closed her eyes, unable to bear the intensity of his. She had given him all she had of herself, and now added a last bit of honesty. Softly then, she said, "I had an education of sorts from the doves, that's true. But all their words did was lessen the fear of the unknown. Women, at least the ladies I know, do not talk about what goes on beyond bedroom doors. And I wanted to know how to please you, Kell. Even if I can't bring myself to call . . . what we . . . what you and I—" Annie burrowed against him, unable to continue.

"Tell me, Annie. You've got to know there's nothing you could say that would shock me. I've heard it all. And no one," he said, kissing her hair as he drew her even closer and rocked his body against hers, "could ever tell you about what we shared. Not even me, Annie."

He stroked her back, cupping her buttocks and pressing her against him, unable to stop the need he had for her. She was damp, silken heat welcoming him with a long, shivering sigh that echoed the tremor of her body.

"Tell me, darlin'," he coaxed, holding himself still while the tiny convulsions began for her.

"Loving," Annie whispered long moments later, her voice muffled against his chest. And she told him between lingering kisses, all the names she had learned, until Kell had to bury his laughter as she crossly added, "Honestly, Kell, sliding carrots up the board, pickling, and having hot pudding for supper only make me wonder how anyone manages to get to bed. Everything they called this had to do with the kitchen."

He thought about answering her truthfully, and settled for a compromise that wouldn't shock her out of his arms. "You're suppose to think about hot and steamy and . . . Annie, love, give me your too shy little tongue."

When the kiss ended, Annie laced her fingers through the long, thick length of his hair and held his head still above her. "I want you to know that you have most admirably made your point. I'm hot and steamed like a Christmas pudding."

"Hold that thought," he whispered, setting her aside and rising from the bed. Within moments he was back with a damp cloth.

Mortified when she surmised his intent, Annie tried to scramble to the other side of the bed. Kell had a charming way of enticing her back. And when he had finished his tender ministrations to sore flesh, thoroughly arousing her in the process, he tossed the cloth aside.

"There's more, Annie. And someday you'll do the same for me. Now," he whispered, ignoring her flush of embarrassment, "we were discussing the kitchen. You taste like honey to me."

He savored her generous mouth as he rolled to his back and lifted her above him. He wanted Annie in a way that had nothing to do with the desire that was a savage, unsated pleasure inside him. He wanted her laughter, her prim and proper ways that drove him both crazy and to inspiring lengths to dispell. He needed her trust, and every bit of generously given pleasure she offered to him. And only to him.

"Sweet. Golden honey. And I want to see how hot it gets, Annie. Melt for me again." He licked her lips, then raised her up so he could claim sweeter flesh. He ignored her shocked cry and decided he had been a very patient lover. He wasn't being selfish. He simply couldn't stop the craving he had to share with Annie what he never wanted with another woman.

He was at his best tumbling every objection she voiced, and when the shocked little murmurs had turned to the infinitely sweet, heated sounds of a contented lover, Kell knew he had been right to demand this intimacy from her.

When she lay spent and boneless beneath him again, Kell thought there was heaven to be had in her arms. He couldn't lavish enough praise on her. Then Annie offered him a last surprise.

She curled tight against him like a sleepy kitten, just about purring as she asked, "Still think eating green fruit will give you an Irish toothache?"

"Annie!"

"Well, do you think I can't cure your Irish toothache?"

"Cure it?" he whispered, bending to her smiling lips. "Oh, my darlin', darlin' Annie, I think you just killed it."

Chapter Nineteen

❧

It was Dewberry's cold nose nudging her cheek that woke Annie. She smiled and gathered the heavy cat's body close.

"I am a corrupt, fallen woman, cat," she sleepily murmured and closed her eyes to the sunlight that seemed to bounce off the virginal white surfaces of her room. Stroking Dewberry, she nestled her cheek against the pillow that still held the enticing male scent of Kell. The slight move of her body brought an instant awareness of the sensual aches that allowed her to call herself a woman this morning.

"Love is wonderful, Dewberry." His soft purr only made her smile as she remembered Kell leaving her before dawn, her lips still carrying the lingering kiss he pressed there.

Caught between the half-world of dreams and waking, Annie fought off her mind's determination to remind her of the import of what she had done. The cat stretched his neck, a plaintive meow telling her he wanted scratching.

Annie obliged him and whispered, "Kellian is my lover." The cat's louder rumble made her laugh as he wiggled over on his back, offering her his stomach to scratch. "You old softie. You're every bit as demanding for attention as he is."

Her smile deepened when she remembered every lover's praise that Kell had whispered through the night. She wanted to shout out her love for him. But it was a secret only the cat could share now.

Annie's hand stilled and she ignored Dewberry's batting paws that took exception. Kell did not want to hear about love. He had no intent of making any promises of forever.

He hadn't made many promises last night. Only those about their lovemaking. He had kept every one of them, too, she reminded herself, wincing when she tried to stretch and bury herself deeper beneath the quilt.

Dewberry rolled over, climbing up on her chest, nuzzling her chin. Annie absently petted him, waiting for feelings of sin and guilt to surface. She had known the temptation Kell offered from the first, even admitted he was a test of her moral fiber and beliefs, one she had failed. But there was a happiness inside her that refused to allow guilt or feelings of sin to rise. She was a soiled dove, truly fallen from grace. But she didn't feel wanton, there wasn't any shame for what she had done. Kell had teased her about it, only to encourage her to show him how bold and brazen she could be. The memory stilled her hand and sent a flush of heat covering her body.

With a gentle nudge, Annie pushed Dewberry back on the bed and struggled to sit up. Kell had said something about saints and sinners. Frowning, she stared at the cat, who watched her with unblinking eyes.

"He was afraid, Dewberry, that I would turn him into a saint." Gently catching hold of his ears in each hand, she rubbed them, to his delight, her soft laughter spilling into the sunlit room. "I couldn't get angry with him. If you had seen his wicked grin and the blaze of passion in his eyes—well, it wouldn't have been right for you to see it—but I can tell you, cat, that Kell was very vocal and quite creative in expressing his pleasure that I'm as much of a sinner as he is."

The cat's purrs deepened to a steady rumble. He stretched out his body, paws and back legs extended as if he were getting settled for a long chat.

Annie watched him, thinking he was the only one she could confide in. Perhaps if the world would never intrude, she might have time to cope with this change between Kell and herself. Change? "Oh, Dewberry, what do I call us?" Then, crossly, "I should have expected you would close your eyes and wash your paws of the matter. You're no help, cat."

What would Kell expect from her now? No demands, of that much she was sure.

A light rap at her door, broken then repeated, warned her that Fawn had been sent to fetch her. Realizing how late it was, Annie called out that she would be down directly. She couldn't invite Fawn into her room, she wasn't ready to face anyone yet.

"Time is what I need to sort this out, Dewberry. And time is what I haven't got." With a great deal of care, she moved to the edge of the bed and swung her legs down. "Oh, good Lord, I forgot about the sermon for this morning!"

It was her belief that she could do anything once she set her mind to it that helped Annie stand up. But even her own belief couldn't make her move quickly. A new respect for the marriage state of every women she knew added a great deal of strength. How could they go about their daily chores with legs that still trembled and desire still brimming so that their insides felt like a fire burned?

"But then," she whispered, "how many do I know that even hinted of finding the pleasure I knew with Kell?"

Concern for any telltale signs that she had left her spinster state behind sent Annie to the mirror for a minute inspection.

"Dewberry, do you think anyone will notice this overbright glow in my eyes? Maybe if they ask I could say that I feel a cold coming on? After all, Emmaline was sick. I could have caught something from her." Her fingertips traced the still swollen, reddened shape of her mouth. Instead of concern, all Annie could feel was the heated imprint of Kell's lips on hers, his taste as much a part of her that desire blazed to life to have him near, kissing her senseless once more.

"Your mistress is a shameless hussy, cat. And that is all she can say about herself." Annie couldn't help but shoot the rumbling ball of fur a look of denunciation. "You don't have to be so agreeable."

Gathering up clothing, Annie chose a high-necked pale-blue shirtwaist, satisfied that it would cover the two small marks that proved what a demanding lover Kell was. She didn't have time to linger, but she wanted to touch them, wanted to remember the passion that had exploded between them and left its mark on her. Not only these visible ones, but those inside as well.

She didn't attempt her corset, hearing the opening and closing of the door below and the greetings that followed. She hurried to tie the tapes of freshly starched petticoats and slipped into her dark blue skirt. With the last pin holding her hair in a loose topknot in place, Annie grabbed up the discarded clothing littering the floor and heaped it on the chair.

The thought of seeing Kell had her brimming with excitement and a little fear. Somehow she would find a way to deal with the man's refusal to make a commitment. He had to feel something more than desire, there had been tenderness between them.

It was only when she went to scoop up Dewberry that she spied the stain on the quilt. Her eagerness to see Kell all but disappeared. Her hand faltered on the cat, who licked her fingers in the hopes of more petting.

"What have I done, Dewberry?"

Her hand moved of its own volition to her waist. What if she had conceived a child last night? Shaking, Annie felt a cold sweat break over her. She had never thought to ask the doves how to protect herself.

The thumping of Aunt Hortense's cane warned her she could not linger a moment longer. She lifted a protesting cat and settled him in the crook of one arm, flipping over the edge of the quilt to cover the stain with her free hand.

Somehow she had to find a way to talk to Kell about this. She refused to let the worry already gnawing at her be her responsibility alone.

All thoughts of being a freethinking, independent woman fled her mind, just as Annie fled her room. What would she do if he refused to marry her? But how could she think of marriage to a man who opposed everything she believed in?

Halfway down the stairs, Annie realized that the small crowd gathered below had fallen silent when they saw her. She set the cat down, and he, coward that he was, ran across the lobby and disappeared through the dining room.

"Annie," Lucinda demanded, coming to stand at the foot of the stairs, "you must do something about those women."

"That's right," several others chorused. "Make them leave."

Bewildered, Annie looked from one to the other, her gaze searching every face turned toward her. Abigail's pursed lips, Velma's frown, Ruth McQuary's impotent fury, all brought a groan of despair from her.

"A moment, ladies," she pleaded, forcing herself down the stairs. But as she took the last step, they converged on her, all talking at once.

Pressing her fingers to aching temples, Annie heard the shrill rise of their voices, and that of the others closing in on her.

"Quiet!" she yelled, as startled by her shout as the women, who obeyed instantly. "One, and only one, of you tell me what has happened now."

Glances were exchanged, and while Annie had expected Lucinda or Abigail to come forth, it was Ruth who spoke to her. Annie couldn't meet Ruth's eyes that reminded her of apple seeds. The dark, small eyes set in a face that was near to the same slightly yellowed shade as apple flesh held a warning gleam. With her feathered and flower-laced hat bobbing up and down so that Annie reared back to avoid having her eyes poked, Ruth began.

"I was the first to arrive this morning. Your parlor is full of those awful women. We want them gone, Annie. We agree that we will not worship in the same room with those shameful creatures."

As if to underscore her announcement, chords were struck on the piano, all bass and sounding like a death knell. Annie shot a look at the closed parlor doors, knowing that Pockets must be in there, for a sweeter tune now seeped into the lobby.

"This is all your fault, Annie. You made those women welcome in your home. How could you think to do this to us?" Velma stated, satisfied with the instant agreement that arose.

Keeping her voice low, both to aid her pounding head and to keep the doves from overhearing her, Annie said, "Last week I spoke to you about showing these women a better way. You have done nothing to contribute to my effort. You condemn them without knowing them, without making any attempt to know them. How can you claim to come to worship the Lord here, or anywhere, when there isn't a Christian soul among you?"

"Annie! We are your friends," Lucinda exclaimed.

"Then support me," Annie countered.

"You haven't seen them. They are a disgrace to every decent woman here. Dressed in their devil's gowns!" Ruth shouted. "Go on and look for yourself, Annie Muldoon. Go see and then come out here and tell us that we shouldn't be affronted by them."

"They are painted, Annie," someone shouted behind her as she slowly made her way to the parlor doors.

"Either they leave or we do," Abner Duffner announced, meeting the look Annie shot over her shoulder at him with a warning glare.

Herman Lockwood, thin and balding, spoke up. "Annie, we care a great deal about you. Especially in the light of you having no menfolk to look after you. Listen to my wife, listen to our good ladies. You don't know the tales I've heard about that man. They aren't fitting for a lady's ears, so I won't be repeating them, but I heard them from someone who would know."

Backed against the doors, holding tight to the handles as she faced them, Annie noted the disappointment on a few faces when Herman stopped. The words she could have easily spoken yesterday stuck in her throat. She was afraid to defend Kell, afraid of what she would reveal about her own feelings. And they were confused at best right now.

The only thing she was clear about was the anger that flared inside her for the small-minded judgments these people were making.

"I can't force any of you to stay. I can't say I'll order these women to leave, either. Each of you has a choice to make, but if you leave me now, don't bother coming back. I told you why I rented the rooms to them. You all shared my dream of building a real church here with a minister of our own to hold services. If you can lose sight of that, we have nothing more to say to each other."

Ruth sobbed above the shocked silence and turned to her husband's arms. Annie opened one of the parlor doors slightly. A quick peek inside showed her the doves sitting in the front row, all but Laine, arrayed in their finery. She had to squeeze her eyes closed against the new onslaught of pain as the pounding in her temples increased. It was indeed an array of garish finery, all bright, clashing colors.

But she was unwilling to expose the doves to more of the unwarranted hostility of her neighbors. Annie inched the door just wide enough for her to slip inside. She had almost made good her escape when the front doors banged open.

Backlit by the sun, a furious Kellian York filled the doorway, Bronc right behind him. He stood there for a few long minutes, his gaze pinning each and every one in place. Annie could see only his face, and it was shadowed by his hat brim. But with the new sensitivity the long night past had given to her, she had a sickening feeling that his appearance boded ill for her.

When Kell finally moved, he looked at no one, spoke not a word, but strode through the path made for him straight to Annie.

"You can't deny it any longer. Someone is sabotaging my every effort to rebuild. What's more, you know who it is."

"No."

"Bronc, don't let anyone leave. I want them all to see this."

Annie couldn't tear her gaze from him. He was wearing the linen shirt she had mended, the same one he had had on the night of the fire. Despite the fury coming off him in waves, despite the fact that they weren't alone, she couldn't control the shiver of sensual awareness in her lover's presence.

She didn't even notice what he was carrying until he set it down in front of her with a bang. She looked from his booted foot on the top of a small keg up to his eyes.

"Do you know what the hell happened last night?"

"Kell?" Annie swallowed, unable to force another sound, much less a word, past her lips. The eyes that met hers were not heated with a lover's passion. They weren't even warm. His gaze was the same winter sage green that had chilled her the first time he had broken into her room. She wanted to cringe and hide from every avid gaze that targeted them. How *could* he ask her such a question?

How *dare* he ask her such a question? Anger surged and took over the bewilderment she felt, for this was not the greeting she had expected from him. She rather ruthlessly disposed of the hurt his words caused. Courage might be in short supply, but any woman could dig deep enough and find enough to cope with a man.

"I have no idea what you are asking, Mr. York."

Kell thumbed back his hat. "Don't you, Muldoon?"

Courage, Annie. Don't give him the satisfaction of seeing how much that hurt. Most especially in front of witnesses.

"I asked," he repeated with exaggerated patience, "if you knew what happened last night, Muldoon?"

"I answered you. No. I don't know what happened. No, I don't care what happened." Leaning closer, Annie whispered, "Muldoon? You dare to call me that now?" She was too furious to care who knew it.

"I'll call you that and more. This nail keg is one of four that have been filled with glue. Useless to me. And not only were my nails ruined, but a stack of lumber was soaked with kerosene. Figured to have more than one fire going at a time, *Muldoon?*"

"You crude, immoral, arrogant . . . arrogant *man!*"

Annie was shouting in his face. She didn't realize that she'd gotten as close as she could until the door hit her rump and only Kell's arms stopped her from falling.

"Annie Charlotte! I've heard enough," Hortense announced, pushing through the door. "I've sat inside and heard yelling. Now, I hear you raving about gales and flues. What is happening?"

"Not gales. Mr. York's *nails* have been glued," she answered, shoving free of Kell's hold and brushing off her skirt. Annie stepped to the side to allow her aunt room, only to raise her eyes to the ceiling when the doves and Pockets, even Fawn, crowded behind her.

"I remember Velma's boy came to clean the flues in the spring. The oldest—"

"York? Mr. York? How can you call me that?" Kell demanded of Annie, yelling to be heard over Hortense's rising voice.

"And my boy did a fine job," Velma said in defense of her son.

"What makes you think any of us did this damage to your nails?" Abner asked Kell.

"I'll call you Mr. York if you can call me Muldoon!"

"Yeah?"

Nose to nose with Kell, Annie threw up her hands. "Yes! And what's more, if you don't like it, I won't even speak to you."

Annie spun on her heels to make a grand exit; unfortunately there was no room to move. Kell's grip on her arm sent her gaze down to his hand, while her chest heaved with indignation. "Take your hand off me!"

"You didn't seem to mind them all over—Christ, Annie, I didn't mean—"

She slapped him. Kell didn't know who was more surprised, him or Annie. The rest he ignored. His grip on her arm tightened.

"Aunt Hortense," he began.

"Aunt? Since when did you give him permission to call you—"

"Since he asked," Hortense answered, using her cane to make room. "I do believe the front parlor would serve us better for a little talk. The rest of you may go. There will be no service this morning. There may never be another one held within these walls."

Annie gaped at her aunt. She was smiling at that bounder. Smiling at him! Taking the arm he offered to escort her into the front parlor while she stood there.

Fine. Let Aunt Hortense deal with him. And let Kellian York scream himself hoarse trying to explain everything to her. She had had enough!

Her escape lasted for two short steps before Kell's grip on her arm brought her up short. With a quick, twisting turn, he had her at his side.

"Come along, Annie Charlotte. Aunt Hortense wishes to talk to us."

Wishing she could faint, for if ever a woman had good cause Annie thought she did, she nevertheless went along with him. It wasn't until they were inside and he had locked the door that he released her.

Annie made a great deal of rubbing her arm and finding the chair furthest from the settee where Kell settled himself.

"I really don't care to hear anything he has to say."

"That's enough, girl."

"Listen to your elders, Annie—"

"And that's quite enough out of you, young man. You've a bit to answer for and don't think I'll forget about it."

"Before we begin," Kell said, his gaze coming to rest on Annie, "I would like to apologize for offending you. I was angry—"

"You are furious," Annie cut in.

"Right you are. I'm furious that someone ruined the wood and the nails to slow down the building. You've got to have some of idea who it was."

"I told you before, I don't. You keep insisting that one of those women here this morning would do it and I refuse to believe that."

"Annie, I didn't put glue in the nail kegs. It's real. I didn't spill kerosene on the wood. I'm only thankful that if someone came along and stopped it from being set on fire, I found out before that wood was used."

"These are serious attempts to stop you, then?" Hortense asked from her chair at Kell's side.

"Serious enough to put someone's life at risk. If one of the carpenters smoked while he worked near the wood—"

"Yes," Hortense said, interrupting him. "There is no need to explain further." She turned to her niece. "I know you wouldn't protect someone at the risk of anyone's life."

"No, Aunt, I wouldn't."

Hortense looked at Kell. "Why don't you tell me everything that has happened since the night of the fire? But

I caution you to remember my health and my age, young man. No need to swear."

Somewhat mollified by his apology, Annie sat and listened as Kell told her aunt everything that he knew, from the wagon of whiskey being diverted and its return to other small incidents that Annie had not known about. When he told about the runway horse that nearly took the child's life and what he found, Annie couldn't keep quiet.

"A needle was stuck in the harness?" she cried.

"That's right, Annie. There were four or five women near the dress shop that day. They were close enough to—"

"No! I refuse to believe this. Aunt Hortense, tell him. He doesn't know our friends. Not one of those women would do such a thing."

"Annie," Kell said before Hortense could answer, "I take no pleasure in telling you this. But you keep denying what's true. One of the *good ladies* of this town is trying to get ride of me."

"Annie, dear, listen to him. Would a man have stolen your cap and left it near the fire? Would a man have need to disguise himself to get rid of the whiskey?"

"Well, if it was Abner or Alan McQuary or even Herman—"

"No, dearest. You're wrong. I'm afraid that I agree with Kellian. What I don't understand is why any woman would go to such lengths to prevent you from rebuilding. Not that I approve of the way you intend to earn your living," she said to Kell, banging her cane on the floor for emphasis.

"Mr. York doesn't need or want your approval, Aunt. He doesn't think what he does is sinful."

Kell felt the grate of Annie's prissed-up voice on each of his nerve endings. Last night she had been all sweet, soft whisperings, and this morning she made a return to Miss Starch and Vinegar. Scorched, indeed. He liked being audacious and wicked. Annie could take her Miss Morals and high ideals with all her proper sterling qualities and . . . and bring them back to his bed anytime. Kell jerked himself upright, blinking and rubbing his hand over his face. He cleared his throat, scowling at the thoughts that filled his head. It was the redheaded petunia's fault.

He combed back his collar-length hair, shooting a resentful glare at Annie. She had him running scared. The fire that left his inheritance a smoldering ruin was a match-size blaze compared to the desire he felt for her. And he the fool who had to prove she couldn't tame wildness and stop his pleasure. No, he had to teach her about finding pleasure and free the wild, sweet body and every bit of passion that she hid beneath layers of clothing.

"I must say that your sober contemplation is heartening. Dare I believe there is hope you are reflecting on a change of your stubborn insistence to rebuild that den of iniquity?"

"No, Annie Muldoon, you most certainly may not. My brother wanted me to have the Silken Aces, and have it I will in spite of every damn—your pardon, Aunt Hortense—obstacle in my way."

"Young man, you know it is wrong to earn money from selling the flesh of others. We fought a war—"

"I've never taken a half-dime from the doves. But no one can expect me to kick them out."

"It's true, Aunt." Annie didn't know who was more surprised; her aunt, Kell, or herself.

"Thank you for your support," Kell said, unable to stop the hard, mocking edge in his voice. "If you can believe that, then why don't you believe that one of those women is capable of attempted murder?"

Annie bit her bottom lip, shaking her head. She sent a pleading look toward her aunt, but she was watching Kell. "It would destroy me to believe it," she answered finally with innate honesty. "But there is someone else you have never accused. Laine."

"Is that the shameless hussy chasing you, Kellian?"

"Aunt Hortense!"

"Don't 'Aunt Hortense' me, Annie Charlotte. I've seen that one switching her tail whenever she's near him. She's the one that brought those doves here. Kyle didn't."

"How did you know, Aunt?" Annie couldn't look at Kell, so afraid she would see that wicked, smug look he sometimes wore.

"Oh, I might surprise you, dear, by all that I know that goes on, not only in town," she said, with a sly glance that went from her niece to Kell. "Yes, indeed, I keep apprized of all the doings in my boardinghouse as well."

While Annie felt the heat that had to be coloring her cheeks, she looked on in amazement when a flush tinted Kell's high cheekbones.

He cleared his throat again, leaning forward with his hands folded between his spread legs and stared at the floor. "Can we get back to the problem at hand?"

"Yes," Annie agreed quickly, "by all means, let's. I asked you if it were possible that Laine could be behind this. I've heard that she thought your brother would have left the property to her."

"True enough. But Li and I ruled her out as the cause of all the stoppages as well as the malicious act of injuring that horse and nearly killing that child. And why the—why would she burn the place down? It makes no sense. I know she gets a cut of what the doves make, and she has something put by, but it couldn't be enough to rebuild the place on her own."

Kell glanced up and saw the shudder Annie couldn't hide. He murmured an apology for his blunt talk, but he was at his wits' and to resolve this. Setting a guard on the site wasn't helping, if he took into account the fact that the man had likely fallen asleep.

"Look, all I'm asking is that you keep an open mind and agree to help me."

"That isn't too much, dear, is it?"

Annie met her aunt's steady gaze, her raisin-dark eyes so direct, that Annie gulped. Her aunt knew about last night! The absolute certainty filled her. Why her aunt was not raving and condemning either Kell or herself, she didn't know. The pounding in her temples increased, and Annie rubbed them, closing her eyes. It wasn't too much to ask for her to keep an open mind and admit there could be a slight, very slight possibility that one of the group hoping to make Loving decent was behind Kell's problems. Her stomach churned from her taking this small step.

"Annie Charlotte?"

Bowing her head, suddenly exhausted by it all, she nodded. "All right, I will talk to each one of them. But after this morning, I don't know if they will even receive me."

"The women of our family do not know defeat, Annie Charlotte. Not one has gone after what she wanted and lost. Even if a few used a broom to get it."

Annie shared a puzzled look with Kell. But she had to ask, "A broom? Why?"

"Sometimes, dear, a woman of spirit needed to chase her intended with a broom until she caught him."

"Oh."

Hortense's smile of reminiscence made Kell stand and head for the door. He wasn't about to get himself trapped. He had a feeling that Hortense told the truth about knowing everything that went on. For the first time, he felt very uncomfortable with the thought that marriage might be expected. Damn Li for ever putting that notion in his head.

Behind him, Annie sweetly asked, "Did the broom always work, Aunt?"

"Oh, my, yes. Any man worth being called one doesn't want to get caught. Sometimes it's necessary to use a broom to whack some sense into him. Men, dear, are all grown-up boys. Remember that. Let them think they're running things, smile and say 'yes, dear.' Then, go 'bout your business of keeping order in his life and your home. The women in our family, barring death, had long marriages. Happy ones, too."

"I'll need to remember that, Aunt," Annie said loudly as Kell slipped out of the partially opened door. "A broom," she added, smiling to herself.

But when Annie rushed from the room to catch up with Kell, she found him waiting just beyond the doors for her.

"You try chasing me with a broom and I'll use it to—"

Impluse spurred Annie to lean close and on tiptoe press a light kiss on his lips. "Good morning." She darted beneath his raised arm before he could hold her. A giggle made her look at the back parlor doors where Cammy and Charity were standing.

"Thank you all for your cooking lessons. The goose has been properly stuffed." Annie rushed toward the dining room, only to stop and look back at Kell. "All I need to do," she said, raising her voice, "is baste it well in a slow-burning oven."

The realization that she was talking about him—about them—with a sassy voice and a look that challenged, sent

Kell after her. But he had waited a minute too long, and
Annie made good her escape.

He went into the back parlor and found Pockets seated
at the piano with Ruby alongside him. Cammy, Blossom,
and Daisy were grouped behind them. Kell's furious de-
meanor kept them very, very quiet.

"Where's Bronc?" Kell demanded.

"He left soon as you closed the doors," Ruby answered.

"Likely he went looking for his little dressmaker," Daisy
added. "She didn't come to service this morning."

"Good enough." Kell's gaze took in the wide-eyed innocent looks each dove returned. "Just so you know and
make no mistake, I'm no damned goose. The male is a
gander. But either one, I'm not about to be trussed,
stuffed, and carved by Annie Muldoon or any woman."

Pockets shifted his unlit cigar from one side of his
mouth to the other and played the opening bars of a slow,
sedate wedding march. Kell snorted and left.

The moment the front door slammed they all burst out
laughing.

Chapter Twenty

~

Kell was running scared. No one was going to make plans for his life. He didn't want roots. Did he? Working at the building site he relished the hard labor, but it was doing little to keep his mind occupied and away from Annie. He should have listened to Li from the first and walked away. No, not walked—but run as hard and fast as he could.

Annie had him thinking that Loving would be a good place for him to settle down despite the series of disruptions that slowed his work. And he wanted Annie— had, he admitted, from the first. And now that he had her, the wanting was worse. Much worse. The woman was bound to drive him crazy. At least he had wrung from her an agreement to help him find out who was behind the fire and the stoppages. He just knew it was one of the women. All he had to do was prove it.

Climbing over the stacked lumber to reach the partially laid second floor, Kell glanced down and did a double take.

There was Annie, the object of his desire. She and Ruth McQuary talked for a few minutes more, then Annie crossed the street and headed for Emmaline's. What was she up to now? he wondered, catching hold of the beam above his head.

To keep Annie in sight—Annie with that enticing hip-swinging walk that had already raised his temperature a few degrees—Kell leaned precariously out from the edge of the wood flooring, all his weight dragging on the overhead beam. A sultry breeze buffeted his body, already overheated so that sweat rolled down his back.

A rueful grin teased his lips. Here he was, like some green-behind-the-ears kid, love-starved for the sight of Annie. If he had any sense . . .

A splitting noise made him look up. The overhead beam, the only thing he held on to, was coming apart above him. The fact didn't really register that the four-by-four couldn't crack, couldn't just split apart on its own. Nothing for a few moments made sense until he tried to catch his balance and pull back from the edge.

But Kell was leaning out too far. He couldn't pull back. Couldn't stop his body's momentum. He could and did curse as he fell.

He twisted wildly to avoid the debris below, then tucked his body tight, steeling himself for the bruising jar.

The impact left Kell stunned. He couldn't draw breath. Someone was screaming his name. Black lights danced behind his eyelids. Why was it dark? It shouldn't be. It was the last thought he had.

Annie reached him first, calling his name as she gently lifted his head to her lap. His face was scraped, a bruise was forming over his left eye, but she couldn't see any blood.

"Get back," she yelled, feeling stifled by the press of bodies.

"Move aside," Bronc ordered, shoving people aside to get to Kell. "What happened?"

"I don't know, Bronc. He was up there," Annie said, without looking, "then suddenly he was falling. Didn't you see?"

"No. Emmaline, get some water."

Annie glanced up to see her friend hovering behind Bronc. Her face was pale, and beads of sweat lined her upper lip, but it was the panicked look of her eyes that made Annie want to snarl at Emmaline.

"Did you see what happened?" Annie demanded of her.

"She couldn't, Annie," Bronc answered. "We were together."

"Wasn't no damn accident."

They all looked up to where one of the carpenters stood on the same edge as Kell had, pointing up to the beam that had split.

"Beam's sawed near through. Kell's weight was all it took to crack it."

Annie shuddered and held Kell tight. She refused to let Bronc move him, demanding that he get Li. He was the only one she trusted to touch Kell.

"Look at yourself, Annie," Emmaline bent low to whisper. "You're making a spectacle of yourself over that no-account."

"Get away from me. Get away from Kell. I didn't want to believe him. I couldn't believe him. It took this," she cried out, "to make me understand he was right all along. One of you," she added, her gaze moving around the townspeople without really seeing them, "tried to kill him."

Kell's moan drew her attention and held it. "Don't

move, Kell," she whispered to him. "Li's coming. We'll take you home."

Annie led the way. She couldn't help but think back to the morning after the fire, when she had stood in her room and watched Kellian York march toward her boardinghouse with a crowd behind him. Li had overridden her objections to let Bronc help him carry Kell. The doves formed a circle around the three men, followed by a curious crowd. Annie had no time for them.

She stood aside as the men entered, waited until Ruby, the last dove inside was out of the way, then firmly closed the door.

"One of you stand guard and don't let anyone in," she ordered, heading for the kitchen.

Fawn already had a basin with hot water and folded linen cloths on a tray. Annie added a small crock of salve and after making sure that the back door was locked, with Fawn keeping watch, she took the tray and went up to Kell's room.

He had come to, groaning as Li examined his right arm.

"Is it broken?" Annie asked, setting down the tray. She went to kneel on the opposite side of the bed, catching hold of Kell's good hand with both of hers. "I'll never doubt you again. I'm only sorry you had to be hurt before I would believe you."

"Annie, don't," Kell whispered, turning to face her. Careful as Li prodded, Kell couldn't help the cold sweat beading his face or the wince of pain. "Damn it, Li, don't settle any scores now."

"As if I would. There is nothing broken. The shoulder is bruised. Let me get this shirt off you. Heat will help, then I will wrap it. I do not expect you to leave this bed for a while."

Kell didn't pay any attention to him. Annie was crying,

softly, silently, but washing the hand she held with tears of remorse.

"Don't, Annie. I've survived worse. This is—" Kell lost his breath when Li ripped the sleeve open, never realizing how tight he gripped Annie's hands until she uttered a small cry. "Be careful, Li. Annie won't take kindly to you hurting me."

"No. No, I won't, Li. I'll never let anyone hurt him again."

"Are we having confession time, Muldoon?"

Annie managed a forced smile. "My feelings have never been in doubt. It's yours that worry me." She leaned over to press a light kiss to his lips, needing to pour all the love in her heart into him.

"Annie."

She drew back at the breathless way he said her name, startled by her own action when she saw him pale. Releasing his hand, she set briskly to work unbuttoning his shirt, then asked Li what he wanted her to do.

"Distract him."

With one hand cupping his bruised cheek, Annie once more turned Kell's face toward her. She scooted up closer so she could whisper in his ear.

"Kellian York, I love you."

"Christ! Now you tell me." He shot a glaring look at Li, who sent shafts of additional pain from his injured shoulder with every move, then turned back to Annie. With his free hand he drew her head closer to his.

"Do you know, Kell, I rather like you this way. Prone and biddable. A woman could get used to seeing her man this way."

"Could she?"

"Oh, yes," Annie said, with a genuine smile before she kissed him again and withdrew just as quickly.

"I don't want roots. Only stayed because I owed my brother." Kell closed his eyes, fighting off the waves of pain that were threatening to drag him under. Annie's scent had him fighting yet another battle. A man could get used to having all that sweet concern just for himself. *And that's the kind of thinking that gets a man caught in a marriage trap,* a small voice of caution whispered.

Li, finished with poking and prodding to his satisfaction, tried to be as gentle as he could as he wrapped Kell's shoulder.

Kell opened his eyes and looked at Annie. "I never made you any promises. I never said I was staying," he added, ignoring her attempt to hush him. "I like being free to come and go as I please. You are an ordering kind of woman, Muldoon. The kind that has to change a man. I'm real set in my ways."

"So am I, but that's enough. You're hurting, Kell. Let Li finish. There will be plenty of time for us to talk. I just want you to know that I was wrong. So very wrong not to believe you. Watching you fall—" Her voice broke, and Annie bent her head to his pillow, taking comfort in laying her head next to his.

She squeezed her eyes closed. Seeing him in pain made the pain hers. The image of Kell falling replayed itself in her mind. He could have been killed. From one moment to the next he could have been taken from her forever. He would never have known that she loved him. The tears came, and Annie did nothing to stop them. She didn't care if her nose ran or her eyes were red.

"Annie, it isn't that bad. I've had worse happen. God's earth, Li, give her some of that whiskey. She needs it more than I do."

"W-whiskey?" Annie repeated. She scrubbed her face

over the quilt in a most unladylike gesture, but at this point she didn't care. Lifting her head, she wiped at the lingering wetness on her cheeks. "You can't have whiskey in my house."

Li was already helping Kell to sit up against the headboard. Annie eyed the bottle he held out to Kell. She managed to stand on unsteady legs.

"Don't drink that, Kell. Now is a good time for you to stop. I'll make you a tea that will ease the pain. You do not need spirits."

"Not now, Annie," Kell warned.

"Oh, yes. Now is the perfect time." Annie glared at Li. "Hand it over."

Li, to his credit, did look from her outstretched hand back to Kell's glowering face.

When Annie saw his hesitation, she knew what she had to do. "Kell, look at me." When she had his attention, she ignored her sniffles and said, "Let's remember who held the cure for your—"

"Annie!"

"Kellian!" she returned. It took all her courage to hold his warning glare and not crumble back down to his side. "I do believe he had made his decision, Li. Give me that bottle."

"Oh, give her that damn bottle, Li. Leave it to a woman to pick a time when a man is down, in pain, and—"

"In love with you, Kell." Annie snatched the bottle and fled the room.

Bronc was pacing the hallway and stopped her flight. "I need to talk to him."

"Li's finished with him now. I'm not, but I'm sure you can go in." Annie took a few steps, then turned back. "Wait. Bronc, you were with Emmaline when Kell—"

"I didn't see it happen. I told you that."

"Don't get testy with me. I never believed Kell when he insisted that one of the women in our group would go to such lengths to stop him. I didn't understand how anyone could risk injury or death. I admit I led the fight to close him down, but I hoped to accomplish it by reason."

"I need to talk to Kell, Annie."

She studied his face in the shadowed light, but it was a sense that he was hiding something and wouldn't tell her that forced her to let him go. Thoughtfully, Annie headed down to the kitchen. There was no help for it; confrontation had begun her day, and she would finish with more than anyone could have imagined.

Finding Laine in the kitchen with her aunt sent a battle gleam into Annie's eyes "And where were you all morning?" she demanded of the woman sitting at the table with a cup of coffee.

"Since when do I need to answer to you?"

"Since someone just tried killing Kell."

"Annie Charlotte, tell me that isn't so."

"I'm afraid it is true, Aunt. Kell was working on his building and someone sawed a beam nearly through. He took a bad fall and injured his shoulder. But he could have just as easily died."

"Is that why you're holding a bottle of whiskey, dear."

"This?" Annie had forgotten she held it. "I took this away from him. Kell needs a cup of medicinal tea. Would you see to it, Aunt? I want to hear what Laine has to say for herself."

Annie caught the betraying tremor of Laine's hands around the cup and the avoidance of her own gaze.

"You can't think I had anything to do with it?"

"Why not, Laine? You have the most reason to want Kell out of the way. I know that Kyle promised the place to you. But when he died you found out that he'd left it all to Kell."

"And Kell was content to let the arrangement I had with his brother stand. Wouldn't put a dollar in my pocket to burn the place down."

Distaste for Laine rose like bile in Annie's throat. She managed to swallow it, barely, and paused to think over her questions. Kell needed her help. He had asked for it. She couldn't let him down.

"You can't deny that Kell never wanted the place to begin with. You could have set the fire, believing that Kell would cut his losses and leave Loving. I know you have money set aside, Laine."

"And what if I do? You didn't give it to me. No one ever *gave* anything to me." Eyes snapping with anger, Laine stared directly at Annie until she made herself calm down. "Not that someone like you could understand, having family to protect you, but I worked damned hard for every dollar. But I didn't set that fire. I didn't try to kill him. If I'd wanted Kell dead, he would be."

"Would be?" The words filled Annie with dread, and she felt as if her insides were quaking. She shot a look at her aunt, busy with measuring pinches of herbs into the teapot. For once Annie was glad of her aunt's deafness.

"You heard me," Laine said. "I'm very handy with a gun. I had to be." She looked up with a smug smile just as the doves filed into the kitchen. "Ask them. We worked a few places together before I brought them here. They can tell you how good a shot I am."

The doves didn't wait to be asked. Most murmured agreement.

"Was there anything else you wanted to ask me before I leave?"

"Leave? Where are you going, Laine?" Ruby asked.

"The coast. I'm tired of small towns and smaller minds."

"Does Kell know?" Annie couldn't help being glad. If Laine was gone, her plans to reform the other women would be easier.

"I didn't tell him. I really don't need his permission. I'm my own woman." Laine rose and came around to stand near Annie. "Finished with your questions?"

"Yes. Yes, you've answered them." Distracted, Annie blocked out whatever Laine was saying to the doves. Some of her questions had been answered, true enough, but more were rearing their ugly heads. She didn't want to believe—even after her impassioned declaration to Kell—but now she had no choice. The culprit was someone she knew. Someone she thought a friend.

Annie's quandary of unanswered questions was shared by Kell and Li once Bronc started talking.

Kell's pain had settled to discomfort after Li had retrieved a fresh bottle of whiskey from his bottom drawer. Whiskey had taken the edge off the pain, but Kell had to struggle not to move as he watched Bronc pace in front of the bed. He concentrated on curbing his impatience every time the man hesitated.

"I know I found it hard to believe at first, but I followed her."

"And?" Kell prompted, ignoring Li's look that counseled patience.

"And I didn't see anything, Kell. It's just a feeling I've got. She's not a woman willin' to listen to reason. Not 'bout you."

"But is she a woman capable of murder, Bronc?" Li asked.

It was a question Annie asked herself over and over as she forced herself to go to Emmaline. Her friend had to set aside their differences and help her. One of the women, and here Annie had a hard time naming them, but Lucinda, Velma, Ruth, and Abigail were the only ones she could think of who had time, opportunity, and reason to get rid of Kell.

Annie went around to the back where Emmaline had a private entrance to her rooms behind the dress shop. No one was at the building site, and she realized after a few minutes that Emmaline wasn't answering the door.

Stepping back a little, Annie glanced from side to side, noting that the windows had both the sheer lace curtain and the heavier drapes covering them. Emmaline was the only one she could talk to now. Determination sent her back to knocking at the door.

Inside, Emmaline sat in her darkened parlor, each knock echoing the pounding in her head. "Go away, Annie," she whispered. "Go away."

But Annie wasn't listening. She began to call out, moving from window to window, rapping to gain attention.

Emmaline covered her ears with her hands, rocking back and forth, wishing the woman would disappear and leave her in peace.

But she knew how futile a wish it was. Annie wouldn't leave. She would have no peace.

"Emmaline! Emmaline, open the door. I know you're in there."

Annie's shouting roused Emmaline to stand. She slowly shook her head, understanding that resistance was futile. She went to the door and drew back the bolt, then stood aside in shadow to allow Annie in.

"You couldn't leave things alone, could you, Annie? You had to interfere. You had to come here."

"Emmaline, what's wrong with you?" Annie stood in the middle of the darkened room, turned to face her friend as she closed the door. The sound of the bolt sliding home was the only sound Annie heard above her indrawn breath.

She saw what Emmaline held. Saw it, but couldn't believe it.

"Emmaline?"

"Sit down. We shall have a talk, then you are going to help me."

In Kell's room, the silence was drawing out, filled with tension as Bronc paused in the telling of his story. Li had gone to reassure everyone that Kell wasn't injured badly and had just returned.

"The first time I spent the night with her," Bronc said, staring out the window, simply unable to face his boss, "she started talking in her sleep. Callin' for Charlie. Took me back some. But when I woke her up, Emmaline couldn't remember anyone by that name. Bad dream, that's what she called it. But I couldn't get back to sleep and sure enough, she woke along 'bout dawn calling for him again.

"She's real shy. You've got to understand that, Kell." Bronc turned, but avoided the other two men's gazes. He slipped his hands into his pants pockets and stared at the floor. "It took some doing, but she finally admitted that she's no widow. Charlie was her husband, still is, for all she knows. He ran off with a sportin' gal an' left Emmaline with debts that cost her home and their business. He was a carpenter."

"I know how hard it is for you to tell us this, Bronc," Kell said. And he knew if it had been Annie, he'd likely want to do everything he could to protect her. Even lie. But the latest accident showed that things had gone too far. The wood and nails could be replaced. His life or someone else's couldn't.

"Still can't believe it," Bronc added, shaking his head and once more turning to the window. "She's so sweet and kind. Don't seem possible. But after today I can't hide this."

When the silence once more grew thick with tension, Li, who was leaning against the door with his arms folded over his chest, turned to Kell.

"Your call."

"Thanks." Kell barely spared Li a glance. "Bronc, she— Christ, I don't know what the hell to do."

"I've got some savings put by. It's all yours. Ain't gonna make up for the trouble she caused, but—"

"Forget the damned money, Bronc. I can handle the loss. The only problem is what to do with her. If she's obsessed with closing us down, Loving isn't the place for all of us. You know the only reason I kept the doves on. If I could find work for them, if they want to leave, I'd be happy with the Silken Aces as a saloon."

Kell caught the look Bronc suddenly shared with Li. "What? You both look like you can't believe me."

"It is most difficult, Kell," Li answered. "A few weeks—no, even days—ago, you would have demanded your pound of flesh or its equal in cash."

"Yeah? Well, maybe some of all the do-gooders in this house rubbed off on me."

"You're willing to let Emmaline go?"

"I'm willing enough, Bronc. Thing is, is she?"

"I could take her away from here. Find me a little place an' maybe start up new. Guess I'm a fool, but I fell hard for Emmaline. First time a woman ain't shy 'bout needin' me to make her happy."

"Much as it disturbs me to interrupt your plans, Bronc,

and yours, Kell, has either one of you thought that Emmaline might not agree?"

"Leave it to you, Li," Kell said with a scowl. "No. Wait. Get Annie. She has a right to know, and Emmaline's her friend. Damn me, but she's going to take this hard. I know, I know," he said, a slicing motion of his good arm stopping Li from interrupting. "She finally admitted it was one of her group. But with Annie I've come to learn that admitting something and believing it can mean a long wait's ahead."

"I will fetch Annie."

Kell offered the bottle to Bronc before Li closed the door. "Have a drink. You'll need it to face Muldoon." He meant it as much as a peace offering, knowing what it cost Bronc to come forth. He wondered whether he could have done it if it had been Annie. Brooding, Kell closed his eyes. He hadn't had time to think about what Annie told him. Love. What the devil did he know about it?

He was as green as meadow grass about love, as Annie had been about men and sex. Since that no longer held true for her, did he in turn understand what her declaration meant? Annie was a woman forever. A . . . even in his thoughts he couldn't quite form the word.

"I'll have a drink, Bronc." One for courage, Kell told himself, savoring the bite and warmth. He waited a few moments, until he forced the word out. *Wife*. Annie was meant to be a wife. The cold sweat covering his body had nothing to do with his injury.

The light rap on the door interrupted his thoughts. "Come in."

Kell wasn't surprised to see Laine. But he was surprised that she was dressed for traveling. Dressed for once almost like a lady. "Going somewhere?"

"I'm leaving, Kell. Denley Wallace is giving me a ride to Forth Worth. I can wait for a stage out to California there."

"Kinda of sudden, ain't it?" Bronc asked.

Laine ignored him and tugged on the ruffled edge of her gloves. Satisfied, she once more met Kell's studying gaze. "You know why I'm going. We don't need to rehash. But before I left I wanted you to know that you're not the man your brother was."

"And I thank the Lord for that. There's money due you, Laine. Guess all I can say is good luck."

She smiled for the first time. "Don't worry about the money. I skimmed a bit more off last night to cover what you owe me. I'll take your good wishes, though; I never had any."

Kell laughed. Not at her, but himself. Li wasn't off the mark at all. He had changed since coming to Loving. Changed even more since he'd met Annie.

"I knew about the skimming, Laine, but take it with the good wishes. It'll make up for everything you thought Kyle owed you and never paid."

She turned for the door, then paused to look back at Kell's prone figure on the bed. "It never would have worked out. My staying on. But I thank you for the offer of a partnership of sorts, Kell. Maybe there's a man out there who thinks like you. Maybe California's the place I'll find him."

"Well, don't that beat all," Bronc said, once she had closed the door.

Before Kell could answer him, Li burst into the room. "Annie's gone. No one's seen her. But her aunt thinks she may have gone to Emmaline."

"Sweet Christ!" Kell struggled off the bed. "Bronc, you'd better pray that woman loves you. Because I'm warning you now. If she touches one hair on my Annie's head, I'll kill her."

Chapter Twenty-one

◈

"I don't understand why you never told me any of this, Emmaline. All this time. I thought we were the best of friends. And not once, not even a hint of the lie you've been living. Why? Just tell me why?" Annie pleaded. She refused to look at the gun Emmaline held on her. Annie was trying desperately not to remember the weapon at all.

She refused to cower in the deep wing chair where she had been ordered to sit. Annie knew how dangerous the situation was, but her need to know, to understand, had prompted her demands.

"Please, Emmaline. I've listened, but—"

"Would you have welcomed me as a friend if I'd said I was an abandoned wife? That my husband ran off with a whore? Tell me, Annie, how you would have lied to me. Tell me about the respect the other women in town would have given me when they found out. And then," she said in a voice that vibrated with fury, "tell me how I would have been given the chance to start a new life for myself without the taint of being run out of town 'cause I couldn't pay all the debts."

"There is no way I can answer you, Emmaline." Annie tried to fight the chill that had her spine quaking. She must remember that this was Emmaline. Her friend. But she had never known her, never knew the secrets she had carried. She was afraid of this woman and Annie had never realized how hard it was to disguise that fear. The thought crossed her mind that she didn't know if the gun was loaded. Annie eyed the weapon in the gloom of the room and decided that she wasn't brave enough to find out by lunging for it.

"Emmaline, I trusted you. I can't say what the others would have done." *Keep her talking,* Annie told herself. Her mouth was parched and she swallowed. Fear had sucked all the moisture from her body. "If you had told me from the first meeting, when we talked about forming the group, how strong your feelings were, things wouldn't have come this far."

"You wouldn't have believed me."

"You never gave me a chance!"

"Sit down, Annie. I haven't decided what to do with you."

With some surprise, Annie realized that she had stood up. Her knees were shaking, and she braced one against the other.

"I don't want to sit. I'm scared and likely the dumbest creature on earth to tell you, but I need to move. Don't worry. I won't make a grab for you, Emmaline. Despite what you've done, despite what you did to hurt Kell, I can't hate you."

"As if I care."

"I think you do. If not," Annie dared to say, "why didn't you just shoot me?"

"Shoot you?" Emmaline repeated, unable to keep the horror of the thought from her voice. "I never wanted to kill anyone. I just wanted them all to go away from Loving. Those women are evil. They do the devil's work, enticing men to lose their wages gambling, sending them home reeking of liquor, mean as sin, and ready to use their fists 'cause a woman can't be what they are."

"Is that what Charlie did to you, Emmaline? Did he hurt you?"

"It was that shameless hussy's fault. Charlie was a good man till he met her."

"If you believe that, why wouldn't you help me when I asked? I wanted your help, Emmaline. I wanted to give those women a chance to live a different life than the one they have known."

Annie paced, thinking she could try to run through the store and get away. But the longer she spoke with Emmaline, the less the idea appealed. Friendship meant more than sharing minor troubles. A friend had to be there when no one else would stand by you. This would all come out, and Annie knew most of the women wouldn't understand. They would turn on Emmaline. There was no longer the thought of risk to herself. Emmaline needed her. She couldn't judge her and not stand ready to be judged herself.

"You know, Emmaline," Annie said softly, drawing nearer to the straight-back chair the woman sat in before the door, "those women can't force men to come to them. They don't go out and hold a gun—"

"You dare tell me that! What do you know?"

"That's the point, Emmaline. I do know them." Annie acted impulsively and came to kneel in front of her. She was careful not to try to hold one of Emmaline's hands, but rested hers on her arm. "They have had hard lives, dear. And like you, they've struggled the best they knew to survive. You had a skill and the desire to live a decent life. That's what I wanted you to show them. Your strength, Emmaline. It doesn't matter to me if you're a widow or not. But you can destroy yourself and all you've worked for if you don't give up this hate."

"You're not going to stop me, Annie." Emmaline shook off her hands and lifted the gun. "Get back in the chair. I'll have to lock you up in the sewing room while I go out."

"You haven't listened to a word I've said! Don't do this." Annie backed away but refused to sit down. "Kell doesn't want the doves here. He's not like his brother. You remember that it was Kyle who let Laine come here."

"I won't hurt anyone, Annie."

"What are you going to do?"

"What I should have done from the start."

The fear slammed back into Annie with such force that she fell into the chair. The sudden bright flare of the lamp Emmaline lit made her throw one arm up to shield her eyes. It was only for seconds. The need to protect Kell, protect everyone, forced Annie to lower her arm. Her gaze locked on the gun that Emmaline held at her side.

For the first time Annie thought Emmaline might use the gun on herself. The woman's eyes were staring blankly ahead, not focusing on Annie.

She wasn't sure where the idea that she could take the gun away from her came from.

Thought became action. Annie lunged up from the chair, free of the fear that had held her. Surprise was on her side. She had Emmaline's wrist shackled with both her hands, unable to enforce her demand with a verbal one, just squeezing as hard as she could to make Emmaline drop the weapon.

Annie had never thought about the amount of strength a woman had. She had never needed to know. Petite as Emmaline was, she was strong. But Annie had desperation on her side, She used her shoulder to butt Emmaline's chest, knocking them both off balance.

The report of the gunshot was deafening in the small parlor.

"Let it go!" Annie yelled, refusing to release her grip. It was stupid to worry about the gun, but that's exactly what Annie did. She didn't know how many shots it carried. The old horse pistol that had belonged to Aunt Hortense's husband looked nothing like this and carried two shots. When the gun went off again and plaster from the ceiling almost blinded Annie, she stopped thinking and fought Emmaline for possession of the weapon with a single-minded purpose.

The wrenching pull of her hair made tears fill Annie's eyes. She tried to ignore the pain, inching one hand over Emmaline's to try and grab hold of the gun's barrel. The hot metal made that impossible.

Elbowing the smaller woman's side, Annie heard her grunt of pain, and did it again, all the while unaware that she was screaming for Emmaline to let go.

Emmaline kept her grip on Annie's hair, driven nearly mad by the thought that Annie would stop her. She pulled harder, crying out when she felt as if the skin and bones of her wrist would snap under Annie's hold.

With her head on fire, Annie shoved Emmaline. She saw too late how close they were to the table where the lamp was lit. Afraid of fire, Annie suddenly released the other woman. To her stunned surprise, Emmaline let her go in almost the same moment.

Annie hurt in too many places. She was dragging air in, trying to moisten her mouth to speak, her throat raw from yelling. She held out her hand to Emmaline, silently pleading with her to give over the gun.

Emmaline backed to the door, her hand shaking, but still in control to keep the weapon aimed at Annie.

"Stay here. No one's stopping me." Emmaline fumbled behind her with her free hand to release the bolt.

Annie pleaded with her, her voice reduced to a hoarse whisper. She heard Kell's shout outside. "Emmaline, drop the gun. If Kell is here that means he knows it's you. Don't do anything more. Please."

"Stand back," Kell shouted, and he and Li readied themselves to kick in the door.

Emmaline slid the bolt free. The force of the door suddenly shoved open behind her sent the smaller woman in a headlong flight toward Annie, and the gun went off.

"Christ! Bronc, you never said she had a gun!" Kell muttered, almost falling into the room.

"Kell," Annie called softly, swaying where she stood. Pain vied for her attention. The stinging burn on her arm was claiming first place as she turned to see the gun fall from Emmaline's hand.

"Annie. Annie, I didn't mean it. You've got to know I didn't mean to hurt you," Emmaline cried out.

Bronc caught hold of her, wrapping his arms around her waist and hushed her.

With eyes only for Kell, Annie tried to smile. Her lips refused to cooperate. "You're hurt, Kell." Her vision blurred, and she wished she could tell him to stay still.

Kell gently wrapped his good arm around her shoulders. He motioned Li away. He didn't want anyone touching Annie. Nausea churned in his belly as he glanced down at the blood on her arm and was hit with the realization that Annie did not know she had been shot.

"I hurt, Kell."

"I know you do, love. Rest against me."

"You were over there, and now," she said in a faint voice, leaning against his warmth, "you're here."

"That's me, here today, there tomorrow. Put your arm around my neck, love. You need to go home."

Kell staggered as he lifted her into his arms. He had to grit his teeth with the pain spearing through his body.

"Let me carry her," Li insisted. "You'll wrench that shoulder and need—"

"I've got her."

"He's a mule, Li," Annie said, resting her head on Kell's broad shoulder. "But he's my mule." Seconds later, as she was carried outside with Li in front dispersing the crowd, she whispered to Kell, "Don't be angry. But I'm going to—" Confused, Annie stopped. Her eyes drifted closed. She wanted to be sick.

Every step Kell took sent jarring pain shooting through her. But there was a blessed pull that beckoned her to fall into a void where there was no pain.

"She has fainted, Kell. Let me carry her now. Annie will never know and I will have less to do."

Annie awoke, unsure of the time, her mind hazy from the tincture of opium Li had insisted she drink. Her arm throbbed beneath the bandage. A flesh wound, he had called it. She knew she was in her room, she remembered being carried here, recalled Kell beside her, whispering and promising her things she could not remember. Aunt Hortense had hovered about, offering all manner of instructions. The more Annie struggled to recall them, the more her head ached. Her throat was bone dry and she wanted water, but the clear thought and desire were harder to act upon.

Her legs felt like the weights from Lucinda's flour scale

were attached, leaving her helpless even to kick off the quilt. That sense of helplessness intensified, sending panic streaming through her.

"Annie? What is it, darlin'? You're thrashing about like you're wrestling demons."

Somehow it seemed right that Kell was here beside her. "Water," she managed to say. With a bounce and jar, Dewberry was on the bed, burrowing beneath her hand, his rumbling purr at once comforting.

She sat up with Kell's help, greedily drinking every bit of the water he gave her, asking instantly for more.

"Do you want me to light the lamp, Annie?"

"No. The dark feels . . . better somehow. Kell, is it tomorrow yet?"

"Should be light in about an hour or so. Why?"

Annie kept her eyes closed, her hand stilled on the cat's furred neck. She thought he had stepped closer to the bed again. "You're still here."

Kell caught the hesitancy and the question underlying those three words. He leaned over and slid one hand through her hair, his long fingers grazing her scalp, producing small, uncontrollable shivers. While her response to his light touch satisfied him, he was thankful there was no sign of fever.

"Where would you expect me to be, Annie?" Her helpless reaction to his caress sent a hot surge of blood pumping through his body, and he fought his own reaction. It wasn't the time or the place to show Annie that a brush with death desperately needed a reaffirmation of life. Loving her . . . loving?

"You said," Annie struggled with the cobwebs in her mind. "Here and gone tomorrow. Or something. I—"

"You expected me to leave? To run out on you?" Kell

jerked back. "You were shot, Annie. Shot trying to help me and you figured I'd—"

"I'm glad you stayed."

There was a smile in her voice. Kell thought the idea was foolish, but that is what he felt. Her restless stirring brought him back to her side.

"Too warm?"

"Yes."

"Fretting, are we?" Kell lifted the quilt and pushed it down to the foot of the bed. "Better?"

"Not a bit."

"I'll light the lamp and mix what Li left for you. It'll help you to sleep."

"I don't want the lamp lit. I don't want to sleep."

Dewberry had had enough. He leaped from the middle of the bed over to where Kell was, rubbing against a man who knew how to treat a cat.

Accommodating the animal with long strokes that set up his rumbling purr, Kell asked, "What do you want, Annie?"

"Does your shoulder hurt?"

"Never mind my shoulder. Tell me what you want."

Tell him. Two little words were all she had to murmur. But every moment that had passed since she had awakened helped lift the drugging fog and left her mind clearer. She wanted him to hold her. She could feel the tension from his near, still body, so close she could reach but inches and touch him. But asking Kell to hold her was a sign that she was not entirely independent, that she needed him. Kellian York would run faster than Dewberry had deserted her if she hinted about need.

But she had told him she loved him. Kell didn't run then.

He wasn't in any condition to run, remember?

That is entirely beside the point, Annie countered to the little nagging voice in her mind. But he never told me that he loved me. Not once.

"Annie, I'm waiting to hear what it is that you want."

"Go away, Kell."

"I can't do that, petunia. Someone has to stay with you." Kell gently nudged Dewberry aside and leaned down.

Annie lifted her hand to push him away. A small moan escaped her lips when she touched his bare chest. "Lord! Don't you ever wear a shirt when you should?"

"I can't fit one over the bandage, Annie. Can't keep cutting them up, either. Had those made by a fancy tailor."

"That's you," she muttered in a cross little voice. "Mr. Fancy—"

"Annie. Annie, stop. I won't fight with you." Kell brushed her hair back, unable to stop the need to touch her. "Tell me what you wanted."

If he had a wife, Annie told herself, he wouldn't need a fancy tailor to make his shirts. He wouldn't ever worry about tears again. But Kell wasn't interested in a wife. She heard him repeat his question and set her mouth in a firm line. She would not ask him to hold her!

Kell straightened, puzzled by her silence. He knew Annie. She wanted something from him. What would—light dawned. "Do you need the chamber pot?"

"Kellian York!"

"Don't try to get up. And what the hell's wrong with me asking? I don't see anyone else in here. You would think a perfectly natural—"

"Ladies do not—"

"Spare me, Annie. And spare yourself. We both know what I think about ladies." The silence stretched out, until Kell, with a shrug of his good shoulder, sat back down in the chair near the bed.

"I can be just as stubborn as you, Annie," he muttered after a few minutes.

"I'm not being stubborn. I do not need to use the chamber pot. There! Are you satisfied, Kell? I said it." Annie glanced at his shadowed shape, swearing to herself that she knew he was smiling. The need to have him hold her had not disappeared. If anything, it had intensified.

Plucking at the sheet with her fingers, Annie asked, "Did you say it was almost morning?"

"Sun should be up soon. Why?"

"After what happened, Kell, would you think me foolish if I said I need to see the sun rise?"

He came out of the chair and scooped her up before she could take her next breath. "No. It's not foolish. I wouldn't mind seeing it myself."

"But your shoulder—"

"It's just a little sore, Annie. Stop fussing over me. I told you I've had worse happen and survived."

Annie nestled her head against the bare skin of his chest. "I can't help fussing. I was so frightened when you fell. I don't want to hurt you, Kell." *I just want to love you.*

His resistance was at an all-time low. Kell hooked his bare foot around the chair rung and dragged it closer to the window. Annie tugged aside the curtain, sighing contentedly when Kell cradled her in his lap. Kell glanced down at her, unable to stop the incredible feeling of absolute peace that stole over him. And with that peace came a sense of rightness, that here is where he belonged, holding his Annie and watching a new day dawn.

His Annie? The possessive thought sent a shudder through him.

"Are you cold?" she asked, all sweet concern as she cupped his cheek.

"No." Kell settled her weight on his lap, thankful that she could not possibly know that his answer was to more than her question. "No" was for the temptation that loomed before him. *Remember, you're a freedom-loving man.*

"Kell, what's going to happen to Emmaline?"

"I don't know. All I could think about was that you were shot and needed help. I haven't seen her, or Bronc, since I carried you out of there."

"What will you do to her?"

"God's earth, Annie! Why all the questions? Can't you just sit—"

"No. I'm worried about her." She slid her hand down from his cheek and sighed. "Emmaline's my friend."

"Damn it! She tried to shoot you!"

"You don't have to yell at me. I can hear you, Kell. And you're wrong. Emmaline wouldn't have shot me. She was scared. Things had gone too far. I so wish," she whispered, once more snuggling close to him, "that she had been honest with me from the beginning."

Kell rubbed his head against her hair. "Annie, wishes don't always come true."

"They do if you believe enough."

It was the unshakable conviction in her voice that set his anger to simmering. He had a strong feeling that Annie was talking not only about Emmaline but also about him. A trap yawned. The very one he had managed to avoid. Damn her! He didn't want to say things that would hurt her.

"Annie, you've got to stop worrying about everyone. You can't make the whole world turn to some wonderful idea you have that everyone needs to be happy. And while I'm at it, you should take some time to understand that for your own protection you need to say no to people. If you don't, they'll keep on getting you involved in their troubles."

"But isn't that what friends do? Be there when they are needed? If it was Li, would you turn your back?" She winced as she turned away and stared out the window. His voice was so sharp, with a cold, final flatness that truly disturbed her. His body was tense and Annie gently shook her head, wondering what had caused it.

"Am I too heavy for you, Kell? I could sit here by myself."

"You're fine where you are. I like holding you. Just stop worrying so much."

Annie leaned forward to see that the gray sky was giving way to a pale blue wash. With another small sigh, she wished she could do as Kell asked and stop worrying about everyone. It was simply easier to say than to do.

Kell missed the warmth of her head nestled against his shoulder. "Annie, don't sulk. I purely dislike a woman who sulks."

"I'm not sulking," she answered softly, but didn't turn to face him. "I'm thinking about what you said. You never answered me about Li. Would you turn your back on him?"

"Never."

"Yet you ask that I do that to Emmaline. There is something you need to understand about me, Kell. I do worry about the people that I care for. I will never change. And I'm afraid of what you'll do to Emmaline. Once you threatened to call the sheriff on me. Will you have her arrested for what she did?"

Kell cupped her chin and urged her to face him. "Are you asking me to just let her go?"

"I'd like to, Kell, but I won't. You have to do what you think is right." She paused, her teeth worrying her lower lip, while she kept her gaze directly on his. "Bronc is in love with her. Emmaline needs someone like him. I'm sure he would be willing to wait for her."

Sliding his hand into the thickness of her hair, he brought her head back to his shoulder. "I'll think about it, Annie. I promise you that."

She smiled against his chest. A few scattered kisses seemed in order, and she most promptly gave them to him. Kell didn't seem to realize what he had just said. *He'd promised her.* And Kell swore that he never, ever made promises to anyone. Her fingers entwined with the soft hair on his chest, a warming glow filling her.

"You'll be able to finish your building now."

"Yeah. About a week more should see the Aces opened for business. I should be able to find a buyer fast."

"A buyer?" Annie couldn't believe what she heard. She struggled to sit up, but Kell kept her in place. Hope flared, bright, beautiful hope. "You are going to give up—"

"I'm not giving up anything, Annie. Just like you to think that." *Tell her. You owe her that much.* "Look, I never meant to keep the place. I just wanted to prove to you and everyone else that I wasn't going to be run out. And I couldn't just leave the doves on their own. Now that they can work again, it's up to them what they want to do."

"Oh."

"That's it? 'Oh.' "

Suddenly afraid of what else he would say, Annie used her fingertips to silence him. "Let's just watch the sun rise, Kell."

Despite her weight, Kell squirmed in his seat. Her voice held a wealth of despairing acceptance. She'd just told him that she worried about people she cared for. But he almost admitted that he was ready to move on and Annie hadn't said a word. 'Oh,' he decided, didn't count.

He expected an argument. Some protest. A little bit of her annoying questioning. There wasn't even a hint of a sob. Not a sign that it mattered if he stayed or left.

All he had was the sweetly scented, warm weight of Annie in his arms. And a slow-burning, most confusing fury that she would let him walk away!

Well, it was just what he wanted. No ties. He didn't even need to hear her tell him that she loved him again.

"Kell?"

"What!"

"There's no need to snap at me. I want to go back to bed. If you'll let me go, I can walk there myself."

"I took you out and I'll put you back. I keep forgetting that you're a regular Miss Independence. You don't need anyone to do anything for you. Well, I've got news for you, Annie." Lowering his head until he was nose to nose with her, Kell forgot what he was going to say. The soft morning light bathed the luscious shape of her mouth.

He gathered her closer to him. His mouth hovered just above hers. A last sane remnant warned him that he shouldn't give in to the temptation to kiss her or he would never let her go.

"Kell?"

He jerked his head back and stood up so quickly he almost dropped her. Kell couldn't get her back to the bed fast enough.

"You need to sleep. You need to be left alone, Annie. You need quiet."

"I do?"

"Yeah."

Annie watched him back toward the door. She wanted

to tell him that the only thing she needed right now was him. She had a funny feeling that Kell had been talking about what he needed.

The shadows were banished from the room as the sun fully rose. She knew it had to be a trick of the light that made Kell appear . . . panic-stricken? Kellian York? Ridiculous!

The man did not know how to run scared. And of what? Surely, he couldn't think that she was going to chase after him?

Annie heard him close the door, but she kept staring at the spot where he had stood. The more she thought about it, the firmer her conviction that Kell had been running from her.

She loved him—sinful, sweet-talking, seducing ways and all.

What was she going to do about it?

It was even more worrisome than the thought of what Kell intended to do to Emmaline.

Chapter Twenty-two

∾

Kell groaned when he found Aunt Hortense waiting for him in the kitchen. He almost turned around and walked out, but she offered him a steaming cup of coffee and some sage advice.

"Sit down before you fall down and drink the coffee. While you do, I'll tell you that you can't avoid me anymore. Young man, I want to hear a declaration of your intentions toward my niece."

"Right now?" Kell hunched over the table, cradling the cup. Just the scent of coffee scattered the cobwebs of sleep.

Hortense, taking the chair opposite him, leveled her raisin-dark eyes at his. "It's as good a time as any."

"Maybe for you. I'm not sure about me." The first sip of the dark, strong brew nearly scalded Kell's mouth. "You sure don't make coffee like Annie!"

"Thank you, Kellian." Hortense set her spectacles in place and lifted her cane onto the table.

Kell set the cup down very carefully and eyed the cane,

then looked at Hortense. "You intend to use a weapon on me?"

"I intend to have the answers I want."

"Were you listening at keyholes, Aunt Hortense?"

"As if I need to at my age. You have turned my niece's life upside down, Kellian. You have caused more excitement in the last few weeks than Loving and its people have seen in years. But, before you tend to all the business that waits, I want to know about Annie."

"What about her?"

"You are being deliberately dense. A trait of most males, I fear. Did you propose to her?"

Kell found himself staring into his cup. "Shouldn't you be concerned with her wound?"

"Annie's body will heal. Women are quite strong, you know. It's her heart I worry about. She'd been hurt once by a man—"

"I've heard about her almost marriage. Rest assured, I haven't stolen your cash box."

"Kellian York," Hortense said, banging her cane on the table for emphasis, "do not try to banter with me. As my niece's guardian I demand an answer. Are you going to make an honest woman of Annie?"

"Annie doesn't need a guardian. Annie is already as honest as a woman can be. And for me," he stated, shoving back his chair and standing, "that's one heck of an admission."

"Ah! We make progress at last. Sit down, Kellian. I'm not finished with you. You haven't answered me."

"And I won't. Not now, maybe not ever." He shot her a glaring look, one meant to intimidate, and found her dabbing at her eyes. "God's earth! Don't cry."

"You don't understand. I'm old. I shall go to my just reward resting easier if I know that my Annie Charlotte will have someone by her side to care for her. She has such a soft heart, Kellian. Too soft at times, and people tend to take advantage of her." Sniffing, she glanced up at him. "Why, just look at you. Annie couldn't say no, could she?"

Kell felt heat flood up the back of his neck and rise rapidly to his face. He had to get the hell out of this place! Never, never in his life had he been reduced to blushing. What was wrong with Hortense? Talking like this to him? She was a good woman, a lady, and ladies didn't use such frank talk.

"Annie needs—"

"What your niece needs is peace, quiet, and sleep."

"Are you talking about Annie or yourself, Kellian?" Her gaze drifted past his shoulder to the doorway. A smile formed, and brightened her eyes. A last wipe with her lace-edged hankie and Hortense tucked it beneath the cuff of her sleeve. "Do come and join us, Pockets, dear."

"Pockets, *dear?*" Kell repeated, turning around. "What the hell's been going on behind my back?"

Pockets, grinning around his cigar, sauntered over to stand beside Hortense's chair. Kell didn't miss his move to place one hand on Hortense's shoulder, or hers to cover that hand with her own.

"Well?" Kell asked, settling his hands on his hips.

"What you see is simply a mutual understanding that even at our age, Pockets and I need companionship."

Still grinning like a fool, Pockets nodded. He removed his cigar and looked Kell over. "Hate to tell you this, Boss. You've got business waiting in the back parlor. Bronc's there with Emmaline." He gazed down at Hortense. "I've shown your ladies group to the front parlor. They want news of Annie."

"She's fine. Everyone's fine. But me." Kell spread his arms wide.

"Are you looking for pity, Kellian?"

"Kell's not a man who'd welcome pity, Hortense," Pockets answered. "By the way, can't find Li anywhere."

"I might of known that he'd desert me too." Raking back his hair, Kell eyed the two watching him. "Someone should feed Annie. As you reminded me, Pockets, there's business waiting."

"One more thing, Kellian. Please keep in mind that my niece has admitted she loves you to distraction. The good Lord knows why. But while Annie may love the sinner, she will still hate the sins."

Kell's grin was downright wicked. "Aunt Hortense, you may not know your niece as well as you think you do."

"Well, I declare—"

Kell closed the kitchen door and never heard what she said. He couldn't avoid tackling the problem of what to do with Emmaline any longer.

Two hours later, Kell emerged from the back parlor and went in search of Li. He still didn't understand why he had done what he had about Emmaline. But it was definitely something more to be laid at Annie's door. The woman was having an unaccountable influence on him.

Finding Li kissing Fawn behind the big cottonwood tree in the yard, Kell whistled a warning and waited until they broke apart before he joined them.

"Did you receive your pound of flesh?" Li asked, cradling Fawn close to his side.

Kell hooked his thumbs in his waistband and rocked back on his heels. "A pound of flesh is not what I've got. You are looking at the new owner of a dress shop."

A rapid-fire explosion of Chinese didn't faze Kell. He was entranced by the smile lighting up Fawn's face. For once she didn't hide from him, but met his gaze directly.

And he had no need for Li's explanation of her hand motions, touching her heart, then her forehead, and pointing at him.

"Fawn believes that love has made you act wisely."

"Love had nothing to do with it," Kell snapped back. "Bronc asked if I would accept it as payment for all the damage Emmaline caused me. He figures to leave here by nightfall. I agree that it's for everyone's best interest that they go. He'll use his money to get started somewhere new. And before you go and get any ideas, I took the dress shop because he insisted. I'm not keeping it. Whatever money I get from the sale will go to help the doves."

Li shared a long look with Fawn, thoughtful for a few minutes. Kell was steaming. He didn't appear very happy with the way things had turned out.

"Kell, I want to make sure I understand. You are going to finish building the Aces?"

"That's right."

Aggressive was the only way Li could describe Kell's voice and stance. If he didn't know better, he would swear that Kell was looking for a fight.

"You plan to stay in Loving and marry Muldoon?"

"Annie. Her name's Annie and I'm not marrying anyone."

"Ah."

"What the hell's that supposed to mean?"

With an innocent smile, Li shrugged. "You are back to calling her Annie, that is all. I did not think I would see the day you would give up your freedom."

"And you won't live to see it. I'm just wrapping up all the loose ends before I quit this place. You've been telling me from the first we shouldn't have stayed here. Now I've come to my senses and agree with you."

Li pressed a kiss to Fawn's gleaming black hair and

gently touched her cheek. Regret laced his voice as he glanced at Kell. "I do not think I can leave Fawn."

"Well, it's not going to be today. I want to find a buyer for the Aces and—" He broke off to see the adoring look that Fawn shared with Li. "I'm wasting my breath trying to talk to you now."

"No, Kell. I have just found a peace that I have longed for and love which I did not believe in with Fawn. If the town will accept us, I want to live here."

"So, like Pockets, you're deserting me too. This is more of that infernal Annie's fault. And don't worry about finding acceptance. Believe me, with Muldoon on your side, she'll make those biddies bite their tongues before she'll allow a cross word against you."

"Annie is a most formidable opponent," Li agreed.

"Don't be saying it like you're warning me."

Fawn touched Li's cheek to gain his attention. She pointed to herself, then to Li. Using two fingers in a rapid, scissorlike motion, she indicated them walking before looking up at the second floor.

"Annie? You want us to go see her?" Li asked.

At her quick nod, Kell answered before Li. "You two go ahead. I've got things to do. And Li," he added, "don't mention that I'm pulling out. I'll tell her myself."

He hadn't taken more than a few steps when Pockets called from the kitchen door. "Kell, you've got mighty ruffled feathers to smooth in the front parlor. Those ladies are demanding to talk to you."

"Tell them to—"

"If not you, they're threatening to go upstairs and see Annie."

"They haven't got the sense the Lord gave mules. Annie was shot! They can't go bothering her now!"

Kell closed his eyes and threw back his head, muttering

curses under his breath. He wanted a drink, craved one, in fact. Opening his eyes to find that Li, Fawn, and Pockets were watching him with intense interest made him think that a rip-roaring drunk would serve him better.

"Kell?" Pockets prompted.

"I'm coming. Tell 'em to keep their corsets tied."

Pockets waited until Kell was abreast of him before he put out a hand to stop him. "I truly hate to kick a man when he's down, but I'd better tell you that Annie's been talking to the doves all along about finding other ways to make money."

"Somehow, that doesn't surprise me in the least. I never wanted them working for me. Right now, if I never saw another woman, it would suit me fine."

And it was a fact he made clear to Lucinda, Velma, Ruth, Abigail, and Aunt Hortense. While the ladies listened politely as he told them about Emmaline and Bronc, they were not happy to hear that Kell intended to finish building his saloon.

Their reaction gave him a perverse sense of satisfaction, since he left out the part about trying to find a buyer for the place.

"We shall have to discuss this with Annie," Lucinda informed him after a whispered consultation with the others.

"Not today you won't. Annie's been hurt, in case you've all forgotten that. She doesn't need to be bothered."

"Hortense!" Abigail glared at Kell. "Since when does he—"

"Did I mention that I might have lumber left over to start your church?" Kell had additional satisfaction as their mouths shut and they faced him as one. "Trust me, ladies. Think of this as everyone holding a winning hand and splitting the pot. It's the best deal you'll get from me."

"Hortense, how can you allow him to dictate to us?" Velma demanded, and her question was echoed by the others.

"Ladies, please." Hortense patted her heart and leaned back in her chair just as Kell rose from where he had been sitting. "This has been a trying time for all. I'm too old to contend with constant quibbling and fighting. We shall trust in the Lord." Hortense saw that Kell couldn't get to the door fast enough. "Yes, that's the best course. Trust the Lord and Annie to manage him." Since the other women were watching Kell, no one noticed the angelic smile Hortense bestowed on him when he shot her a look over his shoulder.

"I told you—"

"Yes, Kellian, you did." Humming a little tune that Pockets had taught her, Hortense wore a contented smile that could have rivaled one of Dewberry's rumbling purrs. And no matter how many questions the ladies asked, she refused to say another word.

Kell gave a passing thought to going upstairs and checking on Annie as he made his escape. His shoulder ached, his head ached, and he realized he had had a bellyful of trying to talk sense to everyone in the boardinghouse.

Pockets came out of the back parlor. "Kell, the doves are still waiting to talk to you."

"Later."

"If you say so. But I warned you. If you don't talk to them, they'll go to Annie."

"If I catch one tail feather of theirs up in her room they'll have to answer to me."

"Where're you heading?"

"Where any sane man goes when he can't find two inches of peace!" Kell's shouting roused the house, but he didn't care as he slammed the door and made good his escape.

Unfortunately for Kell, there was no escape from Annie. He couldn't get her out of his mind. When he hit his thumb for the second time as he tried to work on the building, he tossed aside the hammer in disgust. He eyed the boardinghouse and resisted the urge to go back. He'd been wanting a drink all morning, and here it was late afternoon and he still hadn't had one. That's when he decided he would get drunk—stinking, singing-to-high-heaven drunk.

As he told his second bottle of whiskey, "Ain't a green kid wet behind the ears. Ain't gonna get trapped."

Kell wasn't so drunk that he didn't know what he needed to cure him of his ills. "A pleasure-lovin' woman."

But the only pleasure-loving woman that he could imagine was Annie Muldoon.

He eyed the two empty bottles on the table in front of him and decided that they too were stacked against him.

Chapter Twenty-three

〜

It was late Tuesday evening before Kell was sober enough to approach Annie's room. He had bathed and shaved, wore his second-best shirt and had spit-shined his boots. He had come to a decision.

But it was with alarm that he saw Li coming out of Annie's room. "What's wrong?"

"A little fever, Kell. She will be fine. Fawn and Charity are bathing her to keep the fever down." Taking note of Kell's extremely neat appearance, Li added, "If you want to see Annie, you will have to wait. She did not sleep well last night, so I gave her a sleeping draught."

"It wasn't anything important. But you're sure she'll be all right?"

"I would not lie. It was only a flesh wound. From that she will heal."

Kell had no choice but to accept that Li was telling him the truth. He certainly wasn't going to go into her room now and tell her that he planned to leave. Had to, if he wanted to keep his freedom.

"Well, if she needs anything—"

"Are you worried about her, Kell? Do not. There are many willing hands to tend her. Annie will not want for anything."

Kell grunted in reply. He wouldn't give Li the satisfaction of asking if Annie had mentioned him.

It wasn't until Thursday morning, when he attempted to see Annie again, that Kell realized a conspiracy was going on to keep him from seeing her. Ruby answered his knock, just as she had the previous morning, and told him Annie was still sleeping. When he returned after lunch, both Blossom and Daisy greeted him at the door of Annie's room and told him they had just washed her hair, so she was in no condition to see him.

Kell snatched the supper tray from Fawn, but Lucinda was there, ready to take it from him. "Annie is indisposed, Mr. York. She is not up to having any visitors this evening."

"And what are you?"

"Her friend. A longtime friend with her best interests at heart."

Kell stared at the door that had been closed to him.

"Well, hell!" He turned the handle and found the door locked. "Annie! I want to talk to you." Pressing his ear to the door, Kell waited. There wasn't a peep to be heard from the other side.

It wasn't until the sound of his stomping off down the stairs was heard that Cammy released Annie's mouth.

"You almost spoiled everything, Annie."

"But I want to see him."

"Now, Annie," Lucinda said, sitting close by the bed. "You don't want to see him just yet. Listen to wiser heads, dear. We've all agreed this is the best way to bring him to his senses."

Of course, when Kell made the accusation that they were all in cahoots to keep him from Annie, it was denied. He could have barged into her room and demanded that they be left alone, but Li insisted that any upset could bring a return of her fever.

Kell, with a little modification, adopted Hortense's favorite expression. He'd trust to himself to get this straightened out. And never once did he ask himself why it was so important that he tell Annie about his plans.

Pockets waylaid him early Friday morning. "You can't put off seeing the doves any longer. They need to talk to you."

Drawing on the small remaining store of his patience, Kell followed Pockets into the small back parlor.

Ruby stood by the piano bench, with the other doves arranged behind her. "I've been chose the one to talk to you," she began.

"Fine," Kell answered, leaning against the back wall with his hands in his pockets.

"We all want you to know we think it's a swell thing that you're gonna help build a church."

Kell looked at each dove in turn, his expression stern. He caught the secret little smiles, Cammy's smirk, and the laughter the doves couldn't keep from their bright eyes.

"Glad I have your approval," he finally said. His thoughts drifted immediately to Annie and what she would think about his offer.

"Kell," Pockets called, shaking his arm. "You're not listening."

"Sure I am." He roused himself and looked around.

"We know you're worried about Annie." Pockets dug into his vest pocket and removed one of his precious cigars. "Now you keep this for later. Annie don't like anyone smoking in the house."

"Ruby, please," Charity said, moving up to stand beside her. "Go on."

"You tell him. Kell isn't going to say no. He doesn't own us, girl."

"That's for sure, Ruby. I don't. I never wanted the damn brothel. With Laine gone, I intended to talk to each one of you. I'm finishing up the Aces. The way the work has been going we should be ready to open Saturday night. I'll give you all a choice. Work for me dealing or serving whiskey, but that's all I have to offer."

Charity launched herself at Kell, hugging him tight. "Then I can marry Jessup? He's asked me so many times, and I want to be his wife."

Kell peeled her arms from around his neck, wincing at the twinge of pain in his shoulder. It reminded him that a little rest would do him a world of good. And he swallowed a comment about what he thought of the state of marriage.

Nibbling on her lower lip, Charity backed up. "Kell, you won't hold it against him for stealing your whiskey?"

"Jessup cleared himself when he brought it all back. Why do you women think that men need you to oversee everything? We can tend to business without your interference."

"Because," Daisy answered, "Aunt Hortense said we had to learn to manage men."

"Outside the bedroom," Blossom added, to the laughter of the other doves.

Daisy took one look at the scowl on Kell's face, then glanced at Ruby. At her slight nod, she added, "If you had to ask such a question, Kell, pity the woman you marry.

She'll have her hands full. Or maybe it'll be the other way around."

Kell studied the toes of his boots. He would like nothing better than to fill his hands with Annie's sweet body. He even wanted, no, needed, Annie's hands on him. There lay the danger. He resigned himself to this state of permanent aching while hearing what the rest had to say.

"Is it true that you're gonna sell the dress shop?" Blossom wanted to know.

"Emmaline signed it over to me. Bronc wanted me to have the money, but I don't need it. I planned to give each one of you a share. Charity can have hers for a wedding—"

"No. I mean yes, I want a share. But Jessup and I want to buy this place outside of town. We're gonna be ranchers." She looked at Blossom. "Tell him."

"I want the dress shop, Kell."

He looked at Blossom's serious expression, then at each of the doves in turn. "Annie put you up to this, didn't she? Don't bother denying it. I can smell the conniving witch's hand in this."

"Will you help me, Kell?" Blossom had come forward, but she stopped. She had used up her store of courage.

"You want that shop, I'll give it to you. But you—"

"I don't *want* it. I'll pay you for it."

"Listen to me!" Kell came away from the wall, close enough to grab hold of Blossom's arms. He wasn't hurting her, but he gave her a little shake to catch her attention. "It's not up to me alone. You've got the women in this town, who are the narrowest-minded bunch of biddies you'll ever run up against." Kell let her go. "Do you understand? They won't care if you can sew. Those women will hold your past against you. I don't like it, but face the

truth before you get dreamy-eyed with a head full of foolish notions."

With a glint of tears in her eyes, Blossom shook her
head. "Poor Kell. You're the one who's got no understand-
in'. I'll be havin' Annie on my side."

All Kell could envision was Annie embroiled in getting
everyone's life settled while he was made to wait. Wait?
He was going to hang around Loving that long? He saw
the doves walk past him and out the door. Pockets remained seated at the piano, picking out a few mournful
notes. He didn't even look up when Kell let a string of
curses fall.

For once without his half-chewed cigar, Pockets allowed Kell to finish. "Annie would have tossed you out if
she had heard you. But, Kell, you've got a lot to learn
about that woman."

"You're likely right. But you can't believe that Annie can
make the world right for everyone. She'll try, of that I've
no doubt. And probably make some man gray worrying
over her. But she can't make the townspeople accept the
doves as respectable women."

"Maybe your Annie can't do it alone, but between her
and Hortense they'll sure give it a try. May have a little
hell to pay, but my money's on them." He laughed until
tears filled his eyes.

Kell stood there, wondering why he did. Crazy. Pockets
was crazy. The whole boardinghouse was filled with people who were crazy. He knew that for a fact, for he had
come to count himself as one of them. And it was all Annie's fault.

He groaned. He didn't want to think about Annie.

"You know, Kell, Hortense is a fine woman. She carries
a nice tune, and she don't mind a man having a nip or
two. Joins me now and again. I'm not so old I can't appre-

ciate a good woman. Man needs someone to care about him."

"I suppose the next thing you'll be telling me is that you want to marry her? God's earth, Pockets, I counted on you."

"Still can. But I'm not marrying Hortense. 'Course, living in a town called Loving could make a man change his mind. Figure there might be something in the well water?"

"If there is, I'll be sure not to make any whiskey here. It's liable to infect the whole damn county."

Pockets took pity on Kell's glazed eyes, the distracted way he ran one hand through his hair, and the shadows beneath his eyes. "A last word. Don't let them keep you away from Annie. I have it from good authority that she misses you."

Kell couldn't get out of the room fast enough. But as he crossed the lobby to the stairs, the front door opened. He recognized the drummer who had made his Annie laugh when she served him lunch for a few weeks ago.

"Sorry, we're full up. Can't have a room here. Can't even get a meal here," he announced, advancing on the poor man, who'd barely gotten inside. "The Cozy Rest no longer caters to single men."

"But I've always stayed—"

"Not anymore."

The drummer took one more look at the warning glint in the man's eyes and backed out the door.

Kell brushed his hands together. "One down and the good Lord knows how many more to go."

What was Annie going to do without someone around to watch out for her? It wasn't his problem. Then why, he asked himself, was he hanging around here? Could he really walk away from her? Never tease her again? Never see sparkling challenge in her eyes? Never taste that luscious sweet mouth that gave him as much pleasure as any man had ever desired?

Foolishness. Kell started for the stairs, made it halfway up, and turned around to go back down. He stared at the counter, remembering the day she hid behind it to avoid seeing him. That only led him to recall the reason why— those first charming kisses, the breathless way she said his name, those sweet little sounds that made his blood race.

What sane man wanted a woman who liked lemons? Did he want to spend the rest of his life educating Annie that pleasure wasn't sinful?

No. He had better things to do with his time, with his life.

Like what?

Kell thought about that. North of Loving, the Indian lands had been opened to settlers. It was a big territory worth exploring. A man of his talents, along with the stake he'd have from selling the saloon, could wander at will. He wouldn't have a worry. He wouldn't be saddled with anyone. It was a life he was comfortable with, even happy with, wasn't he? He liked being alone just fine.

Despite what Pocket said, Annie didn't need him. Not once in the last few days had she made any effort to see him, send for him. He had no use for the corset contingent that would likely interfere with his life if he stayed here. Those women would be the cause of a running battle with Annie. A man couldn't sentence himself to living with that.

He didn't need their approval. Didn't want it. Why should it matter to him if Annie turned out just like them?

Oh, what a waste!

But Annie wouldn't be wasted. Some man would come along, like that damn drummer, and Annie—No! He'd be damned if some other man was going to enjoy the fruits of his labor.

And it was labor to seduce her. The result was the most pleasurable, intense lovemaking he'd ever had. He didn't need to wrap it up pretty in his mind.

But Kell was lying to himself and that admission had him sitting down on the step—hard. What he shared with Annie had been more. No matter how he tried to run from the truth—it was still there.

He was running scared from commitment. From the forever kind of promises that a woman like Annie needed—and what's more, deserved.

He was running from . . . *say it, even to yourself* . . . love.

What if he couldn't love Annie enough? What did he have to offer her?

Closing his eyes, Kell leaned his head against the banister. He couldn't answer the questions by himself. Only Annie could. All he had to do was ask her. He'd never lacked courage.

"Are you sure this is working?" Annie asked the doves in her room. "It's been five days."

"Annie," Charity said, "he's just like a mustang that's been corraled for the first time. Kell's testing his fences, and when he sees them holding firm, he'll settle down."

"Yeah," Ruby added with laughter in her voice. "He's roped and still lunging, but that wildness'll be gone quick."

"I rather like his wildness." Annie plucked at the quilt. She felt fine and hated this enforced bed stay, but everyone insisted that if she wanted Kell, she had to stay away from him.

"What if you're all wrong?" she asked when the waiting stretched and tension grew unbearable. "What if he leaves? I—"

The door flew open and Kell filled the doorway. The doves instantly arranged themselves in a line hiding Annie and her bed from his view.

"Out," he grated from between clenched teeth. "I won't even bother to count. Just leave. I'm going to talk to Annie."

As one, the five women turned to look at Annie. "Is that what you want, Annie?" they chorused.

"Yes. Lord, yes."

"He's in a fine temper, by the look of him," Blossom warned, before she stepped away from the bed and started for the door.

Kell stepped aside, glaring at each one as she slipped past him. He closed the door and locked it, then pocketed the key. Turning to Annie, he said, "I've come to a decision."

Annie fussed with the ruffles on her blue bed jacket. She yearned to have it be the decision that would keep them together.

The sharp raps on the door made Kell spin around with a black scowl. "Your aunt," he announced.

"Kellian, open this door at once. You can't lock the door. You can't be alone with my niece."

"She's upset, Kell."

Still facing the door, Kell agreed with Annie, then added, "Don't worry, I have the right answers for her."

"You do? She'll want to know your intentions, Kell, but you haven't even told them to me."

"Well, if everybody would leave me the hell alone with

you for ten minutes maybe I could get around to it. You hear that, Aunt Hortense?"

"Annie Charlotte, I demand that you open this door! I will not have a room locked to me in my house."

Kell stripped off his shirt, smiling at Annie's gasp.

Since his back was toward her Annie made a few hurried moves of her own, then prompted him. "So talk to me."

He turned around and found his breath caught somewhere in his chest. Annie sat up in bed, clutching the sheet up to her chin. He leaned against the door, ignoring Hortense's muttering, needing the solid wood to keep him standing. The soft light filtering through the lace curtains played over the white sheet, Annie's bright blue eyes and the length of her copper-gold hair the only splash of color. She had a sassy mouth, was prickly as a hedgehog, and likely would keep his life constantly upside down and inside out—and enjoy doing it to him.

But she loved him. Annie brought him laughter. She smoothed all the hard edges with her goodness. And he could no longer deny that she had the makings of a pleasure-lovin' woman. Yet, when he spoke, he said none of these things to her.

"You know I'll take care of you."

"I never asked you for that, Kell."

"Well, you've got it. Don't be such a contrary woman, Annie. Your aunt and the rest of them are probably pressing their ears against the door so as not to miss a word."

"All right," she conceded. Annie heaved a sigh, wishing he would just come close enough to hold her. Then this ache of loneliness would leave. He would kiss her, and— No, no. She had to give him his chance to say what he had to.

"But, Kell, I promise to take care of you, too."

"I've never proposed to a woman before."

Her eyes sparkled, and her smile deepened as she watched his nervous move to smooth back his hair. "You cannot imagine how that pleases me, Kell. I like being first in something with you."

"That's not all I've got to say." Glancing at the seam between door and jamb, he leaned close. "Are you all hearing this?"

A smothered giggle that could only have been Cammy's came in answer. Facing Annie, he warned, "We've got lots of witnesses. But sure of what you say, darlin'. I won't let you take back one word."

The graceful power of his muscular body unsettled her. Annie looked up and found him watching her with a heated gleam in his eyes. She lost track of what he had said, lost all the well-meaning advice she had been given. She loved Kell so much, her heart filled with the sheer joy of it.

"I love you, Kell."

Hearing those words again tested Kell's strength of will. Only by exerting force did he stop himself from going to her. If he touched Annie, if he kissed her now, the world could go to hell in a handbasket. Tempted as he was to do just that, for his own sake he had to say his piece.

"I'm not going to change my ways. Even if you think they're sinful. But I'll never want another woman. And that's a promise. Since you say you love me, I'll take that as an unqualified yes, Annie."

"But you haven't asked the question."

"What the devil do you think I've been saying? You're going to marry me, right? Lord knows you went to enough trouble to bring me to my knees. Hiding away in here, conspiring with all of them to keep me away from you."

"Yes, Kell."

"And another thing—Yes? You said yes?"

"Yes. I'll marry you, Kell." Annie raised her voice and repeated it again for the benefit of those waiting out in the hall. Moments of shuffling and laughter ended, and she knew they were finally alone. "They all heard me, so you can't take back your proposal, Kell. And you should know that I don't want to change you."

"You don't?" Kell shook his head. Annie kept him unbalanced. Had from the first. Every time he thought he had her figured out, she disabused him of his notions about *good* women.

"Maybe you don't see the changes you make all by yourself. Offering to help build the church is one."

"Don't go getting any ideas about that, Annie. I just felt that I—well, it was just something to help out, that's all."

"I've missed you terribly, Kell," Annie whispered.

The same longing that was inside him was there in her voice. Her eyes held all the passionate warmth that he knew he would find in her arms. "Hungry, Annie?"

"Oh, yes, Kell. Till I ache."

"You're going to rest today, and let me, only me, take care of you?"

"Resting isn't what I had in mind, but I'll agree to you taking care of me. My wound is nearly healed. And, Kell, I've been . . . restless. Now, don't you think we've done enough talking?"

"I've only been waiting for an invitation."

"You don't need one." Annie's laugh was husky with all the desire that rose as Kell's hands moved to his pants buttons. She shifted her body beneath the sheet, turning slowly to face him. "With all this enforced rest, I'm ready for anything."

"That sassy mouth is gonna get you in trouble, Annie."

She met the blaze in his eyes with one in her own. "It

already has. But there's a sinful, sweet-talkin' seducer who promised to educate me on how to handle trouble."

Kell kicked off his boots and shucked off his pants. "I'm glad to hear you remember that. And he's the only one who'll do your educatin'. Ah, Annie, I sure do like you prone and biddable."

Having her own words returned only made her smile deepen. Very deliberately, Annie lowered the sheet. She loved the way Kell hesitated with one knee on the edge of the bed, momentarily flustered by her boldness. It was gone too quickly, replaced by a look so dark and heated that a shiver of anticipation raised her desire and love for him to a new high.

"You made some promisees, Kell. Like the one to take care of me. I'm very hungry."

"I'll satisfy you, Annie. In every way." The bright look in her eyes wasn't passion alone; love was there, and it wedged open the door to his heart. "I love you, Annie."

"That's all I've ever really wanted." She kicked aside the sheet and welcomed him into her arms.

"Lord," Kell whispered, cherishing her love, "if you sent me a pleasure-lovin' woman like Annie to make me pay for my sins, I'm gonna die a happy man."

Epilogue

After a week of rain, the sunlight flooding through the lace curtains announced that spring had finally arrived in Loving. Annie, rushing to get dressed this Sunday morning, paused a moment as the gold band on her finger was caught in a stream of sunshine. The man who had once offered her a choice between himself and a noose had placed this symbol of his love on her finger. She never tired of looking at it, just as she never tired of loving Kell.

For the past seven months she had been Mrs. Kellian York, but not the only bride in Loving. Charity had wed Jessup first, then she and Kell had spoken their vows. Fawn, after Annie made sure she understood and Li had done a great deal of talking, had married him this past winter. They were so in love with each other that no one could look at them and not feel a part of their happiness. Fawn's silence didn't matter to Li, although he had confessed that he had not given up hope that it would someday be ended.

Just last week, they all attended Ruby's wedding to Denley Wallace. The wealthy rancher had invited the whole town to the day-long celebration of their marriage. Ruby certainly had not let any grass grow under her high heels once Laine had left. She had set her cap and those long legs of hers toward catching Denley. There were even hints that another proposal might be coming any day now; Kell's new barkeep had been walking out with Cammy every evening this week.

A quick look at her watch pin warned Annie that she was late for service. Pinning on her straw hat with its pretty pink-silk ribbons, she tilted the brim at a rakish angle and lowered the veil. The thin netting didn't hide the brightness of her eyes or the warm flush coloring her cheeks. Now, if Kell kept his promise to slip away the moment service was over, she would have nothing more to worry about.

Today was so special. Since the town's population had grown, Kell—with a little prompting from her, Annie admitted—generously offered to close down the saloon on Sunday and hold the church service there. It would be the last time. Their new minister arrived this week and would christen the church next Sunday.

Rushing down the stairs, Annie wanted everything to be perfect today. Unlike her somewhat public proposal of marriage, she wanted privacy to share her wonderful news with Kell.

Exchanging greetings with other late arrivals, Annie felt as if her heart would overflow. She had her dream of seeing Loving with its church and from Kell, more love than she had ever wished for. She stood for a moment at the open doors, seeing a very somberly dressed Pockets take his seat at the piano to begin accompaniment for the first hymn. Annie smiled at her aunt, who sat next to him, ready to turn the pages.

Her winter cold had made one more change. A most temporary one, Kell insisted, the first time Annie had asked. But the starch in her shirtwaist nearly melted when Kell took his place opposite the long bar, and the congregation settled to silence. Annie waited until he saw her, then she took a seat near the door.

She noticed that Kell was as nervous today as he had been the first time. Clearing his throat, he ran one finger around his starched collar. He had not told her what he was going to talk about today, but once their opening song was done and Kell began to speak, Annie closed her eyes.

The wages of sin. Kell's voice carried well as he directed those in attendance to reform their ways and not lie, cheat, or steal. There wasn't a cough, or a restless stirring, but Annie knew there were many who hoped that her husband would one day give up his saloon and his wicked ways.

Well, just a few of those wicked ways, she amended, and asked the Lord's forgiveness for clarifing the request. She never wanted to give up the pleasure she found in Kell's arms. She was a little misty-eyed when she looked at her husband again. Hell-raiser and heaven-sent man that he was to her.

He didn't preach against drinking or gambling. But then, Annie knew he moderated the first and had never been reckless about the second.

As the closing hymn began, she slipped out the doors and went around back of the saloon to wait for Kell. Within minutes, he had his arms around her.

"Kiss me good morning, wife."

Turning in his arms, Annie warned herself that one kiss

would lead to others and she wouldn't get him away. But Kell lowered his head, and she touched her mouth to his.

"Are we so long married, you think that's a kiss?"

"Come with me, Kell. I'll give you lots more." She caught hold of his hand.

"Promise?"

For an answer Annie laughed, and started running behind the buildings, with Kell alongside her.

When they rounded the back of the boardinghouse, Annie stopped. Li stood hugging Fawn near the cottonwood tree. She no more wanted to intrude on them than she wanted them to see her and Kell. But Li spoke, and his words held Annie still.

"Say it again, love. You do not know how I have longed to hear those words from you."

Kell, standing so close behind Annie, wrapped his arms around her waist and tried to pull her away. He had not kept many secrets from Annie since they had been married, but this was one that wasn't his to share. Li had confided to him the frustrated attempts Fawn made to speak, often ending in tears that Li had been helpless to stop.

Annie resisted Kell's gentle tugs. She hadn't kept too many secrets from him since they had been married. If Fawn had not come to her, wanting so much, Annie would have gone and left them alone. But Fawn had come to her . . .

Leaning down, Kell whispered, "This is their time, not one for sharing with us."

Eyes glittering with tears, Annie offered him a trembling smile and let Kell draw her along the back wall of the house.

And on the warm spring air, Fawn's words came to them.

"Fa-wn l-love Li."

"And Li adores—"

Kell silenced Annie's sobbed cry of joy with a kiss, backing away until he was sure they wouldn't be overheard. He held her close, rocking her, understanding how precious those words of love were for Li to hear. Not only for the healing they would bring to his friend, and to Fawn, but for the reminder that he had heard, and would hear, those special words of love every day from his wife.

"Love did that, Kell," Annie whispered, drawing back a little to look up at him. "Will you come with me?" It was so hard to contain her excitement, which was bubbling and simmering with the need to be free. Knowing that Fawn was loved had been enough, but now Annie understood what a truly precious gift it was to express that love.

Skirting the garden and walking with Kell along the lane that led to the meadow, Annie basked in his adoring looks. Settled beneath the dappled shade of the newly leaved saplings, Annie closed her eyes and leaned back against Kell's chest.

Kell brushed aside the fluttering ribbons from her hat hung on a limb above them, contented to let Annie find her own time and way to tell him her news.

"The town is growing so fast," she began. "I'm glad that Daisy and Cammy opened the cafe."

"Are you?" he asked distractedly, kissing a tumbling curl.

"There'll be less cooking for me to do. Less work all around."

"That's important for some reason?"

Annie reached up and cupped his cheek. "Kell, have you noticed . . . something . . . anything a little different these past weeks?"

"Yes. I've still got this unsatisfied craving to count your freckles with kisses." He planted several scattered ones over her cheek and nose. "And you're becoming a stingy woman with your kisses. Especially those wicked ones I'm so fond of."

Annie turned and within seconds had straddled his lap. Draping her arms over his shoulders, she complied by giving him one of those very wicked kisses, deep, and hungry enough to curl her toes inside her high-buttoned shoes.

When she broke the kiss, Kell looked into her eyes and said, "That is what I call a good morning kiss. And I'm going to confess that I've wanted to—"

With a little squirm, Annie shook her head. "I can tell by myself what it is you're wanting. Please, I'm a respectable married woman. I do not plow clover in meadows."

"Naughty, Annie," he whispered with a voice filled with need. "We, love, do not plow clover." He caressed her hips, settling her more fully on himself. "Remind me," he continued, nipping her earlobe, smiling when she rewarded him with a most delicious shiver, "to keep you away from the doves. Mr. and Mrs. York do not plow clover. No hauling or hulling. No plantin' oats. We're not making the chimney smoke. I won't be stablin' a goose neck, a gully raker, a bald-headed hermit or a naggie.

"We, my darlin', raise a little hell." Taking her mouth in a sweet, wild kiss that left her breathless, Kell smiled. "And the only Jack in your orchard is me."

"Kellian!"

"Annie!"

"You do this deliberately to keep me off balance."

Seeing the laughter in her eyes, hearing it in her voice, Kell found that the rapid pulse in the hollow of her throat needed his attention. Nudging aside the pink ruffled edge of her shirtwaist, he paid proper homage to increase its rate, then lifted his head.

"Don't you know by now that it works both ways? You've

brought me to heel like a coon dog with his tongue hangin' out. Of course, what the good Lord blessed you with might have something to do with it. It's these freckles that drive me wild—" he kissed random spots across her face—"and this mouth that got me ready to sit up and beg for a taste—"

"No begging, Kell. Just be nice and listen to me and I'll give you all the kisses you want or need."

"Just so long as you understand that all Mr. and Mrs. York do is make love." One look at the flush coloring her cheeks and Kell couldn't resist teasing her. "I'd bet you're blushing straight down to your belly button."

"A bet you'd win," Annie murmured, but she had to close her eyes against the desire that blazed in his. She wanted him so much, but if she didn't talk to him now . . . "Kell, have you ever thought about your name?"

"My name?" Fully involved with opening the buttons on his wife's shirtwaist, Kell wasn't paying attention.

"Yes! Your name. Don't be dense. I'm trying to tell you something important."

Busy tracing the lace edge of her chemise, Kell thought to argue about what was important, but with the store of patience he had only for his lovely wife, he stopped. One look at Annie's disgruntled expression and he had to bury his head against her curls not to laugh.

"A man should want his name to be carried on, Kell."

"Don't tell me. You've decided to rename the town after me."

"No! Not the town," Annie whispered, leaning back. She lifted his hand from her hip, hesitated, then set it palm side down over the curve of her belly. "You never said, and I never asked before, but do you want children?"

"Children? As in many?"

"Kellian, they come one at a time!" She moved off his

lap and amended, "Sometimes there are two. Please, please say yes, Kell, because we are having a baby."

Annie scrambled up on her knees, cradling his cheeks and lifting up his face. He appeared a bit dazed. "Kell, say something!" She scattered tiny kisses over his face, landing a quick, hard kiss on his lips. "Well?"

"Are you sure?"

His voice was soft, almost hoarse, but Annie heard the uncertainty, the disbelief, but mostly she heard the hope.

"I'm very sure that you're going to be a father."

Kell closed his eyes briefly, and took a deep breath. A father. He was going to be a father. A man with a great deal of added responsibilities. When he looked at Annie, her gaze was so anxious, he had to smile. Swiftly coming to his feet, he drew Annie to stand beside him.

"Are you happy, Annie?" he murmured, enfolding her in his arms.

"Very happy." She rested her cheek against the steady beat of his heart. "I would like to keep this our secret for a little while."

Kell cupped her chin with his fingers and gently tilted her head back. "I love you." He sealed her lips with a cherishing kiss. Feeling her joy, seeing the excitement in her eyes made his doubt vanish, and he laughed out loud. Suddenly lifting her up, he gazed at her still slender waist, and when he saw her radiant smile, he began whirling her around until she shrieked with laughter.

As suddenly as he had started, Kell stopped. "I suppose you'll want to build a school now."

"A school? Why, Kell, I never gave it a thought."

There was a hidden gleam in her eyes that made him shake his head. "I'll just bet you haven't."

"What I've thought about," Annie said, in a voice husky with desire as she bent to his ear, "is could we—"

"Annie! You're going to be a mother!"

Annie nudged her nose against this. "I only asked if it were possible. You're becoming a bit of a stuffed shirt, Mr. York."

"And you, my charming wife, are too fond of wanton ways." Kell shifted her until she was safely cradled in his arms. "You belong home. In bed. With me. All bets are off."

"But who wins—"

"Ah, Annie, my darling Annie, this way we both do!"

Whisper My Name

~

Raine Cantrell

Prologue

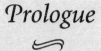

The mountains waited, as did the messenger beyond the small pool of light the single candle shed on the gleaming wood writing desk. Within its light lay a letter, sealed and ready to begin its journey.

The letter was to arrive at the mission off the California coast in weeks; it was the final link that would bring the events of the past together. When the letter's demand was answered—and it had to be answered—there would be no turning back, no stopping what had to be.

Fingering the soft doeskin bag of coins that would make the journey possible, the writer's thoughts drifted back in time.

This was the only way.

Vengeance is mine, sayeth the Lord. But the Lord had not brought vengeance. He had rewarded the secrets kept with riches. If the Lord would not move to do what must be done, it belonged to another who had waited and planned. Too many years, hard lessons of patience learned, and willingly paid, to see justice served. Soon . . .

A motion brought the messenger forward to receive both the letter and the coins. When the door closed softly behind the man, the writer was once more alone, as it had ever been.

There was only one who could destroy this plan for revenge: the wild card. But the deed was done. Too late now . . . much too late.

Chapter One

∽

Saturday night in Florence was no place for a lady. It was no place for Luke either, in his present mood. He took another, longer look at the woman arguing with Chay Booker in front of the stage depot, ever mindful of the wide berth miners and ranch hands gave him. A loner by nature and circumstance, Luke knew it was just as well that no one tried to crowd his space in front of Long Tom's saloon. He was restless, bored, and drunk enough not to walk from whatever came his way.

Swigging a drink from his bottle of whiskey, he targeted a flint-eyed gaze on the woman again. First impressions could save a man's life. Luke had learned early on to size someone up quickly and coldly. And the woman he watched was no lady.

She touched Chay as she talked with the ease of a woman familiar with touching strange men. Most ladies wouldn't put their lily white hands on a man unless they had to. And then only after they trapped him into marriage. She appeared to ignore the whistles and catcalls

that came her way. Ignore them as if she didn't even hear
the miners bent on inviting her to celebrate while they
stood drinks for their less fortunate brethren, or the cow-
boys with a week's pay burning holes in their pockets,
more than ready to raise hell and break anything else that
got in their way.

She didn't even glance up and around to see who was
speculating about her riding ability.

A lady would have been hollering for help if someone
told her they'd like to ride her hard and put her away wet.
That his own thoughts were as crude didn't matter to him.
He was watching her reactions.

She'd come off the stage alone, something else that no
lady would do unless she didn't have a reputation to protect. Eyeing her willowy build again, Luke found himself
adding that there weren't many ladies who turned a man's
thoughts to how she would feel accommodating the fit of
his body and for how long.

The constant creak of the swinging batwings and the
shouts and laughter within the saloon faded from
Luke's hearing. Just as the once-held thoughts of being
a part of it had faded over the years. He stashed his
whiskey bottle between his knees and built himself a
smoke. Just as he brought the match's tip to light his
cigarette, he looked up and found that she was watching him. He didn't even feel the match burning down
until the singed leather of his glove warned him. The
light and heat were gone in the same instant, but Luke
wouldn't forget.

She was tall for a woman, topping Chay by a good
three inches. She had some to go to come near his own
six foot two inch height. But then, he reminded himself,
he had never paid attention to a woman's height. His
business with them was concluded prone and willing,

satisfying a need like eating when hungry and drinking when thirsty.

In the light spilling from the lantern hung near the depot's door, he couldn't see much of her face, half hidden by the shawl she had wrapped around her head and her shoulders. She certainly wasn't dressed like any lady he'd seen. No bonnet, no fancy hat, no parasol, no high-buttoned shoes. The hem of her gown was ankle length, revealing a pair of moccasins. White women didn't wear them.

Curiosity kicked up his interest another notch. Not many women made the rough and dangerous one hundred twenty-five-mile trip into this part of the Idaho Territory. She wasn't someone's wife sent for after a big strike, or a left-behind sweetheart come to be married. That kind of news spread fast and there hadn't been any. But there was another kind of woman drawn to a place like Florence.

Jimmy Jack, the town's half-breed drunk, wove his way through the milling horses being led down to the livery since the hitching posts were crowded with mounts, heading for Luke. The fact that Luke couldn't keep his eyes off her for more than a few seconds sent a shaft of annoyance through him. No corset cinched her waist or hips. She moved with the supple grace of an Indian maid, following Chay back and forth as he unloaded the boot of the stagecoach.

"Got a drink, Luke?"

He took another drag of his smoke and handed it to Jimmy Jack. "Want my makings to save one for later?" A nod sufficed for Luke to hand them over, but he held onto the bottle. "Aloysius should be done shoeing my grulla. You go check on it for me an' I'll leave you the bottle."

Once more Jimmy Jack nodded. Luke saw half his tobacco spill from shaking fingers trying to fill the thin pa-
per. He removed them from the old man, built a cigarette
and tucked it in his torn shirt pocket.

"Molly's got food for you. You make sure to sweep up
for her an' she'll let you sleep in the kitchen tonight. Go
on now, see about my horse."

If his grulla hadn't cast a shoe just outside of town,
Luke wouldn't have bought another bottle of whiskey. He
wasn't about to leave Jimmy Jack more than a drink or
two, so his swigs were hard and fast until less than a quarter remained in the bottle. At least the old man wouldn't
get his belly rotted out drinking swill.

The liquor, added to what he had already, set fire to
his blood. It set him to thinking about the last, quick
tumble he'd had with Tassy that afternoon, before the
sweat and leavings of other men couldn't be hidden by
the lilac water she favored as a washup between customers.

This only brought him back to thinking that the
woman across the street was here to make money from
hungry men. Since he decided for sure that she was no
lady—for he knew firsthand all he ever wanted about
ladies—odds were she was a new nickle-a-ride-mat-
tress-back. He'd never had any truck with virgins and
there was something about her that aroused him.
Aroused him enough to think about plunking down a
few silver dollars for her time.

Jimmy Jack reappeared at his side. "Mornin', grulla
ready." He reached out and touched the rawhide strips
that hung from Luke's gun belt. "You keep?"

"Always. I never forget what you taught me, Jimmy
Jack. Go eat at Molly's." He handed over his bottle, wiped
his mouth with the back of his hand, and moved.

Luke paid no attention to the men coming and going across the street. Two things made most of them step aside for him: his reputation and his name. He had earned the first, and he hated the second.

He sauntered his way at an angle to where the woman stood, idly noting that most of the families who came into town to buy their monthly supplies and pick up their mail from the stage, were already off the street.

He gave thought to the fact that he might be piling up grief for himself like the thunderheads building in the sky above him. Thought about it and dismissed it. Luke rarely denied himself anything he wanted. He only had to want it badly enough. He'd learned early on that everything and everyone had a price.

And he could buy whatever he desired. All it took was a whisper of his name.

Chay disappeared inside the depot office just as Luke came to a stop behind the woman. Tension rolled off her body and collided with his. No cloying fragrance reached him, just the warm, clean scent of a woman. He was struck by the strange thought that there was a wildness in her, as deep and dark as the currents of the Salmon River. Gut feelings were about the only things Luke trusted, so this one came and settled. Fast and hard. The same way his body was urging him to take her.

He was damned to figure why. He hadn't even seen her face. And when she leaned close to the doorway and spoke again to Chay, Luke found that her voice ran through him the same way: deep, dark, and fast. He felt his nerve ends sizzle as if lightning strikes had hit them.

A loud clap of thunder sounded and he looked up, a frown tightening his brow. Storms were wild in these Idaho mountains. A man had to outwit and outrun their fury. For all the arguing she was doing with Chay, there was nothing of anger in her voice. There was a liquid, throaty quality to her every word, that drove itself into his senses like a miner's pick sinking deep into rock. Liquid as hot honey, the slightly accented voice hit him with the same potency as the fancy aged brandy that his brother favored. For the moment, Luke chose to listen.

"There must be someone willing to help me, Mr. Booker. I told you both my money and the letter were stolen in Lewiston once I had my stage ticket. I can't spend the night here. Someone has to—"

"Look. I done tole you once, done tole you too many times, there ain't no one gonna make that trip tonight." Chay came to the doorway. "If I could figure a way to help you, I would. Can't, though. Ain't my job to see to folks once the stage gets 'em here."

"I was assured that the Colfax name meant something—"

"Does. Sure as hell does." Chay stepped out. "Luke? That you standin' there?" Chay ran a hand over his thick red beard, his head jutting forward on his long neck like a turtle coming out of his shell. "By damn! Can't tell where you begin and the dark ends."

Dominica Kirkland whirled around, nostrils flaring like an animal scenting danger. She was unsettled that someone had stood behind her without making a sound. Her first thought was that Chay Booker was right; there was no telling where the man began and the night ended. She was not accustomed to looking up at many men, but he was taller than her by a half a foot at least.

With his presence came a deep sense of darkness, not only from his clothing as he stepped forward, but with a darker, powerful force impacting on her as she looked upon his face. Domini wondered if he had been named for Lucifer, the most handsome of the fallen angels. His features were hard-edged, and there was a consuming blaze of unexplained anger in his eyes.

"You can help, Luke. There here gal's lookin' for—"

"I heard her, Chay." Luke motioned to the man, and Chay slipped back inside the depot office, closing the door.

Domini glanced from the closed door back to the man who stood watching her. There was a dangerous stillness to him, bringing a feeling that nothing going on around him escaped his notice. Including her.

The ensuing silence was meant to make her uncomfortable and it did. She bore with his scrutiny for a few moments more, then spoke.

"Since you heard my request, you know I need to reach the Colfax—"

"He send for you?" *It would be just like Matt to order himself up a new woman. Arrogant bastard that he was.*

"Yes, I was sent for. The letter that was stolen—"

"Well, it don't matter none. You're here." Luke tilted back his hat brim with his thumb. He looked her over from bottom to top, then focused on the way the freshening wind pressed the cloth of her gown against her legs and the flare of her hips. The legs were long, the kind men could dream about, and her hips had a womanly invitation to cushion a man's ride with ease.

"You'll do," he announced.

"Do? For what? I'm only interested in a ride—"

"Same here. No sense in wasting time." He reached out with his left hand and caught hold of her chin with his thumb and forefinger, lifting her face up toward the lantern light.

Her brows and lashes were as black as his own, framing green eyes that tugged at his memory. She wasn't pretty. It was too soft a word for her. Her features were strongly molded on smooth golden skin that didn't owe its color to the sun.

He thought her a breed, then dismissed it. There was a delicate refinement to the angles and planes of her face. Striking was the only word that came to his mind, for he had the unshakeable feeling that a man would never tire looking at this woman through all the seasons.

The very fact that she stood still, and silent, while he took her measure, confirmed his earlier assessment of her. Somehow having his opinion verified didn't dim his interest. If anything, seeing her up close, touching her skin, only brought out tiny claws of need inside him. He brushed his thumb across her bottom lip and released her.

"Let's go."

"Just a moment. Who are you? And why are you willing to give me a ride out there tonight?"

"I'm Luke. An' it's too late to start out there tonight, just like Chay told you. I'll get you a room at the hotel." Luke glanced around and saw the single carpetbag near the door. "That all you got?"

"Yes, that's mine." Domini watched him scoop up her bag. "Mr. Booker said there wasn't a room to be had."

"There's always a room for me." He eyed her ruffled expression. "You coming? There's about three minutes before the storm hits. I've already had my bath an' you'd shiver in the cold slash of this mountain rain."

"Why are you willing to help me when—"

"Sometimes Colfax's interests an' mine ride the same

road. That's all you need to know." He caught hold of her arm.

"I'm not sure I want to go—"

"It wasn't ever meant as an invitation. Colfax sent for you. That makes you Colfax property. 'Sides, this town ain't no place for a woman alone tonight."

Domini stared up at him. The warning and the threat were there in his voice and the still blazing anger of his eyes.

"Do you work for him? Mr. Colfax, I mean."

"I've done some troubleshooting for him in my days."

Her gaze lowered to the gun he wore low on his left hip. She hadn't missed the knife sheathed slightly off center to the left of the small of his back. Domini was no stranger to men and their weapons of violence. If Sister Benedict hadn't believed that she could take care of herself, Domini knew she would never have allowed her to make this most important trip on her own.

Even with all that anger shimmering in his gaze, there was the awareness that she was a woman. She sensed no evil for all that he guarded himself. What frightened her was the desire she had to feel his gentle touch on her face again. Strange how she felt its loss.

"Two minutes and counting until the storm hits."

"I can't pay you."

"Yeah, right. The money got stolen. We'll figure out something."

"All right. I'll come with you."

A loud clap of thunder capped off her agreement. Domini watched him walk away, expecting her to follow. He walked as if he were alone, and she wondered why men simply stepped aside for him. Too exhausted to think about it, she began to follow him toward the far corner where the wind swung the post sign announcing

Tanner's Hotel. Luke took the steps lightly, moving with a grace that drew attention to his lithe, powerful body.

A fat drop of rain hit Domini's cheek and she looked up. She loved the first moments before a storm—when the wind rushed and the clouds piled and billowed before spilling their precious life-giving rain. Exhilaration filled her as lightning split the sky and lit the undersides of the dark clouds. Here was raw power as only nature could unleash. She was distracted by curses as the door behind Luke was flung open and four men staggered out to the wooden porch.

Since Luke stood dead center, and showed no inclination to move, the men split to go around him. Domini saw that Luke didn't even turn to acknowledge being told that he couldn't get a room here; they were full. He just remained where he was, waiting for her.

Domini could smell the incoming rain now, and with it the stench of unwashed bodies. Two on each side of Luke, the men came down the steps toward her. She caught Luke's gaze on her, but sensed he was very aware of the four men. She glanced at the two nearest to her, then back at Luke. He had set her bag down, but it was the only move he had made.

"Bless my bleary eyes! We got ourselves a woman."

Domini stilled, as a fawn hiding in a thicket would still when the hunter approached. Only she had nowhere to hide. To run would have them on her like a pack of wolves. She never once thought to call out to the man who waited for her. She had been on her own for so long that she depended upon no one but herself.

They wouldn't expect her to fight. Violence was against her beliefs, but she had been trapped by men like these before, and the Lord didn't need another lamb. Domini closed out the sound of their voices, blurring in her mind their crude words, just as she had done with the other men when she arrived.

Luke, snared by a fierce hunger that flooded his loins with heat, was caught up in her obvious enjoyment of the coming storm. The four men were circling her now. He waited for her plea. It took a few moments for him to realize that the plea was not coming, and he was filled with an explosive possessiveness.

"Caully."

One man turned at the soft murmur of his name. "That you, Luke? Thought you were gone."

"Well, I'm right here, Caully."

"Didn't mean to cut you out. Plenty to go 'round since we're sharing."

"That's not how I figure it." Luke came down the steps and never once looked at the woman.

But Domini couldn't take her eyes from him. He moved with a mountain cat's grace, supple, primitive, and dangerous. A shiver walked up her spine. She stood forgotten when Luke reached out his right hand and gathered up Caully's shirtfront, and with a twist of the material he lifted the man up on his toes.

"Now, Luke—"

"Now, Caully. Just listen. You don't look. You don't touch. An' you never make the mistake of thinking that I share. Ever."

"Nooo sireee, Luke. Caully ain't gonna make that mistake again. Just let him go and we'll leave, Luke."

"Always said you were a smarter man than some, Ramsey. Take him an' get the hell out of my sight."

"Com'on, Caully, he's wild tonight," Ramsey muttered as he grabbed hold of his friend's arm and hurried with the other men passed Domini.

"Who are *you?*" Domini rubbed her arms, ignoring the rain, and staring up at him.

"About the only man who can get you out of the rain tonight. Coming?"

Never share. Domini heaved a weary sigh. So the battles were not done. But one was better odds for her. Still caught in the tension of the past minutes, Domini hesitated. He removed his gloves, tucking them into his gun belt and held out a hand to her. Rain pelted them both, and she knew as she reached out to take his hand and looked into fathomless black eyes that on some deep instinctive level she trusted this man.

He didn't say a word as he opened the door and ushered her in before him to the hotel's desk.

"Sorry, we're full up—"

"Harold, I need a room."

Domini saw the flustered look of the desk clerk when Luke reached over and spun the register around.

"You never stay in town on Saturday night, Luke."

"I'm here tonight."

"If you're just looking for a place for a few hours, I work all—"

"Harold, you ain't writin' no newspaper. An' room six is no longer occupied by Logan. Don't bother going up. I'll explain to him."

"But he just checked in. . . ." Harold Doverville's voice trailed off. He wasn't about to argue with Luke, he didn't like arguing with anyone. If Luke wanted to disposses one of the Gold Bar C hands, that was his business.

"Send up some hot water." Luke glanced at her. "Make that later, Harold. Much later."

"You can't do this." Domini would have said more, but the cynical twist of his lips silenced her. She had her first look at him in the light. His hair, the little she could see of it beneath his hat, was as black as her own. There was a scar on his right cheekbone, a jagged mark that hadn't been stitched before healing. His eyes were for a woman to lose herself in, and against the sudden racing of her heart, she heard a warning.

Abruptly, he headed for the stairs, carrying her bag. Domini took one step, then another. There was no choice. All the doubts she had about coming here surfaced, but as she climbed the stairs behind him, the certainty that she could trust him returned.

"Wait here." His order was given in the same soft voice he had used all the while. She glanced down at her bag, which he had set beside her, leaned against the wall of the dim lit hall, and closed her eyes.

"Logan. Logan, open the door. It's Luke." He had to repeat it twice before the sounds of swearing revealed that the man heard him.

Domini did not open her eyes when she heard Luke's order for him to get his gear and leave. The protest from Logan that he had a woman with him brought Luke's suggestion that Harold had offered his room for a few hours. She didn't want to see the knowing looks of the man and the woman with him as they left.

She sensed his nearness, although he hadn't made a sound. There were his scents that she had marked without knowing, of damp leather and horse, of whiskey and smoke, of power and aroused male. The rain slashed against the window at the far end of the hall, and she heard its force drumming on the roof. The room would be dry and, once she explained his mistake about her, safe. Domini went inside.

Luke had hit the lamp and stood holding the still smoking match. "I want to see you in the light." He saw the delicate twitch of her nose as she caught the reek of sex and liquor from the tangle of sheets on the bed. Luke walked past her to close the door, securing it with a straight chair wedged beneath the handle.

"Are you giving me a choice?

"About the light? Sure. It's the only one." He came to stand behind her. But he didn't touch her. Not yet.

"You're wrong about me."

"You're not a woman? Fooled me but good," he whispered, smelling the rain that mingled with her clean scent. She stepped away and reflex made him grip the end of the shawl, stripping it and whirling her around to face him.

Straight and smooth, her ebony hair was coiled in a thick mass at the base of her neck. "These have to go." He reached out for the combs and pins. Hunger to taste her lips made him catch her head between his hands, dragging her close.

Domini went still as his fingers touched the delicate flesh just behind her ears. She was suddenly afraid to move, afraid she would lose the shimmering anticipation that trembled to life. It was not submission to his greater strength. His eyes bore into hers, drawing her into his need. There was a natural hard edge to his temptingly handsome features that whispered of hunger and darker passions. Hard-edged, yes, and filled with a simmering promise of danger.

"I've wanted to touch you from the moment I saw you," he murmured.

Domini closed her eyes and saw again his face in the match's flare against the night. Something wild inside her cut loose from its mooring. Shocking, dizzying longing to answer the hunger in him intensified with the slow brush of his body against hers. Stormy excitement rose, each sensation sharp and exquisite. His mouth was closing over hers, and she had her first taste of a man's hunger. It would be so easy to stop him. She had to stop him. But her will, that indomitable strength of will that helped her survive, was dissolving with the emotions colliding inside her.

The generous shape of her mouth was soft beneath his. *Soft enough to ease a man's pain.* Luke rejected the thought even as it formed. There was nothing soft in him. Not anymore. There was only a need to know her mouth, to savor its taste and feed the sweet hot ache that filled him. He'd think later about the strange yearning for her mouth. Luke never kissed any woman, whore or lady. But he wanted her kiss. There was no soft coaxing touches, he captured her lips with his, and felt her explosive answering need meet his demand.

Domini let his kiss take her on a wild, potent ride for long moments. He was a storm, flooding her with a torrent of emotions that had no names. Their harsh breaths mingled like the rush of the wind in a dizzying force around them. But she could not let this be.

Luke pressed his body to hers, his tongue delving deep in her mouth, passion a hot driving force that took him right to the edge. His hips ground against her softness and for seconds before she struggled, he was aware of the plaint yield of her body against his. Her hand slid around his waist, the move a warning flare, but she rocked her hips and he thought she was trying to climb into his skin.

It was seconds before he realized that the cold press on the side of his neck was his own knife blade. He eased his mouth from hers, but didn't move. "Honey, you just made the biggest mistake of your life."

"No. It's you who made the mistake. And," she pressed her point home with knife tip and words, "your life that's at risk." She knew how awkward her position was. He could easily twist away and be free. There was no time to think, or be weak. "I'm not what you think. I tried to tell you—"

"Like hell you ain't." He saw within the darkened green of her eyes that she would use his own knife on him. Her hand wasn't shaking, only her lower lip gave a betraying quiver. Luke brought his arm down hard, slamming into the crook of her elbow and twisted free. She didn't release the knife and it ripped down his shirt, blood welling to fill the long cut. "You bitch!" The words were without heat, but then the heat had disappeared and cold fury replaced it.

"No! I'm protecting myself. You think I'm a whore for sale. I'm not." She backed away from the murderous look on his face, knowing the knife against his gun offered no protection at all. The brass bedstead brought her up short.

"If you're not Matt Colfax's whore, then who the hell are you?"

He made no move to stanch the blood dripping down his arm, or to take the knife from her. Domini couldn't help herself. "You should wrap your arm," she whispered, wary and holding the knife out before her.

"The hell with my arm. Answer me. Who the hell are you?"

"I don't know Matt. Toma Colfax sent for me. I'm Dominica Kirkland."

"The devil you say." Luke shook his head, staring at her with disbelief. "Kirkland? You're Jim Kirkland's wife?"

"No. My mother is dead. I'm his daughter."

He threw back his head, flooding the small room with laughter. There was no joy, no welcome at all when he ceased abruptly and looked at her. "Welcome to hell."